Adventures of City Girl

Carol Maloney Scott

Adventures of City Girl

Copyright Carol Maloney Scott 2025

ISBN: 979-8-9944002-0-3

Formatting by Rik Hall
(http://www.RikHall.com)

For

Nick

*Who gives his mom a chance to play "city girl" every time
she visits Chicago*

Chapter 1

"Hey, lady, can I axe you a question?"

The heavy New York accent disorients me for a moment, and I stare at the gruff-looking middle-aged man in an old Buick and sigh. I know he's talking to me because I don't see anyone else walking down the sidewalk, carrying her five-inch stilettos and limping.

Just little old me adjusting to my new city life, working for a designer shoe company that requires wearing these instruments of medieval torture.

Buick guy doesn't seem to be dissuaded by my silence. "You okay there? Workin' on your feet all day, are ya?"

I stop and consider running away, but that's not happening on these feet. I shift the weight of my Michael Kors tote to my other shoulder and reply, "I'm fine, thank you. Was that your question?"

Even though my mother taught me not to talk to strangers, she also taught me to be polite and helpful. These two things have been a conflict in my life, and I have tried to be a little more specific when teaching my own kids.

Although my daughter would have already given him money and my son would have told him to fuck off.

He laughs and says, "No, I was wonderin' if there's

any good strip clubs in this neighborhood?"

I close my eyes and take a deep breath, knowing this won't make him disappear but also considering what would make a strip club "good" and how I am qualified to make that assessment.

"Hmm, well, I know there is at least one because my brother saw it when I moved into my new apartment, and he said the neighborhood wasn't gentrified enough for me to live here."

Scott's Addition is an oddly named, but also very trendy part of Richmond, Virginia. But its seedier roots still creep up through the cracks here and there, alongside the luxury apartments, craft breweries, and retro bowling alley with live music.

Just as my new acquaintance scratches his chin, presumably at his confusion over the word "gentrified", I hear a voice behind me that would wake the dead all the way in Hollywood Cemetery on the other side of town.

"Lenny, didn't I tell you to stop creeping around asking stupid questions? I swear, does this lady look like she knows where a strip club is? And if you turn on that fancy phone you bought, that Cindy person will tell you where you wanna go."

I turn around and see the authoritative voice is coming from a little old lady in leggings, a long t-shirt, a sweater, and a hat. She's dressed for the slight chill in the early October air.

Meanwhile, my feet are turning blue on the sidewalk. I need to do something about my car situation. Or buy sneakers.

I am tempted to ask who Cindy is and why she's in Lenny's phone, but while they are arguing about

Lenny's manners and how to use an iPhone, I start to slip away, making a mental note to walk home down a different side street next time.

"Lenny, obviously, this woman isn't a stripper, look at her!"

What? Lenny thinks I'm a stripper. I glance down at my skirt and pull it down—it's a little short, but I think Lenny should be asking if I know where to find a good optometrist.

Also, I'm wearing glasses—do strippers wear glasses?

"Hey, no offense, miss, but you're lookin' a little rough around the edges if I'm bein' honest, and those look like stripper shoes, you know what I mean?"

He shrugs his shoulders as if his logic is airtight.

The old lady smacks the hood of his car, and Lenny and I both flinch.

"Now stop this nonsense, or you're gonna have to pick a different neighborhood to spend your millions. Now scram!"

Lenny rolls up his window and floors it down the street.

I wrinkle my forehead and say, "That guy has millions?" Wow, you never know what you'll see around here. "I'm Tara. Thanks for the help."

She waves off my gratitude with her wrinkly, bejeweled hand. Her fingernails are bright green, and there is a huge gemstone ring on every finger. Hmm, maybe she's secretly rich, too.

"Listen, honey, Lenny's harmless. He won the Lotto up in New York and got the bright idea to come down here and live near his Aunt Dinah, now that he doesn't have to work for peanuts in that filthy car wash in

Brooklyn."

I want to ask how a filthy car wash attracts customers who want clean cars, but my feet are screaming for mercy, and it's still another two streets over to my apartment, a foot soak, and a glass of prosecco.

However, my curiosity gets the best of me.

I smile at my feisty neighbor and say, "Have you lived here long?"

Her accent sounds like she just drove down I-95 for the first time and got lost on the way to Florida.

"Oh, me and my Vincenzo have been down here going on fifty years. We used to own a little pizzeria, but now it's a tattoo joint. Lenny is my sister's son, and I feel like I need to keep an eye on him since she passed. He's a little touched in the head." She taps her skull.

"Oh, I'm sorry about your sister." I would be lost if my sister, Beth, died, even though if she saw me wearing these shoes, she'd lecture me about foot health. Sometimes, a podiatrist is the least useful doctor to have in the family.

"Eh, she was crazy, too. Where do you think Lenny gets it? Now, what's going on with you because you are a bit of a mess, honey."

By now, I've plopped my beautiful burgundy purse on the sidewalk and I'm eyeing the ground like it's a chaise lounge.

"I'm on my way home from work, and I parked far away."

She peers in the direction I came from and says, "Car trouble? I could go home and call you a tow."

I am wondering why she can't just ask Cindy on her cell phone, but she may not even own one, based on her earlier comments.

"No thanks, the car is fine." My eyes dart around and look everywhere but at Dinah's bespectacled glare. And yes, she's also sporting jewels on her glasses.

"Then why are you walking home—what's wrong with parking on the street outside your place?" She places her hands on her ample hips, and I can see I'll have to provide more concrete answers before I can move on.

"It's always really…umm…full this time of day, and I don't know how to parallel park. So, I find a spot as close as I can where I can just pull in. And walk the rest of the way."

Dinah laughs and says, "Oh boy, you're new around here too, I see. Where did you learn to drive?"

"A small town in Connecticut. We had a lot of parking lots."

Dinah shakes her head and smiles. "Okay, I'm gonna go up to the corner and get my car and drive you home." She holds up her index finger as I begin to protest—the one adorned with the huge ruby, and says, "And then I want to hear about how you ended up here and what's with the shoes."

She points at my feet and screws up her face. Apparently, I am the most perplexing thing this woman has seen in a long time, and she's related to Lenny.

"Okay, thanks." I glance up at the building behind me because I'd love to duck in there and sit down while Dinah, my elderly rescuer, hobbles up the street, but I see it's a donut shop.

No, I've sworn off those for sure. After seeing them used the way I have, there's no going back, but Dinah doesn't need to hear about how I caught Todd in the back room of The Donut Hole.

"No need to thank me—you made my day. Nothing exciting has happened on this street since they opened that hipster bowling alley that looks like the one from the 50s in Coney Island." She fishes in her pocket and pulls out a key ring that looks like it belongs to the night janitor at a high-rise office building, and fumbles for her car key.

"There, that's the one. Vinny keeps the keys to the cars we had in the Carter administration. Haha…I'll be right back, now don't move. Not that you could, you poor thing. I'll get you home, and I'll wait while you get cleaned up." She nods like it's all settled, and I am five years old.

"There's no reason to wait, I'll be fine and—"

"Nonsense, I'm taking you back to my house afterwards. You look like the last rose of summer had a fight with an alley cat, and Vinny will be so happy to meet you! We can have a big meatball and talk about how you got yourself in this mess. I bet it starts with a man."

"It always does, doesn't it?" I nod and think about how good a big meatball would taste right now, and hopefully that isn't a code word for something I don't want to know about and is, in fact, an actual Italian food item.

Dinah rubs her hands as if she's about to watch the premiere of a new soap opera called Adventures of City Girl and yells out as she ambles down the road sideways, "Don't you worry—I've been married fifty-eight years and if there's one thing I know it's men and how not to kill them. Oh, and also, I can parallel park so you can barely slip a dollar bill between the cars when

I'm done. I'll teach ya!"

She winks, and I offer her my last smile.

I have a feeling I am about to get all the education I need from the most unlikely source.

While I wait, I'll just glare at the donut counter through the window and think about how to phrase my tale of woe to my new elderly friends, so they don't spit out their meatballs.

Chapter 2

"Yes, I can say for sure that's the biggest meatball I've ever seen."

I stare at the behemoth sphere of meat on my plate, smothered in the most heavenly-smelling sauce (or gravy, as my new friend Vinny has pointed out), and my stomach growls.

Vinny, or as he introduced himself, "Vincenzo Bertelli at your service, mi acara", beams from ear to ear, and his gray mustache moves with his smile, making him look like a Disney cartoon character.

"We served these at our pizzeria, and they were a very popular item, right, Dinah, my love?" He winks at his wife as he plops a huge serving of rigatoni on my plate.

I was already having portion-size anxiety, and now it's just a lost cause.

Dinah has about an eighth of one of these meat monstrosities on her plate and a pile of steamed broccoli.

"Yes, everyone loves your balls, Vin!"

I feel my face turn pink as I listen to the elderly couple laugh and flirt like they were teenagers.

Were Todd and I ever that playful?

The answer is no, and Todd sucks.

Dinah pats my hand and says, "Eat up, sweetie. You're too skinny. Now let's hear more about that cheating husband of yours, the bastard."

Vinny sits down at the table with his own sensibly portioned meal and catches me eyeing their plates vs mine.

"What? We can't eat like that anymore; we'd be dead." He laughs again and taps the side of his head. "Ah, senior moment, I almost forgot the mozzarella garlic bread." He jumps up, but before I begin to protest the onslaught of more food, the doorbell rings.

Vinny yells out, "Oh merda, the bread is burning, oww!"

Dinah pops up like she has a spring-loaded butt and yells, "Vin, I told you to use the potholders, not the dishrag."

She rushes to her husband's aid as the bell rings again and someone is now calling from the front stoop.

"Mr. and Mrs. B, you guys okay in there?"

Dinah has Vinny's hand wrapped up in ice and says, "Tara, could you get the door? It's just Shawn comin' to get his order."

Now that I am parted from my gluttonous meal, I am even hungrier, but I'm happy to help. Also, this delays my storytelling, and I still can't believe I am going to spill all the proverbial beans.

All they know so far is that I caught Todd cheating and that his new girlfriend is now living in my house.

Oh, and I started to tell them about the bunny, but not about the donuts.

It's a simple story, the same as every other divorced person, right?

The kitchen is in the front of the old 1920s bungalow, so I quickly reach the door down the short hallway and open it to the most gorgeous green eyes I've ever seen encased in quite the hot man… wait, never mind, he may not be much older than my kids.

"Hey, are the Bertellis here? I heard a lot of yelling. Not that it would be unusual for them."

His smile is as white as his eyes are green, and I stumble to find my voice. "Haha, yes, they're okay. Vinny just had a little cooking mishap."

When have I ever used the word "mishap"?

I stand back and gesture for him to come in.

As he enters the small foyer, I smell faint cologne and something minty, like maybe… mints…

He clears his throat and says, "Yeah, they'd get thrown out of the library. Anyway, I'm Shawn, I'm just here to pick up my order."

He extends his hand, and his grip is firm, as if he respects women as people, but not bone-crushing like he's trying to prove he's as strong as the muscles under his tight, long-sleeved t-shirt suggest. I stare at his deep mahogany skin and perfectly manicured nails and again remember to speak.

"Yeah, Dinah said that. About your order." I can't imagine what they are selling him. "I'm Tara. I live down the street—"

"I know, in the Residences at the Old Iron Works, right? I'm your neighbor. Across the hall and two doors down. Fourth floor? Sorry, I hope that doesn't come across as creepy."

"No, not at all. Especially after meeting Lenny earlier today. I mean, Lenny was creepy, not you. And yes, wow, you're observant. Sorry, I haven't said hello."

He shakes his head and says, "No worries, and you met Lotto Lenny. He's alright, but I'm sure he asked you something ridiculous and/or wildly inappropriate."

Before I can decide whether to tell him that I was mistaken for a stripper earlier today, Dinah comes barreling into the already cramped space and shoos us into the kitchen.

She kisses Shawn on the cheek and says, "Look at you, so big and strong, come in. Vinny has your food ready, and I see you met Tara. I heard you saying that you two are neighbors. See, honey, not all the men are as creepy as Lenny in this neighborhood."

We follow her into the kitchen, and Vinny is sitting at the table with a bandaged hand.

"It's not that bad, she just fusses. I got all your favorites, kiddo." He gestures at the large bag of food labeled with "Bertelli's To Go" on the side.

Dinah says, "When we closed the pizzeria, this one didn't know what to do with himself, so he started his own little in-home catering business. It keeps him busy, so I have time for my hobbies, like playing Bingo at the VFW with Shawn's grandma."

Shawn smiles, but his eyes widen. "Please don't tell her I was here, though." He turns to me to explain. "I order from Mr. and Mrs. B all the time, but then my grandma brings me her version of comfort foods, like fried chicken and peach cobbler. And she doesn't want me 'cheating' with another grandma's food."

"That's sweet, I'm sure you never have to cook."

Now that I really look at him in the light, he's not a kid, but he's still not in my dating pool. Not that I have a pool or even a puddle. But I'd say he's not more than mid-to-late twenties.

Of course, the irony of that isn't lost on me when I think of my husband, who is shacked up with little Nicole Kavanaugh.

"Haha, no, I never do. But I do have to work out a lot." He gestures to my plate. "I see they've already introduced you to the big meatballs."

Everyone laughs again, and now I am sharing the balls joke with people old enough to be my parents and a guy almost young enough to be my son.

Vinny blurts out, "I have a great idea. Dinah, get our young friend a plate, and he can join us for dinner."

He motions to the cabinets behind him, and Dinah is already on it. Maybe a lifetime of eating big meatballs does make you spry.

Shawn waves his hand and says, "I don't want to intrude, but if you don't mind the company...?"

He looks at me, and I sit down because really, I am not used to being around men with this combination of eyes and muscles, and now I'm noticing the perfectly trimmed facial hair... oh well, I can enjoy looking at a hot young guy. I'm sure Nicole is in my jacuzzi tub right now with that asshole Todd rubbing her back and... ugh... he really is a bastard.

"Yes, please join us, Shawn. I was just about to tell the Bertellis all about how I came to be single again."

Dinah smiles and squeezes my arm as if to congratulate me for flirting. Was that flirting? I don't even know anymore. I've spent so much time around couples who either adore each other, like my brother and his wife, or my neighbors on River Road, who all have massive sticks up their butts and mostly tolerate each other until someone gets caught at the donut shop doing very bad things.

Well, that was probably just Todd, but still.

Shawn sits down while Dinah fusses over him. I wonder if the Bertellis have any kids or grandkids. They haven't mentioned any, and I feel like if they did, I would already be viewing Vinny the 3rd's communion pictures.

Now that everyone is settled around the table, Dinah says, "Okay, get some meatball in ya and then let's hear the dirt."

She turns to Shawn and says, "So far we know that her husband, Todd, told her he was leaving her right after their daughter's high school graduation—"

Shawn holds up his hand as he wipes his mouth with the embroidered cloth napkin. "Hold up, sorry, Mrs. B, you have a daughter in high school, Tara?"

I resist the urge to roll my eyes. Shawn damn well knows I'm much older than him. But honestly, it's sweet and endearing and a teensy bit flattering. He could have taken his meatballs and gone home, and he did notice me at the apartment complex, so… maybe he does find me a little bit attractive. Not that I would consider him as a potential… date. Or anything else.

I sigh, trying to put the "anything else" out of my mind and say, "Yes, my daughter, Willow, is eighteen and she's at college now—"

"Tell him where." Dinah smacks my arm.

I've only known this woman for a few hours, and she's already rescued me from bleeding feet, sat on my bed while I freshened up after work, and she's going to teach me to parallel park "that ridiculous gas guzzling SUV" on Sunday.

Look at me with the fun weekend plans!

"She's at Harvard. And my son, Birch, just started his junior year at The Collegiate School." I wish that didn't sound so pretentious.

"Wow, that's impressive. Interesting names. Willow

and Birch." He sits back and stretches as if he's already at his meatball capacity.

"Yeah, Dinah and Vinny immediately said, 'I guess you like trees', but the people in our social circle name their kids even crazier things. My son goes to school with a Zeppelin and a Cosmo."

I instantly regret using the term "social circle" because, as my sister said when I moved into this neighborhood, "Try to remember you're not living around a bunch of bourgeois dickheads anymore."

I think my sister and Dinah would hit it off.

Dinah finishes her broccoli and takes a sip of her prosecco (they broke this out earlier just for me) and rubs her hands like she can't wait to get to the "good part".

"So, where was I? Oh yeah, so the husband tells her he's done with her as the kid is graduating, and that he wanted to wait until the other one graduates too, but he just can't wait that long. And Tara here accuses him of having someone else, and he says, 'No way, what do you take me for?', right?"

"Yes, he was very indignant, but I'm not that stupid. Although I was a little stupid. The signs were there."

Shawn's expression softens. "Like he was less attentive and out late at night? That's what happened to my mom with my stepdad."

I wince at Shawn's "mom" comparison, but he's too young to have had this type of firsthand life experience, so of course, he would compare me to his mother.

And Dinah and Vinny explained that they've been married since they were seventeen and nineteen and ran away from home because she's Jewish and he's Italian. Apparently, there were fathers with shotguns and mothers with wooden spoons.

Everyone has their drama. Shawn will get his eventually, and he'll be wishing his biggest problem was hiding meatballs from his grandma.

I put down my fork and sigh. "No, well, yes, but Todd is a lawyer with his own firm, and he has always worked late, and he's never been overly attentive. But other things happened that should have been suspicious."

Vinny is sitting with his arms folded across his chest, and it looks like he's starting to snooze. I guess I'm not getting to the "good parts" fast enough. Dinah must have tapped his leg under the table now, and he jumps and says, "Yeah, you started to say something about a bunny and a girl in your backyard."

"Please don't tell me this girl was… an actual girl." Shawn is screwing up his face in disgust.

I look at Shawn and grimace, "Oh noooo, it's not that bad. Todd's not in prison. She's twenty-four, so not a girl, but to me she's a girl, I guess."

"Oh, am I a boy then? I'm twenty-five." His eyes twinkle with mischief, and Dinah squeezes his cheek.

"You're all man, kiddo. Look at these muscles, Tara." She squeezes his arm, and Vinny grimaces.

"Dinah, stop… the kid's gonna take his meatballs and run, and we're just gettin' to the good part. Go ahead, honey. So, what happened?"

Thankfully, Vinny diverts the conversation back to my humiliating story instead of focusing on Shawn's manhood, which is not at all questionable.

"I came home early one afternoon from volunteering at the school and saw Todd's car in the driveway. And then I spotted our neighbor's daughter running in our backyard."

Shawn says, "With a bunny? How is that suspicious?"

I shift in my seat and sigh. I don't know why I am embarrassed to tell these stories when I didn't do anything wrong.

"No, I stopped her and asked her why she was running in our backyard, and she said she saw an injured bunny and was chasing it to try to save it." I roll my eyes at the absurdity of it all.

Dinah, Vinny, and Shawn all look at each other, and finally Shawn says, "She was in the house with your husband, and she ran out the back door when she heard you coming home."

"Wow, you should be a detective!" Dinah jumps up and down in her seat, and even though I hate telling people how naïve I was, it feels strangely good to entertain these new friends.

This may be more effective than therapy or scrubbing the toilet with Todd's toothbrush, which I may or may not have done.

Vinny leans forward and says, "In your own house? What a disgrace. So, you didn't even question it at the time?"

"I did in my head for a moment, but sometimes you just want to pretend things are okay, you know?"

Shawn moves his chair a little closer to mine and places his hand gently on my shoulder. Softly, he says, "That guy is a fool, and you're going to have an amazing life without him, just like my mom."

Again, the "mom" talk should dissuade me from my attraction to this very young man, but screw it—his mom is obviously older than me.

And he's just being nice, although the way he just

licked his lips is a little… umm… suggestive, but those meatballs are very saucy, and maybe there was some leftover gravy on his full, delectable lips.

Seemingly oblivious to the awkward mood and my increasing pulse, Dinah says, "So, that's the bunny story, but what about the donuts. That sounds like the good part."

"Well, it's good if you're in the audience, and it's almost funny now, but not quite yet." I squirm in my seat and blurt out, "Did you know the donuts from The Donut Hole are big enough to hang off nipples?"

Chapter 3

"Well, that was some story."

Dinah sips her coffee and shakes her head while Vinny fiddles with the bandage on his slightly burned fingers.

He says, "Not much shocks me, but I would say catching your husband eating donuts off a woman's… I can't even say it… that really takes the cake. Or the donut." He rolls his eyes.

Shawn begins to gather up all the food the Bertellis have packed for us to go, including a package of cannolis, and says, "Okay, well, I think we can all agree that Tara has been through a lot, so maybe it's time to call it a night. And stop talking about donuts."

He winks at me, which makes it almost worth the humiliation because, as I mentioned earlier, Shawn is quite easy on the eyes; however, everyone looks relieved to call it a night, including me.

It wasn't the worst thing to explain to my new friends that my husband was eating donuts off the nipples of our neighbors' daughter in the backroom of her family's donut shop.

But it also wasn't the best story to share, either.

Dinah is helping Shawn pack up and says, "What I don't understand is how they stayed on her nipples. They must be like little doorknobs. That wouldn't work for me at my age."

She glances at my chest, and now Vinny and Shawn are both trying to find other places to look to avoid assessing if my forty-two-year-old nipples are perky enough to be described as little doorknobs.

Vinny clears his throat and says to Shawn, "So who do you like in the football this weekend?

"Which game?"

"Any game, kiddo, just so we can stop talking about… you know… although in my day we called them knockers, not knobs."

Now everyone is laughing because it really is absurd. I couldn't even make this up if I tried.

Dinah wipes her eyes and says through the giggles, "We're sorry, honey. I know it must have been traumatic at the time, but it is funny when you try to picture it. But let's not do that because… well, I think we all have our reasons why."

Shawn kisses Dinah on the cheek and shakes Vinny's hand.

"Goodnight, Mr. and Mrs. B. This food will tide me over until dinner at Grandma's on Sunday for sure."

He turns to me and gestures towards the door. "Are you ready, Tara? You wanna walk home together?"

I inwardly swoon (is that a thing anyone does anymore, or am I reading too many romance novels?) at the thought of going home with Shawn, but then I realize he means would I like to walk down the sidewalk next to him since we both live in separate apartments in the same building.

"Yes, I'm ready to leave." I grab my stuff and hug the Bertellis with a promise to see Dinah on Sunday for my parallel parking lesson.

I don't see how she's going to see out of the windshield of my mammoth vehicle, but maybe she is just going to give instructions, and I'm going to drive it up on the sidewalk, slam into a pole, and scare away the pigeons all on my own.

Shawn holds the door for me, and we step out into the cool, crisp night air.

He inhales deeply and says, "Isn't October the best month? This air feels so good."

I smile and nod, but wince as I realize that even though I switched to the most comfortable flat shoes I own when Dinah took me back to my apartment, my feet are still crying out in agony from the earlier torture in those damn heels.

"Are you okay?" Shawn immediately reaches out for my arm, and now I feel like an old lady who must be helped home. What a way for a young guy to spend his Friday night.

I purse my lips and explain my footwear predicament and how Lenny thought I was a stripper.

"Wow, I was right. That Lenny is somethin' else. But seriously, they force you to wear those shoes to the office? They're not even selling the shoes there, right?"

"Exactly, it's not a store. It's the corporate headquarters. They moved down from New York when the Adrien Monet died, and his grandson took over the company."

He doesn't need to know about my history with the grandson just now, or maybe ever.

"So, it's like a brand image thing?"

I nod as he steers me off the curb, and I settle into holding his arm because why not?

"How did you end up working there? You said you

were a stay-at-home mom for a long time?"

Again, the length of my mom tenure makes me feel old, but I need to get over it. Shawn seems genuinely interested in my story.

"I was, but my sister-in-law, Moneca, is the CFO there, and she pulled some strings to get me an admin position reporting to the Regional Director of Stores."

I leave out the part where Moneca mentioned to Didier Monet, the grandson in question, that Tara Silverthorne was getting divorced and looking for a job, and that I had an offer in less than a week.

I probably could have gotten Moneca's job if I… well, let's just say it seems as though I still have some pull with Didier, after all these years.

We round the corner, and now our building is in sight. It used to be an old iron works, hence the name. It's a very modern space, with lots of glass, chrome, and brick.

When I was given the tour by the twenty-something rental agent named Justin, I said it reminded me of the inside of a tin can, and he said, "Oh, you're so cute."

Despite his condescension, I signed on the spot. This place is nothing like my sprawling French country estate home on River Road. My former dwelling is a beautiful house, but it's not the place for me anymore, and I wanted the exact opposite environment to start my new life.

Shawn opens the door, and I immediately feel the loss of his arm against mine. It's colder, and the heat in the building's lobby is a welcome but insufficient substitute for his body heat.

I am surprised but also annoyed with myself for having these thoughts. Like many newly single women who've been betrayed after long marriages, I decided to swear off men for a while.

I think I've just forgotten what it feels like to be around a new, attractive man.

"So, what do you do?" I've been so focused on myself all night; I haven't asked him a thing about himself.

Shawn puts his hand on my back and leads me to the elevator. In romance novels, the guy always puts his hand on the lower back, and I somehow feel cheated by the mid-back placement of Shawn's warm, strong hand.

The whole time I've been lost in my semi-lustful thoughts, Shawn has been saying that he works from home as a customer service agent for a bank.

"Is that the one where the smaller local bank was acquired by the huge one, and all their customers are angry?" There was a lot of complaining about this in my "social circle".

He points at me and says, "Bingo! And I'm not referring to the fun game of chance the grandmas play at the VFW."

"I'm sure. I thought they laid everyone off. Did you work for the smaller bank or the big one?"

"The smaller one, but my manager says they kept me because I'm so patient with the customers, especially the older ones."

Of course, he likes old people. That's why he's making sure I get home okay.

I smile at him in the elevator, and as we go up to our floor, I notice that we are about the same height.

I am so used to looking up at Todd—even though I am not a short woman at 5'9", Todd is 6'6", so a giant.

A big jerky giant.

I don't want to think about Todd and ruin the moment. Not that there is a moment, but if I just leaned forward the littlest bit, my lips would be on Shawn's. I could trip over something and fall onto his lips, like in a cheesy slapstick rom-com.

I'd probably break our noses or chip a tooth.

And what makes me think he would even want to kiss me? He's just being nice because he's a good person. He was happy to spend his evening with his elderly friends and a new neighbor. A guy like Shawn isn't wanting for female company or friends to spend his weekends with.

It may be my imagination, but Shawn seems to be closer than he was on the sidewalk, and he's licking his lips again, and there is no way he still has meatball gravy on his mouth after a vigorous scrubbing with Dinah's fancy napkin.

The elevator goes ding, and we step off. I am not going to grab Shawn's arm again, and he doesn't offer it.

My apartment is closest to the elevator, and I am acutely aware that it's up to me to invite him in or say goodnight. After our time together, both options feel awkward.

"So, this is you, right?"

He points at my door, and I nod.

"Yep, this is my new home. Well, I've been here about a month."

"I know, remember I was the one who knew you were my neighbor."

He flashes that smile again, and I'm glad I have my bludgeoned feet to blame if I suddenly go weak in the knees.

"Well, it's early, but you probably have things to be

and places to do. I mean people to do and…"

We both laugh, and he says, "Actually, I don't have any of those things, even though I'm not sure what some of them are."

He stands up straighter and says more seriously, "But I don't expect you to invite me in or anything. My mama would be very upset with me if she thought I was trying to get into a beautiful woman's apartment after just meeting her."

That reminds me that I need to have better conversations with Birch about consent and all the things his donut-eating father is too preoccupied to address.

I take a deep breath and say, "Well, we do have dessert to eat. The cannolis, I mean."

"That we do, and I wouldn't mind hearing more stories about your new life, it's very exciting."

I turn to unlock and open my door and compose myself. I've never done yoga, so I suck at breathing to calm down.

Oh, what the hell.

"Sure, let's have dessert. And I'll tell you all about the fun I have planned for tomorrow."

Chapter 4

I can't believe I ever loved this furniture.

Or did I?

My separation from Todd has forced a lot of introspection, and I realize that I did many things because they were expected of me.

Our house was huge, so of course I had to buy big furniture, and I wasn't a decorator, so I let Todd hire one to "help" me.

So why am I surprised that I ended up with a bunch of stuff that doesn't feel like me?

I plop down on one of the enormous velvet couches in my packed storage unit and catch my reflection in the ornate and equally gigantic mahogany mirror situated across from me, leaning up against a… you guessed it… gargantuan dining room hutch.

The mahogany reminds me of Shawn's skin, which I would love to see and feel more of, but then why did I pretend to be so tired I couldn't keep my eyes open last night?

We had a perfectly pleasant conversation while we ate our cannolis… literally… off plates, when we were suddenly too close for comfort.

Well, my body was getting very comfortable, but my brain was sounding alarm bells.

My new apartment-sized furniture is teeny tiny, and

Shawn's knees were touching mine on the couch.

When have knees ever felt that good?

I sigh, and I glance back at myself in the mirror. It's an old family piece my mother gave us when we got married, and Todd "allowed" it in the house because the decorator said it was charming and vintage.

Was there ever a time Todd wasn't controlling and annoying?

Yes, there was, and it was the day I was gazing at myself in this beautiful, full-length mirror, equally gorgeous but clueless… on our wedding day.

I was so young and in love and full of hope for my life with Todd. I couldn't wait to have children and decorate our first home together. I had no real career ambitions of my own. Or at least I didn't give myself a chance to develop any. However, I thought I had time to figure it out.

But my husband's income was increasing in direct proportion to the size of his head, and his self-importance began to slowly squash any blossoming dreams for my own career.

However, the kids came along quickly, and I told myself this was all normal, and if not normal (what is normal anyway?), it was common.

I lean back and check my Fitbit and see that the Lassiters are running late.

I guess they are also more important than I am.

When I moved out of our house, Todd was eager to unload all this furniture that once upon a time he adored because his new girlfriend thought it was for "old people".

I thought about setting it on fire on the driveway, but since I am all about revenge fantasies with no criminal follow-through, I had the movers bring it here, to this storage unit.

And I bought new furniture for my apartment because this stuff wouldn't fit in the service elevator, let alone through the doorway of my oddly shaped tin can of a dwelling.

Despite giving me the cast-off furniture, Todd has been generous with money since the separation, partly out of guilt and partly because he doesn't want our children to shun him forever once they are off Dad's payroll and don't need him anymore.

Willow and Birch are firmly Team Mom.

I wish Birch didn't have to live in that house to continue to attend his high school, but it's convenient and all his friends live close by. Scott's Addition is not a great neighborhood for teens, unless their parents want them to be surrounded by breweries, cideries, and wineries.

Which we do not.

I stand up and rub my arms; it's a bit chilly in here, and I peek out front to see if Karen and Phil Lassiter have decided to grace me with their presence.

When Todd mentioned that I was trying to sell these household treasures at a neighborhood party, Karen jumped on it.

Their twins, Avery and Ally, just started grad school together at the University of Virginia in Charlottesville, and instead of an apartment, the girls have rented (meaning their parents are paying for) a small (Karen's words—it's 2500 square feet) period home near the Downtown Mall, and this furniture would work perfectly.

Even at Harvard, my daughter is living in the dorm

and has nightstands from Ikea.

But the Lassiters ridiculously spoiled daughters solved my problem, and they are about to unload a whole pile of cash on me, which will help me buy a new car. The SUV I am driving is in Todd's name, and I need to get rid of it. Not only can't I park it, but it's also embarrassing to drive around the city in an eco-unfriendly vehicle.

Oh, I hear a car now, so I can finally get this over with and…

Oh boy, it's not the Lassiters.

In the daylight, Shawn looks even more stunning in snug-fitting jeans and a red t-shirt and the sunglasses… and now he's caught me staring.

I wave like an idiot and say, "Hey, what brings you here?"

As if there would be any reason to be here other than to see me. He obviously isn't yearning for a Tiffany lamp or a Royal Doulton soup tureen before my old neighbors snatch them up.

His smile is as bright as the autumn sunlight, and it's directed at me. Me… I feel swoony again.

"Hey, I'm glad you're still here. I thought you said you were meeting your buyers at ten, but I figured I'd swing by and see if you needed any help."

He closes the distance and envelopes me in a hug.

He feels so good that a part of me wants to drag him over to the Queen Anne chaise lounge and pull down the storage shed door and…

Oh boy, I think that could be on the table… literally… as Shawn leads me into the unit and we get stuck in front of my antique dining table, which has never seen any more action than a turkey carving.

Shawn pulls back, and my heart is racing.

"Sorry, I just wanted to get out of the sun and prying eyes. Since last night, you didn't seem like you were ready for this to be a public thing." He gestures back and forth between us.

I take a deep breath and recall our conversation about me not being ready and him being too young and all the other excuses that don't hold much weight. Well, they would if I even believed them.

"It's okay, it's not so much readiness. I'm mostly scared."

He lifts my chin, and as always, our faces are at the same level, and he says, "I have a good idea that would make it less stressful for you. Also, before I tell you about it, I'd like to kiss you."

I look beyond Shawn out into the parking lot, and I still don't see my tardy buyers, and at this moment, there is no reason to do anything but lean forward and let myself be kissed by this sweet, gorgeous guy who, for some reason, wants the same.

Maybe he bumped his head recently.

I lean in to satisfy my desire and curiosity, and "Ow!"

Instead of a kiss, I slam myself into Shawn's shoulder, which is as solid as it looks, and realize I've tripped on the huge ornate leg of this monstrosity of a table.

I rub my head, and he says, "Are you okay? Here. Let's move over to the couch."

He takes my hand, I trip yet again, and we both fall onto the couch, and now one of the lamps next to the couch tumbles, and he catches it before it hits me.

We both start laughing, and now he's above me, and

I say, "Help, help, I'm stuck".

And of course, that's when the Lassiters decide to show up, and Karen starts screaming bloody murder.

"Phil, oh my God, Tara's screaming!" She holds her hand to her mouth before Shawn and I can disentangle and get up and yells, "And there's a strange man on top of her!"

Phil comes rushing in and says, "What are you talking about?" He sees us standing up, calmly straightening our clothing, and says, "Oh, we're so sorry to interrupt—"

"What do you mean, interrupt!" Karen's eyes are bugging out of her head, and she's pushing toward Shawn with her phone out.

"I'm calling 911, Phil, cover me!"

Shawn puts his hands up to protect his face as my five-foot-tall former neighbor in the designer dress and heels tries to climb up his back like a squirrel hiding its nuts in a tree.

"Karen, I'm fine! Shawn is my neighbor. Get off him!"

Now Phil is pulling his wife off Shawn, and his face is redder than the bottom of his wife's shoes.

"Karen, are you insane? Get a hold of yourself!"

He manages to set her down and tries to fix her disheveled clothing.

"I'm so sorry about that. She's a little twitchy since she decided to join the neighborhood watch. I told you no more crime dramas, Karen."

She huffs and yells, "Well, she was screaming for help, Phil!"

I glance at Shawn in total humiliation, but I see a smile forming on his lips.

The ones I was a centimeter away from enjoying before a lunatic attacked.

Karen stomps her foot and says, "What's so funny, young man?" As she fully takes in Shawn's appearance for the first time, she says, "Oh, you are young, aren't you?"

Phil rolls his eyes as his wife starts flirting with the man she almost called the cops on for trying to consensually kiss a woman in a storage unit.

Shawn tries to look more serious and says in a mocking tone, "I just find it a little funny that your name is Karen… and you are a Karen."

I cover my mouth to suppress my laughter and watch confusion settle over Karen's face, and more embarrassment over Phil's.

He leans forward and cups his hand around his mouth to block his wife's view, "You have no idea how unhappy I was when that saying became a thing."

He glances at his walking meme of a wife, and she smacks his arm.

"Just pay Tara what we owe her and let's get going. We have a brunch reservation, remember?"

"I do remember, and I also recall that it took you an hour to put on your makeup."

Karen purses her lips and pretends to busy herself with examining the furniture while Phil writes a check.

"Well, I for one need a mimosa desperately after all this drama. And I'm sure Tara would love to cash this check before the banks close."

Shawn says, "Right, and I might try to steal it while we finish what we started on the sofa."

Karen wrinkles her face in disgust and says, "I told you we should have scheduled the movers right away.

Who knows what condition this furniture will be in by Monday? She's probably going to have a party in here, and then everything will smell like drugs and who knows what?'

"Karen, go wait in the car. I'm pretty sure if they were going to have a party, they would do it in their own homes."

She clutches her pearls (literally, not just an expression) and walks back to the car. "Fine, if we get stuck with a table near the kitchen, you're sleeping in the guest room."

She flounces out the door, and Phil sighs more deeply than a mouse who just escaped a cat's jaws.

Or in this case, a Karen's.

"I am sooo sorry, I'm Phil Lassiter by the way."

He shakes Shawn's hand and says, "I think she's off her meds again because she says they make her fat. I'd much rather she gain a few pounds of fat and lose a few of crazy, but anyway, I deeply apologize for her behavior."

He hugs me, which is something that has never happened and is super weird.

"Tara, I wish you all the best with…?"

"Shawn Allen. I'm Tara's neighbor."

They shake hands, and Phil says, "And between us, most of our neighbors are really disgusted by Todd's behavior. I heard he couldn't even find anyone to play tennis with at the club."

"Oh, the horror." Shawn clutches his non-existent pearls, and we all laugh.

Phil shakes his head and says, "You see what living with my wife has done to me? I used to be in the Marines, if you can believe it. But once I opened an insurance agency and made it big, I became one of the Karens by association."

Phil hurries out to face his fun brunch date when she bellows, "Philip, my mimosa!"

Alone at last, Shawn leads me to the more comfortable sectional couch behind the dining room table.

"I like this furniture maze. It's like the ones at Halloween except the scariest thing is a Karen trying to put a man in jail for kissing his new… hmm… so about that."

Great, now instead of kissing me, he's going to tell me that he's had second thoughts about trying to date me now that he's witnessed the world I come from up close and personal.

"So, I had an idea."

He takes my hand again, and from the way he is suggestively rubbing it with his thumb, it doesn't seem like he's decided to make a run for it.

I swallow my worries and say, "Okay, what is it?"

"I know you aren't comfortable dating me because I'm too young and it could never work and all of that, but what if we just practice dated?'

I blink hard and scrunch my forehead. "Practice date? You mean fake dating? Like in all those rom coms where the guy needs a date to a wedding because his mother wants him to have a girlfriend?"

"No, not like that at all. Actual dating, but we're doing it so you can get more comfortable with dating. No commitment, no exclusivity. You are free to meet what you describe as an 'age-appropriate man', but in the meantime, you are having some no-stakes fun with me."

I lean back into the comfy cushions and rub my temples. "So, you mean we would be dating and doing other things…"

He moves in closer. "Oh yeah, lots of things. Whatever you want—you're in charge."

"So basically, you are just describing casual dating or friends with benefits."

"No, I think the latter is just disrespectful. My mom went through a lot of that. Oh, sorry, I know you don't like it when I mention my mom."

Now is not the time to get into that whole thing, so I nod for him to continue.

"Well, she did, and I don't like it, and if you want to call it casual dating, that's fine. Maybe it's honest dating. I think we're both in agreement that we probably wouldn't work long term."

"Right, you'll want kids in five to ten years, when my lady parts are no longer functional. And I have teenagers, and I'm not starting over after getting this far. Haha…"

He rolls his eyes. "That's not what I meant, about your lady parts… but what do you think of what I just said?"

"I still don't get what you're proposing."

He pulls me closer and says, "I am proposing that we date, but look at it as a chance for you to get back in the game after being with the same man for a long time. I can be your transition guy, but not in a bad way. And this way we can stay friends forever."

"I like this idea, and I do need help. The thought of dating scares me to death. Any time a middle-aged man tries to talk to me in the produce aisle at the supermarket, I pretend I'm done shopping and drop my mangoes and run."

"Exactly, and don't you want your mangoes to get some attention?"

He leans in even closer.

I whisper into his lips, "I don't think we're talking about fruit anymore."

Chapter 5

"Well played, Mom. Well played."

Birch is shaking Shawn's hand as if they just closed a million-dollar deal.

I clear my throat, and my eyes dart around the foyer of my former home. I barely recognize it with all the mid-century modern furniture that clashes with the style of the house.

"Birch, Shawn is not my boyfriend. He's a neighbor and a new… friend."

Even though Shawn and I enjoyed some very boyfriend-like activities in the storage unit this morning, we mutually agreed that we both get to decide what to tell the important people in our lives about our relationship.

Also, thank God there was no mattress on the four-poster king-sized bed in the back of the unit, because I was almost unable to control myself, even when the old lady who frequents the flea markets showed up with a fresh haul at her neighboring unit.

My son, who stands at 6'2" at sixteen, winks at us and says, "Sure, Mom, just a friend. I get it."

When did my baby boy start winking?

"Dad is going to shit in his driving moccasins when he meets you, Shawn, and I can't wait. It's about time he gets a taste of his own medicine."

Now he sounds like he's been talking to my mother.

I place my purse on the entryway table, which looks like something out of the Flintstones cartoon, and say, "Birch, you really need to be more respectful of your father's choices. And really, I'm doing fine. There's no need to be angry on my behalf."

He glances at Shawn and says, "I can see you're doing fine… as in doing this fine man… am I right?"

He raises his hand to high-five Shawn, and he reluctantly complies.

Probably a force of habit.

Also, Birch must be super angry at Todd if he's happy his mother is having sex.

I'm not… yet… but that's beside the point.

I told Shawn coming here was going to be awkward, but he insisted that he wanted to come after I said that I dread visiting my former home and its occupants, except for Birch, of course.

But I need to deal with this vehicle situation. I don't want this SUV, and since I don't own it, I can easily leave it here.

So, Shawn volunteered to drive his car so I would have a ride back after I surrendered mine.

Dinah is going to be disappointed about the parallel parking lesson, but I will still need to learn even after I buy a more practical car for city living.

"Is your father home? I saw his car in the driveway."

I peer around the kitchen, where my son has led us, as if I would miss Todd. He's enormous and well… obnoxious.

"Yeah, he's here. He's upstairs with the donut heiress."

"Birch!"

Shawn smirks and nods his head in the direction of the back staircase.

Oh, there she is.

"It's okay, Mrs… I mean Tara. He's called me worse. Haven't you, little boy?"

My son pops the top of a soda and replies, "Well, considering that you used to be our babysitter and now you're banging our dad on the regular in my mom's house, I would say it's reasonable, wouldn't you, stepmom?"

Shawn grimaces and whispers to me, "Wow, this one has got a mouth on him. My grandma would be smacking his head with her bedroom slippers about now."

We never hit the kids, but maybe a tap of lightweight footwear to the skull every now and then would have been helpful.

The bellowing voice that joins us puts an end to the bickering.

"Birch Silverthorne, you go to your room right now. You're disrespecting Nicole and embarrassing us in front of your mother and her…"

He reaches across the kitchen island and extends his hand, "Todd Silverthorne. It's a pleasure, and I apologize for my son."

Shawn shakes his hand and says, "No need, I'm just here to help Tara out. With the car."

Todd scrunches up his face and says, "Oh, I thought you were her… you know? Tara, you brought your mechanic here to fix your vehicle. Doesn't he have a shop? Also, what's wrong with the Benz G-Class? I paid $140,000 for that vehicle. Take it to the dealership."

"Oh my God, Dad, he's not her mechanic. You're

such a fucking racist. He's her boyfriend."

"Birch, get upstairs now or… or… I'll do something you won't like."

Todd isn't used to disciplining kids. Or even talking to them a whole lot.

Shawn whispers again, "I was gonna recommend beating him with the slippers again, but the kid really has a point. Maybe I'll wait outside."

I take Shawn's hand in solidarity and say, "Birch honey, just go and let me know what night you'd like to come for dinner this week, okay?"

I plead with him with my eyes as he marches up the stairs, yelling, "Fine, but people don't hold hands with their mechanics, Dad. You big—"

Luckily, the door slams before we get to hear him finish that statement.

Todd runs his hand through his still thick mane of graying hair and says, "Okay, again, I apologize. Nicole and I just… woke up… I'm a little woozy. And you said you were here to help with the car."

I turn back to my soon-to-be-ex and explain. "There is nothing wrong with the G-Class, except that it's way too big and expensive for me to park on city streets. It's impractical. And since it's not even in my name, I am leaving it here for you."

I drop the keys on the kitchen island and turn to go.

"Wait, what? You don't want that gorgeous luxury vehicle that I picked out just for you?" Todd eyes the keys and says, "What are you going to drive then?"

"I'm going to buy a car like a normal person. One that I pick out."

Nicole, who has been standing in the kitchen the whole time staring into space, says, "I'll take it. You haven't bought me a car yet, baby."

I gag inwardly. Baby? Really? Is this what he wants at this point in his life? A vapid college dropout who calls him Baby?

I miss Todd less and less the more I see him.

Todd barks at Nicole, "Now you're going to start on me. You have a perfectly good car that your father bought you when you went to college… for the… what, third time?" He leans on the counter, and now Nicole is pouting.

"Fine, I'll just go to my room then, too. You're so unfair."

A second set of much smaller feet stomp up the stairs, and another door slams further down the hall.

Todd opens his mouth to say something, but seems to realize that apologies or explanations will just make him look even more foolish, so he says, "I am going to my study to find the title to the Mercedes. I am going to sign it over to you, Tara, and I want you to get a nice vehicle and keep the rest of the money to do something fun. Maybe go on a nice trip with… Shawn here."

Before I can argue, he disappears into his home office.

I sigh and say, "I'm so sorry for the way everyone I know has treated you today."

He kisses me gently and says, "Tara, your ex-husband and your former snooty neighbors are hardly people in your life. I'm used to dealing with assholes in certain situations, and we'll rarely be in those situations. Plus, your son is awesome, and you are such a badass with Todd. It's pretty hot, actually."

"Really, well, maybe we can get out of here and continue where we left off in the storage unit."

He pulls me close and says, "Or we could go back to the storage unit. We could leave a little something for Karen."

He laughs, and I playfully smack him. "I walked right into that one, didn't I?"

Todd returns to the kitchen with the document in hand and doesn't meet my eyes.

He obviously knows that Shawn and I are not just friends, and he doesn't seem to like it.

He hands me the title, shakes Shawn's hand, and ushers us out the door.

We stand on the front porch when I realize that I had left the keys to the SUV in the kitchen.

"Shit, I have to go back in and get them, and I really don't want to."

Shawn says, "I know, text Birch and ask him to bring them out."

I jump at the good idea, and in a few minutes, my son is handing me the keys and saying, "Sweet, you get to keep the car, and also not keep it and get the cash."

"Yeah, I'm going to get a more sensible car. Your father has been generous with money, you know. I mean with me."

It doesn't excuse what he did, but it is true. I barely need a lawyer for this divorce. Todd's guilty conscience is overtaking his love of money.

Birch says, "Whatever, Mom. He has plenty of it. Nice meeting you, Shawn. Again, sorry for my shitty dad. Maybe I'll see you when I visit my mom for dinner?"

I shouldn't have brought Shawn here. As nice as it is for Birch to like a man I am dating, I am only practice dating, and I don't need to complicate that with my kids.

For instance, Shawn isn't going to carve the turkey when we have Thanksgiving in my apartment when Willow comes home from college.

To his credit, Shawn doesn't seem freaked out by his new fan.

"Sure, man, that'd be great. And try to go easy on your dad. That woman in there is going to drive him up a wall. I don't think she'll be around long."

I tilt my head like a confused puppy. "You don't?"

"Nah, she's a nightmare, and Todd is looking pretty over it. I wouldn't buy any 'World's Best Stepmom' gifts just yet."

Birch laughs, and I can't help but brighten at the idea of Nicole going away, not for my sake—I'm done with Todd. But it would be nice for my kids because Shawn is right—Todd has made a huge mistake, and I don't think the kids are going to let him forget it.

And I have a hot young practice boyfriend who is not driving me up a wall, well… only in a good way.

Who's having the midlife crisis now, Todd?

Wait, is that a good thing?

I hug my son and remind him to tell me which night he can come for dinner, and we head back to our cars.

Shawn says, "I'd love to ravage you here on the driveway to annoy Todd, but I'm sure a Karen is lurking with a cell phone. Maybe even the actual Karen from this morning."

I lean in to kiss him anyway.

"You're probably right, but the good news is that you never need to set foot on this street again. And neither do I."

I open my car door and say, "So, where is this afternoon's dating practice being held? My place or yours?"

Chapter 6

"It's so smart of you to sell this monster truck. It's pretty schmancy, but you can get a little zippy car, and this lesson will be a piece of cake."

Dinah is sitting in the driver's seat of my soon-to-be departed luxury vehicle, and as predicted, she can barely see out the windshield.

"Maybe if you had a phone book, I could sit on it, but then my ass would slide off on a turn. That's just not safe. Are you listening to me?"

While Dinah rants about cars, all I can think about is Shawn and whether I blew it with him.

Even though I'm not even sure what there is to blow when you're practice dating, other than… well…

"I'm sorry, I'm a little preoccupied." I pick the cuticle on my thumbnail and make a mental note to schedule a manicure. Hell, I can get a spa week in Sedona after I trade in this SUV.

"Okay, girlie, spill it. It has something to do with Shawn, doesn't it? Ooh, this is gonna be good."

I explain the whole story to Dinah—about how Shawn came back to my apartment after dinner on Friday, and how we spent the day together yesterday. The kissing… and also the racism… and my overly enthusiastic son.

"Wow, that bastard gave you this vehicle outright?"

She peers at the SUV's interior as if money was going to start spewing out of the glove compartment.

"That's what you got out of that whole story?"

I shake my head, and Dinah says, "Honey, I knew you were gonna end up with Shawn by the way he was looking at you. Practice dating. That's exactly what I was thinking. You need a palette cleanser, like a lemon sorbet. And he's just the guy. So, what's the problem? Also, we need to get to a car dealership before they close to get you a zippy new ride. They close early on Sunday."

I pause a moment to make sure Dinah is done, and she motions for me to reply and makes the 'zip your lip' motion with her fingers.

I don't think that will last long.

"I don't even know where to start. I like Shawn a lot, and obviously, I'm attracted to him. He's sweet and smart and very patient. And it seems like we both have realistic and reasonable expectations."

Dinah puts her hand to her heart, "Oh, you're killin' me with the romance. Stop, I'm an old lady."

I roll my eyes at my sarcastic friend and say, "I'm just saying that I don't have a good reason to put on the brakes. Hell, my son even liked him. But yesterday I pretended I had somewhere to be so we wouldn't end up spending the night together."

Dinah taps her fingers on the steering wheel. "Why would you do that? Playing games when you have just defined a relationship that is totally anti-game playing is just ridiculous. Are you hung up on Todd?"

I screw up my face and say, "No, not at all. At first, I was devastated, but now I know it was for the best."

Dinah counts off on her fingers. "Okay, so which is

it? You're too religious to have sex outside of marriage? You're afraid to get pregnant? Let's see what else? You witnessed a mafia hit, and you're entering the witness protection program soon?"

"Why would that keep me from having sex?"

"I guess it wouldn't, but it was in a show I was watching last night."

As if that is the least bit logical, I say, "It's none of those things. I'm just scared. I haven't been with anyone but Todd since… in a very long time."

Whew, I caught myself there. I almost said not since freshman year of college, and that may be a teensy white lie. Or whatever color an actual lie is.

"All the more reason to get on with it, girl! When you get to be my age and you and your man both have parts that need a jump start and a lube job, you'll see what I mean. It's like we have to go to the local auto parts store to get it on these days. Oh, but back in the seventies — did I tell you about the time at the museum behind the woolly mammoth exhibit?"

"No, let's save that one for another day. And I know what you're saying. I guess I'm being silly. And Shawn isn't pressuring me."

She taps my arm and says, "I think you're just annoyed with yourself for not going for it. You're a free woman now, and I think you deserve all the happiness."

That makes me teary-eyed, and I reach across the seat to hug Dinah, and she says, "Okay, there's no need for all this mushy stuff. Now I have the perfect idea. Let's get you a new car, and then we'll hit one of the local hot spots. There are loads of men there."

"But you just said I should sleep with Shawn."

"Yes but remember you're practicing. Think of it as

if you're learnin' how to ride a bike. With Shawn, you're takin' off your training wheels and riding in the neighborhood. But you've both agreed this isn't the Tour de France for either of you, right?"

I didn't expect biking as the metaphor Dinah would use, but she's full of surprises.

I nod and she says, "So you need to start lookin' at those fancy racing bikes so you can meet the one you want to make it to the finish line with. Just like me and Vin." She gets misty-eyed now, even though she has shunned the "mushy stuff".

"Okay, you're right. I'm going to loosen up."

I jokingly start shaking my hands and wiggling in my seat, and Dinah puts up her hand, "Okay, let's not do that while we're out lookin' for men. You look like you're tryin' not to wet your pants. Speaking of which, let's get to this car dealership. I drank a lot of coffee, and my bladder isn't what it used to be."

We switch seats so I can drive because it's helpful when the operator of a motor vehicle can see the road, and we head to the nearest CarMax.

CarMax is a used car dealership with lots of selection and great prices. I don't need or want anything fancy, and the money from the trade-in will make a nice savings account.

It's not like I'll have to drive my used car to brunch at the country club, and it will be towed because Karen (one of the many) calls the police on a "suspicious" vehicle.

We park the Mercedes SUV in front of the dealership, and already salespeople are wetting themselves thinking of what they can sell us. Little do they know we are here for something "zippy" and cheap.

"How can I help you, ladies? This is quite a vehicle, Ma'am. Are you looking for something for your grandmother?"

I cringe because there is no telling what's going to come out of Dinah's mouth.

The middle-aged salesman's smile is waning as he realizes his mistake a little too late.

"I am not her grandmother, you nitwit. Now, before you get all googly-eyed thinking my friend is made of money, we are here to trade this vehicle in on something practical. Now get to it, sonny."

It's amazing what you can get away with when you're an old lady.

The salesman introduces himself as John and shakes both of our hands.

"Silly me. I'm not wearing my glasses. Of course, you're not old enough to be this lady's grandmother. I mean, not that she looks too old. You both look—"

"Oh, can it, Johnny. Let's just see the wheels."

I smirk and lead the way so that John will close his mouth and stop gaping at the unbelievable nerve of my friend and find me a car. I'm dying to get this over with so I can hit this hot spot teeming with eligible men that my seventy-five-year-old neighbor is going to show me.

John gives us a brief tour of the showroom and the lot. He slows down at one point, presumably for Dinah, and she says, "I can keep up with you, remember how young I look?"

He looks a little sweaty, and it's a crisp fall day.

I survey the insane amount of gently used vehicles before me and ask, "Do you have something zippy? Small, maybe in a crazy color."

And that's how we ended up driving out of the lot in a 2017 Honda Fit in bright orange with a load of cash in my pocket.

Well, an electronic transfer of a load of cash into my bank account.

I could have gotten more at the Mercedes dealership, but I can't imagine bringing Dinah there, plus I wanted something cheap, reliable, and non-pretentious.

Mercedes doesn't make that.

Dinah opens the sunroof and releases her long mane from the bun on the top of her head. Her grey tresses blow in the wind, and she starts singing folk songs from the sixties with the same sentiment.

"This was a find! And low mileage too. You'll be driving this when I'm in my grave."

"Dinah, don't say that! You're going to live a very long time, and I'll want a new car before then."

We laugh and decide this is the perfect time to check out the scene at Dinah's favorite "watering hole", as she calls it.

We pull up to The Hard Apple in our neighborhood. It's a cidery and apparently one of the most popular in town. I can't believe how hopping it is in here for a Sunday afternoon.

The door is open, and people are spilling into the street. I hear laughter and bad karaoke and suddenly feel too overwhelmed to park the car.

Okay, the street is too full, and I never got my lesson, so I'm not too proud to let Dinah park my new zippy vehicle.

As I stand on the sidewalk, I hope no one sees her parking my car, like an elderly valet service.

She comes sashaying down the street laughing. "Two hipsters in beanies just asked if I could park their cars next. Haha… I just found a new side job."

"You didn't do it, though?"

"No, I told them I had a prior commitment as wing woman for the hottest new chick in town."

I smirk at Dinah and say, "You didn't really say that."

"To hell I did!"

I turn around and sure enough, two young guys are straining to get a look at me.

"I thought we were here to scope out the serious dating scene for me."

She shrugs her shoulders and says, "Sure, but who knows how much practice you might need. Best to cover all the bases." She smiles at the patrons hanging outside the building and loudly says, "I can't wait to get my cider on."

Everyone smiles at me, as if I've taken my sassy mom out of assisted living for the weekend.

Dinah makes a beeline for the bar as soon as we're inside. She squints up at the menu board as the young woman behind the counter patiently reads the specials to her.

We both settle on the pineapple cider, and I survey the room. It's an eclectic crowd, although if we take Dinah out of the mix, I am among the older people here. But I do see some men my age, and there are a lot of people who don't look coupled up.

Alexa, the server, gives us our drinks, and we find a small table in the corner to sit down. I think it was previously occupied a moment ago, but was vacated by young men with good manners who were taught to give up their seats for little old ladies.

"Isn't this place the bomb? Do the kids still say that? Actually, I don't care, I say it."

It's not a very big room, and it's crowded. Some people are playing board games, others are singing off-key renditions of eighties hits, and others are just enjoying a beverage with friends on a Sunday afternoon.

The cidery has a nice neighborhood vibe, and I finally relax a bit—until an attractive man with deep auburn hair and lots of freckles on his strong forearms approaches the table.

"Mrs. Bertelli, how nice to see you. Where's Mr. B? Doing well, I hope?"

"Yes, he's fine. I brought my new friend here to mingle and get acquainted with the neighborhood. This is Tara. Tara, this is Patrick. He owns The Hard Apple."

She nods at me, and her face is plastered with a conspiratorial grin. Although I don't think Patrick knew about this meeting. Therefore, she is a solo conspirator.

"Hi Tara, nice to meet you." He offers his hand, and I take it. I think about how it feels strong and warm, but different from Shawn's.

Is this my life now? Comparing how men's hands feel?

And if I take Dinah's advice, I'll be comparing more than hands soon.

But this is what happens when you're a PTA mom one day and a single city girl the next.

I'm not sure if I should thank Todd or go with my original inclination to kick him in the...

"I own the cidery with my partner, Bobby. So, how long have you been here in Scott's Addition?"

Before I can answer, Dinah blurts, "Whoa, look at

the time. Vinny was expecting me a long time ago. He's making homemade pasta and chicken cutlets tonight."

She jumps and maneuvers Patrick into her chair.

"Dinah, Patrick probably has work to do. And you said Vinny was playing poker tonight."

I glare at her as she backs away.

"Oh, I say a lot of things. Patrick, don't forget to come and get your meatballs this week. Bye, kiddos."

And she's gone.

I turn my gaze back to my new tablemate and say, "I drove us here. I think she's going to walk."

Patrick smiles and says, "It's not that far, and she's got a lot of energy for a lady her age." He leans in and says, "But I do think she's super excited about setting you up with someone."

My face must be turning just a few shades lighter than Patrick's hair.

"Oh, I don't know about that."

He says, "I do. Dinah's been trying to set me up with someone since I broke up with my fiancée."

"I'm sorry to hear that." I really don't want to be someone else's transitional person, especially since he's probably not practice dating anyone as a buffer.

Who am I, and what am I even saying?

He waves his hand and says, "Don't be. It was a while ago, and everything is good now. So, let's hear your story, Tara."

He motions for Alexa to bring us more drinks, and I sort through the events of the past few months to decide what to tell yet another new "friend".

"Well, let's see. How do you feel about donuts?"

Chapter 7

"These damn spreadsheets."

I mutter under my breath even though I'm in my office and no one is around.

Yes, this company is so fancy that even someone in my lowly role gets an office. It's tiny, but it has a door and a small window.

Too bad it's on the 5th floor, so I can't escape out the window.

I can't seem to learn even the most basic Microsoft Office voodoo.

At least that's the way it feels to me, a stay-at-home mother suddenly thrust into the throes of the modern office.

I know I said that Moneca, my sister-in-law, got me the job. And yes, as the Chief Financial Officer, she has some clout.

But the reason for my easy transition back into the world of paid employment is probably going to be knocking on my door in the next few minutes.

I can't worry about that now, though. Who can help me with this gibberish? Maybe Shawn knows about spreadsheets.

I sigh when I think of how sweet he was this weekend and how fun it was to spend time with a man who isn't preoccupied with something... or someone else.

But even though Dinah is encouraging me to go for it, I didn't sleep with him last night.

I thought about it after my forced "introduction" to Patrick at the cidery, but when I got back home, I wasn't sure if Shawn was back from dinner at his grandma's house.

I also don't want him to feel like practice dating me is a new part-time job.

I close the spreadsheet and take a sip of my now-cold tea. Ugh… maybe I should slip out and get a cup with lunch before "you know who" shows up again to ask me to have lunch, a drink, or run away to a foreign land with him.

And to think when I was lounging around my parents' pool in Connecticut in the summer, I thought it would be eons before I would meet a man, but it turns out once you leave the suburbs, there are single men everywhere.

I stand up to stretch my legs and peer out the window. The city looks pretty in the fall. Patrick asked me if I like apple picking.

I wasn't sure how to respond to that, but I guess it wouldn't hurt to diversify my practice dating.

Except… Patrick is a man in my serious dating pool. Based on his pop culture references, I would say he is my age or maybe a little bit younger, but he's not a kid or an old guy trying to grab my butt in the checkout line at the supermarket.

That was the extent of my interaction with eligible men in my parents' neighborhood, but they do live in a 55+ community.

I didn't end up telling Patrick the whole donut story.

I don't want awkward nipple conversations with a man who could one day end up… well… you know…

Patrick is attractive and successful, and he was good-humored about Dinah setting us up.

It's fun meeting new people, but also scary. Shawn and Dinah are right about one thing—I am very out of practice, and that's as if I was ever competent enough to stop practicing when it comes to men.

I'm having dinner with my sister tomorrow night, and I'll ask her what she thinks about all of this. I know I don't have to commit to a guy as soon as I go on a date, but it just feels weird to have Shawn texting me and asking me if I'd like to explore one of his favorite hobbies later in the week (and he means an actual hobby, although it's a mystery activity) and Patrick offering to take me apple picking next weekend.

I ponder whether apple picking is a good first date experience—lots of time to chat, walk, focus on the fruit instead of each other's fruit… hmm… but did it work out well for Adam and Eve?

Now I spot Didier getting out of his bright blue sports car in the parking lot below.

Crap, I should have done my ruminating in the café, and now I'm a sitting duck. Maybe I can grab my stuff and get out the door before… shit, a knock on my door already? Did he grow wings and fly up here?

I get ready to rush past him when my boss, Penelope, opens the door and says, "Oh, there you are. I'm off to lunch, but can you stop by my office this afternoon? I have a new assignment for you."

Penelope is the Regional Director of Stores for Adrien Monet Shoes. We not only make shoes, but we also sell them in our own retail stores. She's in her mid-thirties, single, and gorgeous with thick dark hair and an hourglass figure.

I just hope whatever she has for me doesn't involve spreadsheets.

Or PowerPoint. Please God, no PowerPoint.

"Great, I'll stop by later." I smile even though I'm kicking myself for losing my escape window to avoid my next visitor.

I hear him before I see him. "Oui, my weekend was spectacular, mon ami."

I wish someone else would detain him, but no one makes any more than polite conversation with Didier when he's on this floor. Everyone is a little intimidated by the grandson of the founder, and the current President of the company.

He almost runs into Penelope as she turns to leave.

"Where's the fire?" Penelope speaks more freely with the big boss, and she knows something is going on with me and him, but she really doesn't care as long as I do my job and no one in HR bothers her.

Didier pulls his tight turtleneck collar away from his neck and says, "There is no fire, but it is hot in here. I will ask someone to turn down the heat. Who does that? Do you know?"

Penelope shakes her head and says, "I'll text building maintenance." She wags her finger at him, "And don't you take up too much of Tara's time—she's working on an important spreadsheet."

She mouths something behind his back, and I'm sure it's something like, "Let me know if he's bothering you" or "Please don't quit because of this guy".

She waves and backs out of the office. Didier doesn't close the door but quickly sits down.

"You look beautiful. How was your weekend?"

I sigh and sit back down in my chair. I keep thinking that I will find a way to dissuade Didier's interest. A short fling twenty years ago shouldn't have been this memorable.

"It was good, great actually. I met lots of new friends." I would love to say I met some new men friends, but that would only make him pursue me harder. He's always been extremely competitive, which is how I ended up with him in the first place.

I was working for this very company right out of college as a Marketing Assistant. At that time, it felt glamorous and exciting, and I was able to walk in these shoes. We were still in New York, and Todd had been working for a law firm in Manhattan for a couple of years, and we were planning our wedding.

He was working all the time, but I didn't mind because I was excited for our future and busy with my new job and the wedding details.

Todd was working long hours and was extremely stressed. And as if that wasn't enough, his father had just announced his run for the United States Senate and was asking the family to help with campaigning.

Those Silverthornes are all self-centered, but that's a story for another day.

Todd and I grew apart, and about six months before our wedding, he broke up with me.

Just like that—poof… done.

I was shocked and heartbroken, but also super angry. He claimed there was no one else, and less than a year later, I married him, believing that there wasn't, but I can't say the same for myself.

Didier was a handsome Frenchman, just a few years

older than me. He was working in the family business and had much more time and disposable income on his hands.

He was fun and exciting, and I was swept away… until Todd came back into my life with endless apologies and flowers and gifts.

I had wanted a chance to see if things with Didier could develop into something more than play, but in the end, I decided that he wasn't serious enough for me.

It was so incredibly stupid because we were all so young, although Didier was playing the field and wasn't married for many years, and only recently separated from his wife. She moved to Quebec with their adorable three-year-old daughter.

Todd knew about Didier back then, and I am sure he assumes that I got this job now by sleeping with the boss, but I told him that Didier was married and that my sister-in-law was the one who helped me.

This is all technically true, but the sharply dressed man with the thick salt and pepper hair and the thicker French accent (after all these years) is relentless.

Ever since he found out I was single, he has been trying to spend time with me.

Didier frowns and says, "New friends? I would love to hear everything about them, unless they are men. Then I would like them to go away like little bugs flying by my ears, au revoir, little men bugs!"

He swishes his hands in a flourish, and I can't help but smile at his antics.

"Didier, you are still a married man. How do I know your wife isn't going to come home with your daughter and you'll be a happy family again?"

"Oh, that will never happen. She despises me."

I roll my eyes at his dramatic words. "Really? She despises you? I heard you were planning the company Halloween party together."

"This is just for the show. Dominique is very invested in the company's success—she is like a scary bird with the claws and the beak pecking at me to give her the money."

He mimics his wife's bird-like greed, and I glance out into the hallway in the hopes that someone… anyone… will walk by and I can pretend I urgently need to talk to them.

He pulls out his phone and starts tapping. "I will prove to you that my wife hates my guts, as you say." He holds up a finger and places the phone on my desk as it dials a number.

A woman answers and says in beautiful, native speaking French, "Que veux-tu, idiote?"

What do you want, idiot?

I guess she isn't crazy about him.

Didier switches the conversation to English and says, "I am with a beautiful woman, and I told her that she has no need to worry that you and I will be together because you hate me. Please tell her how you feel."

"Yes, I hate you. Whoever you are, strange woman, please occupy my idiot husband so he stops calling me. I am going now."

I stare at the phone and say, "Wow, she's a sweet one."

"I told you; she hates me. So, you see, we are fine. Come to the Halloween party with me as my guest. And let's go have lunch now and talk about our couple's costume."

Would it be so terrible to have lunch with him? And

I do like him—he just comes on so strong, and my resolve can be so weak.

Before I know it, I'll be the Morticia to his Gomez in a few weeks, and then I'll be in Paris in a white dress within the year, walking down the aisle at some cathedral.

Hmm… I guess most women wouldn't find that to be a sad story…

I sigh and say quietly, "Okay, I will have lunch with you, but not today."

I am practicing setting boundaries. No extra explaining—no is a complete sentence!

He stands up and folds his hands, "Merci, I promise I will be a perfect gentleman. I just want the chance to know you again. How could it not be fate for both of us to be single again after all these years?"

I smile and lead him out the door with a promise to send him a calendar invite for lunch sometime this week.

I lay my head down on my desk after he leaves and barely have time to sort through my thoughts when I hear a gravelly lady's voice laced with years of cigarettes and yelling at her many sons.

I sit up and say, "Oh, hi, Roz. How are you? Sorry, I was having a moment."

The office cleaning lady saunters in and points to my trash can.

"I thought he'd never leave. Jeez Louise, he's got it bad. I can't believe you finally caved. Well, I can because look at him. Honestly, I think it's kind of romantic the way he is so persistent. But of course, if you thought he was a rodent, I'd call the exterminator fast… you know what I mean?'

I hardly ever know what Roz means. She speaks her

own language, but she's a good listener and another mom-like figure in my life.

Come to think of it, I have almost as many moms now as love interests.

Maybe I could assign each of them a man for us to talk about. It's becoming too much for one mom.

"I do like him, but he's the President of the company, and that alone is a problem."

Roz says, "Hey, you only live once. When my Jimmy died… God rest his soul… I was crushed, but then I got back out there. I had four or five boyfriends at the same time. You think too much."

She squeezes my shoulder and is off to collect the rest of our trash. She should be a life coach, not a cleaner.

"Thanks, Roz. What are you doing this weekend? Do you like brunch?"

She pats her wide midsection. "Don't I look like I like brunch? Haha… of course… I know, why don't you come over on Saturday morning, and I'll make you the best brunch you've ever had. My little granddaughter will be with me, but she can watch cartoons and play while we talk." She lowers her voice and adds, "Maybe by the weekend you'll have at least one scandalous thing to share."

If only she knew how many scandalous opportunities presented themselves.

Well, at least if it were like a hundred years ago. According to Roz, I should be building a reverse harem.

I agree to her plan, and she gets back to work, and I turn to my computer to do the same.

I don't know how other harem builders can function. Maybe I should just stay single and work on myself.

No, that's boring. I can do it all at the same time.

Starting with this stupid Excel formula crap… and what to do with all these men.

I spend the rest of the afternoon watching training videos on LinkedIn and YouTube (about Excel, not men), and I finally figure out the simple tasks.

Maybe I should use this company as a training ground to catch up on all I don't know and get a job somewhere else. That way, if I did decide I wanted to be with Didier, I wouldn't feel so weird about it.

Although I am enjoying the practice dating with Shawn and all that is waiting for me there, and Patrick's arms will look very strong and sexy while picking apples—maybe he'll have to lift me up to pick the best ones at the top of the tree.

I know for a fact that not even my eighteen-year-old daughter is this boy crazy.

I glance at the time on my computer and realize I never stopped by Penelope's office. She's probably busy, but I should see if it's a good time now.

I am just about to send her a message when she pops her head in my office, "Hey, I forgot we were supposed to meet. I am double-booked for the rest of the day, but I need you to fill in at the flagship store in Carytown."

I blink hard and wrinkle my forehead. "You mean you want me to work in the store, selling shoes?"

Wow, something I am even less qualified to do.

"Yes, that's what I said."

"Oh, I would be happy to help out. Is there a staffing problem?"

"You could call it that. Several people have quit to work at the new mall, and Kenneth is beside himself. You know how he gets? Anyway, we really need all hands on deck, and I thought you could learn a lot more about the business this way, so a win/win."

I've never worked in retail. Not even in high school—I worked at a day care after school, practicing for my mom job.

But one thing you don't have to do when you're selling shoes is spreadsheet formulas, so I'm all in.

"Sounds good, I guess I should get in touch with Kenneth?"

"Yep, I told him to expect you. Is tomorrow too soon?"

I fight the urge to let my jaw drop to the ground, and I agree, because what else can I do?

Penelope is already on her phone as she exits my office, giving me a thumbs-up.

But really, how hard can it be to sell shoes? I've bought a lot, so it can't be that different, just the reverse process.

Except I'll have to wear the uncomfortable shoes while standing all day.

I could just quit and live off the money I got from selling the Mercedes, but then what would I do when that runs out?

Nope, I will do my job to the best of my ability and learn new skills. And if I end up destroying my feet, my podiatrist sister can give me a… foot transplant… I don't think that's a thing. I should check my disability benefits just in case the only solution is an extended break from standing at all.

I email Kenneth and ask him to text me what time to report to the store and anything else I need to know.

Now it's time to go and meet my sister for dinner in The Fan, which is close to her house on Monument

Avenue. I turn off my computer and see that my daughter has called.

I hope nothing is wrong — kids never call unless they want money (she would ask Todd) or they're having a crisis.

I'll call her from the car — while I'm busy collecting moms I need to remember that I am one.

Chapter 8

"Mom, I hear you have a hot, young boyfriend!"

I resist the urge to chastise my daughter for talking to her brother about my love life.

However, when they lived in the same house together for the past sixteen years, they barely interacted at all. I almost had to reintroduce them once a week (or month) at the dinner table.

"Willow, remember your brother Birch, the one who bit your ears like a puppy when he was a baby? Well, here he is all grown up, and now he's had all his shots."

"Willow, you know Birch exaggerates, and he's just trying to get under your father's skin."

"Actually, Dad was the one who told me, but Birch added in the details. It's fine, Mom. We want you to be happy."

I am trying to pay attention to Willow while keeping my eye on the GPS so I can find this restaurant and then find a place to park. Why did I not think of this parallel parking problem when I moved to the city? At least I have a zippy little car now. If I still had my SUV, I'd have to leave in the morning for a dinner reservation.

"Your father told you? Huh… well, he's not my boyfriend, just a guy… you know what, don't worry about it. He's my neighbor, and you'll meet him when you come home next month for Thanksgiving. Did you get your plane ticket yet?"

Oh, there's a spot, no damn it, there's a parking sign with all those arrows about how it's a towing zone under a full moon on opposite Tuesdays and a loading zone any time someone named Tara Silverthorne tries to park there.

At least it's not raining, and since when does the city have this many fire hydrants? Oh great, now Beth is texting me about where I should park, but I can't look at messages and the GPS without flying onto the sidewalk, and what did my daughter just say?

"Wait, you want to come home sooner than Thanksgiving? How can you do that? Your classes aren't online. And aren't you having fun in your dorm? It seemed great when we dropped you off."

At Harvard, the freshman dorms are more like apartments. I killed cockroaches with hairspray in my freshman dorm.

Also, she's in Boston… she can't say that she's bored. I was never bored in Boston.

She sighs, and I know I am about to hear an exasperated rant about how I don't understand anything.

"Mom, fun isn't all there is to life, and I hate it here. Everyone is a smart, rich asshole, and the ones who aren't think I'm a smart, rich asshole."

As a mother of two, Todd's soon-to-be ex-wife, and someone who is trying to parallel park in The Fan at 6:00 PM, I am well aware that there is more to life than fun.

"Honey, you've only been there for two months. It's a big school in a major city; you need to give it time. Also, what will your father say? Oh my God, did you tell him? Or was he just interested in my new non-boyfriend?"

"No, Mom, I'm telling you because I thought you'd be more supportive. Dad is an Ivy League whore."

Oh, a big truck is pulling out of that spot, and now, great, the freaking purple city bus is coming, and I'm in the way. How in the hell should I know where the bus stops are?

"Willow, you can't call your father a whore, even if it isn't in reference to you know who… hold on, I'm trying to park in the city to meet Aunt Beth for dinner."

"Holy shit, Mom, why didn't you say so. I can't believe I haven't heard any crunching sounds or screaming pedestrians."

Who in the family is this sarcastic? Surely not me.

"Haha, very funny. Listen, I think I see a bunch of spots and I only have to walk like four blocks, which is an improvement over my usual… anyway, please try to stick it out until Thanksgiving and we can talk about it then. Our family has been through a lot lately, and it's normal to react to the turmoil."

That sounded pretty therapist-like, but also supportive Mom-like.

I wonder when my children will figure out that I have no idea what the hell I'm doing.

"Okay, I guess I can do that. Can I at least stay with you? And maybe Birch can come stay with us, too? Even he's looking good after being around these assholes. And are Grandma and Papa coming?"

Clearly, this child has never seen the inside of a city apartment if she thinks I can host a turkey-induced coma sleepover for the whole freaking family.

But for now, I say, "Yes, of course. It will be a big happy family reunion… and I have lots of new friends for you to meet, and no, they are not all men."

Dear Lord, if I let her meet Dinah, that woman might suggest she channel her inner trapeze artist and join the circus.

Or sleep with Shawn since I haven't done it yet.

"Okay, I'll book my ticket, but I am getting a good seat and charging Dad's card. You know, I don't even want to be a lawyer. I hate lawyers, I don't even really like laws."

I somehow manage to pull my car right into a beautiful, huge spot on a half-deserted street—this must be where all the people live who work late and go to happy hour because nobody is home.

Did my daughter just say she doesn't even like laws?

I rest my head on the steering wheel and think about how good my bed will feel later with no one talking to me, although I could stop by my hot, young "practice" boyfriend's place. I wonder if they serve energy drinks at this restaurant for women who want sex but can't stay awake.

Also, hopefully, my daughter will come home before she gets arrested for breaking a law she doesn't like.

Once again, she doesn't get that from me because I've spent the past twenty minutes driving around the same streets looking for legal parking.

"Call me again sometime this week. I really want to hear more about your classes and… well, anything good. There has to be something."

Hopefully, she won't call my mother for advice. I don't know how that woman raised a doctor. She's as bad as Dinah, but instead of telling her to be daring, she'll tell her to move to Connecticut, and she'll hire her to answer phones at the real estate firm.

I am angry with Todd, but that might kill him.

Willow promises to call, and now I realize that I must make sure I'm home at least one night this week, and with all this "practice" and possibly "real" dating, I'll have to start scheduling a phone call night for my children and parents.

That reminds me, do I have any Tylenol in the house?

Beth is waving to me from down the street, and it looks like she met me halfway, as if she doesn't think I can find the new trendy Asian fusion restaurant.

I circled it three times so I know where it is; however, I don't know what I will order because when I looked up the menu online, I couldn't understand it.

I mean, it's Mexican and Asian? What the hell…

I finally close the gap between us and look down at my feet. I forgot to change into more practical shoes, and I know Beth is going to make a comment.

"Hey, I was worried you wouldn't find parking."

She grabs me in a big sister bear hug, and then pulls back and says, "Why are you as tall as me?"

As I said, I am not a tiny woman at 5'9", but Beth is Amazonian at 6'0". She looks a lot like Wonder Woman. We both got my father's height, while my brother got my mother's lack of height.

Poor Robert.

I put up my hand and say, "I don't want to hear it. Not everyone can wear orthopedic shoes to the office. We are selling high fashion. Now take my arm so I can hobble the rest of the way with my battered feet."

She sighs and shakes her head, but guides me to the door of Wong Garcia.

We are seated by the window, which is nice for people watching and also for sitting down as soon as possible.

The server asks what we'd like to drink, and I order a ginger ale because one alcoholic drink will put me to sleep, and also, it's too much work to decipher the drink menu.

Beth studies the menu and says, "This food is new for you, isn't it? It's not a fifty-dollar steak."

I squint at the menu — do I need bifocals already? "I eat plenty of cheaper meals, especially nowadays, but I don't know what you're talking about. You're not exactly poor."

Beth lives in a townhouse on Monument Avenue, which I am sure is valued at over a million dollars. Just like my house, I mean, Todd's house. Someday I will be able to say that without any bitterness.

"True, but I am more in touch with my roots and not in the least bit snobby. Speaking of roots, do you know you have some grey hairs?"

I touch my head and say, "I really hope it's the lighting and what, are you Mom now?"

This banter continues as we order our entrees. I am getting something that's a cross between a taco salad and a pu pu platter, and I just hope it stays down.

Being an open-minded, adventurous city girl, I'm about to find out.

I tell Beth about Willow because my kids are my favorite… and safest… subject.

"If she doesn't want to be a lawyer or go to Harvard, you can't make her. You know that, and who cares what Todd says? Is he really in a position to say anything about anything?"

"Well, he is still her father, but I know what you mean. He didn't think through the ramifications of the whole Nicole thing, especially not when it comes to the kids and their opinion of him."

Beth waves off my defense of my baby daddy (I'm thinking that's what I should call him now, but maybe not out loud) and says, "Well, I can't wait to see her when she gets home. We should do Thanksgiving dinner at my house, don't you think?"

Whew, that's a relief. I want to ask if Mom and Dad can stay at her place as well, since I don't have enough room, but I don't want to push my luck. Our parents are a lot of work.

The server brings our food, and it smells amazing. I don't know why I would doubt it—I don't know anything about cooking. All I ever made at home was grilled lean meat and salads so Todd and I could fit in with all the "beautiful people".

The new Tara Silverthorne isn't as boring, although soon she will need bigger pants.

Beth places her napkin on her lap and picks up her fork. "This looks delicious. So, speaking of delicious, when were you going to tell me about your new man?"

"What man? Are you serious? I just met him three days ago, how could you possibly know there's a man?"

Beth laughs and says, "You forget I'm a foot doctor, and that many of your neighbors are my patients because they are also vain, silly women who destroy their feet."

"How do my neighbors know… crap, someone saw me at the house?"

She nods and smirks.

"And in the driveway?"

"I always say the women in your neighborhood need more to keep them occupied than shopping, but yes, one of your neighbors saw you at the house with a very handsome young man."

I roll my eyes and say, "And I'm sure she gave you a few more details?"

Also, what are the odds of one of those bitches having a foot appointment the day after I showed up at my… I mean, Todd's house?

"Oh yes, she did, but I think it's great." She butters a piece of strange-looking bread and says, "He does sound really young, though."

I finish chewing a tasty morsel and reply, "It's not like he's riding a bike with training wheels. He's an actual adult. And nothing is really happening. We're just practice dating."

As soon as I say that, I regret it. Now I have to explain this convoluted, vague concept to my practical, analytical sister.

Also, why did I think bringing Shawn to Todd's house was a good idea?

There. I said it that time. Todd's house.

"Practice dating?"

I attempt to give her the basic rundown of my fear of dating in general, and my need to get comfortable being… intimate (I hate that word) with men other than Todd, and how I don't want to screw up a good prospect when one comes along.

I know I sound insane, but I just keep talking.

"So, you are practice dating so that you'll be more comfortable real dating, and you want this guy to be your transitional man because he's not a serious prospect?"

"Wow, you're good at understanding this."

"It's not very complicated. A little nuts, but that's okay. As long as you're both happy with the plan. So, if you're practice dating, are you having practice sex? Because that seems like the biggest plus of this situation."

Why does everyone want me to have sex?

"That part is complicated."

Beth signals the server for a refill on her wine and says, "It's not really. You're just making it that way. You are not married anymore, Tara. You deserve to do whatever you want now."

She sounds like Dinah and my children, and my inner voice that I tell to shut up numerous times per day.

"I know, but I just met him. He is a nice guy and very good-looking. I don't know what he sees in me, but I guess some young guys like older women."

Beth smacks the table. "I know! He's in the Boy Scouts, and he's trying to earn his 'banging an old lady' badge."

If we were home, I would throw something at my smart-ass sister.

"Come on, Tara, you have to admit that was funny. Instead of helping old ladies across the street, this would be the more… modern version… hahahaha."

"Okay, it was funny, but also sick. Actual Boy Scouts are children. And how about you? You never talk about dating anyone. We don't even know if you're… you know."

Beth lets out an exasperated sigh. "I told you, and I tell everyone that my sexuality is none of anyone's business."

For years, our family has suspected that Beth was a

lesbian and didn't want us to know, but she still won't deny it or affirm it.

I say, "This is all because of that one time in college when Mom found your Melissa Etheridge CD in the car, and it was the same week you refused to wear a dress to a family party."

"She was so ridiculous. I'm surprised she didn't become a detective instead of a realtor with all the snooping she did."

"Yes, obviously those things don't make you a lesbian because millions of straight women listen to Melissa and wear pants, but seriously, you can't even tell me, your own sister, the truth? You know that no one in the family would have a problem with it."

She leans back in her chair and says, "No, it's the principle. I am not required to share any details of my personal life with anyone. When I want you to know, you'll know."

We've had this conversation numerous times, and I guess she's just never going to tell us. She's so stubborn!

Also, not a family trait I inherited.

"Okay, so you like your privacy. But why don't I have any? My shitshow of a life is paraded out in the open for everyone to see."

She places her napkin over her plate as if her meal is now deceased—rest in peace, enchilada fried rice, and says, "You're the one who's advertising your love life like it's a going-out-of-business sale at a used appliance store."

I get a mental image of me wearing a costume, standing on the street with a sign that says, "Last chance, boys—Tara Silverthorne's lady parts are shutting down soon!"

Speaking of costumes, I just remembered the Halloween party and Didier's lunch invitation I agreed to accept. And then that makes me think of work and the store I have to work in tomorrow.

I change the subject and tell her about work, and before you know it, the check is on the table, which of course she snatches.

"You can pay next time, and please, for the love of your arches and heels, do not wear those shoes to the store tomorrow. Don't they make flats or bedroom slippers or something?"

I promise to check out the whole line and get myself the most comfortable impractical designer shoes possible because I agree—Shawn isn't going to want to earn his merit badge if I'm using a cane.

Beth insists on driving me back to my car, even though this is a very safe neighborhood.

I promise to keep her up to date on my love life, but I didn't even tell her about Patrick. Who knows if that's even going to happen. Guys say a lot of things while drinking cider on a Sunday afternoon.

Or at least I assume they do. Todd wouldn't be caught dead in a cidery on any afternoon. He's a wine snob.

I enjoy a short, quiet drive back to my apartment, but everyone on my street seems to be home now. I'm surprised more people aren't out having fun.

I mean, I'm exhausted, but I am one of the oldest people in my building.

When that hipster rental agent showed me the apartment, I asked about the demographics of the tenants, and he said there was a good mix of people and that there were other older residents, like the lady in 1C who knits him sweaters like his grandma.

He's just lucky I don't own any knitting needles—comparing me to his grandma!

I park around the corner and realize that I must walk past The Hard Apple to get home.

If I weren't so drained, I might pop in, but that would make me appear too eager.

Plus, if I go straight home, I could see what Shawn is up to, but he's probably not home yet.

He texted me earlier and said he was watching Monday Night Football with his buddies at the pool hall.

I hope pool isn't the hobby he wants to introduce me to on our date—no, that would be silly. And he's not going to want to introduce me to his friends—this is just practice dating.

I'm slightly limping again as I approach the entrance to the cidery. Unlike yesterday, it's pretty quiet, and there is only a faint hum of conversation coming from inside.

I don't want Patrick to see me walking past. I can't be tempted to prolong this night. I have to get home to soak my feet, and I also don't want to seem like a stalker.

There are already too many things to worry about with this whole "dating" nonsense. Maybe I'll read some articles tonight for confused divorced women.

I want to hurry past the door but not look like I'm running from the cops.

Knowing me, I'll fall flat on my face, and Patrick will have to come out to carry me to safety and call the paramedics.

I have definitely watched too many cheesy rom-coms.

Instead, I hobble at the pace I can manage and glance

into the cidery. I don't see him, so maybe he's in the back. Oh, there he is.

He's at the bar talking to a pretty blonde with very long legs.

Well, of course, he's a good-looking man who owns a bar and obviously meets women every night.

But that doesn't mean I can't go apple picking with him, or whatever, right?

I narrowly escape detection when he laughs and turns his head slightly towards the door.

Whew… I'm pretty sure he missed me, and he knows I live in this neighborhood anyway, so I'm just being silly.

I have more practical things to focus on. Once I get home, I am going to go online and order some vitamins. And I need to get to the grocery store so I can start eating healthily again. Meatballs and Mexican pu pu platters are delicious, but this woman needs a salad or twelve to keep up with this new lifestyle.

I am almost home when a familiar Buick pulls up beside me.

"Hey, lady… oh, it's you. Still with the shoes, huh?"

Lotto Lenny shakes his head as if he's qualified to judge my life decisions.

"Good evening to you, too. Did you have another question?"

"Yes, as a matter of fact, I do. Are there any bookies in this neighborhood?"

"Bookies, like for gambling?"

He screws up his face and says, "No, I wanna go to story time at the library. Of course, for gambling. Oy vey!"

Where is Dinah when I need her to discipline Lenny?

"I don't know. Your questions are outside my areas of expertise."

"Yeah, I think I may need to find a different neighborhood. Damn gentrification."

Poor Lenny. He's trying to figure out where he fits, just like me.

"Hey Lenny, can I ask you a question?"

"Sure, let me guess? You wanna know how much money I won, right?"

"No, that's none of my business. I'm just wondering why you don't buy a new car. You could probably afford something really nice. Not that this car isn't… nice."

He laughs and says, "Oh, it's a genuine piece of shit, but I like it that way." He lowers his voice and looks around. "This way, I stay incognito if you know what I mean. If I had a fancy set of wheels, the chicks and the feds would be crawling all over me."

He winks and waves as he drives off, but abruptly stops and backs up.

"I almost forgot; I just saw your new boyfriend at the pool hall."

I almost started the "he's not my boyfriend" speech, but what's the point?

"He was watching the game, right?"

He shrugs and says, "If that's what they're calling it now."

Chapter 9

"Look at her. There's a gal who knows how to walk in heels." Dinah nods her head across the street.

I lower my sunglasses to get a better look at the graceful blond walking down the sidewalk, headed in the opposite direction.

"Wow, yeah, she is steady on her feet."

Dinah purses her purple painted lips and says, "Not sure where she's going in that get-up, though?"

You see all kinds of things in the city that you'd never see on River Road, but this woman is dressed a little… sparsely… for the weather and the time of day.

"Maybe she works at the strip club that Lenny was looking for."

I hate to stereotype her based on her appearance, but where else would a woman in a tube top and a hot pink mini skirt the size of an ace bandage be headed at 8:30 on a Tuesday morning?

I also see a spot of pale blue on the sole of her stilettos. Interesting. She must make a lot of money in tips if she's buying Monet shoes.

Dinah slaps my arm, "That's it, I bet. No wonder Lenny was trying to find that place. I didn't know strippers were that attractive. I thought it was just on TV."

Having no experience in this area, I just shrug my

shoulders. I have better things to worry about than what anyone else is wearing.

Such as Lenny's comment about Shawn last night. I haven't talked to Shawn yet, and I don't know how or if to approach the subject of a "young chick hanging all over him" at the pool hall.

After all, we are practice dating and made an agreement that we can both do whatever we want. We haven't even slept together yet, and I can always back off any time I want.

So why does it feel so icky?

I can't worry about it right now, because in a couple of hours, I need to begin work at the store. They put me on the eleven-to-seven shift, supposedly so I can cover lunches and breaks. I think my training is going to consist of someone showing me where they keep the shoes, and I'll be fed to the shoe-buying lady wolves.

But really, how busy can a store that sells shoes that cost hundreds of dollars be on a Tuesday?

I am joining Dinah on her morning walk because I am not used to going into work this late, and I don't want to waste the morning lounging around in my pajamas.

Plus, I've been eating way too much lately, and I am determined to stay in shape. I noticed Todd was a little thicker around the middle — probably from all the free donut samples.

I shake that thought out of my head and tune back into Dinah's running monologue about her day.

"Oh shoot, I think I have a doctor's appointment today. What time is it?"

I glance at my Fitbit and say, "It's 8:35, but why don't you just check your calendar on your phone?"

She laughs for a good thirty seconds, including some light wheezing and thigh slapping, and finally says, "I don't bring that thing on walks. And even if I did, how would it tell me if I have a doctor's appointment?"

Recalling her "Cindy" comment, I guess I shouldn't be surprised that she isn't too tech savvy.

"There is a calendar app on your phone. Do you have an iPhone?"

She shakes her head and says, "No, why would I have your phone? I have a little purple one in the kitchen drawer."

I hate to be one of those people who chastise old people for not using the latest gadgets. I have teenagers, so I know how much tech shaming goes on. I didn't know how to make an Instagram story, and I thought I'd never hear the end of it.

So, what if I posted a video of me cursing at my foot? It got a lot of views before Birch took it down and threatened to block me.

But Dinah should really carry her phone in case of emergencies.

"Oh, so you don't carry it. What if Vinny needed you in an emergency?"

She waves off my suggestion and says, "If he has an emergency, he should call 911. I'm not a doctor."

Hmm, that's a fair point, except she was certainly acting like one when he slightly burned his hand.

"But what if you have an emergency while you're out alone?"

"I'd just start screaming like it was 1985 and someone would call 911 on their… oh, I see where you're going with this." She crinkles up her face deep in thought. "But I still don't like people being able to track me down. I like to fly under the radar."

Now she sounds like Lenny, which reminds me of Shawn and what I'm going to do.

Also, with the volume of her voice and the brightness of her lips, she is never going to fly under the radar. Her lips could be seen from space.

We finish up our walk with me telling her that my mother is coming to visit next weekend, even though they are coming in a little over a month for Thanksgiving.

This is not the most opportune time for Liz Lunsford to swoop down, but knowing her, she'll be on the phone with her real estate clients all weekend.

We're interrupted by Vinny pulling up in his old delivery van and honking the horn. Once Dinah is done dramatically clutching her heart, she gets in and thanks Vinny for remembering her doctor's appointment, laughing as always.

This does not seem like the most efficient way to do things, but then who am I to say anything? They've been together for fifty-eight years, and they're a lot more stable than I am.

I wave goodbye as I see Lenny's ancient Buick cruising down the next block with a woman... oh come on, that gorgeous blond is in Lenny's car?

I hope she knows him, but again not my problem.

Dinah is probably right—Lenny did find the strip club after all, without help from me or Cindy.

I continue to the end of the street and decide to go home and get ready for work. I am going to wear my uncomfortable shoes, but I intend to scope out the whole line and see if I can get away with something more practical. After all, being a man, Kenneth, the store manager, doesn't have to wear these stupid shoes at all.

I open the door to my little oasis from the world and sigh. It really is a cute apartment, and I've done my best to make it cozy with throw pillows in soft blues and taupe and a patterned rug from the pretty home furnishing store next to the Adrien Monet store.

Most of my new furniture is cheap and disposable, but it looks nice for now.

My bedroom is up a winding spiral staircase, and yes, I am smart enough not to tackle it in my work shoes.

I start pulling outfits out of my closet, and while I am not going for the look of my blond neighbor, I do need to spruce up my wardrobe. It's pretty bland.

I never got into spending a lot of money on clothes for myself. I bet Nicole is making up for my thriftiness with Todd's money.

However, I do have a windfall from the SUV sale, so I will find a few new pieces of trendier clothes on my lunch break. Dinner break? Hmm… I wonder when I get a break if I'm covering all the other breaks.

This retail world is a mystery.

I settle on simple black pants and a floral silk blouse, along with my black Monets.

I'm going to carry them, so I don't wipe out on the stairs. The soles of all of Monet's shoes are a robin's egg blue. Adrien was trying to copy the concept of the signature Louboutin red with his own flair for color.

They are beautifully crafted shoes, but I wonder if they reflect the way a real woman lives.

Sure, well-paid strippers and social climbing show-offs love them, but what about young mothers, old ladies, pregnant women, and just plain large women?

I grab my black Kate Spade city tote and make my

way slowly down the stairs. At least the store is on one floor.

I wrestle myself into my Monets, hop into my zippy little car, and park in the lot a block away from the store. I'm probably not supposed to do that because parking for customers is scarce in Carytown, but I don't care.

Before I even reach the door, I see Kenneth outside on his phone. He is gesturing wildly, and I wonder if I should give him a moment to finish up, so I don't awkwardly eavesdrop while trying to get to the door.

He turns and spots me, and now he is flailing even more manically, waving me to the door like I'm about to slide into home plate for the winning run.

"Thank God you're here!"

He opens the door and leads me inside the empty store.

"Thank… you… is there a problem?"

Kenneth is often overly dramatic on the weekly team meeting calls that I moderate for Penelope, and I don't see what could possibly be wrong. The store is immaculate, and I don't see any fires.

He throws his hands up in the air. "Is there a problem?, she says. Yes, there is, as a matter of fact. That was my contact at the wine bar, and she said the Ladies Who Read book club is just finishing up their meeting."

"Oh, why is that bad?"

I shrink a little as he bellows, "Because when those bitches are done pretending that they know how to read and drowning themselves in a full-bodied red blend, they sashay their asses over here to shop."

I put my purse down on the counter and try to catch Kenneth's eyes, as if I were emergency services, talking him off the ledge.

"Don't you want people to shop in the store?"

He sighs like he's trying to suck in the entire contents of the sales floor and says, "Yes, but Isla and Darby both called in sick—I swear they have a thing going and gave each other the creeping crud—and all I have is you to help me with the assault of the Real Housewives of Carytown until Gwen comes in at three, and by then the store will be destroyed and there will at least one customer who passed out trying to buckle the straps on her kitten heels."

"Wow, they're already drunk before eleven o'clock?"

I don't know why I say this, because some of these women are probably my old neighbors. They were always trying to get me to join ridiculous clubs, but I preferred to go to the gym or volunteer at the school.

Also, I do know how to read and shun breakfast binge drinking.

Kenneth shakes his head and again leads me to where he needs me to go, which is the back room.

"Okay, I am going to give you a very quick course in bringing half our inventory to the floor all at once and telling entitled… ladies... that these shoes will make them look like queens, even if they have toes like a mother elephant."

I take a deep breath and enter the cavernous space. I can do this. There are absolutely no Excel formulas involved in shoe sizes, and at least Didier doesn't just pop into the store.

Just as Kenneth begins showing me the section where they keep the small selection of flats—see, I knew it—we hear a familiar voice from the front of the store.

"Bonjour, where are my shoe people?"

Shit, why does he know I'm here? I would think that "presidenting" would be more time-consuming, but that's probably what all people with that title want us to believe.

Although maybe he can oversee charming the women while Kenneth and I haul shoe boxes and take their money.

I see by the look on Kenneth's face that he also recognizes the French accent and wishes he could run out the back door.

He whispers, "For the love of beautifully crafted footwear, why does that man have to show up now? Did the store look dusty? How is my hair?"

Kenneth shifts his head from left to right, and I assure him that his perfectly styled tresses are going to pass the test and remind him that Didier is probably not here to spy on him.

"Ohhhh, I get it. The rumors are true, then. So, did you guys… you know…?"

I push my new boss back into the store before he completes his rude hand gesture, and now I hear another man's voice talking to Didier.

Do we sell men's shoes, and I don't even know it? It wouldn't surprise me because I haven't seen a single shoe yet, except for the two pairs I own. But I am getting those flats before I leave today if I make it through the descending horde.

Crap, I already spot them milling around on the street, laughing and plotting footwear peril as Kenneth rushes to shake Didier's hand.

Before I can even say hello and explain how busy we are about to be on my first day, I see who else is here to visit.

Didier says, "I was just talking to this young man, Tara, mon amour. He claims he is here to see you. Is this true?"

I roll my eyes. "Why wouldn't it be true, Didier?"

He stumbles over his words. "Oh… only because he is so young and doesn't look like your son, who I have seen… in the photos on your desk… and know what he looks like. Not like this."

I am about to yell at him for assuming anything about my visitor when I catch Kenneth ogling Shawn out of the corner of my eye.

As usual, Shawn looks delectable, but is there anyone here who isn't lusting after someone?

Shawn smiles and says, "Hey, I'm Tara's friend, Shawn." He waves as if everyone is acting totally normally and looks at me, "I just wanted to see if you'd like to meet me on your break. What time do you—?"

As Kenneth starts to offer him a job and the key to his apartment, and Didier insists that he is the one taking me out on my break, the door bursts open, and the "Tara's meal break standoff" doesn't stand a chance against the rush of designer handbags, Chanel No. 5, and slurred speech.

One of them shrieks, "Marilyn, isn't that the French guy who owns this company? He looks like Justin Trudeau!" She puts her hand to her face and yells again, "Oh my God, and look at the cute young stud he fell on top of."

I don't think I'm getting any meal breaks today.

Chapter 10

"Fine, you can wear those, but if we get a secret shopper in here, I'm pretending you don't work here and calling the police."

Kenneth flares his nostrils and huffs.

All I did was ask if I could wear the sparkly flats from the new holiday collection instead of the hooker heels.

Also, I really don't think we have secret shoppers, and Didier was still here while I was trying them on. If the CEO is okay with it, then the store manager needs to calm the hell down, especially after the onslaught of shoe mania we just endured.

I sigh and say, "Agreed. If I am caught wearing less comfortable footwear outside of our major brand line, I will gladly surrender to handcuffs."

I glance at my Fitbit and see that it's almost time to meet Shawn at the deli for my meal break.

He hung around for a few minutes after Kenneth pulled Didier off him and the vultures, I mean valued shoppers… stopped gawking and trying to touch his chest.

We tried to have a semi-normal conversation, but with so many bejeweled hands sticking shoes in my face and yelling out their sizes, I said, "Meet me at the deli at four," and he nodded and ducked out before anyone else could "woman handle" him.

I know it seems like I'm exaggerating, but it was truly crazy for about an hour, and I was thankful that Didier stayed around to distract the shoe and man-crazed mavens so I could get my bearings in the back room. It's bigger than the sales floor, and it could use better organization.

The shoe boxes are even beautiful at Adrien Monet—they are color-coded by collection, and all the colors are a muted palette, kind of like trendier Easter egg colors. The tops of the boxes are sculpted on the edges in curlicued designs that make them look like crowns or tiaras. Apparently, keeping the shoes in the boxes and arranging them in massive designer closets is a thing on Instagram.

Of course, the main reason Didier stayed is because he saw Shawn and now thinks he is his new competition. The web is feeling more tangled, and I think I'm the black widow spider. I should be glad it's been easy to get male attention, but it feels more confusing every day. And now I have to decide if I am going to say anything to Shawn about what Lenny told me. It seems ridiculous now that Shawn has met Didier and obviously thinks there is something going on there.

We're just practice dating.

Kenneth interrupts my train of thought. "Okay, go meet the young stud. Gwen is finished in the stockroom, and she can cover for you out here. When you get back, I'm going to have her train you on the register."

He unlocks the drawer under the counter, and I grab my purse. I hope Gwen is a good teacher because I have never been on the other end of a cash register in my life. It can't be too hard—no one pays with cash anymore, so

I won't have to touch money — yuck.

The sidewalk is quiet at this time of day as I walk a block to the deli. The stay-at-home moms and crazy drunk divas are all home by now, and the working people are still at their desks. If I were still married, I would be at the kitchen island asking Willow and Birch about their days or driving someone to the mall or an appointment. I'd be perusing the refrigerator and planning a simple, healthy dinner.

I miss the active mom days, and I don't like how they were cut short so abruptly, but my life is a lot more interesting now. I'm just not sure if interesting is overrated.

As I open the door to the popular eatery, I am accosted by delicious, indulgent smells and spot Shawn at a booth near the back on his phone.

I smile and approach him, even though he is still talking. I am not going to ask who is making him smile like that. It's none of my business.

He gestures to the seat opposite him, and I busy myself with arranging my purse and jacket, hoping he will end his call before it gets awkward.

"Okay, yep. No, I can't tomorrow night. I have a date. Yes, I do… wouldn't you like to know. Haha… okay, love you too. Bye."

He places his phone face down on the table and says, "Hey, you survived. That was wild in there. And that French guy is heavier than he looks." He rubs his neck as if he's sustained an injury and laughs. "I was telling my mom, and she was rolling. I don't think her friends are quite as shoe crazy."

I clear my throat and say, "Oh, your mom. That's nice. Yeah, it was a bit much, but Kenneth assured me that it isn't an everyday occurrence, and I got him to let me wear flats." I lift my foot and shake the sparkly black shoe.

"Wow, how kind of him." He leans across the booth and says, "Now when I kiss you, I won't have to stand on my tippy toes."

His eyes sparkle almost as much as my shoes, and I look away. I'm sure that his mother was on the phone, but he has a date tomorrow night, probably with the girl from the pool hall. Crap, now my phone is beeping.

"I'm sorry, I just need to check this in case it's one of my children."

I wince at how old that made me sound. Not only does Shawn have much younger girlfriends, but even his mom is probably cooler than me.

Shawn picks up his menu and glides one across to me. "Oh yeah, when is Birch coming over for dinner? I thought you guys could come over to my place after and play some games."

"Um… he's coming on Sunday, I think…" Great, Patrick is texting me to go apple picking on Sunday. But that's got to be a daytime thing, and it's not like we are going to have the most romantic first date in history where we spend the whole day together and end up asleep in each other's arms.

There is no way in hell that's happening because now I will need to ditch him in time to make my son's favorite Olive Garden imitation sausage potato soup and watch him kill flaming skeleton zombies with my young practice, maybe soon-to-be lover.

Shawn is pretending to be engrossed in the menu to give me some privacy, but he is peering at me now, and I know my face is flushed.

Why do I have to be so white? It's inconvenient while juggling men. I haven't even responded to Didier's text about lunch yet, but I am hoping to get that out of the way tomorrow on my break, when I will explain to him that I am not going to be Jane to his Tarzan at the Halloween party. I need to nip his attraction in the bud, and I am also scared of Morticia, I mean Dominique.

"Everything okay with the kids?" Shawn reaches out and touches my hand, and now the blush has moved to another part of my body. I really wish he didn't have this effect on me, but between his looks and his... soul... spirit... something that makes him fully present and attentive — it's all too much.

I put my phone back in my purse and say, "Yep, Birch is coming on Sunday night for dinner. I'm sure he'd love to see you. He needs a break from Nicole."

I pick up the menu and begin scanning it. Finally, a server comes out of the backroom holding a mop. I guess she didn't even know she had any customers at this odd time of day. Normally, the wait would annoy me, but after a half shift on the shoe floor, I am already feeling a kinship with service workers.

"Hey, sorry about the wait, folks. What can I get you?"

Just as Shawn says, "I'll have a BLT and water is fine," I blurt out, "I also have a date on Sunday."

The server pops her gum and looks back and forth between us, probably trying to figure out if we are a couple and if a fight is about to break out before she can put in our order and get back to mopping.

Shawn grins and says, "Okay, but what do you want to eat now?" He glances at the uncomfortable server who is still smiling like someone who can't wait to tell the kitchen staff about the old woman cheating on her young boyfriend.

I sigh, put the menu down, and look the server in the eye. "I'll have a corned beef on rye, no pickles, and a side of potato salad. And a Coke."

Why not just go whole hog on the food therapy?

Shawn raises his eyebrows as the server scurries away. "So, Tara, it's fine that you have a date. You know that, right? Remember our agreement?"

I place my hands on the table and fiddle with my straw wrapper as our drinks arrive quickly and our server again departs quickly.

"Yeah, I know. I'm sorry, this is just a lot to get used to. I'm going apple picking with a guy I met in the neighborhood the other day." I almost told him that Dinah set us up, but I don't want it to seem like she's my practice dating pimp.

"Apple picking? That's cool—I used to do that with my grandma when I was little. Not that it's not fun for a date too."

I stifle my annoyance and say, "Well, I'm sure you're taking your date somewhere more fun tomorrow."

The server rolls her eyes as she brings our food—that was quick. She really must be dying to know what's going on here, but to her credit, she walks away. Then I notice she stops at a nearby table to wipe away non-existent crumbs.

Shawn picks up his BLT, takes a bite, and after chewing enough to satisfy his proper table manners, he says, "Well, you're about to find out because I am going on a date with you tomorrow."

"Ohhh..." I absently release my tight grip on my

humongous sandwich, and some of the corned beef falls onto the plate. "So, you don't have a date with anyone else?"

Shawn wipes his hands on the paper napkin and gulps his water. "Not this week. Or anytime in the future that I know of. Maybe the server is single."

He laughs as she overhears him and returns to her mopping.

He leans across the table and takes my hand again, and I've pretty much lost my appetite. At least for food. Well, on second thought, that potato salad looks good. Just the right ratio of mustard and mayonnaise.

"Tara, look at me. Are you sure you're okay with our arrangement?" He snaps his fingers. "You know what I think? You saw Lenny this morning, didn't you?"

I decide that now is a good time to fill my mouth with tasty meat so I can worm my way out of this conversation. But I am such a bad liar. If I were Todd, I would have gotten caught long before the donut shop incident. And I'd never think of a bunny on the fly, like Nicole.

Shawn takes small bites of his BLT while I finish chewing, never breaking eye contact. He's enjoying this torture way too much if the smirk at the corners of his perfect lips is any indication.

I take a slug of Coke, which burns my throat, but in that satisfying way when you're a former Coke addict.

And yes, I mean I drank a lot of Coca-Cola as a child. Do I look like someone who does drugs? I can't even go apple picking without guilt.

"Okay, yes, I did. I saw him last night after having dinner with my sister, who is definitely on board with practice dating. She thinks it's going to become a hashtag."

I'm stalling, and even the server is repelled as she comes back out, presumably to see if we need anything.

I want to yell, "Yes, I need a backbone and someone to sit under the table and tell me the right thing to say".

Shawn says nothing, so I continue, "Lenny told me that he saw you at the pool hall with some buddies and that there was, and I quote, "a hot little number doin' a dance on your lap and hangin' on you like a hooker on a slow night.'"

His eyes widen, "Wow, he's descriptive. And nuts. That was my cousin Shonda. She's got ADD and can't stop bouncing around. And before you say anything, he was partially correct. She's like my third cousin or something, so she thinks if we hooked up it would be fine."

Now it's my turn for the stoic silence. I am not asking if they hooked up. I've eaten far too much corned beef to stomach that story.

"But obviously, we have not hooked up. I've known her all my life, and she's always been a wild child. Before I left, she moved on to other laps. I tolerate her because our moms are cousins and best friends."

I feel so stupid, but I need to say something before the check comes, and I have to go back to the store, and I don't even know anything about this date I am supposedly going on tomorrow night. And that's if Shawn hasn't decided to cancel practice dating because I can't handle it.

"You don't owe me an explanation at all. And I know these things are going to come up. So, let's just forget it. I would love to go on the date tomorrow. You said you were going to introduce me to your favorite activity?"

He stands up, and just when I think he's chosen now to realize he has to go to the bathroom, he comes around to my side and sits next to me, squishing me up against my jacket and purse.

He puts one arm on my back and cradles my face in the other. "It's my favorite public activity, and it's a surprise."

I swallow hard and don't move a muscle for fear the server will come back and he won't tell me about his favorite private activity, which I can only guess is not killing flaming skeleton zombies.

I take a deep breath and whisper, "I get off work at seven tonight."

Chapter 11

I don't even know what's happening.

It's a Wednesday morning, and I am not in the office, but on my way to the grocery store to pick up essentials I have run out of, like food, before going into my retail job at eleven to work in the stockroom.

Oh, and I just left my twenty-five-year-old lover sleeping in like a teenager after the absolute best sex of my life.

Some would say turning back the clock is a fun thing, but worlds collide in this scenario when your teenaged son is also texting you what he wants for dinner on Sunday while in the bed of the previously mentioned... ahem... lover, and your daughter in college asks you to send her a copy of her medical card because she can't find it and needs to go to the gynecologist.

I am walking to the grocery store, because isn't that one of the perks of city living?

Oh, and meeting hot young men with bodies like characters in superhero movies or ads for bodybuilding shakes.

I pull my jacket a little tighter around my body to combat the slight chill as I round the corner past The Hard Apple.

I'm a reasonable person, and I fully grasp the

concept of dating multiple men as a societal norm, but I don't know if I can go apple picking with a man on Sunday after everything that happened last night.

And that will likely happen again between now and Sunday.

I have never been with a man like Shawn. Todd was young when I met him—I am horrified to think he was only a little younger than Shawn, and that was around the same time that Shawn was getting his diaper changed and learning to walk—but Todd was a tall but somewhat gangly young man.

And Didier was lean but not very muscular or strong.

And my high school boyfriend was just a skinny kid.

But Shawn… I didn't know another human being's body could be that hard… and I mean everywhere. But also, soft and warm… and he's also so damn nice and…

I shake these thoughts from my head as a shiver hits me again. Isn't this all normal? It's normal, right? I bet other divorced women go through this, but in my experience, they seem to struggle with finding a new partner, and if I joined a divorced women's group, I would be attacked with wine glasses and pitchforks if I told them about Shawn.

And the others.

So, if I logically know that I have found something rare and amazing, so amazing it would inspire raging jealousy in other women in my situation, why can't I just enjoy it?

I'm at the grocery store now, and I just realized that I am limited in what I can buy because I have to carry it all home.

All of the small shopping carts are taken, so I grab a

huge monstrosity for a family of five and enter the bright store. I really need to get some pre-made salads or something healthy. Since moving into this neighborhood, it's been takeout and big meatballs galore.

Now that I'm here, I do wish I'd made a little more effort with my appearance. I did run back to my place to take a quick shower, but my unwashed hair is in a messy bun, and I'm wearing old jeans and a faded sweatshirt from one of the kids' elementary school fundraisers.

Normally, I wouldn't be caught dead in this getup, especially in my old neighborhood with the pearl-clutching Karens, but Kenneth told me that I'll be working in the stockroom today, and it is truly filthy back there. I've been wanting to get my hands on it. As a mother of a teenage boy, I am experienced in extreme cleaning.

Okay, now where is the produce section? Oh, right here. They have a whole wall of premade salads and fruit cups, and other things that might keep me fit and give me enough energy to keep up with my practice boyfriend.

I do hope I don't see anyone I know, but what are the odds in this neighborhood? I hardly know anyone… oh son of a bitch.

I duck behind the huge banana tower as I peek towards the organic frozen food section, and who is there but Patrick… and he's talking to that same woman from The Hard Apple. Hmm… are they shopping together?

This is exactly why this dating multiple people thing is stressful. For some reason, my mind relegates Patrick to The Hard Apple. It has never occurred to me that he is a free human who exists in other places and doesn't sleep next to the big machines that make the cider in the back room.

And so, what if he's dating that woman? I just left Shawn's bed. This is going to get complicated very fast. I just wanted to get a few things and be on my way, and now I am paralyzed.

Also, I look like crap, and I just realized that I am having my meal break today with Didier, and with the way I'm dressed, we'll have to go to the Golden Corral.

But I am definitely not trying to impress Didier with my appearance, so maybe this look will work to my advantage.

Patrick's "friend" is laughing and touching his sleeve as they pick out gluten-free bread and fake chicken. I don't remember him being that funny. Also, she's dressed like she just stepped off the runway, or at least she doesn't look like she slept in a dumpster, unlike me.

But actually, I slept in a very warm and cozy… ugh… I need to put that out of my mind for now.

Good, it looks like they're walking further into the store, and I think I have everything I need.

As I sneak over to the checkout, looking around like I just stuffed my pockets with a stash of contraband cucumbers, I pray that Patrick and the model are engrossed in picking out the most environmentally friendly toilet paper, far away from my escape route.

I am aware that constantly shifting my eyes from the door to the back of the store is the very definition of being shifty-eyed, which is, of course, a very suspicious behavior, but I don't fully appreciate my own weirdness until I spot the young mother in line behind me widening her eyes and tilting her head.

"Ma'am, are you okay? Did you forget something you needed? We could get it for you, right, girls?"

Two little blond things at her side nod enthusiastically, as if helping crazy ladies is part of the community service they're learning at the Montessori preschool.

I shake my head to snap me out of my ridiculously uncharacteristic behavior and reply, "Oh no, I'm fine. Just in a bit of a rush." I attempt a smile and then realize that I now probably look even crazier.

I don't want to give these children nightmares, so I settle down and engage with the cashier who is patiently waiting for me to insert my debit card and get out so she can wait on more desirable customers. I want to check out quickly before the helpful woman behind me tries to pay for my groceries, assuming I have as little money as I do decent clothes and normal eye movements.

I thank the cashier and push my cart out at a calm pace towards the exit, and glance back to see the little girls waving. I wave back and think of how cute my own kids were at that age.

Now that I'm on the sidewalk, a quick survey of my purchases tells me that I bought way too much to carry these bags home. It's almost a mile to my apartment, and I'd rather not have to deal with exploded lettuce all over the sidewalk when I inevitably drop some bags.

Just my luck, Patrick, or the woman from the checkout line will drive by as I'm chasing rolling tomatoes into the gutter.

So, what can I do? Okay, Uber is a thing. I've never used it, but I could download it. But then I'd be standing here for who knows how long while I try to add a form of payment.

And why does the sun have to be so glaring? Maybe if I just roll the cart a little ways around the corner, I can get out of the path of the sun and Patrick, who must be about ready to emerge from the store.

If he offered me a ride, I would be mortified. I am guessing he arrived in a car like a sensible human, or maybe his hot friend drove, and then I would sooner abandon my cart and make a run for it. Free salad for all!

Okay, there's the app store. Now type in Uber… there it is. Wait, what the hell?

I pushed the shopping cart to angle it out of the path of pedestrian traffic on the sidewalk, and now it won't budge.

Is the wheel stuck? No, it was fine up until now. Shit, I can't just leave it sitting here like this, and what if the Uber parks across the street to wait for me? I'll look positively unhinged because the only way this thing is moving is if I pick up the whole cart. I start slamming it a little more aggressively just as the mom and girls walk by with their little bag of snacks.

Mom says, "Oh, Ma'am, you can't take those away from the store. Can I call someone for you? Girls, stay by Mommy. I need to call an Uber for this nice lady."

"No, thank you. I was just about to call my own Uber, but the cart is stuck."

She wrinkles her forehead, but does seem to see the problem I'm having. "Hmm… that's odd. I could go back into the store and ask someone to come out and help. Oh, wait, here comes a man now. Sir, can you help us?"

I get a sick feeling that when I turn around to see the helpful man-savior, I'm not going to like what I see. I didn't see a single other man in that store except for…

"What seems to be the problem, ladies?"

I sigh when I see it's just a store worker, and I relax as he patiently explains to me that the carts are equipped with a security system, so they lock up once they leave the store's perimeter.

"It's like an invisible dog fence, but for carts. I'll disable it, and you should be able to move the cart back to the front of the store to wait for your ride."

He bends down to perform some kind of security magic, and I laugh, "Haha… silly me… I had no idea that was a thing. Did you know?"

I smile at the young mom, and she says, "No, we didn't know that. Right, girls? But honestly, I've never tried to steal a shopping cart. Not that you were stealing it. It was the sun, of course. You couldn't see your phone. So much shadier over here."

I open my mouth to talk my way out of this nonsensical situation, and we all jump as someone pulls up to the curb, laying on the horn.

I glance up and see Dinah peering across the passenger seat to the scene on the sidewalk.

"What the heck is goin' on here? Is that you, Tara? You look like sh… poop." She waves to the little girls, who are more excited by the second. The old lady was about to say a real curse word!

"What happened to you? Oh, wait, I bet I know. Throw your stuff in the back seat and hop in." She rubs her hands together with glee, and I know why.

She assumes my haphazard appearance is related to last night's activities and not an upcoming shift in the stockroom, coupled with an ignorance of city shopping norms.

I thank my helpers and start grabbing my grocery bags. I give one to each of the girls to put in Dinah's car because they have been promised a service opportunity, and it seems like the least I can do. I open the back door, and the mom hovers close as the girls neatly place the items in the car.

Honestly, if I were this woman, I would be worried that we were some kind of incognito kidnapping ring, too.

Dinah turns around in her seat and says, "Aren't you little ladies just the cutest and so sweet to help this poor unfortunate woman?" She winks at me, and I purse my lips.

The kids mumble rehearsed polite words, and Dinah says, "Hold on, I think I have some candy."

My eyes widen, and I shake my head. I know this woman is drawing the line at accepting candy from strangers. You can tell Dinah never had any kids if she doesn't know that golden rule.

The mom perks up and grabs the girls' hands. "No, thanks, we need to be going, and we have plenty of candy at home."

She turns to me and says, "Have a great day," as I hear one of the girls whisper, "No, we don't, Mommy."

I sigh and get in the car, reclining the seat back as Dinah is now pointing at the front of the store, "Isn't that Patrick? Oh, roll down the window again. Or maybe I should just honk, but that seems to scare people for some reason."

"No honking. No window. Please just drive."

She looks at me more closely and says, "Hmm… yeah, we need to get you out of here. You're messin' up my matchmaking efforts in that outfit. And what's with your hair?"

She guns it away from the sidewalk, and I hang on to the door handle.

"I'm working in the stockroom today, and I just wanted to get a few groceries, but I bought too much. And I was trying to get some exercise, and then I saw Patrick and the shopping cart locked up."

Dinah shakes her head and smiles as you would when a crazy person rambles nonsense.

"So, am I to take it that someone literally banged your brains out last night?"

"Dinah, oh my god… really?"

She throws her hands up, which should be on the wheel, and says, "Well, I'm just callin' it as I see it. But you probably should've waited until you had a day off, hahaha… anyway, you should come to karaoke at The Hard Apple tonight. After you wash the stockroom dirt off, of course."

We pull up to my apartment building and Dinah expertly parallel parks in a tight spot right up in front. She must be able to see better than her constant squinting while driving indicates. I'm still marveling at her parking job when her last comment sinks into my brain.

"What? I am not singing karaoke. And Patrick was with a woman. And yes, I know I was with another man, but I have a date with that man tonight, and he says he's going to show me his favorite hobby."

"Didn't he already do that last night?"

We grab the bags from the backseat, and I tell Dinah to shush because he could easily be outside, or on his way outside, and I don't really want him to see me in this state either. That's why I left him sleeping.

And I definitely don't want him to hear me talking about our… whatever we are doing… with Dinah. Her voice could easily carry to the 4th floor, so I put my finger up to my lips and she glances around.

"That boy is still sleeping… but when he wakes up, he'll be looking for you."

The twinkle in her eye makes me laugh as we bring the groceries into the building. I am being very silly—Shawn knows I talk to Dinah. It's kind of impossible not to—she's like human truth serum in a feisty old lady's body.

We reach the hallway, and now Dinah is sneaking into my apartment like a cat burglar. I'm surprised she doesn't pull her hat down over her face like a ski mask.

I glance down the hall at Shawn's door and smile. He really is amazing, and we will have fun tonight.

I watch Dinah as she's already reorganizing my fridge to fit my purchases. Karaoke, really? Never in a million years. But it may be worth it to go one day to see Dinah perform.

I thank my nutty friend and we both head downstairs—me off to work and her back home to see if Vinny is up for mid-morning fun time. Her words, not mine.

I guess if I am inspiring her with my love life, it's a win for all.

After a peaceful drive to the store, I park in the lot because I still haven't worked on my street parking skills and breathe in the fresh air while I walk to the store. It's such a beautiful day—maybe Kenneth will let me keep the back door to the stockroom open to air out the receiving area.

"I said you would be working in the stockroom, not

on the porta-potty cleaning crew. What happened to your hair?"

Kenneth looks me up and down at the door. I really don't understand why he feels the need to greet all his employees for their shifts at the door, like some kind of management butler.

He's probably afraid we will change our minds and run back to our cars.

He also checks the street for signs of large shopping hordes. After the other day with the book club ladies, I don't blame him.

I walk past him and say, "Hello to you, too, boss. That stockroom is filthy. Now direct me to the cleaning supplies, and I'll get to it. Cleaning before organizing."

He saunters towards the back of the store and starts vaguely pointing in different directions. "Um… I think there could be some over here. Maybe under that shelf. I don't know, I don't really do cleaning. Anyhoo, Didier called and told me that you must be allowed to take your meal break at four because he is meeting you here. I am assuming you didn't know that?"

He raises an eyebrow at my appearance and then snaps his fingers. "Or you did know, and you are hoping to repel him with your disheveled appearance. That's smart, girl. Okay, I'll leave you to it."

Finally, some peace so I can think about my problems with no interruptions.

"Tara, we're getting a big shipment, so I called in all the part-timers to help!"

Kenneth bellows this news from the front of the store, and I resign myself to an afternoon filled with a bunch of young people who will mess up the place as I'm cleaning it, just like my children.

Maybe the flashback to my old life will be a welcome distraction.

Chapter 12

"Hey, you're my neighbor, right?" A pretty blond woman walks down the hallway from the direction of Shawn's apartment.

I knew I should have looked at the time before I stepped out into the hall.

In my haste to be on time for my date with Shawn, I ran home from work and rushed through my primping routine, which was extensive because I worked in the dirty stockroom all day.

Feeling like I was going to be late, I left my apartment in haste, and now I'm standing in the hall, realizing that my date lives two doors down and I look silly and overly eager.

But if I go back inside now, Shawn might catch me and think I'm being even weirder.

Although I am 100% being weird.

I smile at my neighbor and say, "Oh, I'm just waiting for my date. He's um..."

"Oh, I know who you're waiting for. I heard you guys the other night."

My face immediately reddens, and my eyeballs widen in alarm. Is privacy really so lacking in apartments that she heard us?

She laughs and puts her hand over her heart. "I didn't mean... I didn't hear... anything inside the apartment. These walls are like concrete. I meant I heard you talking in the hallway. It sounded like you were having fun. I don't think Shawn dates a whole lot, and he's such a great guy. So cute too! I'm Cassie, by the way. You've probably heard me yelling at my dog to pee outside or trying to calm a crying toddler. '

"It's nice to meet you, Cassie. No, I haven't seen any dogs or little ones, but I'd love to meet them."

I decide not to comment on Shawn because I feel self-conscious that she's sizing me up and wondering why a hot young guy would want to date me.

I would, however, be open to her ideas because I still don't get it.

Cassie looks at her phone and says, "Well, have fun. I gotta run. I have a rare babysitter tonight, and I'm meeting a friend at karaoke night. See you soon."

I wish her a good night as well and watch her walk to the stairwell.

Huh... why did she say she'd see me soon? Maybe she just means in the building. She seems nice, and I could use some new friends.

I'm hoping none of my other neighbors decide to go out right now because I am still a few minutes early, and there is no sign of Shawn. I could go knock on his door, but that feels too forward, even though the events of last night should have erased any awkwardness.

Hmm... or has it just taken awkward to a whole new level?

Speaking of awkwardness, my early dinner break with Didier was bizarre, but I wasn't expecting anything else.

I calmly explained to him that I just want to be friends, and he said, "It is because of the man with the hard body. I understand. When I fell on him, it felt like I landed on a how you say... a table where you eat with the bugs."

"You mean a picnic table?" I said.

"Yes, picnic where the bugs eat your food and make gross times. His body was hard like that."

Sometimes I wonder if it's still a language thing with Didier, but after all these years in this country, I think he's just one odd bird.

We talked about the upcoming Halloween party, and we decided that I would go but not as his date, and we were not doing couples costumes.

This will be the first time that his lovely, soon-to-be scary ex-wife is attending a company event, and I would rather not be the reason the whole staff has to witness anything unpleasant. She claims that she wants nothing to do with Didier, but she called him four times during our dinner. I would rather not draw undue attention to myself from the French shoe queen.

Didier said I should bring the "hard man" and that he wants me to help him find a new woman.

"If you meet any new lovely ladies, please arrange an introduction. I want to date outside of my circle. It is full of greedy social creepers."

I said, "Do you mean climbers?"

He waved his hand and said, "Yes, but they are creepy while they are climbing. My body and bank account are not big mountains."

We parted as friends, and I assured him that I would keep my eyes open for eligible women who would use his body and financial resources in a non-creepy way.

Whatever that means. I never said my previous fling with Didier made any sense, and I think it's now obvious why I married Todd, who could at least make his brain and mouth work together.

Ugh... his mouth makes me think of the freaking donuts again.

Anyway, I could set someone up with Didier. He is handsome and rich, and he's a good guy, if a little hard to understand.

Hmm... Cassie seemed nice, but she's a little young for him, and I'd hate to get a single mother involved with someone with as much baggage as Didier. I wonder why she hasn't dated Shawn.

As if I conjured him by thinking of his name, he startles me. Shoot, he caught me leaning against the wall and staring into space. But at least I am wearing a cute, shortish skirt and a tight, lightweight sweater showing a little cleavage. I've upgraded my bra collection from the sporty variety to the ones that do a better job of squishing and pushing.

"Are you ready? You look like you're waiting for a bus." He leans close to my ear and whispers, "I can give you a ride later, but I thought we'd walk now. It's a nice night."

He kisses the sensitive skin on my neck, just below my ear, and I think I let an audible whimper escape.

I am a little embarrassed about the bus comment, but Shawn never makes me feel silly. He's like a warm blanket—like a very hard blanket.

Well, more like firm. Or maybe like a heated blanket. Or one of those weighted ones?

I realize it's my turn to say something, but between my blanket fantasies and Shawn's body, it's difficult to find words. The spot on my neck is still warm and sending more warmth to other places.

I take his hand and say, "I'd love a walk. Where are we headed?"

A few minutes later, I remember why I don't like surprises.

As we stroll down the block that contains The Hard Apple, I get that weird feeling again and hope I don't run into Patrick. I was lucky this morning to escape him with all the grocery cart shenanigans.

But I needn't have worried about seeing him as I passed by the bar, because the cidery was our destination.

Crap.

Now that I'm being ushered into the building and greeted by noise and off-key singing, I realize the level of hell I have entered.

Dinah spots me and drags Vinny with her. "There you are. Aren't you excited about karaoke night?"

"What? No, I mean... sure." I glance at Shawn, who is taking my coat and shaking Vinny's hand. I turn away from them and loudly whisper, "Did you tell him to bring me here?"

Dinah plasters a "who me" look on her face and says, "Who, me? Of course not. Shawn comes to karaoke every week. It's the place to be in the neighborhood on a Wednesday night."

"Then why didn't you tell me this is where Shawn was bringing me for our date?"

She shakes her head and sips her monstrous pint of cider.

"That's none of my business. I never interfere in my friends' love lives." She slaps her leg and says, "Okay, what are ya gonna sing? Vinny and I are doin' Sonny and Cher like we always do, so you and Shawn can't pick "I Got You Babe" as your song."

I open my mouth to speak and then close it again. There are so many things to unpack in that question, I don't even know where to begin.

I thought moving to the city would be a more anonymous life and give me the chance to meet lots of different people.

It turns out that Scott's Addition is just an urban, more diverse version of my wealthy suburban street, where everyone knows everyone's business.

Every new person I have met in the neighborhood is here, including Dinah and Vinny, Cassie, my neighbor, the practice boyfriend I am sleeping with, and the owner of the establishment, who is next in line for... well, whatever we decide to do after apple picking.

I think I even saw Lotto Lenny and the stripper from the other day at the bar.

Shawn asks me if I'd like a drink, and we find a table to drink our ciders.

"So, are you surprised?"

His twinkly eyes make it hard to be mad at him, and how would he know my aversion to public singing?

When the kids were little, I took them to a children's class called Musical Munchkins, and the leader, Miss Joanie, would play the guitar and we'd sit in a circle and sing. Then the kids would bang on instruments and march, and the moms would hand out the Tylenol.

The moms were expected to sing, but there were enough overzealous performers that I could get away with moving my lips or whisper-singing.

And if Miss Joanie asked for soloists, I pretended to have laryngitis. Of course, my son didn't help by saying, "Mommy, you can talk. You just yelled at me in the car for smearing applesauce on Willow."

Caught in another daydream, I remember that Shawn asked me a reasonable question and say, "I am surprised, but I'm sure it will be fun. Do you like to sing?"

I'm hoping I can pretend to be too tired and need to go home before I can get a turn. There are a ton of people here, and it looks like there are already a lot of people in the queue. Names of upcoming singers are scrolling on a board, and there is a line of people waiting to sign up.

"I love to sing. My mom and grandma are in the church choir, so I was involved in a lot of church music growing up, but then, of course, I branched out on my own. I love all kinds of music."

"Well, you'd better get up there and claim your spot so we can get home. You promised me a bus ride."

That really didn't come out the way I intended it—there is nothing sexy about a bus ride, and who is the bus in this situation? I may need to take a class in flirty banter. However, anything that gets me out of here before someone shoves a microphone in my face is sounding good.

"Oh, I'm not worried. I'm a regular. I'm on permanent rotation. I'll be up right after our friends, the Bertellis. Come on, let's get closer to the stage to show them some love."

As we get closer to the makeshift stage, I see Dinah and Vinny getting ready to start. Dinah is sporting a long black Cher wig, and Vinny has his own black Sonny Bono wig. The black mustache already comes standard on Vinny. Come to think of it, he's almost eighty—he must dye that thing.

"Aren't they so cute?"

I am startled by another male voice close behind me, and turn to see Patrick smiling at me and gesturing to the stage.

Obviously, he is here on what seems to be one of the cidery's most popular nights. I wonder if he sings, too. I feel like I stumbled into the cast of an off-off-Broadway play by accident.

"Oh, hi, yes, they are adorable. And pretty good singers too. Um... this is my... friend... Shawn."

I touch Shawn's shoulder to alert Patrick that we're together. I certainly don't want Patrick to think I'm here alone. I can't end up juggling two dates in the same room. That takes the whole casual dating thing a bit too far.

As the two men face each other, I remember that, of course, they already know each other (Shawn's on permanent rotation), but I guess it still makes sense to make my relationship with Shawn clear.

As if the word "friend" makes it clear.

The guys shake hands, and Shawn says, "I hear you and Tara are going apple-picking on Sunday."

I almost spit my drink as Dinah hits one of the high notes of the song. "I've got you to love me sooooo."

This couldn't get much more awkward.

"Yeah, I'm taking her up to the orchard out past Charlottesville. Do you know it?"

"Yeah, I used to go with my grandma, and I think I went there on a school field trip once. Not really my thing. But hey, you're the apple guy!"

They click glasses and laugh as I do the math in my head and realize that he probably went on the field trip a few years before I was chaperoning my kids on school outings.

Between the continuous age revelations, the bizarre camaraderie of my dates (yes, plural), and the need to escape musical humiliation, there is only one place to go—especially with Dinah coming off the stage. If she asks me what song I'm singing, I will tell her the one about the grandma getting run over by a reindeer.

She's not a grandma, but she will get the sentiment.

The ladies' room is tucked in the back, and luckily, the crowd is big enough that I can get lost in it on the way, despite being taller than the average woman, and the old lady who is surely looking for me, both to praise her performance and to further interfere in my weirder by-the-minute love life.

I open the door and almost walk right into... yes, you guessed it... Patrick's model friend.

"Oh, hi, excuse me." She steps back and subtly looks me up and down. "You look so familiar, but I just can't place you. I'm Bobbi..."

Just as I'm about to say, "I'm Tara" and pretend I suddenly don't need to pee and get the hell out, the door opens again, and thankfully, I jump out of the way before Bobbi and I are getting intimate on the bathroom floor. Patrick really needs to expand the size of the bathrooms in this place.

The newcomers are my neighbor Cassie and another black-haired woman, who I assume is the friend she was meeting. They are hanging on each other and singing an impassioned version of the Sonny and Cher classic into their hairbrushes, pointing at each other on all the "babe" references.

At least they know how to have fun.

Cassie awkwardly jabs her brush back in her purse while her friend tosses hers on the ground and runs to a stall. "I'm peeing myself!"

Bobbi is smirking, but not in a nice "aren't they cute having a good time?" way. It's more of an "I can't believe my lover owns this stupid bar and I'm stuck here with these idiots" kind of way.

Now I won't get a chance to find out if the lover thing is true because Cassie is hanging on my arm. "I can't believe you're here. You were just in the hallway. That's my bestie Raven on the toilet."

Raven yells something unintelligible, and Bobbi is looking for a way to get around us to the exit, but with Cassie swaying, it's not easy to find an opening.

I sit Cassie down in the tiny chair in the corner and say, "What did she say?"

"She said you should come to tarot card night at her apartment. She lives downstairs from us. Witchy Eve, it's called. Raven is sooo good at it. Hey, maybe she can predict your future with Shawn."

Bobbi touches up her lipstick in the mirror and turns to me. "Good luck with that."

As she opens the door, Dinah comes flying into the restroom like she's also got a peeing emergency, but I should know better. She's here for me.

"Tara, what are you doin' hiding in the bathroom talking to Patrick's ex-fiancée?"

Bobbi waves on her way out.

"What, she's his ex-fiancée? Bobbi? But they were grocery shopping together. Are you sure he's not married?"

"Oh, would you stop it? I know everything—when are you going to get that through that pretty little head of yours? Now, it's time for Shawn to sing, and he's stalling so I could find you."

"Oh, he really wants me to watch? I guess that makes sense."

She pushes me out of the ladies' room and says, "Of course it does. He's singing for you, dummy."

Cassie yells, "I'll text you about Witchy Eve!"

Dinah scrunches up her face and says, "I have to watch you constantly, don't I?"

As I see Shawn getting ready to sing his opening notes, I also spot Patrick and Bobbi going into the back room together. I need to find out what's going on there before apple picking or any other kind of temptations, but now is not the time.

Now is the time that I hear my practice boyfriend singing the old Motown song, "My Girl" by the Temptations, in perfect pitch, complete with the hand gestures towards me with Dinah pushing me up to the front of the stage as if I were a vacuum cleaner or a lawn mower.

I have never had a practice boyfriend before, but this doesn't feel like practice. It feels real, and now everyone in the room is staring, and Lotto Lenny is raising his glass to me across the bar, and all I can think is—at least I get to ride the bus later.

Chapter 13

Mid-week partying is for younger people.

That's why my practice boyfriend was up and making breakfast while answering calls from people who can't remember their banking passwords, while I was struggling to keep my eyes open long enough to kiss him goodbye on my way to my early shift at the store.

Today I have been tasked with reviewing the online job applications for the store, and scheduling interviews for ME to hire new employees because:

A) I have experience recruiting volunteers for painful PTA activities.

B) Kenneth only likes the "fashion" part of his job, not the "manager" part.

C) I may have caused an employee or two to quit, due to my "mom" attitude.

Whatever.

I think this will be a great chance to help attract the right kind of employees who really want to work. And anything that keeps me away from the corporate office and spreadsheets is fine with me.

The stockroom and office areas are so clean and tidy now, and I love it that I'm dressed in a cute dress, I'm sitting in fancy, uncomfortable shoes, and I'm still here in the store amidst the buzz of retail activity.

Kenneth loves helping the customers—he truly has

a gift for matching the shoes to the person, and his over-the-top personality is a hit with women of all ages.

I glance around the small office, and I am so in love with the small improvements I made yesterday. Just a couple of cute succulents on the desk, an adorable pen holder in the shape of a shoe, and a cozy, bright cushion for the desk chair—and it feels so homey. I can think in a space like this.

I take a deep breath and open the store's applications folder on the office laptop. This should be fun.

Ugh… the first applicant's name is Shawn. It's not my Shawn—well, he's not my anything, and it's a common name.

I am just trying to distance myself a little, but I stayed at his apartment again last night because how do you walk away from someone who sang a romantic Motown hit for you in front of everyone in the neighborhood?

This is getting more confusing all the time, but I tell myself that it's just a cute song and he probably thought I would like it, not realizing that it's a song that his grandfather sang to his grandma.

I'm not that old. He could have easily picked a '90s rock ballad, like Aerosmith's "I Don't Want to Miss a Thing", but he probably doesn't know any of that music because while I was in high school, he was busy being a baby.

And Patrick—there's an odd one. I thought he had disappeared with his ex into the back room for the night, but nope. He was back out there socializing with his guests and applauding the singing efforts of his most loyal patrons.

And before we left, while Shawn was in the men's room, he found me so we could firm up our plans for apple picking on Sunday.

And what's even crazier—Shawn came out of the bathroom and "caught" us, but just shook Patrick's hand, put his arm around me, and said goodbye.

While Shawn was saying goodnight to Vinny, I told Dinah I feel like I am destined to be the main character in one of those silly reverse harem books my friend Christine is always reading.

Dinah said, "We should all be so lucky."

She squeezed my arm, and I realized that no one seemed to think any of this was a problem.

Speaking of Christine, I am having drinks with her and our other friend, Michelle, tonight at a rooftop bar in the neighborhood. I haven't been there yet, but it seems to be a popular place to hang out. I originally balked at the idea, but apparently, they have heaters, so the cool people don't have to hide indoors when the temperature drops.

I'm enjoying all this fun, but I could use a night in. I thought it could be tomorrow, but I'm on the evening shift at the store. At least if my night out with the girls goes long, I can sleep in.

Alone.

I told Shawn I'd be out late, and he should go out with his friends. I don't want him to spend all his time with me. It's not healthy.

When I said that, I could have sworn his green eyes looked a little sad, but he reverted quickly to his normal, happy self.

Maybe if he goes out without me, he'll meet a nice young woman, and this will just have been a fun experiment.

A palette cleanser.

I sigh and go back to the job applications. This Shawn works at a carwash, so I really don't think our brand is right for him, and I don't need anyone just for the stockroom.

Listen to me—I don't need anyone. As if it's my store.

The next application is from someone named Rosie who works in the Macy's shoe department. Okay… this is more promising.

My phone buzzes on the desk, and I see it's Roz texting me about brunch on Saturday.

I miss seeing her in the office, and I'm sure she'll have some gossip for me. And it will be nice to meet her granddaughter. Maybe I'll bring her a gift. I wonder what little girls are into these days. I know, I'll ask my neighbor Cassie.

After a couple of hours of staring at the computer, I am ready to stretch my legs and search for some lunch. Therefore, I am switching shoes. There's no way I am teetering on these heels just to grab a salad at the café on the corner.

I confer with Kenneth quickly before I leave and tell him that I have a few interviews scheduled and I'm finding some good candidates.

He says, "Just remember, they are not interviewing to be your children."

I laugh at him and say, "Hey, that's an idea. We could hire my children."

His contorted face tells me what he thinks of that idea—hahaha…

Birch knows nothing about fashion and Willow… I

need to make some time to have another talk with her. I'm not sure if her silence means "All is well and I am staying in Boston" or "I am packing my stuff to move back home and not telling you until Thanksgiving."

I've wanted to say something to Todd, but I don't know what he knows, and I don't want to "out" my daughter to her father as someone who doesn't like the law. Or laws. Or Harvard. Or Boston.

All his favorite things.

Well… except Nicole and… donuts.

The café is busy for a Thursday, but I spot a small table in the back and sink into the cozy booth. Once I order my veggie salad with salmon, I start playing with my phone because isn't that what solo diners do nowadays?

Honestly, I don't know what they did in any days, because before my divorce, I rarely went anywhere alone. It's kind of nice.

What can I look up while I'm waiting? I know, this whole non-monogamous dating thing. I still think it sounds like something along the lines of the reverse harem, or the traditional harem, or some kind of harem.

But I am keeping an open mind. It does seem smart not to jump into a committed relationship so soon after my divorce, and I'm doing everyone involved a favor by testing the dating waters before I commit.

This way, no one gets hurt.

Hmm… this is very interesting… there are different types. It's NMD, but I keep wanting to call it WMD, but that's "weapons of mass destruction," and my dating life isn't that bad… yet.

Here's a handy list of the different types. Okay, everyone knows about polygamy. That's an old one.

And I definitely don't want more than one husband or to be a sister-wife.

Although I used to think it would be nice to have someone else help with the kids and the housework.

Swinging is another oldie but not a goody for me. I am not interested in swapping anything, except makeup tips or comfortable shoe recommendations.

God, I do sound old.

Some of these types must be more of my style.

Hmm… triads or throuples? What the hell? Okay, so that's if Shawn, Patrick, and I were all dating each other? I don't see any evidence of that happening.

Also, throuple sounds like a disease. And triad sounds like something from a science fiction movie.

"The triad is landing on the enemy planet, and all the citizens have come down with throuple."

The server brings my salad, and I cover my phone and blush, as if she cares what I'm looking at. And for all I know, she's the girlfriend of the hostess and the fry cook.

I take a gulp of water—is it hot in here? Or is it all the creative relationship combinations on my phone raising my core temperature?

I get a few forkfuls of salad in my mouth for fortification before I read on.

Now this makes much more sense as a definition of non-monogamous dating—an arrangement where people have multiple consensual romantic, sexual, and/or intimate connections.

So, it doesn't have to be sexual with half the eligible men in the neighborhood, but it can be, and I'm still in the clear?

So many options.

I peer out the window and watch the world go by, thinking—if I'm in the clear, why does everything feel so muddy?

My phone buzzes again, and I jump, knocking it onto the tile floor. I awkwardly reach over on my side to grab it, but a cute little boy gets to it first. Before he can wipe his snotty, cheesy paws on it, his mom takes it away from him and offers me a disinfectant wipe—all while the phone just keeps ringing.

"It's fine, really. Thank you for helping me." I smile at the sweet cherub face as I answer the phone and immediately stop smiling.

"Hello, Mom."

I know what you're thinking. And I do love my mother, and sometimes I even have fun with her. But she can talk… I mean more than any human I've ever met. And I need to get back to the store soon, and I haven't even told her I'm not working in the office anymore.

"Hello, my favorite middle child! Are you busy? I just have a few minutes between showings, but I have a couple on the hook for a million-dollar sale if they can stop arguing about granite vs. marble countertops, and now I hear her yelling about how carpeting is a toxic germ spreader, but he needs to keep his tootsies warm, so tile is out of the question. Anyway, they'll work it out, and it will be cha-ching for me. Haha… so are you all set for my visit?"

I mentally know that she is coming next weekend, but emotionally, I am stuffing it like the woman Kenneth was helping, trying to cram her size nines into a seven.

And yes, my emotions are spilling out and about to pop, just like the feet of our customer—hopefully she didn't kick Kenneth in the privates when her foot ricocheted out like a spring-loaded sausage.

Again, it's not that I don't want to see my mother, but my life is a little complicated right now, and with her and my father planning to come for Thanksgiving, I don't understand why she feels the need to visit a month sooner.

Especially when she is successfully shaking down Connecticut's wealthy home buyers for commission money every weekend.

Yes, I know she works hard, but does she really deserve to earn that much money to referee couples' squabbles? In a good year, she makes almost as much as Todd does when the squabblers make it to the divorce stage of their drama. Come to think of it, she benefits from that as well when they sell their houses and buy more houses.

The whole world is one big round of divorce lawyers and real estate agents getting rich off couples' misfortunes. And then there's the wedding industry, but at least that one is pleasant and hopeful, when people are first starting out. Hmm… there's a career idea…

While I'm daydreaming, my mother has been babbling on and on.

"…and he really has the most amazing blue eyes. You know, some older men lose that sparkle, but not Peter. So, I just don't know what to do."

My stomach does a little somersault, and I say, "Who is Peter, and why are you looking at his eyes?"

My father's name is Simon, and my mother has been with him for almost fifty years. And his eyes are brown.

She'd better be talking about some senior citizen client who has his heart set on a house with faulty plumbing, but I have a feeling the moral dilemma is even worse than shaking down the elderly for cash.

Okay, well, that's a debate for another time because that probably is worse than my mother lusting after someone named Peter.

"Haven't you been listening to me?"

Um, no, that's why I asked, woman!

I obviously don't say that and give her my rapt attention and plenty of silence to fill, which she usually has no problem doing. Silence and Liz Lunsford are not well acquainted.

"Mom, who is Peter?" I am trying hard not to grit my teeth, but even the people in the booth next to me are frowning at the look on my face. They wouldn't be so judgmental if they had Liz for a mother.

"I was telling you—Peter is a new agent in our office. I was assigned to help him… you know, learn the ropes in this office, and well… he's just so handsome and attentive. He hangs on my every word."

"And you don't think that has anything to do with the fact that you make a quajillion dollars per year selling real estate and Peter wants his piece of the pie."

She huffs loudly and says, "You know, you're just like your father. So rigid in his thinking. Not everyone looks at the world so cynically. There are some true romantics left."

"You've been married to Dad for forty-eight years and not once has his lack of romanticism seemed to be a problem for you. I mean, he's an actuary. They don't even let romantic people have that job."

While there are probably some lovely people who celebrate Valentine's Day and whisper sweet nothings who work at my father's Hartford-based insurance company, the profession does seem to draw the more serious types, since they spend all day figuring out the statistics of horrible things happening—like the odds of your lifetime marriage imploding over some joker named Peter with sparkly eyes.

"Tara Ann Lunsford, I love your father, but you know I'm almost seventy, and when a handsome young man comes along and pays you some attention, it's hard not to take notice. I am so flustered at the office, and that's just not me at all. I've even been tinkling."

"Tinkling?"

My exasperated hussy of a mother sighs and says, "Yes, tinkling. You won't be so smug about it in a few years. Menopause is coming for you, and you carried two children."

I push the rest of my lunch away and put my head on the table. She is far beyond menopause—at least I hope so for my future's sake.

"Are you telling me that this Peter guy makes you pee in your pants?!"

Oh boy, that was loud. Now the little boy who found my phone is yelling, "I peed in my pants, too, Mommy! Hahaha… that lady is talking about pee pee in the pants!"

"There is no need for you to take that tone with me. I am coming to you as a woman in need. I can't discuss this with my friends. And your sister may be a lesbian, and she would tell your father in a heartbeat."

I take a deep breath and concentrate on modulating my voice to a lower tone. "Mom, listen to me. First of all, Beth's sexual orientation is none of our… never mind. You said this guy was old to have sparkly eyes. Then you just called him a young man. Please don't tell me you're falling for some young kid who sees you as the grandma you are."

"Of course not. He's a perfectly respectable fifty-two."

I do the math quickly, and I don't like the number I come up with—seventeen years age difference.

Now who's the hussy? But wait, I may be foolish enough to be lulled into a fake romance with a younger man, but I am no longer married. Ha, take that, Liz!

Before I can lodge any further protests, Mom says, "I don't expect you to understand. I know you're lonely after your divorce, and it's hard for you to imagine being the object of such intense male attention, but that's why I need to come see you. I just need a little break from Peter and your father and get my head on straight. Although I can't say I don't have fantasies of it getting messed up…"

Before my lunch makes a reappearance in front of these peaceful diners, I signal the server for the check.

And the irony! Liz thinks she's the only one with lustful men? Wait until she sees my reverse harem. Well, two men probably aren't enough for a proper harem, but I could easily drum up a third if my old mother still has it going on.

"Okay, this conversation is over. I will be happy to talk to you about this more next weekend, and in the meantime, please don't do anything foolish."

"I won't, I promise. Even though your father is going to tell me how many people die in airline fatalities every year before I leave, I'll be strong."

I have no smart retort for that one because we've all been on the receiving end of Dad's doom and gloom.

He'd better figure out how to up his sparkle game before he becomes a statistic of mildly incontinent cheating wives.

Chapter 14

"I love this place. There are no children here", says my oldest and dearest friend, Christine, who has five kids. I'm glad she's taking a little time for herself tonight.

"That's why it's called a rooftop bar and not a rooftop playground," replies Michelle as she casually tosses a straw wrapper at our mutual friend.

Michelle is drinking tonight, but she drinks a full glass of water for every glass of wine because, as a single mother, she can't possibly deal with preteens and her job as a massage therapist with a hangover. According to her, a perpetual state of Zen is the key to her success.

I say, "That's silly—a rooftop playground would be soooo unsafe."

We all laugh at my pathetic attempt at humor, but judging by the behavior of some of the patrons, including my already tipsy friends, I am wondering if a bar at this height is smart for adults—at least some of the ones I'm seeing, like the guy who is trying to get his girlfriend to reenact the famous Titanic "flying" scene in the direction of Broad Street, ten stories below.

Wow, that guy pulling them back to safety is as tall as Todd. I'm glad someone is a sober adult… oh crap, it is Todd.

Todd doesn't go to trendy bars.

I don't want my friends to notice him because then

this will devolve into another Todd-bashing session, and while he deserves it, I don't want to waste any more of my precious time on this earth thinking about my ex. One thing I don't see is Nicole. I wonder if there's trouble in paradise. Shawn may have wisely predicted that her days were numbered, and it's not a big number.

I return my attention to my table, and Christine and Michelle have moved on to a heated debate about which of the bartenders is the hottest.

Christine says, "I like the tall blond guy. What, he's the opposite of my short, dark, hairy husband."

Michelle puts her hand to her forehead. "Andy is cute, Christine. I'd do him if he wasn't your husband."

"Eww, don't say that. All he does is create more pregnancies." Christine gulps her pina colada and stops talking as we all glare at her. "What?"

I say, "You're not pregnant again, are you?" I wince at my choice of words because it's none of my business how many children Christine and Andy have, and I know she must be sick of people judging her for her aggressive breeding. Oops, there I go again with the judgy talk.

Christine's eyes widen, and she says, "No, get those devil words out of your mouth. And you're right, Michelle, Andy's still got it, but a girl can fantasize."

She goes back to staring at the Viking impersonator mixing drinks while Michelle shares her preference for the lean, older guy with short, black hair and facial hair grooming to die for.

And by older, I mean old enough that he remembers when we didn't have cell phones, unlike Thor, who had one in middle school.

And of course, that makes me think of Shawn. I

wonder what he's doing tonight. Maybe I don't want him to be out having fun and meeting age-appropriate women.

Michelle stands up and says, "Well, I'm going to get more wine and see if I can get the number of the hot guy with the beard."

"I thought you said you'd sworn off men for a while after the guy who was secretly sleeping on his mother's couch and collected turtles."

Michelle's dating life is one of the reasons I was afraid to even attempt it after Todd and the donut incident.

She waves off my comment and says, "I'm not getting it for myself—I'm getting it for you."

I swallow a swig of wine and the lump in my throat.

"Um, well about that…"

Christine grabs my hand and loudly whispers, "Ooh, we were waiting for you to tell us about your new man."

Michelle sits back down as I tell them all about Shawn, Patrick, and non-monogamous dating.

They share a loaded glance after my whole speech, and I say, "What? You think I'm crazy? Slutty? Delusional? Spit it out, I can take it."

Michelle says, "No, I think it's a great concept, and I've dated more than one guy at a time. But inevitably, you're going to 'catch feelings', as the young people would say. Like Shawn. And that's what I'm concerned about."

"Oh, well, of course I like him, but I know the limitations. It's just practice dating."

Christine says, "And I was practice pregnant five times."

"Come on, you seriously don't think it's possible to be involved with a man without falling in love?"

I am grasping now because this is the first time anyone has cast any doubt on my plan, but these ladies are my contemporaries. It doesn't matter if my teenage children or my elderly friends think it's all fun and games.

Michelle jumps in. "Oh, I think it's possible for some people, but you can't delude yourself into believing that after a lifetime of monogamy, that you're suddenly going to embrace the counterculture. And it sounds like Shawn is perfect for you, except for the one tiny problem of his age."

I suddenly want to go home and crawl into bed with a bottle of gin.

Or with Shawn.

Holy shit, I may be catching feelings.

"Well, what am I supposed to do now?"

Christine says, "I think a good start would be for all of us to sashay our 'still in pretty good shape' asses over to the bar and get you introduced to another possible man for your harem. The more options, the less focus on any one of them." She grimaces and says, "God, I hope that's not why I have so many children."

Michelle is assuring the now weepy Christine that she's a wonderful mother, as I casually glance over at beard guy and make eye contact. He smiles, but in a smoldering way, not all toothy and peppy, like his partner, Thor.

I'm sure he gets this constantly. Female bartenders get hit on, but so do men. They know it's an unfortunate part of the job, and they play along to keep their patrons happy and score big tips. And I'm sure some see it as a perk of the job.

Before I can protest, my friends have each grabbed an arm and are propelling me towards the bar and guaranteed embarrassment.

I also make the quick decision to play along because I notice Todd milling around, and I would rather not run into him tonight. If Todd is out drinking solo, we won't have a friendly chat. He's an asshole drunk because he only indulges when something is wrong, like the time he didn't win Lawyer of the Year, and he told his partner's wife she looked like a giraffe's ass and promptly fell off his chair.

Luckily, his speech was so slurred, I was able to convince them he said that she has Jennifer Aniston's ass.

We're at the bar, and Michelle is ordering another round for all of us, and she physically places me on a stool. I guess we aren't going back to our table, which was far away from the new man to add to my harem.

Christine sits down next to me while Michelle loudly says, "So, Tara, tell us all about your new single life."

I roll my eyes, and the beard guy smirks as he shakes another cocktail. Maybe this is why Michelle attracts the wrong type of guys. Her approach really needs work.

He is cute, though. No, cute is the wrong word. He's too masculine to be cute. Crap, he caught me admiring his forearms. I love men's arms. They're so strong and defined and… what is he saying?

"I'm James. You ladies seem to be having fun."

I'm sure he says that a hundred times a night.

Michelle is the only one of us who seems to recall how to speak, so she says, "We are, this place is awesome."

She introduces us while Christine is distracted by her phone.

She types furiously and says, "Great, I have two puking kids and the baby has explosive diarrhea. Guess I'll be heading home." She pops her phone in her purse and looks up to three sets of eyeballs in various degrees of shock and disgust.

The funny thing is that James appears to be the most amused and least disgusted. Oh… maybe he's married and has five kids at home too. Duh… not all bartenders are single. Why do I always default to TV show stereotypes? I really don't get out much, do I?

Michelle wrinkles her face and says, "Really, Christine?"

"I know, sorry, that wasn't sexy talk. Not that anyone is going to talk about anything sexy at all. Well… maybe someone will later, but clearly not me."

Michelle downs her wine and says, "Okay, let's share an Uber. My boys are probably lying on the floor playing video games online with forty-year-old men who live in their mother's basements. Hey… I may have even dated that guy."

We hug goodbye, and I decide to stay. I can walk home, the night is young, and well… I'm really not young, but young enough, and maybe I do want to talk to James. The happy hour crowd is thinning out on a Thursday night, and soon he probably won't be as busy.

I stare into my almost empty wine glass and turn away from my friends' retreating forms, and back to James.

He really is a good-looking man, and it can't hurt to talk to him, right? This is what I said I wanted to do —

meet different men and figure out what I want at this stage of my life.

He is standing there cleaning off the bar with the proverbial rag and smiling at me. But not a big toothy smile like Patrick, or the open kind smile of Shawn.

This guy has mischief in his eyes.

"Hey, I'm sorry about my friends. They have young kids and don't get out much. Well, not that I do either. Actually, I do now, but I didn't. Before."

If James would stop that smirky smiling, maybe I could shut up and stop awkwardly explaining my life.

He leans forward just a tiny bit and says, "I work at a bar. They were very tame, trust me. So, all I know about you is that your name is Tara, and you have a new single life. Anything else interesting?"

As I am searching my mind for a witty, non-goofball reply, I catch the biggest doofus of them all in my peripheral vision.

Todd places his drink down on the bar next to me, but because he is enormous and does everything while taking up as much space as humanly possible, it appears more like he slammed his drink on the counter. He tends to break things—the classic "bull in a china closet".

"Now that those nitwit friends of yours are gone, I have a bone to pick with you."

James looks back and forth between me and my ex, and I suppose that, based on my reaction, reprimanding Todd seems like a good idea. I hope this place has a bouncer.

"Hey buddy, slow your roll. That's no way to talk to a lady. You're comin' in a little hot."

Todd screws up his face and regards James with disgust as he replies, "Thank you, bartender, for that valuable life lesson, but I will talk to my wife any way I want."

James glances at me again, and before he can say anything to further escalate this insanity, I say, "Todd, I am not your wife. It's the booze talking. For a jolly green asshole, you could never hold your liquor."

I wish someone we know was here to witness this exchange, because the old Tara would have placated him and tried to get him to leave, so as not to cause a scene. But I am sick of that and ready to give an Oscar-worthy performance, even if my new pal James is the only spectator.

James folds his arms and holds up a finger in the "wait a minute" gesture to his Nordic god colleague, who appears to be going on a break.

I thought for a second that James was going to intervene, but now I think he's enjoying the show. Maybe he's turned on by feisty women.

As I've been saying a lot lately, who am I anymore? Tara Silverthorne does not think about turning on anything but the coffee maker or her YouTube workout video.

"Don't play games with me, Tara. And where is your boyfriend tonight?"

My face flushes, and now James has to be thinking I am the loosest woman in the bar and he's getting lucky tonight if he keeps talking to me. Good thing Todd doesn't know about Patrick. This reverse harem novel is writing itself.

"I don't have a boyfriend. I'm just dating because I'm an adult who thinks before she acts, unlike you and the donut heiress. And since you are living with her, where is she tonight? Are you sick of her immature crap and you're out to see who else you can latch onto?"

I hear James say quietly, "Go on your break, man, I can wait to leave until you get back." He gestures to the show, and the blond guy just shakes his head and walks off, as if to say, "old drunk people are the worst".

"No, Nicole is actually having dinner with her parents tonight, and I choose to avoid that unpleasant activity."

"Gee, I wonder why. Would you love it if your twenty-four-year-old daughter was shacked up with a middle-aged man with two teenagers?" I don't know why I am involving James in this argument, but his gaze is so intense, and I feel like he's in it whether silent or not.

James says, "My daughter is a little girl, so it's hard to say, but I'd probably be unhappy."

Todd huffs and says, "Why are you involving this… person… in our discussion?"

I squeeze my temples to hold off my growing headache and say, "I was talking to 'this person' before you came over and started yelling at me. So, let's hear about your 'bone to pick' with me. This should be entertaining."

Todd bows in mock deference and says, "My pleasure. I'd like to know when you were going to tell me that our daughter is planning on dropping out of Harvard after two months and abandoning her lifelong dream?"

I nod my head and say, "You mean 'your lifelong dream for her.' There, I fixed it. I know you're drunk, so you must be confused. Did she call you?"

"No, I heard her brother on the phone with her, which was highly out of character for Birch, and since he wasn't saying 'dude' or 'yo' or 'sweet', I assumed he was talking to a girl. So, I listened at the door and heard him talking to Willow. After a few minutes of grilling and a couple of minor threats, he spilled it."

James says, "Hold on, Tara, you have a daughter in college. Wow, and I thought you were too young for me."

James is examining my face as if he's getting ready to paint the new Mona Lisa, and I'm so glad I've kept up with my expensive face creams. It's funny, but I thought James looked young; however, because of Shawn, everybody looks old. It's so confusing.

Todd points at James and says, "Now you're screwing bartenders, not just young mechanics?"

"Shawn is not a mechanic, you imbecile!"

Now we're yelling, and people are noticing.

I take a deep cleansing breath and say through slightly gritted teeth, "Todd, if you want to talk about our children, you can call me when you're sober, or we can arrange a meeting at one of our homes for privacy. Now go away so I can live my life happily without you. I'm sure Nicole needs rescuing from Mommy and Daddy Dearest by now."

Todd pulls up to his full height and says, "Well, fine. Whatever, to hell with all of you!"

He storms off, and I can't help but feel a little sad. Todd is a better father than that display showed, and I'm embarrassed for him. And me.

I slump back on my stool and say, "I am way sorrier for that than my girlfriend's sexy reference."

I smile, and James laughs. "He's a piece of work. How long were you married? He's not dangerous, is he?"

"Todd? No, I think he's frustrated with his bad life choices, and he's taking it out on everyone. He normally doesn't even drink or go to bars. And our daughter is going through some stuff. I should be home on the phone with her now, instead of at a bar."

I also think, "at a bar and adding to my man harem," but that would sound bad on many levels.

"Don't beat yourself up. You need to have time for yourself. I bet your daughter is a smart girl. Harvard doesn't take dummies, right? And she has a strong mom, so… she's probably gonna be fine."

"Thanks for that. I appreciate you not intervening once you saw I had it under control with Todd."

"Yeah, I don't go for that macho bullshit, but with working in a bar and in my previous line of work, it's something I look out for."

I stand up and say, "Well, thanks again, I'm just going to close out my tab and go home. I'm no longer very good company."

"What, no… please stay. Austin will be back from his break in a few minutes, and then I'm off for the night. We could sit on the patio on the couches and look at the sunset. But no more drinking… it's not good for the bad emotions. I'll grab us some water. I'd love to hear more about you."

I'm tired and beaten down, but I also know if I go home in this shape, I'll end up in Shawn's bed, and that's probably not best for me either. I promised myself I would give him some space. And James is intriguing, and I'm not getting any bad vibes.

"Okay, I'll stay. Who can resist water and a rooftop sunset?"

Chapter 15

Days off on weekdays are bizarre. Although I've been working for such a short time since my separation from Todd, workdays in general are bizarre.

It's Friday mid-morning, and I've cleaned my apartment, which doesn't get dirty, and I've looked at the news on my phone. I called Dinah to see if she wanted to go for a walk, but she was taking Vinny to the doctor. She says it's nothing serious. I guess when you get old, a lot of your married life is spent taking each other to the doctor.

This is one of the many reasons that Shawn is too young for me. If we stayed together, when I'm seventy-five, like Dinah, he'd only be fifty-eight. And he will have his mother and grandmother to take care of—he doesn't need another old lady in the mix.

One would think I'd be too tired to have all this anxious energy after practically closing down the rooftop bar last night with James.

He offered to walk me home, but even though we had a fantastic time, I don't want strange men to know where I live. It's bad enough that Todd knows where I live—he's strange enough.

I called an Uber and didn't mention that it would only be driving me a couple of blocks. After the grocery store fiasco, I downloaded the app and set up my payment information. It's a must for city living, especially for a bad parallel parker who gets inebriated on two drinks.

Of course, the irony was not lost on me that I refused a walk home from a guy that I agreed to date in favor of a stranger driving me alone in his car, just because a company that makes billions of dollars said he was safe.

I plop on my couch and face the tiny, sunny balcony off my apartment. I even opened the sliding glass door to let some air in. Soon it will be too cold to do that.

And yes, I agreed to go on a date with James. I couldn't resist when he told me about his favorite local cover band in town that plays all my favorite 90s and early 2000s rock music.

James is a year younger than I am, and he has a young daughter. I didn't ask about her mother, but he assured me that he's not married. I didn't want to pry any more than that. We just met, but I gave him an earful of my woes that he probably didn't need. However, he was a good listener.

But you know… bartender… hairdresser…

I really should be shopping for my Halloween costume today, but I asked Shawn to come to the party with me, and now I need to coordinate with him on a couple's costume. That would be a good excuse to go over to his place at lunchtime, but he is working, and what about all that space I was talking about?

He texted me last night to ask if I had a good time with the girls, and I didn't answer until after midnight, so hopefully he believes my friends would stay out that late on a Thursday.

But then I reminded myself that I don't owe him any explanations, and he didn't offer any details on his night.

Maybe he was on a date. Maybe a hot young woman is waking up in his bed right now, grabbing coffee, wearing one of his shirts and nothing else, while he answers customer service calls wearing a big grin.

Regardless, it would be wrong for me to just knock on his door. That is behavior for girlfriends, not practice girlfriends. Or whatever I am.

I also tried to call my daughter, but she is probably in class or avoiding me. I can't blame her—I can only imagine the epic fit she's going to get from Todd, if she hasn't already. She is an adult, though, technically. But she can't keep her plans from us for much longer. Even if Todd is going to blow up, I'm her mom, and I'm here to help her.

Instead of trying to find someone to talk to, I start going over last night in my head and think about every word James said as if I'm in high school. Why not? I never got this much action in my younger years. The universe owes me some romantic indulgence. I found three new grey hairs yesterday—it's now or never.

I told James about Shawn since Todd blurted it all out. I know I didn't have to explain myself, but I wanted to, and it's not often I can get useful input from a man. I don't have any men friends. I work with a gay man and a man who was in love with me up until the other day. And I can't discuss this with my brother. That would be too weird—we don't have that kind of relationship.

After explaining the whole non monogamous dating thing to him, he said, "So, basically, you're just dating. You've never dated anyone without a commitment?"

Suddenly, my mouth was very dry, even though I was drinking lots of water. I wasn't crazy about his insinuation that my carefully researched modern relationship information was insignificant, but then I felt like I was channeling my father.

I can tend to bust out statistics from time to time, too. We're all a product of our environment.

I put my empty glass down on the outdoor glass coffee table and said, "I need more water."

Before I could jump up, he rested his hand on my leg gently and said, "I'll get it. I don't want you to go."

I guess he could sense that I was not only thirsty but ready to go home.

I settled back into the comfortable lounge, and he came back with a fresh glass of ice water.

"Here you go." He watched me as I took a sip, and I realized that he was waiting for me to answer his last question. He's good at listening but also good at asking questions.

I said that out loud, and he laughed. "Well, I did retire from the police force last year. So, I am used to interrogating people. I'm sorry if it came across that way. I was just trying to say that it's awesome if you've been lucky enough to find love and make it stick right away. But that's not how it works for most people."

I sighed and said, "Yeah, you're right. This is all very new to me, and I don't want to make bad decisions. I should probably give myself a break and try to have some fun."

James smacked his hand on his leg. "Exactly. So, what do you like to do for fun? You probably like hanging out with your kids, right? I know you have two, the dropout and the snitch. Any others?"

I almost spewed my water at his reference to Todd's descriptions of Willow and Birch. And of course, we had the usual "tree name" conversation, and he said his daughter has an unusual name, too.

I never got around to asking what it was because he moved on quickly to hobbies and interests. I know a lot of men aren't as into talking about their kids as mothers are, but I thought it was a little weird. Although he was a cop, and that could make someone very protective of their children. I've lived a pretty sheltered life.

I was excited that we liked the same music — and I am not naïve enough to assume that would be the case just because we're the same age. There are many genres of music from every time period.

He got excited when he started telling me about all the bands I should see.

"I can't believe you've never seen any of these bands, especially Girl at the Rock Show. They play Blink-182, obviously, and The Offspring, Green Day, and all the pop punk bands. And then they do the old, mellow stuff, like The Goo Goo Dolls and Matchbox Twenty."

I know I surprised him when I said I had seen some of those bands in concert many years ago.

"See, I wasn't always a boring suburban mom."

He sat a little closer, and I thought he was going to kiss me, and I wasn't sure I wanted that after knowing him for a couple of hours, and also in a public place.

Luckily, he just put his hand on my shoulder and said, "They're playing next week at The Fanclub. Wanna go with me? We could have a fun trip down memory lane."

The Fanclub is a bar in The Fan neighborhood, and the reason I know this is because sometimes they have all-ages shows, and Willow and Birch have gone to see bands there. It never occurred to me that I could go there.

I agreed to go and then hoped I hadn't already made plans with someone else. I need to pay more attention to my calendar. It used to be dictated by nothing but school vacations and PTA meetings.

He walked me outside after we compared the sunset photos we had taken on our phones—his were better than mine, but he didn't say that. I mostly take pictures of food in the grocery store and send them to the kids, so I don't hear complaining when I come home with the wrong snacks.

I again thought he might kiss me when we were waiting for the Uber, but he just opened the door and said goodnight with a little wave.

I tried not to sigh too much in the car so the driver wouldn't give me any funny looks.

And now I am working on convincing myself that I am not trying to see Shawn today, so I can rid myself of some of the sexual frustration that I'm still carrying from last night.

That just seems wrong on so many levels, but James was intoxicating like no other guy I've ever been with. He has a little of that edgy, bad-boy thing going on, but not really. He was a police officer, and he has a little girl.

And he was a perfect gentleman.

But that beard and those arms and that hand on my leg…

If I had this much sex drive in my late teens and early twenties, I would have ended up with someone much more exciting than Todd.

But who knows—the pendulum could have swung so far in the other direction that I was visiting my ex in prison instead of running into him drunk at an upscale bar.

I also need to stop calling Todd my husband. I yelled at him for calling me his wife. In Virginia, you have to be separated for one year before you can get divorced if you have children. Birch qualifies as a child since he's under eighteen.

It doesn't matter either way. It's not like Todd is itching to marry Nicole, and I may never get married again. And as for more children, that's not in the cards for me at my age.

Todd had a vasectomy (I wonder if Nicole knows about that), and I haven't been on the Pill since Birch was born, and my doctor doesn't want me on it at my age. But early menopause runs in my family, so I am assuming that I can make do with alternate birth control methods until my lady shop closes down.

And since that clock is ticking in more ways than one, I really do want to visit Shawn.

But not just for that reason. I miss him.

Yikes, that's not good. I would never tell him, though. But it's been a couple of days, and I do live a few doors down and we are both in our apartments right now, presumably alone—unless my earlier theory was correct, in which case I could just say I was there to borrow… hmm… a cup of sugar?

Okay, it's not 1950.

I bounce up off the couch and head to my bedroom to make myself more presentable. I text Shawn to ask if he's had lunch (it's not even eleven, so of course he hasn't), and he says, "No, why don't you come over. I'll order us something on DoorDash."

I honestly don't even know what that would be. I have heard of these apps, but we never ordered food to be delivered to our house. I cooked my bland, healthy meals, or we went to a restaurant. So, there are more apps I should download now that I live in an apartment in the city and work in retail like a Gen Z kid instead of the Gen Xer I really am.

I'm putting the finishing touches on my makeup to achieve that balance between I am making an effort, but I'm not going overboard, when my phone pings again.

It's Shawn again—he probably wants my lunch order. I hope he's going to get something healthy, but you can get a salad anywhere.

I grab my phone to read his message and… uh oh…

"Hey, I'm really glad you texted. I've missed you."

There are those feelings I said I wouldn't catch, but not only did I catch them, I'm holding on to them tightly.

The question is, am I going to throw them back and engage in a good old-fashioned game of catch with a guy who was playing with Legos on my wedding day?

Chapter 16

"Are you trying to sneak out on me?"

Shawn peeks his head over the side of the bed where I am currently rooting around underneath for my shirt from yesterday, wearing my bra.

Fortunately, I found my underwear. I'm a bit more comfortable with Shawn than I was last week, but still not enough for him to see my wobbly parts with the morning sunshine streaming through the window.

I backwards crab walk out from under the bed with my purple long-sleeved t-shirt and quickly pull it over my head.

"Um…no, I just didn't want to wake you, and I have brunch with Roz this morning, remember?"

He rubs the remains of sleep off his face and says, "Oh yeah, well, it's kind of early. You have a little more time." He wiggles his eyebrows and opens up the covers with an invitation to rejoin him, like Vanna White showing the contestants what they won.

I really doubt he even knows who that is.

I am scanning the room for my purse… did I even bring a purse? At least the key to my apartment… where did I leave that?

"I'm sorry, I want to take a shower at my place and get dressed and… you know…"

"If I didn't know better, I'd think you were trying to

wash me away. But that's not the case, right?"

"Of course not. But I really have to go. Have you seen my keys?"

I lean over to give him a chaste closed-mouthed kiss because no one has used a toothbrush yet, and he runs his hand up and down my arm, making soft circles with his thumb on the exposed flesh of my wrist.

"How about you take a shower here?"

I sigh and sit on the bed.

"Shawn, what are we doing?"

"You came to my apartment. I could have come to yours. Actually, why don't I ever come to yours?"

He smiles, but his mouth relaxes into a grim line upon gazing into my eyes and seeing that I'm not interested in joking.

"Tara, what's wrong? Every time you leave here, you get distant, and you look upset. But right up until that time, we laugh and have fun. What's the problem? Are you rethinking this?"

He sits, and I lie back down longways across the bed with my hand on my forehead.

"I don't know why I do that. I really like you and I missed you, too." I put my hand up and add, "Don't make a big thing about that. Please."

I touch his strong, bare arm in apology while he stares forward toward his pile of clothes on the floor from last night.

I sit up and work to catch his eye and say, "Shawn, I want you to have a normal family and marriage. A happy life that I can't give you." He starts to open his mouth, and I put one finger gently against it. "Please just listen."

He sighs and says, "Okay, I'll listen. But then you

need to give me the same courtesy."

I nod and continue. "We are having an amazing time. You are by far the best man I've ever been with—not that I've been with many, but you know what I mean. You light up a room, and there is absolutely nothing wrong with you."

Shawn wants more out of life—I know he does. He spent a lot of time last night explaining to me how he is going to go back to school to get his MBA, and he's applied for a broker training program at the bank.

I listened and encouraged, but all I could think about was how he would be perfect for a professional young woman who wants to start a family with a great guy.

He laughs and says, "You haven't known me long enough. Just ask my mom and grandma."

"And see, that's another thing. You've mentioned your mom being young when she had you. How old is your mother?"

"Why does that matter?"

I purse my lips and narrow my eyes, and he finally says in a whisper, "She's forty-two. She had me when she was seventeen."

I'm sure it is the fact that I haven't eaten anything yet or brushed my teeth, but the confirmation of that information leaves a horrible taste in my mouth. I am the same age as his freaking mother.

"Tara, age is just a number."

"Spoken like someone with a low number."

He gets up and pulls on his sweatpants, as if clothes are required to be taken seriously in this conversation.

He stands before me with that muscled chest and that sad face, and I just want to hug him and give him a lollipop, but I also want to take off my clothes and take him up on his shower offer.

"You know, I am an actual adult. And I know what I want and what's important to me. Not everyone wants a traditional family. Actually, correction—not everyone needs that to be happy. Families come in all shapes, sizes, and configurations. Children come to parents in many different ways. And a hell of a lot of people who have a 'traditional family' are divorced, with their kids in therapy because of it. So please, if you don't want to see me anymore or have any feelings for me, just say that. But don't give me this bullshit about how you are the bad older woman who is wasting my time and keeping me from my white picket fence and 2.4 children."

He storms out of the room, and I really wish I had taken a moment in the throes of passion to fold my clothes neatly in one place last night. If I had, Shawn wouldn't have caught me searching under the bed. I would be home in my own shower, and Shawn would be asleep with good thoughts about our fun day together yesterday.

I follow him out to the living room because that's where the door is, and he's standing by his kitchen counter, staring out the window with his arms folded.

I walk up behind him slowly and say, "Hey, I'm sorry. You're right. I don't have the right to presume what you want. But I don't want to hurt you, and I don't want to get hurt either."

He turns around and gently puts his hands on my shoulders. "I only suggested practice dating, or whatever that dumb shit was, because you were freaked out and we had just met, and you are a fish out of water in your new life. You know I wanted you to be mine from the start. But I don't want to make your decisions for you, any more than I want you to make mine."

Now my eyes are getting teary, and my makeup is already a smeared mess. And that damn sun is so bright today, everywhere in this apartment.

He touches my chin and looks into my eyes. "You are a genuine person, and I can tell how you feel in every touch, every glance, every word. You can't fool me. There are no guarantees in life. And I don't want to give up on a good thing."

I throw myself into a hug because I need it, but also because I can't look into his eyes anymore.

He embraces me and rubs my back. "Now, am I still invited to dinner tomorrow with your son? I promised him some video game action?"

I laugh and wipe my eyes, pulling back. "But you go to your grandmother's for dinner on Sunday."

"I do, but that's in the afternoon, after church. As a matter of fact, I may even go to church tomorrow with the women in my family. We could use a prayer or two. I'll be over whenever you want me. Just text me when you're ready—you need some alone time with your son."

I run my fingers through my destroyed hair and say, "Why are you so nice?"

"I think a better question to ask yourself is, why is it so surprising to you that a guy can be nice?"

I take a deep breath and gingerly reach for my keys on the counter. "I really do have to go."

I give him one more hug and a quick kiss. "You know we have solved absolutely nothing."

"Life isn't about solutions, it's about living. Now go have a great day. Oh, and tell Patrick I said hi tomorrow.

Bring me some apples. I like the Fuji ones."

I shake my head in mock exasperation. "Seriously? You're bringing up my date with another man after this conversation?"

"Yep, I am. I want you to be sure, Tara. And I think you need to see that age has nothing to do with love."

My heart does a flip-flop like I'm falling out the window upon hearing that word.

Now it's really time to go.

"Okay, I'll bring you some apples. Maybe if I have time, I'll bake a pie. For tomorrow. Birch likes pie. Have a nice day. I mean… this was fun… bye."

I slam the door harder than I intended to, and I wince at my unhinged reaction to a man using the L word in relation to me… us?

I hope Roz has something alcoholic at brunch.

Chapter 17

"Can I have a sip of that fancy drink?"

Roz takes her granddaughter by the hand and says, "No, sweetie, yours is in your sippy cup. And it's much better than what Miss Tara and Grandma have. Grownups drink yucky drinks."

Roz's granddaughter wrinkles her face suspiciously and sips her apple juice.

Grandma and I are having much-needed mimosas.

I know I could tell Roz all about Shawn and my dilemma, but I don't want to become one of those divorced women who bring their drama to every party. Plus, Roz's husband was a police officer killed in the line of duty, so I don't expect her to have much sympathy for my boy problems.

Roz is putting the finishing touches on the quiche, waffles, fruit, bacon, and other assorted delicious treats while little Mae stares at me from her booster seat at the kitchen table.

Roz refused to let me help with the food, and I am content to keep this cute little pixie occupied. Her blond curls are held back with yellow daisy barrettes, and her wide blue eyes are staring like they are trying to absorb every piece of knowledge the world has to offer.

As a mother of teens, I forget what it's like to be in the presence of pure innocence, a blank slate who finds everything fascinating.

When I arrived, she came running to meet me and told me, "My name is Mable, but you can call me Mae."

She was bouncing around on her pink sneakers when Roz joined us in the entryway of her small bungalow home, wiping her hands on a dish towel.

Mable seems like an old-fashioned name for a little girl, but I guess it's a retro thing. And with kids named Willow and Birch, I really have no business judging baby name choices.

The food is finally ready, and Mae and I dig into her grandma's creations.

"Roz, this is so much better than brunch at a restaurant. Wow."

Mae crams a piece of waffle dripping with syrup into her mouth and says, "My favorite restaurant is Chuck E. Cheese."

I smile because that reminds me of the many invitations to Chuck E. Cheese birthday parties I endured when my kids were small. I used to pray over the invitation that it was bowling, gymnastics, or bungee jumping. But it was often the den of childhood mania where we would suffer… I mean, celebrate.

I reach over to cut up her waffle into smaller pieces and hope that Roz doesn't take offense.

"Oh, that's one of my favorite restaurants, too. I really like the games."

Mae's eyes light up as we start discussing the merits of the various amusements and how unfair it is that you need one thousand points to win the lava lamp with the furry purple lampshade.

"But I got a cool purple bouncy ball last time. It's in my bag. Grandma, can I get down so I can show Mrs.

Tara?"

Roz helps her down, and she goes running into the spare bedroom down the hall.

"Slow down, little missy!" Roz shakes her head. "I have seven grandchildren, but she's the sweetest one."

"Wow, seven. That's a lot, but I guess not really since you have five sons, right?"

Roz is scraping Mae's leftovers onto her plate, and I take that as a cue to help her clean up the remains of our brunch.

"Yes, I do have five boys. Can you believe it? And Mae is only one of two granddaughters. It's special having a little girl around, but she's a ball of energy."

Roz peers down the hallway where Mae appears to be amusing herself by talking to her dolls, having forgotten all about the rubber ball.

Roz lowers her voice and says, "Mae doesn't have a mother. I forgot to mention that, and I'm so glad you didn't ask her anything about her mommy."

I drop the napkins in the trash can and say, "Oh, that's terrible. May I ask what happened to her?"

Roz sits down again, and by the look on her face, I'm sorry I asked.

"She overdosed. It was a bad situation. My son… got involved with this girl, and she got pregnant and well… it was a mess. He does his best, but Mae spends most of her time with me when her dad is working."

I glance down the hall as Mae is bouncing towards us with an armful of toys. "Mrs. Tara, do you want to see my dollies?"

I smile and say, "I would love to see your dollies."

She takes my hand and pulls me into the living room as Roz silently mouths "thank you".

I leave her alone to finish cleaning up the kitchen, sensing that she needs a minute to recover from that trip down memory lane.

I intently listen to Mae tell me the names of her dolls and all of their jobs — one is an airline pilot, and the other is a farmer, so it seems like someone is teaching her about girl power and choices.

As I'm thinking about what Shawn said about unconventional families, I am grateful that Mae chooses this moment to climb onto my lap.

I don't want her to see the tears forming in my eyes as I feel my ovaries weeping as well.

We spent another hour or so playing with dolls, dump trucks, and sock puppets. We finish off the morning with three stories before Roz can convince Mae that it's naptime.

We tuck her into the bed in the guest room, and she says, "This was the bestest brunch date."

Roz and I just smile at each other in mom solidarity, knowing how much we both appreciate this sweet little soul, and how it reminds us of our own children.

I didn't realize that I missed this, and now that adds another doubt to my dating game.

Instead of wanting a man who is content to remain childless, maybe I should be auditioning for a stepmom role.

As Roz and I share a cup of tea, she says, "You're going to be the best grandma someday."

With that reminder of my age, my ovaries settle down and go back to sleep, and then I head home with no idea what I'm going to do for the rest of the day.

Patrick texted me to confirm our apple picking plans tomorrow, and I am content to let that be for now. After all, it's just fruit.

On the drive home, I can't help but think I need a hobby that doesn't involve men or worrying about my future. I can't even imagine how I am going to fill up the rest of this day without giving in to the urge to see Shawn.

And laziness and proximity are not good reasons to spend more time with someone than is healthy.

Plus, I really don't want to pick up our conversation where we left off. Those feelings I was hoping not to catch are bubbling up to the surface more and more.

As I pull up to my apartment building, I spot Cassie with a stroller and a tiny wiener dog on a leash. She looks a little frazzled.

"Mitzi, I swear, would you just pick a place to pee. They're all the same." She turns to the child in the stroller and says, "Hold on, Everly, Mommy is trying to get Mitzi to do her pee pees. We'll get more juice in a minute."

I lock my car and join the trio on the sidewalk. "Hey, Cassie, can I help you with anything?"

Upon hearing another voice, Mitzi is even more distracted and pulls on her leash to attack my ankles and kneecaps with excited jumps and kisses.

I bend down to pet her and say, "I'm sorry, I made everything worse by distracting her. She's so cute—look at that frosty face. How old is she?"

Cassie is rooting around in a diaper bag hanging from the back of the stroller and comes out with a new juice box. As she fiddles with the straw, she says, "She's an old girl. She'll be fifteen next month. She was my grandmother's dog. Other people inherit money and jewelry, and I got an arthritic, incontinent dachshund."

She gently hands the juice box to the little girl in the stroller, and she says, "Dank u."

Everly looks to be about two, and with her chubby cheeks and wispy dark hair, she may even be more angelic-looking than Mabel.

"Oh, isn't she sweet? Hi Everly. What a pretty name."

She smiles shyly and again says, "Dank u."

I feel my ovaries waking up again, but is that such a bad thing? It's not like I'd want to start all over with a baby at my age, but it's fine to enjoy little ones, and maybe in ten or more years, I will be a grandma.

I stop petting Mitzi, and she finally walks over to the edge of the sidewalk and pees in the grass.

"Good girl, Mitzi. Let's go get your treat." Cassie looks relieved, like she's dying to get inside.

"Do you need help? I was on my way in." I gesture towards the baby and the dog, and while I'm not sure what assistance I could provide, Cassie's exhausted expression draws out my motherly compassion.

She tucks the blanket tighter over Everly's legs and pulls up the slack on Mitzi's leash.

"Thanks, but I've got it under control. I need to get Everly inside for her nap. Believe it or not, Mitzi likes to walk a little more, but if Everly doesn't get a nap, there will be hell to pay with the crankiness later."

I glance at the little dog with the soulful brown eyes and say, "I could walk Mitzi a little more. If she's healthy enough at her age to walk, it's probably good for her." Hell, it's good for me, and I don't do it enough.

"Are you sure? Her listening skills aren't the best."

I reach down and hold out my arms, and Mitzi hops right up into my embrace.

"That's the best part of little dogs. If they don't obey, you can just pick them up. Right, Miss Mitzi?"

She licks my nose and puts her paw on my chest. This is more dangerous than babies, because I can easily get a dog without giving birth to one.

Cassie thanks me profusely, and I tell her I'd be happy to babysit Mitzi and/or Everly any time. I know she doesn't believe me because when my kids were young, I was too tired to see that it's actually fun to occasionally spend time with needy little beings.

I guess that's why grandparents always say they enjoy their grandchildren more than they did their children, because they can give them back.

Mitzi watches her mommy and sister go back inside, and for a second, I think she's going to start whining, but she looks up at me with her tail wagging and turns around to set off down the sidewalk at a slow but steady trot.

I hope she doesn't poop because I forgot to ask Cassie for poop bags.

"You're not going to make a poopie, are you, Mitzi?"

I'm not looking where I'm going, and I almost walk into someone standing on the corner waiting for the light to turn green. I didn't even realize we'd gotten to this busy intersection so fast.

I look up to apologize, and it's the scantily clad woman who has been hanging out with Lenny.

She's dressed a little more demurely today in tight workout leggings and a hoodie.

"I'm so sorry I walked into you. I'm not used to walking a dog."

She puts her phone back in her pocket and says, "I've seen her around. But with a woman with a baby, right?"

I explain that Cassie is my neighbor and I'm helping her out. The woman pets Mitzi, and the old girl is in heaven with all the new and exciting attention.

"I'm Roxanne. I think I saw you at karaoke the other night. At The Hard Apple?"

The light turns, and we start to cross. I'm holding Mitzi on a short leash because I don't want her to get too far ahead on my watch.

We start talking about karaoke night, and before long, I'm telling her about Shawn and Patrick and my divorce.

She's so easy to talk to that we find ourselves at a coffee shop after a good thirty minutes of walking. I pick Mitzi up, and Roxanne offers to go inside and grab us some coffee while I sit at one of the outdoor tables with Mitzi.

It's warm enough for her if I hold her. She doesn't have very thick fur, but she's sleepy, and my body heat seems to be comforting to her.

When Roxanne comes out to the table, she sits and says, "So, now I will address the elephant in the room. Yes, I work at the strip club."

I almost spray the hot coffee I'm blowing on as I look up in mild alarm. "Oh, that's interesting. You're a friend of Lenny's, too? I mean, I don't really know Lenny, but I'm friends with his aunt. Dinah."

"Yeah, I know. I've seen the two of you walking in the mornings, and I know you saw me in my work clothes. Well, the ones I wear before..." She leans forward and says, "Sometimes I feel like saying hello, but you don't seem like a woman who lives in the same world, you know what I mean?"

I swallow a gulp of coffee, and now my tongue is burning. Great.

"I am living in a very different world now, but I like it. I was a bit too sheltered and… well… so what's it like being a stripper?"

She laughs at my genuine curiosity and says, "It's a job. A sucky one, but it pays well. I wanted to be a pastry chef, but it turns out that satisfying other appetites is a more lucrative career path."

I must be blushing now because she adds, "Too much information? Sorry, I just tell it like it is."

"I understand. I just told you my whole life story in under half an hour."

We finish our coffee, and I look down at a sleeping Mitzi and say, "I should get her back home. I took her from Cassie so fast we didn't even exchange phone numbers. I hope she's napping with her little girl and not worried about where we are."

"I'm sure she appreciates the help. You seem like a good egg for a fancy lady."

As I argue my current lack of fanciness, she says, "Hey, you said you need a hobby, right?"

I am a little afraid of what kind of hobby she will suggest, but I doubt it has anything to do with taking off my clothes, since that's a business activity for her.

"Yeah, something other than men would be a good idea."

As we walk down the sunny sidewalk, she points with her long fuchsia fingernail and says, "I have just the thing. Come to my painting class this afternoon. Sometimes we even have a nude male model, so we could combine your interests."

My laughter wakes Mitzi up, and she licks my neck.

I can't help but think that this new world I'm living in has many surprising perks.

Chapter 18

"They all look the same to me."

We've been up and down so many rows of apple tree varieties that I don't even know how to get back to the store or the parking lot.

Patrick, on the other hand, is like an apple scientist.

He places his hand over his heart and says, "That is fruit sacrilege."

He takes my hand to lead me to the exciting Fuji section, where we apparently have not yet been.

We're having a fun morning, and I can't help but get caught up in his enthusiasm as his big, warm hand leads me along the sunny path.

We are both wearing jeans and flannel shirts. Yesterday, Roxanne and I grabbed a light dinner after her painting class, and we discussed my upcoming date in depth. She had surprisingly good advice and knowledge about what to wear on an apple-picking adventure.

She did recommend wearing the flannel over a sexy tank with a little cleavage showing, but I told her that would require a shopping trip.

Patrick also fancies himself to be a photographer, and I've had more photos taken of me today than on my wedding day. It seems odd to me for someone to want pictures of a first date with a virtual stranger, but maybe it gives him something to do. He is not that big of a talker.

"Okay, reach up in the tree and pretend you're picking that apple, and look back at me slightly. Yep, just like that."

A family of four walks past, and I feel like an idiot — a middle-aged woman posing with apples in a flannel shirt. Wow, what an Instagrammable moment.

I look down at my full basket and say, "Do you think we have enough apples?"

We both start laughing because Patrick doesn't seem to think there is any such thing.

He runs his hand through his thick red hair and says, "Yeah, I guess we do. I'm afraid my enthusiasm for this activity is becoming a turn-off. How about a hot donut?"

I wrinkle my brow and realize that he's offering to buy me one of the orchard's signature fall delights, and donuts do not normally have a sexual connotation.

Thanks again, Todd.

Also, why do I think about sex non-stop now that I'm single?

Roxanne said she thinks I am needlessly obsessing about it and that maybe I should put the brakes on with Shawn… and others.

When a stripper gives you such advice, you really take it to heart. I mean, her whole livelihood is based on an interest in sex.

But mine isn't, and I have not developed the skills needed for the non-monogamous dating version where you bang everyone on random days of the week.

I agree to the hot donut because it will also involve sitting down at an outdoor table with a stunning view of the multi-colored mountains.

Patrick parks me and our apples at the table and goes off to place our order.

I check my text messages, and there is one from Birch about dinner and one from Willow asking me to call her later when her brother is visiting.

Hmm… I wonder what that's about.

I'm surprised that I haven't heard from Shawn, but I am going to leave it be and not text him. If he wants to show up later, he will, and if he doesn't, it's probably for the best.

This date with Patrick is what a date is supposed to be – two people getting to know each other. Not an instant love affair. Shawn's youth makes him impetuous, and he doesn't think about his actions the way I should at my age. After my divorce, the last thing I need is reckless heartbreak.

But then why do I keep checking my phone to see if he still cares after I walked out on his serious talk?

I sit back and sigh as Patrick weaves his way through the crowds with what looks like a bucket of donuts.

"I got a bunch, so you can take some home. If you pop them in the microwave, they're almost as good as fresh out of the oven."

I grab a napkin and a warm sugary treat and force myself to forgive donuts for their part in my divorce so I can enjoy them again like a normal person.

"Hmm… this is delicious. Wow."

Patrick smiles and says, "Yeah, apple cider donuts are the best." He pulls out his phone and starts looking at the photos he took this morning.

"This is a good one, but there's a lot of glare on your

glasses in the sunlight. Have you ever considered wearing contacts?"

I hate that question because it implies that my glasses are unattractive. I have tried contact lenses, but they bother my eyes, and I think my glasses are fashionable.

I can't help but say, "Well, since I've never aspired to be a model, the photo glare hasn't been a big issue for me in my life."

His half smile tells me that he's not sure if I'm being bitchy, or if he overstepped. Really, I'm just messing with him.

"Sorry, I didn't mean to imply that you don't look good in glasses. But I'm sure you'd be even prettier without them. Not that you're not pretty with them. Sorry, but I just get a little…"

"Obsessive about your apple pictures?"

"Haha, yes. I'm always looking for good shots for promotional materials for the cidery, but don't worry. I would never use your image without your permission."

Huh, I am beginning to wonder if I am on a date or if this is just a business trip for him. Also, doesn't he know that glasses are fashionable now?

He leans forward to grab another donut and says, "So, I hear you met Bobbi, my business partner."

"I ran into her, but we didn't talk. Dinah said she's your ex-fiancée." I lick sugar off my lips while I search the table for a napkin. I catch him watching me, and I wonder if all things apple-related are a turn on for Patrick. If I baked a pie, he'd probably be on his knees.

Not that I can really bake pies, I don't know why I keep saying that.

"She is my ex, and also my business partner. It's

complicated."

"When Dinah first introduced us, I remember you said you were getting over a breakup with an ex-fiancée."

"Yeah, that's why it's complicated. Bobbi and I broke up a number of years ago, but we've stayed friends and business partners. Amy, my girlfriend, didn't like that, and she made my life very difficult. So now she's an ex, too." He pauses and looks at the mountains before adding, "I'm sure you can see why I like to make sure anyone I date understands about Bobbi up front."

The new casual Tara will not worry about this. There are many fish in the sea, and I am not even sure I want to reel this one in. I may have to date twenty men before I find love, or maybe more. I can't worry about the baggage of every single guy I meet.

And the only reason Shawn has no baggage is because he was wearing a backpack to school not too long ago. Life hasn't beaten him down yet.

Crap, that sounds so cynical. At some point, I'll find my happy medium between needy love and bored disinterest.

I lean forward and say, "Patrick, you don't owe me an explanation about Bobbi. As long as you're not married now, that's all I care about."

"Okay, but I have to ask about Shawn. You two seemed pretty 'together' last week. Am I too late to this party?"

"Haha... no, not at all." I could explain the non-monogamous dating thing to him, but I feel like it would sound really stupid. I keep thinking of James saying that I was just describing normal dating.

"It's none of my business either, but I don't want to get involved in some messy love triangle."

Now that sounds like something someone my age would say. I think non-monogamous dating was invented to make messy love triangles sound more acceptable and pleasant.

I assure him that it isn't the case, and he seems satisfied. He wants one more selfie in front of the mountains, which turns into another mini photo shoot.

I even take my glasses off for a few, because why the hell not?

On the way back to the car, he asks me if I'll go on a weekend trip with him.

"Um… well… I don't know about that."

He explains that he wants to show me his favorite town, Berkeley Springs, West Virginia.

"It's barely over the border, and it's a cool town. They have mineral hot springs and lots of spas. Hiking. Little shops. Also, the town has absolutely no apples."

I can't help but laugh at that, but I am not sure I want to go on a trip with him. I barely know him.

But Dinah did introduce us, and she seems to be a pretty shrewd judge of character, and Patrick assures me that he will book separate rooms at his favorite inn.

"Sure, why not? But you must promise to take no more than one hundred photos per day."

He blows out an exaggerated breath and says, "Okay, but we'll have to find other ways to occupy our time. I mean with separate rooms as a boundary, of course."

And then he kisses me outside the car, and while it's not electrifying, it's… nice.

He pulls back and pushes a stray strand of my hair

behind my ear. "I think we'll have fun, and it will be nice to get away from this town. It's like we live in a little village with all the nosy bodies."

I can't argue with that logic, and maybe it would be nice to get away.

As we get in the car, I'm thinking about my mother coming next weekend, and then Halloween is coming, and who knows what's going on with Willow.

But I can find a free weekend to explore a different kind of relationship. Maybe this is just what I need to pour some cold water on my feelings for Shawn.

However, Shawn has never asked me if I've ever tried contact lenses.

Chapter 19

"Hi Mom, where's Shawn?"

My youngest child gives me a big hug, but he doesn't waste time getting to the point. Birch has never been known for subtlety.

"Hi sweetie, how about 'how are you, Mom, what's new?' Even 'what's for dinner?' would be a more sensible first question."

I roll my eyes as Birch hangs his jacket on the hook by the front door.

"Sorry, Mom. I just brought some games and wanted to see if Shawn was bringing his PS5 over to play."

I look at the plastic bag in his hand and the hopeful look on his face, and it reminds me so much of his younger self. I wonder if there will ever be a time when I don't look at him and see a little boy who wants attention.

I walk into the kitchen, hoping to avoid the question on the pretense of stirring something on the stove, but the Cornish game hens are in the oven, not on the stovetop.

And yes, I was going to make three in case Shawn shows up, but then I didn't want that one lonely little chicken symbolizing his absence if he doesn't, so I made four.

Birch could probably eat all three extras if offered.

My son places his bag of amusements on my coffee table and says, "Mom, did you break up with him already?"

I sigh and walk back into the living area, where Birch is leaning back on the couch, taking off his size eleven sneakers, before I admonish him for wearing shoes in the house.

I sit next to him and fold my hands in my lap. I'm trying not to look like a mom getting ready to deliver a life lesson, but that's basically what's happening.

"Honey, Shawn is a great guy, but we're not really dating. He's just a good friend, and he's really too young for me. And I know you're going to remind me about Dad and Nicole, but I don't want to make the same mistakes he made. And anyway, I'm not really interested in a relationship, and it's probably best if… oh hell, I don't even believe a word I'm saying. Except the stuff about your father."

I allow the many decorative couch pillows to swallow me up to avoid my son's well-meaning gaze. How much information is too much for a kid his age? Should I be helping him to learn about reality and overcome his teenage naivety? Or is my private life off limits if I want to avoid him telling his therapist about how his inappropriate divorced mom is the reason he can't commit to a woman?

"Mom, you need to chill. I saw the way you looked at each other. I'm not five years old. Did you tell him not to come over? I could go over to his apartment and knock on the door. Which one is his?"

Before I can tackle him on his way to the door, we hear a knock, and Birch hangs back, either attempting to look cool and not so eager or to allow me to answer my own door.

I don't want to tell him that the desire to look cool isn't something you outgrow, as I casually saunter over to the door while my heart is doing a tap dance. Yes, I did just experience an adrenaline spike while picturing my son asking my "boyfriend" to come over and play, but I'm also excited… and nervous to see Shawn after our last encounter.

But it could just be Cassie asking me to watch a baby or a dog, or both. I did offer, after all, but Birch can't kill mutant zombies with a two-year-old or a senior wiener girl.

I open the door and there he is, wearing a light blue button-down shirt and navy-blue slacks, and the biggest smile. In his arms are a big gaming console, a bag of controllers, and a bouquet of yellow and white chrysanthemums.

"Hey, sorry I didn't call, but I thought it would be alright to stop over after dinner at Grandma's. And I wouldn't be opposed to a second dinner—something smells good in here."

I smile nervously as he peers beyond me to Birch, and he seems to be asking me with his eyes how he should greet me. I go in for a hug and a kiss on the cheek.

"You brought flowers." Nice way to avoid everything he just said, Tara.

"I did, here you go. They were selling them at church this morning. My mom and grandma were so excited that I went with them today, but they did pester me about who I was buying flowers for."

"Thanks, I'll put them in some water."

I take the flowers and notice that Birch is heavily

engrossed in reading the description on the back of one of his video games, presumably to give Shawn and me some privacy… and also to look cool. The "looking cool" thing is hard.

While I'm in the kitchen, Shawn greets Birch with some kind of handshake that's cooler than a normal handshake, but it makes me happy that he showed up, especially for Birch's sake.

Although am I just making it worse by allowing Shawn to form relationships with important people in my life?

I baste the chicken and begin cutting up potatoes to boil for mashed potatoes. I call into the nearby living area, "Hey guys, I have some food prep left to do, so if you want to fire up the games, go ahead."

"Yep, Mom, we'll fire them up… they take a while to heat up."

I should scold him for making fun of my use of an old-fashioned saying, but I'm just happy he's back to teasing me and we're not talking about the state of my love life.

And honestly, having Birch here is a nice buffer so I can avoid any serious talk with Shawn.

Yes, I know I am in denial of all my issues.

As I put the last spud in the pot of boiling water, my phone rings, and it is another issue I haven't been properly addressing.

I wipe my hands on a dish towel as I cradle my phone on my shoulder. "Hey, Willow. It's so nice to hear from you. Your brother is here, and I'm making dinner."

"I know, that's why I'm calling. I wanted to talk to both of you. Is he playing games with Shawn?"

I sit down at one of my kitchen stools and say, "How

do you know about that? Never mind, I guess one day you and your brother were bound to grow up enough to stop arguing and start conspiring. Yes, he's here, and they are occupied. Why don't you tell me what's going on first before we have a full audience?"

"Fine, I'm sure Dad told you that I have decided to leave Harvard. But there are two things he doesn't know."

Please don't let it be that she's pregnant.

"Okay, well, you know you can tell me anything." I glance out into the living area, and no one seems to be missing me, so I take a deep breath to steel my nerves for the next announcement.

Whatever happened to the days when kids asked their parents if they could do something, as opposed to informing them of what's happening next? My mother wouldn't have stood for this.

"So, I talked to Grandma…"

Okay, so much for that theory. But to be fair, my mother isn't who she used to be anymore.

All the Lunsford women are changing, except my sister. She's a rock, and I kind of feel bad for her because I have a feeling that we will all be descending upon her shortly with some surprises.

"What did Grandma have to say?"

"She said that she's coming to your place to stay for a while, and I thought I could do the same and we could all hang out together. Won't that be fun? Three generations of women starting over."

Leave it to an eighteen-year-old to romanticize her grandmother leaving her grandfather after fifty…wait a minute. She's staying here for a while?

"Willow, define a while. She said she was coming to

visit for the weekend. And you realize that even though I have three bedrooms, this is a small apartment."

"It's bigger than my dorm suite and I guarantee you and Grandma won't come home stoned at three in the morning and burn popcorn and set off the fire alarm."

I would normally agree with that statement, but who knows what my mother is up to these days? Damn, these handsome younger men for making us think we're younger than we are.

But here I am saying things like "fire up the games," and I doubt Shawn is going to be turned off. I just caught him smiling at me from the couch with all those teeth and those eyes. He smiles so hard with his eyes.

Shit, now my daughter is thinking I don't want her here while I am internally debating whether or not my young lover is still hot for me.

Maybe I should take a solo trip to Tahiti or something. Like that woman in Eat, Pray, Love. I could pick three places that start with the same letter, like she did.

Tahiti, Turkey, and Toledo.

I need one boring one to keep it real.

I interrupt Willow's long speech about how she can't stay with Dad because that bitch Nicole is worse than her roommates, and on and on.

"Mom, I'm not being dramatic. I can't live under the same roof as her. She's a freak, and Dad has lost it with her. I need some stability to plan my next move. You don't want me to end up working at Wendy's or on a stripper pole, do you?"

That makes me think of Roxanne. Now that I know a stripper personally, I don't think we should say things like that anymore, but that's a conversation for a different day.

And at least the girl still has goals. There are a lot of solid life choices that don't have to involve an Ivy League school or a law degree.

"Sweetie, of course, I want you here. You're right, it will be so much fun for the three of us to be together. What a gift."

I do mean it, but my mother is the wild card here, and we are going to have words. Lots of words. I am happy to help my family in need, but she really needs to clue me in if she's leaving my father and plans on moving in with me.

And how's that going to work with Peter?

This is so absurd. My poor father. He probably has no idea and is watching football right now, spouting game statistics while my mother is wishing he would disappear or at least place some bets if he knows how to statistically predict the outcome of the game.

"Do you really mean it, Mom? I'm so excited! I am going to pack up and come home this week. There is a guy here who is doing the same thing, and we are going to rent a truck and come home together."

My potatoes are starting to boil over, and it's time to start mashing them. I'm grateful because I need to get out some frustration. If she is leaving school because of a freaking boy…

Birch calls from the couch, "Mom, is that Willow? Come out and put her on speaker phone."

I don't want to question her about this boy in front of the other boys in the living room, so I decide to table that piece of the puzzle for now. At least she isn't moving in with this guy, although maybe that's the next step in the new plan.

Going to the mineral springs town with Patrick is starting to sound better and better as an escape from reality.

"Your brother wants to talk to you. I'm putting you on speaker phone." I turn off the potato burner and dump the contents into a colander before I walk to the living room.

Now that we are all seated around the coffee table, I hit the speakerphone button, and Willow starts chatting away about her plans, and Birch introduces Shawn. I lean back in my chair and rub my temples, seeing that I'm not really needed for this part of the conversation.

The oven timer goes off, and I get up to attend to the hens. Shawn looks up and quietly says, "Do you need any help?" and I shake my head and motion for him to stay on the couch and talk to my children. I give up, they seem destined for fast friendship.

I pull the hens out of the oven and set them on the stovetop, grab the masher, and start pounding on the potatoes.

I know many people use a blender, but I do it the way my mother taught me. We don't like whipped potatoes in this family—we prefer a few lumps.

Hmm... the lumpy potatoes are a strange but apt metaphor for our lives right now. I don't anticipate smooth sailing in my new living arrangement, even if it will be a little bit of fun.

As I open the fridge to grab the butter, I hear everyone in the living room laughing.

Is Shawn just like one more kid? No. No, he's not. He's just a very pleasant man who happens to be well-liked by everyone, so of course, my children adore him.

I will not allow myself to feel guilty. There are no

guarantees in life, and Willow and Birch will be more resilient as adults, having gone through some things with their parents. The most important thing is that we love them and we're honest and… oh my God, what did Shawn just say?

"It sounds like we're all going to be one big happy family."

Yes, my pretend boyfriend just said that to my children.

Maybe it wouldn't hurt to start researching group therapy now.

Chapter 20

Shawn ran into his living room, popped open the blinds, turned on his computer, and answered a call in one fluid motion.

I am sitting on the couch with a cup of tea, marveling at the speed and resilience of youth. He doesn't even sound tired or like he's missed a beat.

Yes, I slept at his apartment.

And yes, I said I was going to try to keep my distance.

And it goes without saying that there was lots of sex, and I am glad that I don't have to be at work until two.

I can't help but smile at Shawn and stop at his desk to hug him and kiss him from behind while he explains how to stop payment on a check to a lady whose loud voice is bleeding through his headset.

I rinse my cup in the sink and catch a glimpse of myself in the window. I need to get home and get ready for the day. Luckily, when Shawn's working, it's easy to slip out.

I am going into the office today to meet with my boss about the new job they have created for me. I am going to be the Regional Talent Acquisition Manager.

This is a fancy title that means I am going to oversee hiring people for our stores on the East Coast, and I get to work a split schedule from my home, the office, or the store in Carytown. I'll be conducting mostly Zoom interviews for store employees, including managers.

It's a nice compromise between an office job and the retail world, but I'm not sure what kind of career I'm building. I am grateful to Didier for looking out for me, but at some point, I need to stand on my own two feet.

But in the meantime, it's kind of fun interviewing people, and I think I'm good at it. I've already gotten a couple of people to start working at the local store, and Kenneth says I am so much better at sifting through "everyone's bullshit," as he put it.

I'm just about to get dressed and grab my purse when Shawn ends his call, having diverted money away from a shady contractor that Mrs. Henderson on the phone did not want to pay.

"Hey, don't leave. I was just gonna hop in the shower, and I thought you could join me since you have some time. And before you say it, I have excellent shower products, and you know you don't wash your hair every day. Come on, don't you want to get all soapy with me?"

He wiggles his eyebrows, and damn it, I'm toast.

I do have hours to kill, and why not enjoy myself? I'm drawn to Shawn, and it's not just his body and his smile. He's such a good guy, it's insane. I can actually picture him with my kids and my mother and carving the damn turkey on Thanksgiving at my sister's house.

But it's all wrong for him. I know it is. Just like my son and daughter are too innocent to see how this is not a good idea, Shawn is also naïve and living in the moment.

Unfortunately, when the moment is this good, it's hard not to roll with it, and before I can feebly protest, I am led into the steamy water with an equally steamy man.

As I'm focusing on the sensations of Shawn rubbing his decadent coconut and pineapple scented body wash all over my skin, I hear a commotion.

He hears it too because he starts rinsing me off with the sprayer, which would normally also be sexy, but now it feels rushed. He turns off the water and pulls one of his white fluffy towels off a shelf and hands it to me.

"Did you hear something?"

I don't know why I'm whispering. There is no one here, and if it's a robber in the apartment, they obviously know we're here because they can hear the shower. The bathroom door is wide open.

Shawn puts his finger on my lips to shush me, and we hear some movement in the kitchen.

"Oh, shit."

Before he gets a chance to tell me what he's just realized, or I have time to look for the closest weapon, we hear a voice coming from the doorway of the bathroom.

"Shawn Francis, I told you not to take such hot showers. It's bad for your skin. Let me find your lotion."

That does not sound like a robber. It sounds like…

"Grandma, seriously? You just walk in while I'm in the shower."

Oh my God. Oh my God. Oh my God.

I'm a forty-two-year-old mother of teenagers, and I am about to be discovered in the shower with a boy by his grandmother.

"You don't have anything I haven't seen before, but it's not like I didn't peek in first to see if you were decent." She pauses a moment and then says, "Oh hell, those are not your underthings there on the floor. Shawn Francis, do you have a woman in there?"

"Grandma, I will be out in a second. Please close the door and wait in the living room."

She huffs loudly and says, "I brought you some pie from yesterday. You ran out of the house after dinner so fast yesterday you forgot your leftovers… and I see why. Now, before I leave, I just want to see the face of the woman my grandson is foolin' around with. Come on, I can stay here all day until it's time for bingo."

Oh my God, this is the lady Dinah plays bingo with.

"Grandma, come on, this is very embarrassing. I'm a grown man."

While this woman is totally out of line, I can see Shawn's family has a different level of boundaries than I'm used to, but we aren't doing anything wrong, and we are all adults.

Plus, I am not standing naked in a shower freezing while some stubborn old lady waits to see me.

Shawn is quietly apologizing to me, and I rub his arm and whisper in his ear, "It's okay, we all have crazy old ladies in our families. Wait until the weekend when my mother shows up."

I open the curtain just enough to peek my head out, and before I can even introduce myself, Shawn's grandmother says, "Why are you so old?" At the same time, I am thinking, why is she so young?

This woman looks much more like she's Shawn's mother, but then I remember that his mother is my age, and so Grandma is probably barely in her sixties. Shawn did mention that his grandmother was married at seventeen, and she was disappointed that his mother didn't do the same thing when she got pregnant.

Shawn is fuming now and opens the curtain with the towel wrapped around him, making sure I stay out of sight. He steps out of the shower, and Grandma has the good sense to back up. I'm sure he has never laid a hand on any woman, but I think she realizes she's gone a bit too far.

"Out, now. And I don't want to hear about how I'm sassin' you or whatever nonsense that's going to come out of your mouth next. And I want my key back. This is an invasion of privacy and…"

I can barely hear him as he ushers Grandma out of the bathroom and closes the door.

Hopefully, she's on her way out, but from the raised voices, it sounds like she's sticking around to make her opinions known.

I grab another towel and step out of the shower, quickly locking the door.

I glance in the mirror, and I don't think I look that old, but I suppose she was expecting someone who looks very different, and I was a shock.

But still, how rude. And I was standing there thinking I wanted to ask her for some skin care tips while she looked at me like I crawled out from under a rock.

Oh well, the bigger problem is that I am alone in the bathroom with nothing but dirty underwear and Shawn's blue shirt from yesterday.

I guess that's what I'm wearing.

I get dressed, if you could call it that, towel my hair a little bit, and walk into the melee.

Shawn is rubbing his face in frustration and says, "Grandma, you apologize to Tara right now."

The elegant sixtyish lady purses her lips and sighs. "I apologize. I was just shocked, that's all. Shawn didn't tell us he had a new… friend. His mother and I are just very protective of him. What I was said was rude and uncalled for. I mean, you are clearly old enough to be his mother, but I guess that's none of my business."

I stand there in Shawn's shirt with my wet hair and glasses and wish I could have met this lady looking a little more put together.

Or never met her at all. I had never even considered that I would meet Shawn's family. Between last night and this morning, this is getting real in a bad way.

She adjusts her purse strap on her shoulder, and Shawn follows her to the front door. I don't know if he really made her give him his key, but I'm guessing there might be a trip to Lowe's for a deadbolt installation coming soon.

I go into the bedroom to find my own clothes and get out of here with what's left of my dignity. She is probably wondering if I can speak since I didn't say one word. But I couldn't think of anything to say that wouldn't be rude, fake, or pointless.

If the situation were reversed and I walked in on my son in a similar situation… I would like to think I would react more politely, but I know I would be thinking the same thing.

Shawn walks into the bedroom while I'm putting my shoes on and sits beside me. He places his hand on my leg and says, "Tara, I am so sorry. That woman is so bossy and opinionated. I mean, I love her, but she treats me like a kid, as you can see."

"It's okay, I understand. She was shocked, and I don't blame her. She isn't expecting her handsome young grandson to end up with an old white lady, is she?"

"Hey, no one said anything about you being white."

I sigh and shake my head. "I know you're not that naïve. I didn't say she hates white people, but you know she was expecting a very different-looking head to pop out from behind that shower curtain."

He stands up and starts pacing while his work headset is strewn across the bed.

"You need to work, and I need to go home and get ready for my meeting."

He says, "No, I don't want you to run out again. We need to talk about this. Tara, I know my grandmother thinks that I'm just casually dating all flavors of women—she actually said that. But I want her to know… and my mom… and everyone that I really want to be with you."

"Shawn…"

"No, listen to me, please. I know you feel it too."

I wring my hands and put my rings back on my fingers while I glance around to make sure I didn't leave anything behind—just in case I don't ever return.

"Shawn, this is not a good time to have this conversation, but I think what happened here today is just one example of what is going to happen over and over again. My kids are not a good benchmark for the world's acceptance of our relationship. They're young and they like you. Actual adults are going to ask the same questions that I've been asking, and while I know you're going to say it's no one's business, we have to live in the real world. Relationships are hard work, Shawn. You need to think about what you're sacrificing here."

I hug him, and he melts into me. I even feel a little damp on my cheek, and I'm afraid that's coming from his eyes and not left over from the shower.

"Okay, I won't push it. But please don't shut me out. Maybe we can take a breather and just be friends for a while. I mean, I want more, but I don't want to lose you."

I look away at the bed we just slept in, and I know that being "just friends" with Shawn is going to be next to impossible, but if agreeing will get me out of here right now…

"I'm not going anywhere, except home to get ready for work. Now, please get back to work—you need that bank to pay for your MBA, and you have pie to eat. Your grandmother may be a hard ass, but I bet she bakes with love."

I squeeze his hand and walk out the door. I know he's watching me, but I don't turn back.

I owe Shawn more than what he thinks he wants from me.

At my place, I get dressed in a trendy maxi dress and my company's signature heels and put on my makeup.

I'm all dressed up to play the part of the serious businesswoman at a fashionable shoe company, and I have time to kill. If I stay here, Shawn is likely to think of something else he wants to say and come over.

How am I going to create distance between us with him living down the hall?

The arrival of my daughter and mother is starting to sound more appealing. Shawn may be around, but that's a big buffer when it comes to sleepovers and shower sex.

I check the time, and I doubt Patrick is at The Hard Apple, and I don't want to run into Bobbi again anyway, but I know where I can go for some private peace and quiet.

The rooftop bar is open, and it's warm enough in the sun to sit outside. I find the couch where James and I whiled away the night the other day, and open my purse. I brought my Kindle, but I guess I should buy something if I'm going to sit here.

I look over at the bar and squint in the bright sunshine. Before I can get up to approach the female bartender, James appears from a door beyond the bar and says, "Hey, you're day drinking now?"

"Haha, no, just enjoying the beautiful weather. I was going to grab a lemonade or something. Do you work during the day?" I wasn't thinking I would see him, but was I secretly hoping?

He is wearing his usual tight jeans and T-shirt. This time, it says something about the police department. It looks old and soft, frayed at the edges.

"Nah, I was just helping check in a shipment. I'm actually meeting my mom here. She's dropping off my daughter. She stayed with her this past weekend."

"Oh, okay, I'll get out of your way then. I brought my Kindle. It was nice seeing you."

I think I've had enough of meeting anyone's family today, although I doubt James' mother would make any rude comments to me as I'm an age-appropriate woman for her son, fully dressed in broad daylight.

But maybe he would rather not be forced to introduce me to his child. He did seem private about that the other night, and I respect that. Shawn may be too young for me, but James has baggage. I could hear it in his voice.

It's always something. Patrick is probably a secret arms dealer or a foreign spy.

James says, "No worries, I have a few minutes. Let me go up to the bar and get your drink. Lemonade, you said?"

"Daddy, Daddy!"

A little voice is screeching on the otherwise silent patio. Little footsteps are running, and I turn to see an older woman chasing a cute little girl. "Don't run, I think your shoelace is untied."

I am about to make my escape when the little girl stops mid-run and says, "Hi, Mrs. Tara. Do you work with my daddy?"

It's Mae. And Roz.

What are they doing here?

Ohhh… James is one of Roz's many sons. And Mae is his daughter.

Why, oh why?

James approaches with my lemonade and wrinkles his face at his child hugging my legs.

"Either you're really good with kids or you've met before?"

"Mrs. Tara came to Granny's house for brunch. We played with Barbies and ate waffles."

James looks at his mother, and Roz says, "What a small world." She shrugs, and I can see she has questions.

Is there anywhere I can go in this neighborhood and not get entangled in some very attractive man's family?

"Roz works at my office, and yes, I met Mabel on Saturday."

James picks his daughter up, and she wraps her little arms around his neck. "You mean, Maple?"

"Oh, I thought she said her name was Mabel."

He laughs and says, "That's an old lady's name. My little lady's name is Maple because she's sweet like maple syrup, right?"

He tickles her, and as she's giggling, I make the

connection.

"Oh, that's why you made mention of the tree names."

James puts Maple down and says, "Yeah, I thought it was a cute coincidence. Ready to go, sweetie?"

Roz is standing there with her arms folded, and I have a feeling I will have a little explaining to do, but unlike Shawn's grandmother, she seems hopeful that there is a love connection here, as opposed to being disgusted by my existence.

One mother's old tramp is another's potential daughter-in-law.

"Daddy, is Mrs. Tara your girlfriend?"

Mrs. Tara doesn't understand how she's gotten herself involved with this many families.

I don't think this is what the non-monogamous dating people had in mind at all.

Chapter 21

"I don't know if I believe any of this hooey, but it's kind of exciting."

Dinah stage whispers louder than most people talk, but I know Cassie and her friends are well aware that many of the women who attend their Witchy Eve events don't really believe the tarot cards are predicting their futures or guiding them.

Except so far tonight, everyone's readings seem to resonate with their problems.

I brought Dinah and Roxanne along. I invited Roz, too, but she has a date tonight, and after taking care of Maple all weekend, she deserves a little fun time.

Yesterday at the rooftop bar, it was weird. I know James told me he had a daughter, but seeing him with Maple (I've got her name right now) and putting his story together with what Roz told me was maybe more information than I needed.

Plus, Maple seems to really like me, and James didn't seem to be encouraging that. I know we just met and we're not even really dating (our cover band date is this Thursday), but I'm a nice mommy lady and I don't see why he wouldn't want his child to have other positive women in her life.

But again, I guess he doesn't know me, and I am too trusting. Maybe now that he knows that his mother and

I are friends, he will soften up.

My work meeting yesterday went well, so I don't think I'll set anything work-related as my intention for my reading. We haven't done mine yet, and I want to ask something useful but also not too private. A bunch of these women are Cassie's friends and live in this building. They surely know Shawn, or at least know who he is.

If you are a female with a pulse, you would notice him.

Cassie's friend, Raven, is the leader of this event, and she has black hair and she's wearing flowy red pants and a big black tunic with little silver moons all over it. I guess this is the tarot reading uniform.

She's about Cassie's age and is a pediatric nurse at the hospital. I hope she doesn't use tarot to help with any of her diagnoses.

Cassie brought both Everly and Mitzi the wiener dog with her tonight, and that's the highlight for me. Everly is sleeping in her stroller, but Mitzi is sleeping on my lap. This dog loves me.

I'm petting her soft little head as Raven turns to me and says, "Okay, Tara, it's your turn."

She sits cross-legged on the floor in front of a huge, round glass-top coffee table, shuffling the deck of tarot cards. I noticed the box they came in, and this is apparently the mermaid tarot deck.

I don't know if the mermaids can help me, but the artwork on the cards is beautiful.

"You need to set your intention and then pull three cards—one for your past, present, and future as it relates to your question."

Everyone is staring at me. I don't want to say it out

loud, but half the women in the room already know my business, and the other half have shared way more personal things than I would. I now know that Ashley's husband's erectile dysfunction will be cured, and it's time for Nina to come out to her parents.

I squirm, and Mitzi wakes up, yawns, and resettles herself. I wish I could be like Mitzi—her biggest worry is when the next treat is coming.

"Well, I think my question is… hmm… have I already found the love of my life?"

I wince at how cheesy that sounds, but I want to know if any of the men I am currently seeing are the one. But now I realize the cards might think that Todd was the one, and I blew my chance to find someone else, wasting all those years with him.

Okay, I'm taking this too seriously.

I pull my cards and lay them face down on the table as instructed.

Raven gestures for me to turn over the first card. I do so and gasp.

The Hanged Man.

That does not look good, although that one represents my past.

I point at it and say, "Is that supposed to be Todd, my ex-husband?"

Raven laughs and says, "No, you're taking this too literally. The hanged man means that you need to accept the consequences of your decisions, get over it, and move on. So, in your case, you need to accept that you married the wrong man and let that shit go. Make sense?"

I sigh in relief. I don't want anything bad to happen to Todd, like I'm putting a hex on him. He already has a witchy little woman living in his house—no other punishment is needed.

"Yes, that does make sense. I'm trying hard to do that."

Roxanne squeezes my knee in support and refills my wine.

Dinah says under her breath, "I could have told you that without cards… sheesh…"

Raven says, "Turn over the next card so we can see the guidance for your present circumstances."

This one is the Three of Cups, which depicts three mermaids holding chalices up in the air, as if in a toast.

Raven gets excited and says, "This is a great card. This signifies calling your family together to support you. And when you do that, you should trust the results of being with them will be just what you need."

Roxanne says, "Ooo, I just got goose bumps. Your daughter and your mother are coming to stay with you this weekend, right?"

I can't deny that they are, but how are they going to help me with my love life?

Raven adds, "I know you're probably thinking this isn't answering your question because it's not about men, but this could mean that your female family members will inspire you with their love and wisdom to see the truth. Or maybe you'll realize that finding a new man isn't the most important pursuit for you right now."

I'm not sure how a college dropout and a runaway grandmother can help me, but I can be open-minded.

"That makes sense, I guess. Can I flip over the last card now?"

Raven gestures for me to go for it and closes her eyes in concentration. Hopefully, she's not going to guess what the card is before I turn it over because that will be just too creepy.

I turn the card over and… oh, great.

The Fool.

Wow, this is even worse than The Hanged Man.

"Does this mean I'm being foolish because of a man? Oh my God, I am, aren't I? Shawn is far too young for me. I knew it."

My heart is beating fast, and there are multiple sets of eyes on me, many of which look like they'd like to share their opinions. But the one rule of Witchy Eve is to hold back any advice or judgments unless the person receiving the reading asks for them.

Raven opens her eyes and studies the card. "Tara, it's likely quite the opposite. This card invites you to let go of preconceived ideas and remain open to change. So, maybe your assertion that Shawn is too young is incorrect and a product of your upbringing and societal norms."

Always unable to follow the rules, Dinah blurts out, "Yeah, I like that one. Finally, she's talking some sense. No offense, honey."

Raven smiles at Dinah like she's the cutest old sage and says, "Wisdom comes from many places. However, this card could also be asking you to examine whether a man is needed at all. I guess that the need for a partner is another preconceived idea you hold on to. Perhaps your mother and daughter will inspire you to explore the joys of being single."

"But my mother has been married for almost fifty years."

Raven gathers up the cards to shuffle for the next person's turn. "That doesn't mean she can't tap into her solitary joy."

Raven does not know my mother, but I am starting to think maybe I don't know myself.

Unfortunately, I think I have as much chance of figuring it all out from this reading as I would if I asked Mitzi.

Chapter 22

"There are some interesting characters here tonight. What's that guy doing?"

I am at the Fanclub on a Thursday night like a cool person with James, and we are watching the surprisingly good band, Girl at the Rock Show.

The guy I am referring to is holding a drink and swaying to the music, but now he is doing some kind of limbo thing but there is no limbo pole, and it looks like any minute he and his cocktail are going down, and not in any good way, like when the band was performing, "Sugar, We're Goin' Down" by Fall Out Boy.

I was proud that I knew that one because it's "new" music, and then I looked it up on my phone and saw that it was from 2005, the year Willow was born.

James is drinking a beer and bobbing his head to some Green Day as I point to the "dancer" who doesn't look okay.

I'm really not a "girl" at a rock show—more like a mom.

"Oh, that guy? That's 'swaying dance guy'. I'm not sure if he's always drunk or has a different problem, so I try not to stare. He's harmless."

I want to say not to himself, but I rein it in. "So, you've seen him before?"

James laughs and says, "At every bar in town."

It's a little hard to talk over the music and crowd screaming their appreciation, so I concentrate on my own dance moves to make sure they don't make me look too impaired.

As hard as it is to believe, Todd and I are not big dancers.

I wore heels tonight and a sexy-ish black dress I found on sale at Kohl's.

I know, not the chicest store, but I am a woman on a budget now, and I'm not too snobby to save a buck. Plus, I learned about something called "Kohl's Cash," and I think I'm hooked. I also bought a new set of bath towels with little turtles on them, a Halloween wreath for my apartment's front door, and some basic long-sleeved t-shirts in like twelve colors.

I was a little worried the dress was too much, so I took a photo and sent it to Michelle, who told me to go for it since I still have the figure for it.

Christine said she wished she had the figure for it, but she can't stop getting pregnant.

And while I was on my way down the hall to ask Cassie's opinion, I unfortunately ran into someone else with an opinion.

Of all the times for Shawn to be leaving his apartment with a bag of trash on the way to the trash chute, he had to pick that one—the one where I was modeling a sexy-ish dress for everyone I know to see if it's sending the right or wrong message for a first date with a man who is not the guy I am sleeping with who is on his way to the trash chute.

Also, my mother AND daughter are coming to stay with me tomorrow indefinitely.

No stress here!

Shawn is so sweet, though. He just told me I looked great and to let him know if I need any help getting ready for my family visits.

He didn't even ask where I was going, and I don't know if that just means he takes this non-monogamous dating thing super seriously, or he has decided to put me in the friend zone after I ran out of his apartment on Monday.

Cassie also told me the dress was fine, and I should wear it, so I took everyone's advice.

But my feet hurt a bit, and this dance floor is getting more and more crowded as the night goes on—apparently, going out early is still an old people thing, and the younger crowd comes out later. I am hoping that at some point, the old people go home, and it evens out.

Although maybe James and I qualify as old people.

He doesn't look old, though. I've noticed several women checking him out, including some young ones.

He's a lot of fun and a nice guy, but there is something a little distant about him, and I can't quite put my finger on it.

After the show, we are going to get late-night pizza at a very good place my kids love, so maybe we can have some conversation, and I can feel out the situation.

The band is taking a break, and that causes half the people to run to the bar and the other half to the restrooms.

James turns to me and says, "Can I get you another drink?"

I look over at the bar and say, "No, that's okay. It's so crowded. I don't want you to go to any trouble."

He squeezes my arm and whispers in my ear, "It's no trouble, and I'm a bartender, so I think I can get another bartender's attention."

His face lingers near mine a little longer than necessary, and I am acutely aware of the sweat on my neck. It's not like I was going wild out there, but it's hot as hell in here.

"Okay, thanks, I'm going to find the ladies' room."

I don't actually need the bathroom as I haven't drunk enough, and I have been sweating. I'm probably dehydrated. Jeez, I'm glad I didn't say that.

I slip into the bathroom, and there is a line for the stalls, but I squeeze in by the sinks and grab a paper towel to blot the shine on my face and fix my lipstick.

Someone is throwing up in one of the stalls, and her friend is insisting on going in there to hold her hair.

Two other women are loudly whispering in the corner about a guy who apparently "ghosted" one of them, and now he's outside, and they don't know what to do.

So much drama on the singles scene, but surely someone here is married.

Now I am discreetly looking at hands to see how many of these women are wearing rings on their left hands.

Hmm… it isn't many.

When we first arrived, James pointed out another regular bar patron, "cowboy hat dancing man".

This older man apparently grabs women and forces them to dance with him. James told me that I should be careful if I ever go out without a man and never leave alone or accept a drink from a stranger.

At first, I was a little offended, but then I remembered that he used to be a cop; this advice sounded like what I was told by my mother and older girls at college. It makes me worry more about Willow, but she is more streetwise than I am.

I am not sure how that happened growing up on one of the safest, most affluent streets in the Richmond area.

I guess I should go back out to find James. As I turn to leave, I notice all the posters on the walls for other upcoming shows—maybe this would be a fun place to hang out regularly. I forgot how much I loved live music… oh wow, that's concerning.

There is a big sign instructing women on what to do if they feel unsafe in the bar and they need someone to walk them to their cars, or if the police need to be called.

If you go up to the bar and order a drink called an "Angel Punch," that sets the wheels in motion to eliminate the perpetrator and protect the victim.

James wasn't kidding.

I am so proud of the owners for offering this service, but also very angry.

If I see "cowboy hat dancing man" bothering any women who are saying no, I am going to order an "Angel Punch" for him.

I squeeze my way out the door and find James talking to a bunch of guys, holding two drinks.

One of the guys says, "Oh, there she is—you really do have a date."

James hands me my drink and introduces me to his friends, and I promptly forget all of their names.

They are mostly former police buddies, and it makes me feel a little safer knowing they hang out here off-duty, especially for the women who are here without dates.

We can't stay home forever just because we don't have dates or don't want dates.

It's still hard to hear because during the band break, they play loud pop and hip-hop music, so I just smile politely. I'm sure James isn't too concerned about me meeting his friends. We are still virtual strangers, although I bet his mother is going to have a lot more to tell me about her son now.

The band resumes, and we find a place near the stage this time and go back to the swaying and bopping and general fun times, and as James stands behind me and rests his hands on my hips, I forget about ladies' room warning posters, dehydration, and other mom concerns.

Maybe there could be more than pizza on the after-show menu?

God only knows that after tonight, my privacy is about to be swallowed by a generational sandwich.

Chapter 23

"Woo, hoo, anybody home?"

My mother's voice echoes throughout my apartment with the cavernous ceiling.

Liz has landed.

I'm in the bathroom staring in the mirror, giving myself a mental pep talk.

I have spent more time on my appearance than I have on any recent dates. I don't know why I am so hell bent on impressing my mother and assuring her that divorced Tara is fine.

If anything, I should present myself as a mess, so she doesn't get any serious ideas about leaving my father for the hot real estate guy.

I don't have time to make myself look disheveled, so I take a deep breath, inhaling more hairspray residue, and head out with a big smile on my face.

I sent Willow to meet her grandmother downstairs and help her up with her bags. They haven't seen each other in a while, so I thought that it would be nice.

I also thought it would be my last moment of peace or quiet for some time.

I am happy to have Willow home, of course, but I am worried about her and need to make time to dig into her life choices and help her with her new path.

But I am also on a new path, and now my nutty

mother is here, and she seems to be veering off her well-worn path.

I just hope we don't all crash and burn now that we are under the same roof.

I hear voices, and one of them sounds a lot deeper than I was expecting.

Maybe Dad did come after all, and this senior citizen love crisis drama is over.

I stand in my entryway, looking at my mother hugging my daughter and Shawn carrying my mother's suitcases.

This is wrong on so many levels.

I plaster a smile on my face and say, "Hi Mom, how was your flight?"

She refused to let me pick her up at the airport because she loves riding in Ubers.

She says that the drivers are fascinating, and she always learns something new every time she steps into one.

Apparently, she has learned the Turkish alphabet, what to feed a pet snake, and the best recipe for shrimp and grits.

"My flight was lovely. I sat next to the most interesting people. Did you know that Pluto is no longer a planet and that the Polish monarchy was abolished in 1795?"

I shake my head, even though I think I did know about Pluto.

I think she does this to counteract my father's constant habit of quoting probability statistics.

Yes, Thanksgiving is going to be a real hoot, especially if she also has more facts about cheating on your husband in your seventies.

But one problem at a time.

"Shawn, why are you carrying my mother's bags? We can get those, right, Willow?"

I widen my eyes at my daughter, and she says, "Mom, chill. Grandma didn't think he was the help — we just ran into him downstairs, and he figured out who we were and offered to help."

I know my face is turning multiple shades of red, green, and who knows what.

It's not that I was planning on hiding Shawn from my family — after all, Birch already knows him, and Willow knows about him.

But I was hoping for a little family adjustment period before introducing my complicated love life to my mother and daughter.

"Hello, my darling Tara!"

Mom grabs me, and I am hit with a whiff of perfume that may be more than the walls of this apartment can contain. Thank God for the sliding door to the patio.

She peels off her navy-blue coatigan and says, "My Uber driver was a dog trainer and had the cutest little Yorkie in the front seat. So well behaved." She puts her hand to her heart and says, "There was a young woman with a baby in a stroller and a little hotdog when we pulled up, and she was having a devil of a time getting that little thing to listen, but I didn't say anything."

That's hard to believe. My mother must really be out of sorts if she is refraining from interfering in other people's business.

Also, poor Cassie. I offered to help her, and now I have a houseful of my own problems. Maybe Willow would like to do some dog or babysitting.

Shawn is still holding my mother's suitcases (yes,

plural—not a good sign at all), and I motion for him to put them down.

He looks a little uncomfortable and points to the door. "Okay, I will let you ladies enjoy your day. Have fun. It was so nice to meet you, Mrs. Lunsford and Willow.

Mom waves and says, "You don't need to leave. I'm just going to freshen up. And thank you so much for coming to our aid."

She's so dramatic—Willow is more than capable of getting two suitcases into the elevator and down the hall. Sheesh…

I wring my hands and say, "Willow, can you help get Grandma settled in the downstairs bedroom? I thought that would be better for you, Mom."

Mom puts her hands on her hips and says, "Do you hear this, Shawn. My daughter thinks I am too old to walk up the stairs. Can you believe it?" She leans towards him with a grin and says, "I can assure you that the Lunsford women have longevity and lots of spunk."

Oh my God, now she's winking at him.

Willow says, "Come on, Grandma. I'm already set up in the upstairs spare room, but if you want to switch, I don't mind."

Clearly, my mother doesn't know about the spiral staircase, but you know what? Willow won't let her fall down the stairs so she can see for herself that she belongs downstairs.

"Well, let's just check it out, if you don't mind, sweetie. I don't like to sleep near kitchens and living rooms. I can't bear the TV noise."

I shake my head and say, "Mom, I rarely watch TV, and there are TVs in the bedrooms. But sure, why don't you go check it all out and let us know what you'd like to do."

She nods, and Willow takes the suitcases. Shawn has a puzzled look that seems to be asking if he should go with them, and I slightly shake my head no, and shout it out with my widened eyes.

I want to talk to him before he leaves, and it should take more than a few minutes for my mother to pick her favorite room, as if she's an honored foreign dignitary visiting the White House.

Willow and Mom are off to tackle the staircase, and I shoo Shawn out into the hallway.

Hmm… I need to remember to be quiet out here, too, because I forget that other people live behind all these other doors.

Shawn takes my hands and says, "Hey, I hope you're not upset that I met your mom and daughter. Honestly, I just saw two women with suitcases and offered to help. But then I noticed they looked like different versions of you."

"It's fine, I would have introduced you to them eventually. As you can see, my mother is a bit exhausting, and I still haven't had a proper chat with my daughter about what the hell she's doing with her life."

"That's why I was going to get out of your hair."

I don't say anything right away, and he tilts his head, like a puppy dog.

"I just wanted to tell you that when you saw me in the hall last night…"

"In that smokin' hot dress."

He wiggles his eyebrows, and I can't believe he doesn't care why I was wearing that dress.

A part of me thinks there is no way he is into me if

he doesn't care, but then he keeps telling me that he wants me to meet other men, so I know what I want.

Oh my God… is my daughter doing the same thing, sleeping with all the boys at the same time?

I shake my head and return my thoughts to the present. "Well, I mean, it was just a normal dress, but I did have a date with a guy I met. We just went to see a band. Nothing happened."

Shawn pulls me in for a hug and says, "Tara, you need to stop this. You can do whatever you want. If there's a better man out there for you, I want you to find him. You deserve to be happy."

It's a good thing neither of us is leaning up against my front door because Willow yanks it open and says, "I think we need help. Grandma is holding onto the banister and practically flipping off the staircase, and there's a lot of swearing."

We all rush back into the apartment and find my mother halfway up the spiral staircase, hanging her head off the side with a big mass of rock-hard hair-sprayed tresses cascading over the edge.

"Mom, I told you to take the bedroom downstairs. There's a full bath, too. With a tub. You don't need to go upstairs ever!"

Willow has her hand over her mouth, and her grandmother is yelling, "Who has a fucking spiral staircase? It's not a seventies porn studio!"

Even Shawn looks like he's blushing as he tiptoes up the steps and says, "Mrs. Lunsford, may I help you back down the stairs?"

She reaches out her hand behind her back, and Shawn steadies her as she slowly rights herself and leans on him on the descent.

Once she's on level ground, she straightens her shirt and reaches up to touch her hair, which I am glad she can't see.

"Thank you, Shawn. I think I got a touch of vertigo. It's probably from the plane."

Willow leads Mom to the back bedroom, and I tell them that I will make some lunch and get us situated.

Mom yells, "Oh, I know, we should have a slumber party tonight."

Willow says, "Sure, Gran," while I hot-foot it back into the hallway with Shawn before he gets an invite.

I know my face is flushed, and I need to calm down, but now I am hosting a slumber party. Who are we inviting?

Shawn rubs his hands up and down my arms and forces me to make very calming, but also arousing, eye contact.

"Hey, it's okay. Remember my grandmother? We all have crazy families. It's just life. Now, please don't worry about anything, and I don't need to hear about your date."

"Okay, I'm sorry. Well, I'm not sorry because I didn't do anything wrong."

Shawn grabs me and kisses me, and of course, that shuts me up in more ways than one.

He touches his forehead to mine and says, "Now is that better?"

"Yes."

"Good, now I am going to go to the gym and let you spend some intergenerational quality time with your ladies. And no, I do not expect to be invited to the slumber party."

He laughs, and I give him another little kiss. I watch

him walk down the hall, and right before I open the door, he says, "So was it a fun date?"

I sigh and say, "It was fine." I turn towards the door again, but he's still standing there.

"Maybe after we finish painting each other's nails and watching rom-coms, I could sneak out and we could look online for our couples' costumes for the party."

He smiles broadly and says, "That sounds like a plan, my girl."

I watch him walk away, and as I go inside, I think about how I kissed James goodnight and I didn't tell Shawn, but it was kind of a weird night.

It's not like I was going to go home with James, but he was so drunk by that time, I don't think it would have been any fun.

I'm not even sure if that was a normal amount of drinking. Maybe most single people drink like that on a Friday night out. The bartenders were sure busy, and I saw more people swaying than the guy who has that word in his nickname.

It doesn't matter, I guess. It's all part of the learning process.

And I am trying to be a good student.

Chapter 24

"That mother of yours is a character."

Dinah shoves another handful of popcorn in her mouth.

We're in the kitchen in our pajamas, preparing snacks for our guests. Dinah's are covered in penguins.

When I looked at her funny, she said, "Tara, they mate for life. There is no more romantic bird. Plus, my mother used to take us to see them when we were kids."

I felt kind of like a jerk complaining about my mother. I am sure Dinah misses hers, and I should be happy to have this time with mine.

I called Dinah right away because she's close to my mother's age, and it's always a party when she shows up. They both want to teach the rest of us how to curl our hair with electric rollers.

I hope I don't look like a poodle when I sneak out for my rendezvous with Shawn later.

And so Willow wouldn't feel overrun by old ladies, I invited Cassie (yes, she brought her baby and dog). Mom said since they are all girls, they should come and also wear pajamas.

Yes, Mitzi the wiener dog has pajamas. Apparently, Cassie's grandmother loved to dress her up like a doll.

And then just to mix it up, I invited my new friend, Roxanne. She said she hadn't been invited to a sleepover party by a woman in many years and was so excited.

I could say the same, but until I met Shawn, I hadn't been asked to one by any man either, whereas I bet Roxanne gets daily wanted and unwanted offers.

We're laughing about my mother's antics as I pull some freshly baked cookies out of the oven.

Okay, they are made from premade dough, but still pretty tasty.

Wait, what did Dinah just say?

"I said, my mother is a character, too."

I smile sympathetically and say, "I'm sure she was. When did she pass away?'

Dinah finishes her handful of popcorn and wipes her hands on my dish towel. "She's not dead. Oh, I get it, you just assume because I'm so old that my mother is dead. She's just a super old lady. Ninety-eight and still kickin'. She would love this. We'll have to do it again the next time my sister brings her down from Brooklyn."

Wow, my mother was trying to sell Shawn on the longevity of the Lunsford women, but I think maybe we should see if there are any available women in Dinah's line.

My awkward apology for assuming that Dinah's mother was long dead and buried is interrupted by Willow and Cassie, laden down with trays of Italian food.

Vinny dropped it all off, and the girls went down to get it. I'm glad they didn't run into Shawn again, but he's probably out having fun until our booty call.

Hmm… I guess that's not fair to be bitter about it. He can't sit at home chanting like a monk just because I'm not available. He's in his twenties.

Cassie says, "Whew, Mrs. B, your man makes a lot

of food, and it smells delish." She grabs a water out of the fridge and says, "Hey, do you have a bowl I could use to give Mitzi some water?"

I reach above the fridge and pull down some plastic bowls I dug out for the ice cream sundaes we're making later.

"Here, this should work."

Cassie begins filling up the bowl for her thirsty fur baby and points her finger at me. "Oh, and we ran into Shawn. He was on his way out. Looking fine as always."

Willow laughs and says, "Yeah, he didn't ask to help, but I think the sight of us in our pajamas freaked him out enough to stay away."

Yeah, that or he was late for a hot date with a woman who hasn't even heard of wrinkle cream yet.

We put the trays in the oven to keep them warm, and the girls help me with the snacks as we all relocate back to the living room.

My mom has Everly on her lap, and she says, "Oh Tara, don't you wish you could have another one? They're so cute at this age."

I wish she wouldn't say things like that. I am trying to enjoy myself, and I am still not entirely sure that Willow isn't home to spring a surprise pregnancy on me.

She has gained a lot of weight in her short time at Harvard, but that has to be due to stress-eating. She hasn't been gone long enough for that to be a baby in there.

But the last thing she needs is fat-shaming, so I am just going to be supportive and not give her grief about everything all at once.

We arrange the snacks on my big coffee table, and Roxanne has the remote, showing everyone the movie selections we can pick from.

While I was in the kitchen, they had apparently narrowed it down to a top three.

I don't really care, as I've seen every 90's romcom and that seems to be the genre the group is gravitating towards.

It sure was a simpler time.

Dinah plops herself on the couch next to Mom, and little grumpy Mitzi makes a small snort of annoyance since she has to scoot over. However, once Dinah starts petting her head, she settles back down.

"So, Tara, how did your date with Patrick go?"

I give Dinah the stink eye, but when has that ever worked?

Mom says, "Who's Patrick? I thought you were dating that lovely Shawn I met. Tara, are you spreading yourself all over town?"

She laughs, and even Everly gets the giggles.

Many women would worry that their mother would frown upon such things, but mine just loves to joke around at my expense.

Also, I think she is realizing how many men she missed out on, but really, my poor father!

I grab the wine, pour a generous glass, and launch into an explanation of my apple-picking date with Patrick.

Mom is rapt with attention but looks disappointed.

"So, girls, tell me, is apple picking a euphemism for a biblical reference, or did my daughter really go on the most wholesome date imaginable?"

Willow says, "Grandma, stop, you're embarrassing her. And no, she went to the apple orchard. I think it's a romantic date."

Now I see why my sister refused to come tonight. She's smart enough to stay away from our mother in large groups. Liz loves an audience.

Beth said, "No thanks, I'll see her next weekend."

How long is this woman staying in Richmond? She has houses to sell.

While the younger women are trying to divert the conversation back to picking a movie, my phone, which is face up on the coffee table, pings and flashes another man's name.

"Whose James?"

Would they believe that he's my gardener? No, I don't have a yard.

Doctor? Nope, I wouldn't use his first name on my phone.

Boss, no, they know that's a woman.

I sigh and grab the phone before the message preview shows up. I don't know James well enough to guess what he might say or send.

It's safe to say that a dick pic would steer this evening in the wrong direction.

All eyes are on me again as I explain that James is just a guy I met when I was out with my girlfriends.

"We just went to see a band play at a bar. No big deal. It was fun. A little loud."

Cassie is putting Everly down in her napping cot she brought along, and says, "Ooh, that sounds more like a real date. Tell us what happened."

"Nothing happened!" Shit, I need to turn this phone off. He keeps texting me. I might as well see what he wants.

"Okay, he just wants to know if I want to go to another show with him in a couple of weeks. I told him

I was busy with a slumber party, and he said I should bring all of you."

I guess he's not that into me if he wants a group date, but maybe that's for the best. I am still not sure how I feel about his drinking.

Of course, as soon as I mention the invitation, I am full of regrets because everyone wants to go, including Dinah and my mother.

Which means that she intends to still be here in two weeks.

Wait until she finds out that I am planning a weekend away with Patrick.

Luckily, even though this is a sleepover, everyone is going home. We just wore pajamas to pretend.

If we get this movie and Italian feast going, we can fire up the hot rollers, and I can be in the comfort of Shawn's arms and put these other men out of my mind.

I know, I don't believe me either.

Chapter 25

Shawn is sleeping peacefully, but I am already feeling edgy, and I don't know why.

After all our guests went home last night, both Mom and Willow insisted that I go over to Shawn's place.

I suppose there is no reason to hide what I'm doing, but it feels weird and somehow wrong for me to leave my old mother and young daughter to sleep in some guy's bed.

They assured me they were going to watch one more movie and go to sleep, but Willow was already off to FaceTime with this mysterious boyfriend before I was even out the door.

Oh my God, I hope my mother wasn't Facetiming anyone because if she was, it was not my father. He goes to bed at 9:00 every night, even on weekends.

I think it's because people who go to bed and get up at consistent times have a higher probability of living longer.

It's kind of easy to see how Dad isn't a barrel of laughs, but my mother married him and stayed with him all these years.

I shake off the quilt and head to the bathroom, but I am not going to sneak out on Shawn this time. We had fun last night just talking… well, not just talking… but the talking part was nice, too.

I told him the highlights of the evening, including everyone reciting the "you complete me" speech at the end of Jerry Maguire.

Shawn was looking at the costumes in the many online stores, hoping to dress us up as everything from Fred and Wilma Flintstone to a hooker and her pimp.

I kept reminding him that this is a work event, and while my company isn't very conservative, I still don't want to be known as "the one who wore THAT outfit."

Also, I can't help but feel a little apprehensive about meeting Dominique. I don't know why, but she seems scary. Even if I wanted to give it a try with Didier again, I would not be able to get past his soon-to-be ex-wife.

I just don't want her to demand that I be fired because there is no way I could replace the salary and flexibility I have found at this job.

My resume is nonexistent, and I don't want to work a minimum wage job.

I sit on the closed toilet and rub my face as if that will provide me with an answer. At least I'm not snooping in Shawn's cabinets. I really don't want to find a box of tampons or a bunch of hair scrunchies and wonder who they belong to.

I do need to get more serious about my own path. I am sure everyone in my life is wondering why my divorce isn't final yet and why Todd has not been forced to part with more of our money.

Even if I just get my half of the house equity, I will be set for quite some time.

And there is plenty of other money in investments and retirement accounts.

But even though Todd did a terrible thing, I can't find the anger anymore to try to rob him blind.

My lawyer keeps calling me, and I continue to put off the final settlement.

I can support myself until Birch graduates from high school, and maybe then I'll ask Todd to sell the house. I'm sure Nicole would love to move to someplace more exciting and away from her parents and all the neighbors who know her as the donut knocker girl.

Oh well, I can't worry about any of this now—not with my mother and daughter staying with me and juggling three men.

Although I'm not sure whether James counts as a juggling ball or not. He seemed to be into me, but he isn't asking me out on a proper date. But then it is kind of sweet that he wants me to bring my family and friends to the club for the next show.

It's too bad I didn't analyze my marriage to this degree, or a career choice. I would have been divorced a long time ago and made something of myself.

I think about taking a shower here, but all my stuff is at my place, and I'm not ready to go home yet anyway. I am going to rejoin Shawn and enjoy the luxury of my new life for once.

It's still early, and I am sure at least Willow is still out cold, so our little Carytown shopping trip isn't going to happen for a while.

I wish I were going with Willow alone, but I am going to talk to her today, no matter what. I need to know what plans she has for her future, and I want to meet this boyfriend.

When women make sudden life changes, and there is a guy involved, you know he must figure into the equation somewhere.

I gently climb back into bed so as not to wake

Shawn, not that I wouldn't like more one-on-one time with him.

He's going to look amazing in our vampire costumes. I went with that because it's sexy but mostly covered up, I won't freeze or get fired, and vampires don't cross any lines of cultural appropriation or mockery.

I mean, there was a sexy nun and priest outfit—who are the people who would wear that to an office party?

And there is no way I am doing French maid, Swiss milkmaid, Pocahontas, or any other ethnicity used to demean women.

Shawn said I was taking it all a little too seriously, but he doesn't understand. I have spent so much time living near and associating with assholes, and I don't want to be one, even by accident.

I stare up at the ceiling, and I know I can't sleep anymore. I guess I'll do what everyone does in bed these days—look at nonsense on my phone.

Oh, I have texts.

Wow, Willow is up making eggs, and Mom is curling her hair. I guess she must have slept on it, "funny". She will no doubt blame my pillows.

I need to have a talk with her, too. What is she doing here, and what are her plans? All those houses in Connecticut can't sell themselves, and she hasn't mentioned my father once.

I tell Willow I will be home soon. I am cozy back in the nest now, and I kind of wish they were sleeping in at my apartment. We don't really need a shopping trip, but I don't know what else to do with my mother, and I know she will want to stop at the Monet store and meet everyone.

Another text pops up, and it's from Patrick.

I wonder if he wants to talk about the weekend away. No matter how evolved and modern I am now, I am not planning a weekend away with one man while in another's bed. That's crossing a line.

Isn't it?

I squint at the screen and… wait… what is he saying?

I sit up and read it again, and it makes zero sense.

He's in Vietnam, and he wants to know my shoe size.

Patrick is either tripping on something and thinks he's in a foreign land, or there is a shoe store in Richmond called Vietnam that opens early on Saturday mornings.

Hmm… neither of those makes sense.

I know, maybe it's an autocorrect error.

I don't answer because I don't even know where to begin. He never said anything about going to Vietnam, and while he doesn't owe me explanations about his plans and whereabouts, that seems like a significant thing that was coming up, and you'd think he'd mention it.

As much as I'd like to think I know all these guys I've been dating, they are all virtual strangers.

Even sweet, gorgeous Shawn. I mean, sure, Dinah vouches for him, but she only knows him as her bingo partner's grandson and a meatball customer.

I don't want to leave without saying goodbye, so I lean over and kiss him on the cheek… not the head… that feels like something I would do with one of my children.

He stirs and just pulls me closer. I almost begin to

protest, but I don't need any eggs, and as I keep saying, the stores aren't even open yet.

Except the ones in freaking Vietnam, apparently.

He opens his eyes for just a moment, but I can tell by several clues that he isn't ready to send me off on my fun shopping trip just yet.

And I'm not ready to go.

But as Shawn draws me closer, I can't help but wonder what Patrick is doing in Vietnam and why he is buying me shoes? I work for a shoe company.

I clear my mind long enough to enjoy a little more time with Shawn before I face all the issues waiting for me down the hall.

Chapter 26

"What is she doing in there?"

We stopped at Wawa on the way to Carytown because my mother said she had to go to the bathroom.

It's not a long drive, so I am not sure why she didn't go before we left or just waited until we go to lunch, but maybe I will have a weak bladder when I am almost seventy, too.

Willow is in the backseat with her face in her phone. "She said she had to go to the bathroom. Maybe there's a line."

I suppose that's possible, but I have a bad feeling that she wants privacy with her phone, and I know that's not to call my father or work on a real estate deal.

She said she spoke to Dad briefly this morning, and she took a real estate call in the car when we first pulled out of the neighborhood. Willow and I had to open our windows and hang our heads out like dogs to escape the volume of her voice.

"That house just gets the most superior morning light. And the butler's pantry is sooo elegant, don't you think? The sellers are very motivated."

I could practically see the dollar signs in her eyes as she charmed her client, but maybe I am just jealous that everyone has found their life's purpose but me.

I turn around again and patiently say, "Willow, will

you please go and see if Grandma is okay?"

She puts her phone on the seat with the screen down and rolls her eyes. "Fine, I will go stalk Grandma. Do you want anything? I have Dad's credit card."

"No, I don't need anything, and you should watch what you buy. You can't try to get back at him by taking his money just because he's upset with you."

Willow shakes her head and says, "Mom, chill. I'm just kidding. For someone who is getting a lot of action, you are sure uptight."

She closes the door and heads into the store, and all I can think about now is how maybe she's grouchy because she's hanging out with old ladies and not getting any action.

I peek at her phone out of the corner of my eye, but I am not going to do it. Spying on my daughter would be even worse than spying on Shawn. I'm sure I will find out all about this new boyfriend and her very sensible plans.

No one in my family emerges from Wawa, so I lean my seat back and close my eyes for a minute, letting the sun's rays warm my face.

It's a little chilly for late October in Virginia, but the sun is shining brightly, so this day should go smoothly, and everyone should be in a decent mood.

This morning, when I left Shawn to go home, I found Willow at the breakfast bar eating eggs, and my flustered-looking mother flitting around in and out of rooms getting ready.

"Oh, I just never know where any of my stuff is when I travel."

Before I went upstairs to take a shower, I asked Willow if we could talk later, and she said, "Maybe if you're still up, but Kelso is picking me up for dinner, and I am going to look at apartments with him."

She quickly took in my shocked expression as I tried to keep my eyeballs from rolling out of my head, and she quickly added, "For him, Mom, not for us. I've only known him for a few months. Jeez, have a little faith in me."

I apologized and hugged her, and once I was in the shower, I thought how old is this guy that he is getting his own apartment? Maybe his parents are wealthy.

As I was getting dressed, another text came in from Patrick, and he asked if I got his first text and said, "I am in Ho Chi Minh City on business, and I'll be back in a few days. Let's talk about our trip when I get back. Also, what about your shoe size?"

So, Vietnam was not a typo, but what kind of business trip does a cidery owner need to go on in Vietnam? I mean, do they have special apples there?

I text him back my shoe size and wish him safe travels.

I hear them before I see them, and just as I am about to nod off in the car, my mother and daughter come barreling in. It looks like my mother did some grocery shopping there.

"Oh, I just love Wawa. I can't believe we still don't have one. Look at these beautiful pastries, Tara. And I also picked up some magazines and bought a lottery ticket. So fun!"

We all put our seatbelts back on, and I say, "Well, I'm glad you're enjoying your shopping trip so far. Willow, your phone has been lighting up."

I probably shouldn't have said that because I'm sure she thinks I was spying but I did not lay a finger on that phone, and yes I was sitting on my hands while daydreaming, but let's see how you handle it if your eighteen year old daughter drops out of Harvard and comes home the same week your mother is having a late life crisis.

Whew… my brain didn't even take a breath on that speech.

"I know, Mom, it's Dad. I'm going to give in and have lunch with him tomorrow. I guess I do owe him an explanation."

I widen my eyes and hope she doesn't see them in the rear-view mirror. She owes me an explanation, too, but doesn't seem to have a problem waiting to deliver it.

But of course, I haven't been trying to steamroll the girl like Todd. For a successful man, he is really a ding-dong sometimes.

My mother jumps in and starts telling Willow what she should say to Todd, and now I am wondering if my daughter has been more forthcoming with her grandmother than me. However, Mom was hanging out with Willow last night while I was otherwise occupied with my hot young… whatever he is.

Now that we've pulled onto Cary Street, Mom is oohing and aahing at all the shops.

"Oh, this area is just darling. I think you brought me here once years ago, but it looks so different. Oh, look at that beautiful lingerie shop. Where are we parking, Tara?"

I explain that all of the parking is on side streets except the lot that belongs to the new grocery store. The whole shopping area is just a few blocks in total, and it's not like my mother is feeble. I am dying to know if Willow caught her on the phone in Wawa, but I don't really want to introduce the concept of Grandma being a cheating hussy to my children.

They get enough of that at their dad's house.

We park and all reach for our sunglasses as we get out of the car. It is a bright, brisk day, and I take in a deep breath of fall air. It's kind of fun to be in this neighborhood without reporting to work, and if I'm lucky, Mom will forget about the shoe store, and I won't have to visit on my day off.

"Grandma, there's the lingerie store you were pointing to. Do you want to start there?"

Mom squeals like a little piglet and grabs Willow's arm. On second thought, maybe this will be a long day even without working.

And what does my mother need in a lingerie store? She has acres of nighties and robes, and about ten pairs of fuzzy slippers. She may be a hardworking real estate shark by day, but she's a fancy lounging lady by night. I've seen her closet in their West Hartford home—Dad jokes about the statistical probability of her side of the closet caving in from the weight of her treasures.

Yes, this is humor for an old man actuary, but it still doesn't mean she should trade my father in for some middle-aged realtor with a puffy hairdo and more white teeth than I've ever seen in one mouth.

Yes, of course, I Googled the guy. He looks like an older Ken doll, but I am guessing Peter is anatomically correct.

We enter the small shop, and there are a couple of women shopping solo and a young woman straightening lacy bras on a display table.

At a volume only needed to yell across a football field with a wood chipper going in the background,

Mom looks at the employee and says, "Excuse me, do you have any of those pee-pee underwear for old ladies who can't hold it in but want to look sexy?"

Willow starts coughing, and I slap her on the back. She's probably choking on her reply to that outburst, but the store employee doesn't blink an eye. I guess they get even nuttier customers in a lingerie store than we do in the shoe store.

She smiles a perfectly natural smile and says, "Oh yes, ma'am, we do have some very pretty ones with moisture-wicking right over here."

I give Mom an evil eye that I would normally have reserved for the kids when they are pushing me to my limit, but she is oblivious and clearly enjoying the shock value and being the center of attention.

Willow goes to the opposite side of the store and is looking at sleepwear, but I feel compelled to follow my mother before she makes a bigger fool of herself.

As Mom is going on about how lovely the fabric is and how years ago her mother just had to wear Depends like a big smelly diaper, I see a glimpse of recognition on the girl's face with a head tilt.

"Is that you, Mrs. Silverthorne? You probably don't remember me, but you used to be my neighbor. I live next door to Nicole's family." She covers her mouth and says, "Oh, sorry, you probably don't want to hear that name, but just so you know, my family was very upset about what happened. We've started getting cupcakes instead of donuts."

I smile and nod. I know people mean well… or at least I think they do… but I don't need to be told that my former neighbors are on my side. It's over and almost comical that Todd is stuck with an unemployed, almost child in the house when his actual kids are nearly grown.

"Oh yes, I do remember you. You have some younger siblings, right? You're the oldest? Riley?"

"Yes, you have a great memory. Not that you wouldn't because you're not that old." She starts turning red when my mother looks up, and I hope she doesn't start telling her I'm too young to forget things because she has forgotten that she's been married for almost fifty years.

Willow comes over and also recognizes Riley. "Hey, I thought you were going away to college."

Riley laughs and says, "Really, because I heard you dropped out of Harvard." She covers her mouth and says, "Oops, that's probably a sore spot, sorry. I'm taking a gap year, and I don't need this job, but I have to get out of the house. After the holidays, I'm going to do some traveling. A bunch of us are going to Switzerland in January — you should come."

I know that Willow was only an acquaintance of this girl in school, so I am not too worried that she is going to ask Todd for money for an international ski vacation tomorrow.

I guess I should be grateful for Kelso, the mystery boyfriend. He seems to have followed her here, so hopefully that keeps her grounded long enough for me to influence Willow's next move.

My mother is laden down with pee-pee pants, and now she's looking at see-through nightgowns, and I am doubting that those are intended for my father's viewing pleasure. He would probably give her the statistics of catching a cold in the Connecticut winters, walking around half-dressed.

As we continue to browse, Riley excuses herself to

help other customers.

Willow looks worried. "Mom, are you okay?"

"Yes, why wouldn't I be? Honey, I don't care if people mention Nicole. It's a small city. As long as I live here, I am bound to run into people who know our family."

Willow holds up a pair of cotton pajamas with kittens on them, and I am at least glad someone has some sensible shopping inclinations on this trip. I am waiting for my mother to ask if they have any nipple bearing corsets.

And no, I am not taking my mother to that kind of store. I may be participating in the non-monogamous dating thing, but I am not going to a sex shop with the woman who gave birth to me.

Willow adds the pjs to the pile, draped over her arm, and says, "Yeah, you do seem to be quite chill about the whole thing now. I'm proud of you. But you know, it's hard for Birch at school. Nicole is not the biggest asshole in her family. Her younger brothers are all vying for that title."

Before I can question her further and wonder if I should be concerned, Mom yells out, "Tara, what do you think of this garter belt. Too much?"

Chapter 27

"Please, please tell me your costume. Is Shawn going as the Superman?"

Didier puffs out his chest in imitation of how my date will look dressed up as the muscular superhero.

I am at the office today and therefore getting nothing done. Whoever said people who work in the office are more productive has never worked here.

"I told you that our costumes are secret. What are you and Dominique going as?"

Didier jumps up and yells, "I told you I am not going with that shrew of a witch woman. But I cannot make her stay home. She is like… how you say? A letch?"

I wrinkle my brow as my "Didier to English" translator goes to work.

"You mean a leech?"

"Yes, yes, a creepy crawly that suck the blood. I do not even have a date; it is so frustrating. Do you have any single women friends?"

I do, but how would I sell Didier? He's rich but wildly eccentric, and is still married to a beautiful, scary lady who has him by the balls?

"I do know some single women, obviously, but I can't think of anyone you would like right now."

My phone mercifully starts ringing, and I glance at it. "Oh, this is my son's school. I have to take it."

He nods and says, "Okay, I hope the boy is well. Go home if you need to. It will give you more time to think of the single women." He winks and walks out the door.

I answer the incessantly ringing phone with a cautious hello. I never get calls from the school about my kids.

"Hello, is this Mrs. Silverthorne?"

Ugh… I hate that title, but I am stuck with it for now, so the answer is yes.

"Yes, it is. What's going on?"

"This is Principal Richards' office. We need you and Mr. Silverthorne to come down to the school for a conference. Birch is being detained with another student for fighting."

"What? Fighting? Is he okay? Is the other boy okay?"

"Yes, no one is injured, but Principal Richards feels that this is a sensitive matter that should be addressed in person."

A sensitive matter? Oh God, I hope it's not racial or homophobic or… what am I saying? Birch would never start a fight, and he has no biases. He didn't even blink an eye at me dating Shawn, who's young enough to be my son if I were a teen mother.

I did not raise a bully, and even Todd, for all of his faults, isn't that much of an asshole.

I tell the robotic-voiced admin that I'm on my way. Before I can even make it to my car, Todd is calling me.

I don't know what's worse—getting called to the principal's office or having to see Todd in the middle of a workday. He's going to be so pissed off that he has to interrupt his day—his job is sooo important.

"Hello, Todd. I'm on my way to the school. You really don't need to come if you're busy. I can handle it."

Please be in court.

"What? Of course I'm coming. Why is Birch fighting? This is outrageous!"

I can already tell that he is setting this up to be my fault. It is typical of him to blame any and all problems with the kids on me, the stay-at-home mom.

I can't wait until he talks to Willow at lunch today. We talked last night, and he is going to love her story. She's giving up Harvard for… oh, never mind, one child disaster at a time.

"How would I know, Todd?"

As I back out of my parking spot and pop on my sunglasses, I spot a coworker that everyone calls Chatty Chelsea, and I peel out of the parking lot before she can approach the car.

I can't stop to yap about what the cafeteria is serving today or hear a long story about why she's late.

No one cares if you ran out of clean underwear, Chelsea!

Todd huffs and says, "You are his mother, Tara. Has he said anything about enemies at school?"

I want to say, "No, only at your house", but bashing Nicole isn't going to help.

However, I am so tired of being the bigger person. For once, I would like to be a very tiny, petty person. Like a mean little witch… hmm… maybe that should be my Halloween costume.

"Todd, he lives with you. You spend more time with him than I do—theoretically."

"What is that supposed to mean? I have a thriving law practice, and a lot of people rely on me. And you're out there selling shoes. That's hardly equal."

I rest my head on the steering wheel while stopped

at a light.

"This is a ridiculous conversation. I am going to hang up now and let you think about why I am selling shoes and why I don't live in our house and why there is no longer a responsible mother in the home!"

I end the call and throw my phone onto the passenger seat. It's just not as satisfying as when we had phones you could slam down when you hung up on an asshole.

Maybe if I'm lucky, he'll get a call from a rich client and have to turn around and go back to the office.

Or Nicole will ask him to come home because she can't find the forks in the kitchen to eat her ramen noodles.

Anything to get him to go away and let me calmly handle this. Under most circumstances, I can be civil with Todd, but when it comes to accusations about my mothering abilities, he can kiss my ass.

I am listening to some calming meditation music and doing some deep breathing exercises as I pull into the parking lot of Birch's elite private school.

I don't see any sign of Todd yet, but he could already be inside demanding answers and justice.

I hope he isn't threatening to sue anyone.

I report to the front desk and am sent to the principal's office.

It's funny that it is just as scary as a parent as it was as a child, although I was rarely in trouble at school.

My strong-willed sister was more likely to be in hot water, but then we all laughed because the school had to deal with our mother.

Hmm... why didn't I swing by my apartment and pick up my mother? She could be helpful in this situation, but no… I want her to go home to Connecticut someday, and she doesn't need any deeper involvement in this mess that is my family.

It's bad enough I had to leave her alone with Willow. Who knows what life lessons she is learning from Grandma Liz?

At the door, I am beckoned in by Principal Richards, and I see that my son is sitting next to his father, and holy crap… Nicole's family, minus Nicole.

Oh, I didn't mention that Birch's new stepmonster has a brother in his grade at the same school. Willow tried to tell me something about this when we were shopping, but I didn't dig deeper.

Kanyon Kavanaugh is a big kid, but nowhere near as big as Birch. He has a smug look on his face, and it mirrors the snooty faces of his parents.

I nod at them calmly. "Hello, Lilith. Roger. So, what happened here?"

Birch jumps in and says, "Mom, what do you think happened? This asshole attacked me out of nowhere because my 'disgusting old father is'… you know… with his sister."

I can't help but blush and feel embarrassed for Todd. His face is as beet red as his power tie, and I know he would probably like to disappear.

Take that Todd… my mothering is not the problem!

The Kavanaughs are neighbors of Todd's, and our kids grew up together. As previously mentioned, Nicole even babysat for Birch at one time.

I almost feel sorry for Todd for putting himself in this situation, but then I remember the bunny and the donut shop, and my sympathy wanes.

Principal Richards glares at Birch and says, "Watch

your language, young man. And yes, you may have been provoked, but you certainly didn't walk away." He gives both boys the stink eye, and I realize what this is really about.

Mr. Nosy Pants wants to dig into our personal family business in the name of the school's reputation for educating fine young ladies and gentlemen.

I could just gag… I can't believe I was ever a part of this world.

Kanyon is trying to defend himself now, and his father shuts him up with a death stare.

He says, "My wife and I would prefer to handle this at home. I'm sure you can imagine this is a delicate situation, given our daughter's relationship with our neighbor."

Lilith makes a big show of grabbing her purse and adds, "Yes, Principal Richards, we do have Kanyan in counseling, but there isn't much we can do until our lovely daughter comes to her senses."

She flares her nostrils at Todd as the principal clears his throat.

"Well, yes of course. We don't want to interfere in family matters, but the boys need to coexist peacefully. And yes, I do remember your daughter from when she was a student here…"

He clears his throat again. He is either catching a cold or he is choking on his own bullshit.

"… she was an exemplary student."

I can't catch my eyes before they start rolling. Nicole was always a delinquent. One time when she was babysitting Birch, I caught her showing him how to make smoke circles, and our liquor cabinet was mysteriously empty.

Not that those are such horrible crimes, but she wasn't being groomed to be the next Mother Teresa or Rhodes Scholar.

Todd stands up with his red face and yanks on his tie, "We will also deal with this at home. My relationship with Miss Kavanaugh is a private matter."

Principal Richards seems sorry that he forced this little confrontation and dismisses us before things can escalate, but not before suspending the boys for two days for fighting.

The boys are not thrilled with the news, but all of the parents accept it, just so we can get the hell out of this uncomfortable situation.

The Kavanaughs run out the door first, which leaves me and Todd sitting in our naughty chairs.

I feel like someone needs to say something polite. "Well, thank you, Principal Richards, for this enlightening meeting. But as long as Birch's father is involved with the Kavanaughs' daughter, I think there is going to be some contention between the families. Birch, I think you should come home with me for a few days and give your dad some space to work things out at home."

Birch and I stand to leave, and Todd is on our heels.

"Are you kidding me right now with that little performance? I don't have anything to 'work out' at home. And it's just fine for you to have a young boyfriend, but I'm the bad guy here. Her brother needs to grow up, and I am so sick of all these judgmental neighbors. Roger Kavanaugh would probably jump at the chance to dump Lilith for a…"

He finally notices that his soon-to-be ex-wife and son are glaring at him like he has three heads, and he stops spewing stupidity.

"Todd, you sound like a spoiled child. Now Birch is coming back to my place for a few days, and then we will have a family meeting to decide what is going to happen next. Birch, you can go over to Dad's and get some clothes later. Willow can drive you."

Birch is looking at his feet and is uncharacteristically quiet. He probably doesn't want to say anything to blow his chances of a vacation from Nicole by further antagonizing his father.

Todd opens his car door and tosses his suit jacket and tie into the back seat.

"Fine. Birch, we will talk about this when you come home." He stares at his phone and says, "I need to go anyway. Nicole is blowing up my phone, and I have court this afternoon."

Birch and I watch him fly out of the parking lot, and we slowly amble over to my car and get inside.

"Are you okay, honey?"

Birch avoids eye contact while fiddling with his seatbelt and says, "You're not mad, Mom?"

"I don't have the energy to be mad, and honestly, what were you supposed to do? You had to defend yourself. I'm so sorry your family is so embarrassing."

He leans back in his seat and stares out the window.

"It's not your fault, Mom. And I still love Dad, you know. But why did he have to…"

I squeeze his shoulder, and as I am about to offer more platitudes that probably won't help, I glance down at my phone, and now Nicole is texting me.

Seriously?

I pick it up and read out loud:

"Hey, Tara, sorry about the school thing. Principal

Richards was always a little prick. Anyway, Todd is really going to be upset when he gets home. I want to make him a nice meal. Does he have any food allergies?"

Birch's eyes widen, and he says, "Holy shit, are you thinking what I'm thinking?"

"That Nicole hopes he has a nut allergy, and she can kill him with a nice walnut salad topper?"

We both can't help but laugh at that. Tara isn't smart enough to kill Todd, and why would she want to? It's not like they're married, and she would inherit... oh God, did that fool change his will?

I don't care about me, but the kids better not be forfeiting their inheritance to that bimbo.

"It is funny, Mom, but I have never seen Nicole cook anything so... it's a little off brand for her."

I have to agree that it's suspicious, but maybe she is grasping at straws, trying to figure out a way to keep Todd happy as his life continues to fall apart due to his involvement with her.

I text back and say:

"The school thing is under control. Todd doesn't have any allergies that I know of, except maybe rat poison, haha... seriously, just kidding. I mean not kidding... no one can eat rat poison. But of course, you know that. Just don't grind up any cherry pits in his coffee, and he'll be fine."

I don't know if she will get the reference to Ozark, which is one of Todd's favorite shows, but I had to add something a little sarcastic to let her know that I think her question is a tad bit suspicious.

And dumb.

And with just enough snark to diffuse the tension but not enough to invite more conversation about

cooking tips like we are gal pals.
    What a dopey girl she is.

Chapter 28

It's Thursday, and I am bored out of my mind.

I have been going into the office because it's impossible to get any work done with my mother and Willow in the apartment.

Unfortunately, Birch had to go back to Todd's house because, after I dramatically took him home with me after the fighting incident, I realized there was nowhere for him to sleep, except the couch, and he's too tall for that.

I lean back in my expensive, ergonomically sound desk chair and rub my temples.

This job is tedious and silly, and I do appreciate the help I received in getting hired to do anything after being home for basically my whole adult life, but it's kind of a joke.

Anyone could do what I am doing, and before they created this position, the store managers hired their own staff, and it worked out just fine.

I suppose I should be grateful that Didier is generous, but with no strings attached. I should try to find a woman to set him up with, but what I really need to do is focus on my family.

Birch wouldn't have to live with Todd if I had been more insistent about my staying in the house and Todd moving out.

But my desire to escape the humiliation of living in that neighborhood got the best of me, and I read too many books about divorced women starting over, and it looked fun and exciting.

Boy, am I easily duped.

I have met some great people, though, but I feel like I'm neglecting my friends as well.

And Shawn… oh what a mess that is now.

If my life were simpler, it would be so easy to just jump headfirst into a real relationship with him and see where it goes, but simple is not on the menu.

No, instead, I am making life even more complicated by trying non-monogamous dating.

As much as I don't like being controlled, I wish someone would stage an intervention. My friends and family all seem to envy my chance to start over, and I can hardly complain about a cast of attractive men who want to date me.

And Shawn is just so damn nice. Even when I don't give him enough attention, he's there. He has been coming over to the house and hanging out with Birch after work, playing games, and talking about how to deal with bullies. He drives him back and forth so he can spend more time away from Nicole.

And my mother just thinks he's the cutest thing.

And Willow… I suppose I should be glad she doesn't have a crush on him, but luckily… or perhaps unluckily… she has finally shared why she left Harvard, other than her dislike of legal studies and the law in general.

I am glad her lunch with Todd was cancelled due to her brother's schoolyard brawl, and in true Todd fashion, he has gotten preoccupied with work, and I suppose Willow has not rescheduled yet.

But it's only a matter of time before he finds out that she is dating a twenty-seven-year-old MIT graduate who just took a new engineering job in Richmond.

What are the odds of her meeting someone like this in her first week in Boston?

And you might wonder how she would meet such a man.

He's the brother of one of her classmates and came over to make sure his little brother was settling into Harvard nicely.

I know. Couldn't she have gone for the brother?

Willow has always been mature for her age, and it's not like it's illegal. She's eighteen, and how can Todd or I say anything about age gap romance?

Well, we can because we're her parents, and I did, and Todd is going to bust an artery.

She said she wants us to meet him, and I agreed. I was hoping to get my mother to go back home and come back for Thanksgiving and not include her in any of this… at least for now. She did say she has plans to go back to school, but Todd isn't going to like those, either.

I stare at my computer and begin screening more resumes from eager young people, moms with school-age children, and retirees who want to work part-time.

How did I think a job at a shoe company was going to be satisfying or an actual career path for me?

But I know it's all my own fault. When I moved out, Todd offered to sell the house right away and give me half of the money.

Yes, I will get half of everything, and alimony, and I am still working, like an even bigger dope than Nicole.

I know Todd blew up our marriage in spectacular

fashion, but it still feels wrong to take half of everything he's worked for. Yes, I did raise the children and run the household so he could focus on his law practice.

But truthfully, that was fun for me, and I had plenty of downtime to do things I wanted to do, and my stress level was nowhere near his.

I've been stubbornly trying to prove to myself and everyone else that I can make it on my own.

The truth is that with the money I got from selling the Mercedes SUV, I can live comfortably for the next year, plus my alimony covers my rent and basic expenses.

I would feel guilty quitting this job because people here have bent over backwards to accommodate me and teach me some marketable job skills.

Perhaps it is time for me to ask Todd to sell the house or buy me out. That would be a gigantic additional mortgage for him at today's market value, but again, I am not the one who caused this mess.

And I know it takes two people to wreck a marriage, and I am sure I contributed to the overall unhappiness in our relationship, but I still want what is owed to me.

With that nest egg, I won't have to work for a while. Maybe I could go back to school for something… after the kids are more settled.

I check the time, and it is almost time to go home. If Shawn comes over, maybe I should talk to him about my plans. Not that we are a couple with a future, and my plans will affect his life. But he's so calm and reassuring. I know he will understand and offer an unbiased viewpoint.

I start to shut down my computer and gather my things when Roz pokes her head into my office door.

"Hey there, kiddo! Workin' in the office a lot lately? I guess your full house would do that to a person."

She laughs, and I offer a weak smile.

"Mind if I grab your trash? I'll come back to vacuum later."

I gesture to my guest chair, and she looks at me with a puzzled gaze.

"You want me to sit down on the job? What's going on?"

I tell her about Birch fighting and my mother being weirder than usual, and my daughter dating a grown man, and my general life confusion.

She folds her arms across her ample chest and says, "Tsk… tsk… you've really gotten yourself in a pickle."

She wrings her hands and looks towards the door and the empty hallway.

"What's wrong? Did I overwhelm you with my tales of woe?"

I am smiling to diffuse the tension, but a lone tear leaks out of Roz's eye, and I realize that maybe I shouldn't attack people with my own problems before I see how they're doing.

She grabs a tissue off my desk and dabs at her mascara-smearing eyes.

"I'm sorry, Tara. You have enough of your own problems, and I figured you'd find out from James soon enough. You are seeing him soon, right?"

"Yeah, we have plans to go see a band, but what's wrong. Is Maple okay?"

My chest tightens, and my stomach makes a flip just thinking about that sweet, innocent little girl with no mommy.

Roz waves her crumpled tissue and says, "She's fine.

Little ones don't notice what's going on if you try hard enough to protect them."

"Oh no, is James sick?"

That's just what Roz and Maple need—they are all hanging on by a thread anyway with their odd work schedules, and soon Maple will be in kindergarten. She'll need a more stable home life.

Like my son needs and will get once I buy my own house, and he doesn't have to live with Todd and the vapid stepmonster.

Roz laughs bitterly and chokes back another sob. "Yes, I suppose you could call it that. My son is an alcoholic. Actually, two of my sons are alcoholics, and so was their father. The others are sober and in AA, but it's always a long road. James is checking himself into a long-term treatment facility."

Wow, I did not see that coming. He does seem to drink quite a bit, and he's got that brooding, ex-police officer thing going on, but that's just a stupid TV show stereotype. I just thought that raising a little girl as a single dad is hard, and he needs to blow off some steam to cope. And he wanted me to drink water when I was upset.

Thank goodness Maple has Roz.

I lean forward and squeeze Roz's shoulder. "I'm so sorry. Can any of your other sons and their wives help out? I'm assuming Maple is going to live with you full-time?"

She composes herself and says, "Yes, she is. My sweet little darling." She stands up, grabs the trash, and starts tying a knot in the new trash bag. "And no, none of my sons and their wives are suitable guardians for Maple. They all have their own issues, and too many kids for their own good. Maple needs attention and extra loving."

I nod in agreement, and I'm about to offer to help if I can. If I quit this job, I will have plenty of time on my hands to do something good for others.

James wasn't a serious love interest, but I do care about him and Maple, and I could provide Roz with some support until James...

Ugh... is he going to beat this? What are the statistics of someone getting sober and staying that way?'

My father would probably know, especially if it is related to alcohol-related car accidents.

Roz has changed the subject now and is telling me about the rain that's coming, and that I'd better get to my car before I get soaked and catch my death... when my phone rings.

"Hey, sorry, Roz, this is my son calling. Let's talk about this more tomorrow."

She smiles and scurries out of the office, probably feeling like she already shared too much.

"Hi, honey, what's up? Calling to ask me to bring home some of those chicken wings you guys like for video game time?"

For a moment, there is silence. "Birch? You're coming over later, right?"

"Mom, you need to come to Dad's house right now."

I sigh and say, "What did Nicole do this time?"

"She poisoned Dad."

Chapter 29

I could seriously throw up.

I jumped in the car so fast that I didn't have time to text Birch back or call him.

In my haste, I fumbled my phone like a drunk juggler and dropped it while backing out of my parking spot. Now I can't reach it unless I hit a light, which I have no intentions of doing.

How could Nicole have poisoned Todd? Where would she even get that idea?

Shit.

I was only joking, and I told her not to poison him, but I gave her a few good ideas, didn't I?

No, there must be some other explanation.

I am shaking my head, and I must look like a crazy woman talking to myself. The guy in the car to my left is staring at me.

"Yeah, buddy, well, trade places with me for a day and we'll see who's crazy!"

Oh, now we're stopped at a light. I was trying to yell on the fly. At least now I can bend down and contort my body to grab my phone and ow… I banged my head because now some jackass behind me is beeping at me. How short are these lights?

I turn around and scream, "Oh, are you late for your 7-11 hot dog and Slurpie?"

Okay, deep breaths. There is a 7-11 up ahead, but he could be taking his sick mother to the doctor.

Birch didn't say Todd was dead. Surely if his father were dead, he would call and not text, but you never know with this generation.

Maybe he's in shock. Or Nicole tied him to a kitchen chair.

Okay, that one is dumb—Birch is twice Nicole's size and brain power.

Also, why is Todd home during the workday?

I finally pull onto my old street, and I can already see the ambulance lights in the distance.

I glance at the text again. He said poisoned, and, being a kid, he is an expert texter. It's not like he wrote "she posed for Dad" and it autocorrected to poisoned.

Also, Birch would just go to his room, like I am sure he has done many times, living in that house with the two of them.

I park the car one house up since the driveway is completely blocked with emergency vehicles, including police, which I did not notice at first.

As I jog to the front door, Birch is coming out and runs straight for me.

My tall, man-sized boy hugs me fiercely and says, "Mom, thank God you're here. Nicole poisoned Dad, and he's in the ambulance, but they won't let me ride with him. And the police are trying to take down Nicole in the kitchen, and she's screaming for her parents."

I hold him tight and say, "Okay, did the EMTs tell you anything about his condition? What he ingested?"

I glance over towards them, and they look like they are getting ready to speed away. I'm sure someone who is left behind will update us, like the police who are inside with Nicole.

Birch looks too frantic to answer me, and I grab his hand and run into the house. "Let's go inside and see what's happening. Then I'll take you to the hospital to see Dad. We're not divorced yet, so they will talk to me about his condition."

I need to keep my wits about me for Birch's sake. And Todd's.

I mean, he did epically fuck up our lives, but I don't want him to die.

The scene in my once adored home is straight out of a TV show.

And a bad one. Like the old Jerry Springer show meets Cops.

Nicole is answering the question, "what they're gonna do when they come for you" by rolling around on the ground while a female officer wrestles her arms behind her back and slaps the cuffs on her.

Her face is red, and her makeup is all over her face as she screams, "It was her! She told me to do it!"

I look behind me for the person Nicole is accusing of this crime, and I realize she's gesturing toward me with her wild-haired head.

The other police officer, a mid-forties man with huge muscular arms, says, "Are you the victim's wife?"

I want to say yes, and I am also the victim's victim, but I don't want to call any more attention to my distaste for Todd at the moment.

"Yes, I am still legally his wife. Tara Silverthorne. We're in the middle of a divorce, though. A very amicable divorce for sure. Um… is he okay? Do you know his condition?"

Nicole is still yelling and fighting while the female

officer sweats and grimaces.

Muscle guy says, "He's stable, but it's a good thing your son came home. I doubt this one would have called an ambulance."

Nicole screams, "I told you, I thought he was sleeping."

"Okay, that's enough!" The male officer helps lift Nicole off the ground and says, "We will now add resisting arrest to your list of crimes."

She finally stops fighting and bursts into tears. "I didn't mean it. He just came home for lunchtime… you know… and she told me to do it. Look at my phone!"

My face flushes, and I know I am the shade of red that indicates massive guilt.

But is it a crime to joke about a crime?

"Let's start over. I'm Officer Brian Hennessey, and this is Office Claire Pointer. We were called by your son in response to him finding his father unconscious and non-responsive on the couch. Miss Kavanaugh said that she poisoned Mr. Silverthorne because you told her to."

Birch is glaring at me, and I need to quickly talk my way out of this insanity.

"Um… no, I did not do that. She asked me if Todd had any food allergies, which I thought was an extremely odd question, and I made some sarcastic jokes via text. Nicole, are you really that stupid?"

Officer Pointer says, "We read the texts and apparently Miss Kavanaugh misread them, thinking you said he likes ground-up cherries in his food."

"Jesus, Mom, now you're like that crazy lady on Ozark? Are you also growing poppies for heroin in the backyard?"

I am about to explain that I don't currently have a

backyard, but giving any credence to that accusation is a road I don't want to go down.

Let's just stick with attempted murder for now.

Officer Pointer rolls her eyes, apparently thinking I do not seem to be a producer of hard narcotics.

"Anyway, yes, we saw that you were attempting humor with the texts, and we don't know if she truly misunderstood or is just using this as a convenient excuse for her crime. We're taking her down to the station for questioning, and she will be detained."

I blow out a deep breath and hold onto the back of the sofa where Todd was having his cherry pit nap.

"So, she'll be able to call a lawyer and her parents? I need to take my son to the hospital to check on his father and call my daughter."

They both assure me that it isn't my responsibility to worry about the accused and that they will also have more questions for me later.

I guess I should be grateful for the concession. I could be dragged off with Nicole. Who knows what else she's going to accuse me of doing? She's trying to take me down with her. It's not completely implausible that an ex and a current girlfriend could work together to get rid of a wealthy man no one wants anymore.

I squeeze Birch's arm and say, "Come on, let's go see your dad."

He's walking me out of the house as if he's the one holding me up, even though I think his distress outweighs mine.

In the years to come, he'll be helping me cross the street or walk to the bathroom, unless I'm serving twenty to life with Nicole.

Oh my God, can you imagine if they put us in the

same cell?

What terrible thoughts… damn that Nicole for causing even more trouble.

Birch is quiet as we get in the car, and I see I have a text from Shawn.

"Hey, sorry about Todd, WTF? I'm bringing your mother and Willow to the hospital. Meet you there."

I wrinkle my forehead at my phone. "Birch, how does Shawn know about what happened?"

He's looking out the window and quietly says, "I texted him when you were talking to the cops."

He seems so much younger than his sixteen years when he's emotional. He has the body of a man, but he's still a kid.

A kid whose parents have fucked up his life.

But now is not the time to discuss boundaries with Birch, and I'm not even sure what Shawn is to me, let alone my family.

So, I just smile and say, "Good idea, thank you."

Because for all my confusion and angst over my relationship with Shawn, he is the most stable, reliable person I know right now… and I need more of that.

Chapter 30

"You'd think she could have at least finished him off."

My mother is whispering with her hand cupped around her mouth, but her concept of subtlety is as delicate as a bull at a tea party.

I turn to her and say, "How could you say something like that about the father of my children?" To her credit, she does look visibly chastised, but who says things like that?

I need sleep and a vacation.

Todd suffered mild poisoning from ground-up cherry pits. Apparently, Nicole was too lazy to grind up enough to kill him.

Murder is hard work.

He is a big man, and I heard her yelling that it wasn't like cracking a walnut and she'd just gotten her nails done.

Priorities.

Shawn was already at the hospital with Mom and Willow when we arrived.

The police were also hanging around. I didn't really understand why. The victim and the accused are both secured, although I'm still out here running around as a free woman.

I squeeze Shawn's hand as a silent thanks for being here, and unfortunately, I have to leave him alone with my mother, while the kids are in the room with their father, who is thankfully in stable condition.

I lean into him and say, "I'm going to go talk to the police and get this over with."

My mother says, "Are you sure you don't want to bust out of here? In the movies, people hop on the medical supply cart, or they get a sheet off a body and play dead."

Shawn suppresses a laugh and says, "Don't worry about anything. I will drive everyone home if needed." He looks at my newly flushed face and adds, "Not that you won't be able to, of course, because you didn't do anything wrong."

I love the faith he has in me and the judicial system.

Mom and Shawn head to the cafeteria, and I can hear her telling him that she knew I shouldn't have married Todd, and why she should have tried to stop me.

I may not need to decide the nature of my relationship with Shawn. Just a little more time spent with my family, and it will be over before it starts.

I approach the officer who is patiently waiting for me. Maybe it's a good sign that they didn't pounce on me immediately, but now that Todd is not dead or on the way to the morgue shortly, I think it's time to face this problem.

She introduces herself as Office Laken Franklin and gestures down a side hall as I follow her to the conference room that the hospital has apparently provided.

"So, Mrs. Silverthorne, why did you want Miss Kavanaugh to poison your husband?"

I clear my throat and cross and uncross my legs before answering.

She's really coming in hot with the questions. No time wasted on idle chit chat with this one.

"Um… I didn't want her to… do that. As you can see by reading my texts, I told her not to poison him. Surely you can see that it was a joke. The mention of poisoning. Nicole never texts me, and she caught me at a bad time after my son was in trouble at school for fighting."

Sure, just tell her about the whole history of family violence.

Office Franklin is writing in a little notebook with a raised eyebrow. Doesn't the police department have money for iPads? They still use those little notebooks? Even Chick-fil-A takes orders with an iPad. Fast food restaurants are more advanced than local law enforcement, and I am supposed to trust this woman to see the truth?

"So, you were not involved in a plot with Miss Kavanaugh to eliminate your husband and split his money. Instead of doing it yourself, was it worth setting her up as the fall guy?"

"What!?"

I lower my voice as soon as I realize how much I've raised it.

"Of course not. Nicole and I don't get along very well. Which I am sure you can imagine, given our situation. My husband had an affair with our neighbor's young daughter, and now he's living with her."

I go on to give Officer Franklin an unnecessarily thorough account of my situation, and while she can hardly keep a straight face when I get to the parts about the bunny and the donuts, I wish I could make myself stop talking.

What more could I say to make her think I hated

Todd and wanted him dead, alongside his young lover, who was likely getting sick of sleeping with an old guy?

To my great relief, she closes her notebook and says, "Okay, Mrs. Silverthorne. I believe you. For now. But if we have more questions, we will be in touch."

We shake hands because it feels like the thing to do with a person in uniform who has just freed you from the prospect of a life behind bars.

Although I have never been interrogated for attempted murder before, so maybe I am being overly polite.

She turns to leave and says, "Oh, and off the record… she thought if he died, she would get his money. She has no idea what a will is, or legal marriage, or much of anything. She thought the bunny and the donuts were her ticket to an inheritance."

I nod my head in agreement that Nicole is not right in the head. As much as I can't condone what she did, I do hope her parents get her a good lawyer and some psychiatric treatment.

Wait, she told the police about the bunny and the donuts?

They'd better hope for an insanity defense because I don't think general stupidity will hold up in a court of law.

I sit back down in the empty conference room and take deep breaths. I know I should rescue Shawn from Mom babysitting duty, but it's suddenly so nice being alone in this room.

This is the kind of solitude I pictured when I moved into my apartment as a single girl in the city.

I'll stay a few minutes longer and fantasize about that life that doesn't seem possible.

Hopefully, Todd will be fine, and he'll realize the error of his ways. I certainly don't want him back, but it will be better for my kids if this Nicole thing ends.

Of course, I won't be able to throw his relationship with a twenty-something in his face anymore, but Shawn is like a wise old sage compared to that nitwit.

I sigh and click the lone pen sitting on the table. Maybe I should find a piece of paper and leave a note saying I'm leaving town for a while.

Oh, wait… never mind, the cops will surely revisit my guilt if I do that. No one will see that I am a victim of the circumstances around me.

I drop the pen and lay my head on the polished wooden table. I do not want to be a victim. This is bullshit.

My heart flutters as I hear someone at the door of the conference room. After a quick knock, it opens before I can say anything.

I hope the cops didn't find a recipe for cherry pit delight at the house, and they think it's in my handwriting. Nicole could have learned to copy mine—she has a lot of time on her hands.

My eyes adjust as I lift my head and say, "James, what are you doing here?"

He's dressed in a white T-shirt, jeans, boots, and a leather jacket. I really don't have a thing for bad boys, but he's got the look down to a science.

"Tara, are you listening to me? Are you in shock? I mean, I know your husband is kind of an asshole, but I'm guessing you're pretty shook up. I came as soon as I heard."

I stand up and roll my shoulders back. Maybe if I ask nicely, he'll give me a neck massage.

What? We're all alone here, and it's been a tough day.

Seriously, what is wrong with me? Shawn brought my mother and daughter here and is currently waiting for me with an overbearing woman while he thinks I am being interrogated by the police… for the attempted murder of my ex-husband.

Who is that loyal to a non-monogamous girlfriend? Or whatever the hell I am?

And how many men would even care about any of this? Well, I guess right now it's two. Two men are acting like they care.

"How did you find out? This isn't already on the news, is it?"

I can just picture my old neighbors on Todd's street gossiping in the cul-de-sac with their plastic champagne flutes in hushed, judgmental tones. "Well, of course, that girl was going to snap eventually. He's old enough to be her father."

James quickly closes the gap between us and wraps me in a bear hug. Okay, this feels nice, and I am entitled to all the comfort I can get, right?

And yes, I have not forgotten that he is a single father who is getting ready to check himself into rehab, and he's breaking his mother's heart.

But I am sure I am not supposed to know that.

He is talking into the side of my head, and I feel his breath in my ear. We should probably get out of here and check on everyone else, but it's nice when someone checks on me.

But Shawn is out there, too… waiting to check on me.

Come to think of it, Todd never did much checking

on me in the past twenty years.

I really hope Patrick doesn't also show up. It wouldn't be proper to talk about a romantic weekend with my whole man-harem present and my kids and mother.

It's so hard to focus on James' words while he's holding me like this, but he pulls back and says, "Yes, it's on the local news. And I was out having a coffee with a buddy on the force, and he told me about it. Right away, I recognized the last name. So, Todd's gonna make it?"

He's still holding me at arm's length with a soft grip on my upper arms, and the contact is still a little intoxicating, if I'm being honest.

"Yes, I think he's going to be okay. My kids are with him now. I should probably go check on them."

He motions for me to walk ahead of him out the door, and I stop after a few steps.

"Hey, do you happen to know Officer Franklin?"

He narrows his eyes and says, "Yes, why?"

I tell him what happened and about her line of questioning, and he blows up.

"What the fuck? That's what she opened with? Unbelievable. And I'm the one who…" He stops talking and runs his fingers through his thick dark hair, making it stick up all wild and look even sexier, if that's even possible.

I want to ask him to finish that sentence. I am getting the feeling that James was asked to leave the force, and it wasn't because of his dad dying and deciding on early retirement.

Maybe that's when the drinking started.

I calm him down with assurances that it all worked

out fine, and she did seem young. "Maybe she was doing the bad cop thing, and she didn't realize that it doesn't work if you're by yourself. She gave in pretty quickly once I explained the absurdity of the situation."

He rubs my arms again and looks into my eyes. "Okay, well, you let me know if you need any help. I still have some good contacts."

I look away, towards the door, and say, "Thanks. It was so nice of you to come, but I really need to go."

"Oh sure, I won't keep you."

He follows me out the door and down the hall, back into the waiting area.

Just as we round the corner, we almost run right into Shawn with my mother behind him.

That would be quite the awkward pile-up.

Once we all stop and get our bearings, I am about to introduce James when Shawn steps back and throws up his hands. "You know this guy? Seriously?"

Oh my God, what now?

"Shawn, this is my friend James. He came to check on me because of… the incident with Todd."

Shawn shoves his hands in his pockets and rocks on the balls of his feet. I notice that James has also not extended his hand for a friendly shake.

Shawn says, "Okay, I'll let you get back to your friend." He turns to Mom and says, "Mrs. Lunsford, call me please if you and the kids need a ride home, and I'll come back. Your daughter might be otherwise occupied. Good night."

Mom stares at Shawn's retreating form and says, "How many lovers do you have in this town?"

Chapter 31

"Hey, can I come in?"

I poke my head into Todd's room after saying goodbye to my mother and kids in the waiting room.

Willow was adamant that Todd wanted to see me, but I was kind of hoping to put it off.

She said, "Mom, he was so touched that you came right away."

Huh… touched? He better not be too touched because although I don't want him dead, I also don't want him back in my bed, and it seems like the Nicole thing is over after the attempted murder.

Birch was concerned about Shawn's whereabouts, but I didn't want the kids to know what happened. My mother wanted to call him to come pick them up, but I put a stop to that. I don't want any more favors from him if he's going to act like a child.

After all, he is the one who is young and super modern. Non-monogamous dating my ass. I knew it was a bunch of crap.

I gave Mom my keys, and she took the kids home. I said I would get an Uber.

I have had enough "help" from people I know for one day.

Todd isn't responding, but I'm sure he's all right because I don't hear any monitors beeping scarily, and no nurses are trampling me on the way to his bedside.

I hear movement now and see that he is shuffling his way back to bed from the bathroom.

"Tara, I didn't see you there. Come in."

I take a few steps into the room and awkwardly try not to stare at my very tall ex in a skimpy hospital gown.

"You're allowed out of bed? That's great. When will you be able to go home?"

Shit, now that the words are out of my mouth, I realize he's going home to an empty house and his live-in home health care aide is in jail.

He slowly eases himself back into bed, and I avert my eyes to give him some privacy. I don't want him to think I'm trying to see anything, although this is really not the time for those thoughts.

"Yeah, I'm going to live. Lucky me that I shacked up with America's laziness murderess."

That seems like a joke, but isn't it too soon for joking?

I smile nervously and say, "Well, I'm just glad she didn't know what she was doing."

He doesn't reply right away as he adjusts his blankets, so I add, "Todd, you know I wasn't trying to get her to poison you, right?"

He places his hands on his legs after adjusting his pillows. "Of course I know that. If you wanted me dead, you would have done it yourself by now."

My face must look alarmed, and he says, "I'm joking. I know you wouldn't want anyone to die. You're too good a person… too good a mother… for that kind of hate."

He gestures for me to sit in the hard plastic chair, and I slowly lower myself onto it while casually scooting it a little further away from the bed. A bit of distance feels like a good idea right now.

"So, Willow said you wanted to talk to me? If you're tired, I can come back tomorrow or…"

He reaches out and touches my hand, and I am compelled to move a little closer, just so he doesn't fall out of bed trying to reach me.

I guess I am not going to be able to avoid some level of intimacy tonight, no matter how hard I try.

"Tara, I know saying I'm sorry doesn't even begin to cover it, but I am. I have behaved like a fool and dragged you and the kids into my mess."

I open my mouth to stop him because I'm not sure where this speech is going. I am willing to forgive as long as this isn't going to become a plea to get me back.

But that would be delusional on his part, right? He was poisoned; he didn't hit his head.

I wiggle my hand free and pretend I need a mint from my purse, which I kind of do because my throat is dry from all this post-marital discomfort.

Is that a thing?

I unwrap my mint, pop it in my mouth, and position it so I can still talk. "I can't say that it's okay, but it's okay. It is what it is. It probably wasn't the smoothest breakup, but it was looming whether or not Nicole was in the picture."

He leans back against his adjustable hospital bed and sighs loudly. "You're right, and I know you probably don't want to hear it, but I feel terrible about Nicole as well. I was the true adult in this situation, and I led an already confused young woman astray. I don't want her to go to prison." He cradles his head in his hands and adds, "I hope her parents can get her the help she needs."

I plaster on my best empathetic face and say, "Sure, I understand. She seems quite troubled. Are you sure you aren't going to take her back?" I raise my eyebrows as he chuckles and says, "Absolutely not. I know it's not funny, but I have learned my lesson. No more immature, silly girls for me, and no more cheating. I need some time on my own to figure out my next steps, and also, I need to reconnect with the kids, if they'll let me."

Even though I've been trying to keep my distance, a mention of my kids causes me to instinctively reach for his hand.

"They will. This whole situation shook them up, but they love you, and they are old enough to make sense of this and move on. But I do think that Birch should come live with me for a while."

He agrees, and we talk about how good it will be for the kids to be together again under one stable roof.

We also need to get our act together and meet Willow's boyfriend and guide her onto a new path before she wastes all her talents. Apparently, Willow did have a heart-to-heart chat with her father.

Todd grins as he nods his agreement with all my excellent parenting points.

"What an insane situation. Our eighteen-year-old daughter's boyfriend is older than yours."

I feel my face flush at the mention of Shawn. My first inclination is usually to insist that he's not my boyfriend, but I think we are now beyond that level of bullshit.

I squirm in the uncomfortable plastic chair and fold my arms across my chest. "You know, I feel almost as stupid as you. I mean… well, you know what I mean."

He sits up straighter and says, "Tara, you know I

was just teasing. Just because my younger partner turned out to be a childish maniac who tried to poison me, it doesn't mean that Shawn is a bad guy for you. He seems mature, and I know the kids love him. What does your mom think?"

We both burst out laughing and earn a glare from a nurse walking by the room.

"Shh… people are sick here." I put my finger to my lips, and Todd says, "Yeah, some people have a tummy ache from mild cherry pit poisoning."

We can't stop laughing now because it is all so ridiculous. I finally regain composure and try to wipe off what's left of my already smeared eye makeup with a tissue from Todd's bedside table.

"That was good. I needed a laugh. But seriously, Tara, don't compare yourself to me. No one is negatively judging you, and if they are, then fuck them."

"Wow, you hardly ever swear."

Now we're laughing again, and I know I am going to get thrown out of here soon.

Todd clears his throat and says, "You deserve every happiness, and the kids have also told me that you don't like your job. It's high time we sold the house so you can have your full fair share of our assets. Birch isn't going to live in that house anymore, and we don't have to wait until our divorce is final."

"Yeah, I've made some silly choices, too. I didn't even really need a job with the alimony and savings. And even the money from selling the Mercedes. I just wanted to have a different life—single, independent working woman's life. But with my work history, it's impossible."

"Well, that settles it. I am going to call the realtor

tomorrow and get things moving. With the money from the house and your other assets, you should be able to take some time off to figure out what you really want to do. It is absolutely possible for you to find a satisfying career." He pauses and sheepishly adds, "If that's what you want. I know I have had a tendency to tell you what to do, and I have never had any right to do that."

I smirk and nod my head. "Yes, you have been guilty of that, but in this case, those are wise words. I'm confused about my so-called career and my so-called love life, but most importantly… I am not done being a mom. Our kids still need me. They need us. I hope we can start doing a better job of co-parenting for Willow and Birch."

He looks like he's going to cry, and it could be caused by whatever drugs they have him on, or maybe he is grateful to salvage something of the family he once had.

We talk about his plans to get a condo downtown near his office and my intention to buy a small house at some point, but big enough for the kids, as long as they need their mom.

"Well, it can't be too big because I don't want to encourage my mother to visit and stay too long. Maybe the guest room should double as the boiler room."

We laugh together again as I share Liz's latest craziness.

Todd says, "I hope you aren't comparing yourself to your mother. She's lusting after a younger man while married to your father for a million years. Do you think she's serious?"

The nurse pops her head in the doorway and tells me that I need to say goodnight. Visiting hours are over.

I nod and promise to be on my way.

"No, I think she's confused. I haven't had enough time to talk to her about it at any length. I've been neglecting my family with all this dating and my silly job. I'm sorry it took your attempted murder for me to have a wakeup call, but it has."

I kiss him on the cheek and squeeze his shoulder. "It wasn't all bad, right? You and me?"

His eyes are shiny, and I regret getting sappy. I don't want to see him cry. Even though he hurt me badly, there were good times, and now maybe we can be friends… or something like friends.

"Yes, we had some amazing times, and we have two great kids. That's been more your doing than mine. I promise to help in any way I can… and to support you while you figure things out."

"Thanks, Todd. Get some rest. I have so much drama to go home to. I wonder if I could fake an injury and get a nice, peaceful hospital bed for the night."

He puts his fingers to his lips. "Shh… don't jinx yourself. Go home and get some rest. You'll feel better in the morning."

I put my purse on my shoulder and zip up my jacket as I walk to the door.

"Good idea, and you know what? I just may be able to start eating donuts again."

Chapter 32

I can't believe what a day this has been.

I'm standing outside the hospital in the cool night air, fumbling with my phone to call an Uber. After everything that's happened—Todd being poisoned, Nicole getting arrested, and that weird confrontation between Shawn and James—I just want to get home and crawl into bed.

My phone screen is completely black. Of course it's dead. Of all the times for my battery to die, it has to be now when I'm stranded at the hospital at nearly midnight.

I could have let Shawn take my mom and the kids home, and I'd have my car, but I don't need him if he's going to act like a big baby.

I'm contemplating whether to go back inside and ask to use a phone when I hear the familiar rumble of an old engine. A beat-up Buick pulls up to the curb, and the passenger window rolls down.

"Hey lady, need a ride?"

I've never been so happy to see Lotto Lenny since the day I met him, when he asked me for local strip club recommendations.

"Lenny! How did you know I was here?"

"Aunt Dinah called. Said you might need a lift home. Hop in."

I slide into the passenger seat, grateful that Dinah somehow has a sixth sense about these things.

Also, she probably heard about it from the news. Old people are always glued to the local news.

The car smells like cigarettes and pine air freshener, but right now it feels like a sanctuary.

"Thanks for picking me up. I don't know how Dinah always knows everything that's happening in this neighborhood."

Lenny chuckles as he pulls away from the hospital. "That woman's got more connections than the FBI. Haha... but seriously, it's on the local news. She said something about your ex getting a taste of his own medicine. I don't know if the guy deserved to be poisoned, but I kept my mouth shut. It's best with the women in my family."

I lean back against the worn vinyl seat and close my eyes. "It's been the longest day of my life."

"Yeah, well, heard you got quite the soap opera going on. Your ex getting poisoned by the donut girl, and then some love triangle drama at the hospital? Dinah's eating this up like it's her favorite TV show... but she's also worried about you."

My eyes snap open. "What do you mean, love triangle drama?"

Did Shawn tell Dinah why he was so mad to see me with James?

"She made me drive her over to your apartment because it's too late for her to be walkin' the streets. Wanted to talk to your mother. By the way, she's a fine-looking woman for an old lady. Your mother, I mean. Anyway, she said something about your young boyfriend getting all bent out of shape when he saw you with some other guy who used to be a cop. Your ma said he stormed out looking madder than a wet cat."

I have no idea what Shawn's problem was with James. Also, can't my mother ever keep her mouth shut?

Sure, I'm dating multiple men, but that was Shawn's idea in the first place. The whole "practice dating" thing was supposed to be no-strings-attached, right?

"I don't understand what his issue is," I mutter.

"Maybe he's figured out he doesn't want to share you anymore," Lenny says with a shrug. "Sometimes it takes a little competition to make a man realize what he's got… or else he really hates that fucking guy for some other reason."

We drive in comfortable silence for a few minutes, passing the quiet streets of my neighborhood. The cidery is dark, the coffee shops are closed, and even the die-hard bar patrons seem to have called it a night.

"You know," Lenny continues, "when I won all that money, I thought having more choices would make me happier. Turns out, too many choices just make you crazy. Can you imagine how many chicks want to get with a lottery winner? I don't know, maybe you should give the kid a real chance."

"When did you become a relationship expert?"

"Hey, I watch Dr. Phil. And Oprah reruns. Those people know what they're talking about."

We pull up in front of my building, and I can see that my windows are dark. At least my family has called it a night.

"Thanks for the ride, Lenny. And for the advice."

"No problem. I live to serve the women of the night… wow, that came out wrong. You take care of yourself. See ya, kid."

I wave goodbye and head into the building, feeling oddly grateful for his blunt wisdom. As I reach my floor and walk down the hallway, I spot a familiar figure sitting outside her apartment door.

Cassie is slumped against the wall with Everly asleep in her stroller and Mitzi the wiener dog curled up beside her. She's clearly been crying—her hair is pulled back in a messy ponytail and her eyes are red and puffy.

"Cassie? What's wrong?"

She looks up at me with shame in her eyes. "Tara! I'm sorry to bother you. I didn't think anyone would be in the hallway at this hour."

Mitzi immediately perks up when she sees me, her little tail wagging frantically despite her obvious exhaustion.

"It's okay, what's going on? Did you lock yourself out? Once I get my phone charged, I can call the building guy to let you in."

"Everything is falling apart." She wipes her nose with the back of her hand. "My grandmother's estate lawyer called today, and apparently, there was a lien on her house I didn't know about, and Everly's daycare just raised their prices. I need that stupid house to sell. And now Mitzi needs new medicine for her bladder problem, and I just... I can't handle being a single mom to a toddler and take care of a fifteen-year-old dog who needs to pee in the middle of the night. I feel like I'm drowning."

I sit down on the floor next to her, suddenly struck by how my problems pale in comparison to so many other people's issues. I am about to receive the proceeds from a multi-million-dollar house sale, so I can stay home and find myself, and here is someone who really needs help.

"I'm going to ask you something, and I want you to really think about it before you answer," I say, reaching over to scratch Mitzi's graying muzzle. "What if I took Mitzi off your hands?"

Cassie's eyes widen. "What do you mean?"

"I mean, what if I adopted her? You'd still be able to see her whenever you want—we live in the same building. But you wouldn't have to worry about vet bills or walking her when Everly's sick or having to leave Everly alone in the apartment to take Mitzi out... or waking her up."

"Are you sure? She's a lot of work, and she's not getting any younger."

"Neither am I," I say, and Mitzi responds by climbing into my lap. "Look at her—I think she's already decided. Do you want my house to be your retirement home, sweet girl?"

Cassie starts crying again, but this time it seems like relief. "That would be... God, that would help so much. But I feel terrible asking you to take on my problems."

"You're not asking—I'm offering. And it's not a problem, it's a solution. For both of us. I need at least one uncomplicated relationship in my life."

We talk logistics for a few more minutes—I'll come by to get Mitzi's food and toys, and we'll schedule a vet visit to discuss her bladder treatment. When Cassie finally heads back into her apartment with two little sleepy heads, I'm left alone in the hallway with my keys.

I unlock my door as quietly as possible, expecting to find my mother and Willow asleep in their respective bedrooms. I guess Birch is on the couch with his feet resting on the end table. I never even thought about where he is going to sleep. Liz needs to go home; there is no more room at the inn.

The apartment is completely silent and dark except for the streetlight filtering through the blinds.

I'm tiptoeing toward the kitchen, setting my purse down as quietly as possible, when I see a dark shape on my couch that does not look like my son.

"AHHH!" I scream before I can stop myself.

The figure bolts upright, and I hear a familiar voice say, "Tara? What the hell?"

It's Shawn. My heart is pounding so hard I can hear it in my ears.

"Oh my God, you scared me to death! I didn't see you there!"

I slap my hand over my mouth, suddenly panicked that I've woken up the whole building, let alone my mother and daughter. I listen for footsteps or voices, but thankfully, everything remains quiet.

Shawn runs his hands over his hair, looking dazed. "Sorry, I must have fallen asleep. Your mom let me in. She said you'd want to see me when you got home. Birch is crashing at my place."

I sink into the armchair across from him, my heart still racing. "What are you doing here? I thought you were mad at me."

Even in the dim light, I can see him frown. "Mad at you? Why would I be mad at you?"

"Because of James. At the hospital. You seemed upset, and then you just left."

Shawn leans forward, his elbows on his knees. "Tara, I wasn't mad at you. I was mad at him."

"What? Why? You don't even know him."

"Actually, I do know him. James was a racist cop who got himself in trouble and had to leave the police force."

Uh oh… There is definitely a bad story here, but how could I have known?

"I had no idea!" I wince as I realize my loud whispering is starting to negate the whole concept of whispering.

Shawn stands up and says, "I'm sure you didn't, but seeing you with him… I don't know if this is gonna work out."

"What do you mean, racist cop?" I whisper, leaning forward in my chair.

Shawn's jaw tightens, and he looks toward the window before meeting my eyes again. "A few years ago, James and his partner pulled over my cousin Marcus for 'driving while black' in the wrong neighborhood. You know, the usual bullshit excuse—said his car matched the description of a vehicle involved in a robbery."

My stomach drops. "Oh no…"

"Marcus is a college kid, clean record, drives his mom's Honda Civic. But James roughed him up anyway, claimed he was resisting arrest when all Marcus did was ask why he was being stopped." Shawn's hands clench into fists. "My cousin ended up in the hospital with a broken nose and three cracked ribs."

I feel sick. "Shawn, I had no idea. I never would have—"

"I know you wouldn't have. But seeing you with him tonight, after everything that's happened…" He shakes his head. "It just hit me wrong. And it's making me realize that maybe I can't handle this whole non-monogamous thing as well as I thought I could."

My heart starts racing for an entirely different

reason. "What are you saying?"

Shawn stands up and starts pacing in the small space between the couch and coffee table. "I'm saying that I'm starting to feel too much for you, Tara. Way more than I should for someone who's just 'practice dating' me."

"Shawn—"

"No, let me finish." He stops pacing and faces me. "When I saw you with James tonight, I wanted to punch him. Not just because of what he did to Marcus, but because he was touching you. Because you looked at him like you cared about him. And that's not fair to you when you're supposed to be figuring out what you want."

I stand up too, reaching for his hand. "Maybe I already know what I want."

He pulls back gently. "Do you? Because three hours ago, you were in another man's arms. And not just any man—a man who represents everything I hate."

"I didn't know about any of that!"

"I know. But that's not the point." He runs his hands through his hair again. "The point is that I can't keep pretending this is casual for me. And you need space to figure out your life without me pressuring you."

Tears are starting to form in my eyes. "So, what, you're just going to walk away?"

"I think we need to cool it for a while. Give you time to really think about what you want without me confusing things."

"Please don't leave. We can talk about this in the morning when we're both thinking more clearly."

Shawn shakes his head and walks toward the door. "I'll send Birch home in the morning. He can sleep at my place as long as your mother is here, but..." He pauses with his hand on the doorknob. "I think some distance would be good for both of us right now."

"Shawn, wait—"

But he's already gone, closing the door softly behind him.

I sink back onto the couch where he was just sleeping and let the tears fall. Everything feels like it's spiraling out of control. Todd in the hospital, my mother having a late-life crisis, my daughter dating an older man, and now this.

I curl up on the couch and pull the throw blanket over me, breathing in the faint scent of Shawn's cologne that still lingers on the cushions.

Maybe he's right. Maybe I don't know what I want, but losing him doesn't feel like the answer.

I must have fallen asleep, because the next thing I know, I'm being woken up by the sound of someone trying to tiptoe through the living room.

"Mom?" I mumble, sitting up and squinting in the early morning light.

My mother freezes like a cartoon burglar caught in the act, her suitcase in one hand and her purse in the other.

"Oh! Honey, I was trying not to wake you. What are you doing sleeping on the couch?"

I run my hands over my face, trying to orient myself. "What time is it? Where are you going?"

"It's about six-thirty. I'm catching an early flight back to Hartford." She sets down her suitcase and perches on the edge of the coffee table. "I have some unfinished business to take care of in Connecticut."

"Unfinished business? You mean like your life with

your husband?"

She smooths down her hair, which is perfectly styled despite the early hour. "Your father and I need to spend more time together, yes. And I need to talk to Peter… plus he's getting all the big listings."

I blink at her, still trying to process. "Are you leaving Dad?"

"I don't know. But I can't keep running away from the situation by hiding out here." She looks around the apartment. "Speaking of which, where's that lovely Shawn? I was hoping to say goodbye."

Fresh tears threaten to spill over. "He left."

"Left? What do you mean, left?"

I give her the abbreviated version of last night's conversation, and she tsks disapprovingly.

"Well, that's disappointing. I was looking forward to having him at the Thanksgiving table next month." She pats my knee. "But mark my words, that boy will be back. He's too smitten to stay away for long."

"I don't think so, Mom. This felt pretty final."

"Nonsense. Sometimes men need to storm off and beat their hairy chests for a while before they come to their senses." She stands up and grabs her suitcase. "Trust me, I've been married to one for almost fifty years. Although I guess in my situation, I'm the one with the hairy chest, haha…"

After she leaves, I sit in the quiet apartment feeling completely lost. Willow is still asleep, and without Birch and Shawn, the place feels eerily empty.

I need to get out of here.

I throw on some clothes and decide to go for a walk, maybe grab some coffee, and clear my head. Without really thinking about where I'm going, I find myself walking toward Dinah and Vinny's house.

It's not even seven in the morning, but I can see lights on in their kitchen window. Those two are early risers, and Dinah always says the coffee pot is on by six.

I knock softly on their front door, not wanting to wake the whole neighborhood. After a moment, I hear footsteps, and the door opens.

But it's not Dinah or Vinny standing there. It's Roxanne. She's wearing an oversized T-shirt and looking like she just woke up.

"Tara? What are you doing here so early?"

I blink in confusion. "What are you doing here?"

Before either of us can answer, Dinah appears behind Roxanne, wearing a flowery bathrobe and slippers.

"Oh, good, you came for breakfast!" she says cheerfully, as if finding me on her doorstep at seven in the morning is perfectly normal. "Come in, come in. We have so much to talk about."

I step inside, still trying to process why Roxanne is at the Bertellis' house in what appears to be sleepwear.

"I'm sorry, I'm just confused — "

"I know, but you have been too busy with your own stuff. We were all giving you space." Dinah explains matter-of-factly. "Roxanne is staying with us while she gets back on her feet."

"Now," she says, ushering me toward the kitchen where the smell of bacon and coffee is already filling the air, "let's get some food in you and figure out what you're going to do about that boy of yours."

Chapter 33

"Eat, eat! You look like a skinny ghost," Vinny says, piling scrambled eggs onto my plate.

I'm sitting at the Bertellis' kitchen table, which is covered with enough food to feed a small Italian village. Dinah is pouring coffee, Roxanne is buttering toast, and I'm trying to process everything that's happened in the last twenty-four hours.

"So let me get this straight," Dinah says, settling into her chair with her own plate. "Your mother ran back to Connecticut to decide if she wants a boyfriend, your ex-husband was poisoned by his child bride, and now Shawn is giving you the cold shoulder because you were hugging a racist ex-cop?"

"That's about the size of it," I sigh, picking at my eggs.

Roxanne shakes her head. "Men are such drama queens. I should know—I've been surrounded by them for years."

Vinny laughs and pats her shoulder. "This one's got sense. That's why I'm teaching her the catering business. She's going to take it over and make it something big, aren't you?"

Roxanne grins. "Yes, and I can't thank you both enough. Lenny has been such a good friend to me, and he wanted to give me money, but I need to do something real for myself. So, he suggested this great plan. And hooked me up with the Bertellis."

"Wait, so you're getting out of..." I trail off, not sure how to delicately reference her current profession.

"Stripping? Yeah, I'm done with that. Turns out I'm actually pretty good at organizing events and managing people. Who knew?" She takes a sip of coffee. "Plus, Mr. Bertelli makes the best meatballs in Richmond. We're going to corner the market on authentic Italian catering."

Dinah nods approvingly. "It's the perfect solution. Vinny doesn't want to give up his passion, but he can't do it like he did when he was younger. And we don't have any children to pass on the family business. Lenny can't boil water, so Roxanne here is our new adopted daughter and business partner."

I find myself smiling for the first time since last night. "That's wonderful, Roxanne. Really."

"So, what are you going to do about Shawn?" Dinah asks, cutting straight to the point as usual.

"I don't know. He said he needs space, and maybe he's right. I've been so confused about everything." I set down my fork. "Speaking of confused, do you have any idea why Patrick would be in Vietnam? He texted me from Ho Chi Minh City, which doesn't exactly seem like apple country."

Dinah and Vinny exchange a look. "Vietnam?" Dinah says. "No idea. That's odd. You sure he's not just pulling your leg?"

"I don't think so. He sent pictures." I shake my head. "I don't know if I even want to date anyone anymore. I thought James was this fun, interesting guy, and it turns out he's a terrible person. What does that say about my judgment?"

Roxanne reaches across the table and squeezes my hand. "It says you're human. We all make mistakes when it comes to men."

"But what about his little daughter? If he's as bad as Shawn says he is, what kind of environment is that for a child?"

I am not going to mention the fact that he's going into rehab. Someone has to respect someone's privacy around here.

"Roz will take good care of her if it comes to that," Dinah says firmly. "That woman's raised an army of boys, and she has countless grandchildren. One more little girl won't break her."

I nod, but I still feel terrible about the whole situation. How could I have been so wrong about someone?

Suddenly, I glance at my phone and nearly choke on my coffee. "Oh shit, it's Friday! Sorry, but I completely forgot. Didier keeps finding random assignments for me, and I promised I'd help out with inventory today." I start gathering my things. "And I need to tell him I'm quitting."

"You're quitting?" Roxanne asks.

"Yeah, it's time. Todd and I are selling the house, so I'll have enough money to figure out what I actually want to do with my life instead of pretending to be a career woman."

Dinah nods sagely. "Good for you. That job was never right for you anyway. I knew it the day I saw you hobbling down the sidewalk in those ridiculous shoes."

"The only problem is tomorrow night is the big company Halloween party, and Shawn was supposed to go with me as my date." My stomach lurches. "Now I have to face Didier's terrifying French ex-wife all by myself."

Dinah says, "Oh, what's she like?"

"Dominique? Like a beautiful shark in designer clothing. And Didier's been begging me to help him find a new woman, which I've been completely useless at." I pause, looking at Roxanne thoughtfully. "Hey, do you like quirky French men who are obsessed with shoes?"

Roxanne nearly spits out her coffee. "Are you trying to set me up with your boss?"

"Ex-boss, hopefully. But think about it—he's handsome, he's rich, he owns a successful company, and he's looking for someone who's not a social climber or a gold digger."

"And I'm a former stripper who's learning to make meatballs," Roxanne says dryly.

"Exactly! You're real. You're independent. You're beautiful and smart, and you don't need his money." I'm getting excited about this idea. "Plus, you could help him with company events. It's perfect!"

Dinah claps her hands together. "Oh, I love this! The sophisticated French businessman and the former exotic dancer who teaches him what really matters in life."

Vinny rolls his eyes. "You watch too many movies, Dinah."

"So, what do you say?" I ask Roxanne. "Want to come to a Halloween party tomorrow night and meet a French shoe mogul?"

Roxanne considers this for a moment, then grins. "You know what? Why not. What's the worst that could happen?"

"Famous last words," Vinny mutters, but he's still smiling.

I finish my breakfast feeling lighter than I have in days. Maybe I can't fix my own love life, but at least I can try to help someone else's. And who knows? Maybe Roxanne and Didier will be perfect for each other.

Stranger things have happened. In this neighborhood, anything is possible.

Chapter 34

I feel ridiculous.

Standing in the middle of the hotel ballroom in half of a couple's vampire costume, I'm acutely aware that I look like someone who got stood up for Halloween. The flowing black cape and dramatic makeup that seemed so perfect when Shawn and I picked out our matching outfits now just make me feel like a fraud.

At least Roxanne looks amazing. She's dressed as a 1920s flapper in a stunning beaded dress that hugs her curves perfectly, and I notice that Didier hasn't taken his eyes off her since we walked in.

"Tara! Mon dieu, you look... dramatic," Didier says, approaching us with his enthusiastic signature energy. He's dressed as a French artist, complete with a beret and paint-splattered smock. "And this must be the beautiful Roxanne. You are even more stunning than Tara described."

Roxanne smiles graciously as Didier takes her hand and practically kisses it. "Thank you. I love your costume — very authentic."

"Ah, but it is not a costume! I am actually quite the painter in my spare time." He gestures toward his outfit. "Tonight, I am Didier the artist, not Didier the shoe man."

I can practically see the hearts floating around his

head.

"Didier," a cool voice says behind us. We all turn to see Dominique approaching, looking effortlessly elegant in a sleek black dress, her dark hair pulled back in a perfect chignon. She's not wearing a costume at all.

"Dominique, you remember Tara?" Didier says, his enthusiasm dimming slightly. "And this is her friend Roxanne."

She gives us both a polite nod that conveys complete indifference.

"You didn't wear a costume," I say, trying to make conversation. "Don't you like Halloween?"

She looks at me with barely concealed amusement. "My costume is famous fashion designer."

"Oh, which designer?" I ask, genuinely curious.

"Me. I am a famous designer, and I am here as myself," she repeats, looking at my vampire cape with what can only be described as amused disgust. "Some of us don't need to play dress-up to be interesting."

Ouch. I feel my face flush under my pale vampire makeup.

Before I can think of a comeback, I look over at the entrance to see a familiar figure walking in. My heart skips a beat.

It's Shawn, dressed in the other half of our vampire costume—the Dracula to my vampiress. He looks amazing in the black cape, but I'm more shocked that he's here at all.

He spots me across the room and makes his way over, ignoring the curious stares from my coworkers.

"Sorry, I'm late," he says when he reaches our group.

"I... I didn't think you were coming," I stammer.

"I ran into Willow and her boyfriend in the elevator

on my way out. We got to talking, and I went back inside and changed into my costume." He glances around at the group, nodding politely to Didier and Roxanne before his gaze settles on Dominique, who is studying him with obvious interest.

"You need to meet this guy, you know, Willow's boyfriend." Shawn continues, his attention back on me. "Kelso seems like a good one, but I think Willow's feeling a little neglected. She mentioned that you haven't had much mother/daughter time lately."

My stomach drops. The last thing I need is for Willow to do something even more outlandish to get my attention. Dropping out of Harvard was dramatic enough.

"Et qui est ce bel homme?" Dominique interrupts, stepping closer to Shawn with renewed interest.

She sees a hot, young guy, and she suddenly has to speak French?

"This is Shawn," I say reluctantly. "Shawn, this is Dominique, Didier's ex-wife."

She extends her hand with a smile that's much warmer than anything she's directed at me. "Enchantée. I am surprised you are here with..." She gestures vaguely in my direction without finishing the sentence.

Shawn shakes her hand briefly but takes a step back. "Nice to meet you."

The tension is thick enough to cut with a knife. Didier looks uncomfortable, Roxanne seems amused by the whole dynamic, and I just want to disappear.

My phone buzzes in my small clutch purse, providing a welcome distraction. I pull it out to see a text from Patrick: "Just got back from Vietnam! Can we meet for lunch tomorrow? Need to talk about our Berkeley

Springs weekend."

I stare at the message, trying to process. Patrick still wants to take me on a weekend trip? After everything that's happened, a romantic getaway feels like the last thing I should be considering.

"Everything okay?" Shawn asks, noticing my expression.

"It's just Patrick. He's back from his mysterious Vietnam trip and wants to have lunch tomorrow."

Why am I mentioning more men to the man who is breaking my heart? I knew this was going to happen.

"Vietnam?" Dominique perks up with interest. "How exotic. What was he doing there?"

"I have no idea. Something about business, apparently."

Didier, clearly trying to diplomatically change the subject away from other men in my life, turns back to Roxanne. "Would you like to dance?"

As they head toward the dance floor, I'm left standing with Shawn and Dominique, feeling more awkward than ever.

"So," Dominique says, looking between us with barely concealed amusement, "are you two here together, or...?"

"It's complicated," I say at the same time Shawn says, "We're figuring it out."

Her smile is predatory. "Ah, I see. How... interesting."

This is going to be a very long night.

Chapter 35

I'm sitting on my couch with my second cup of coffee, staring out the window at the quiet Sunday morning street below.

The party turned out better than I expected once Shawn showed up. We actually had fun together—dancing, laughing at Kenneth's over-the-top Cher costume, and watching Didier completely lose his mind over Roxanne. She handled his attention perfectly, charming but not desperate, interested but not overwhelmed.

I couldn't bring myself to tell Didier I was quitting. He was so happy, practically glowing as he showed Roxanne around and introduced her to everyone. And honestly, I didn't want to give Dominique the satisfaction of seeing him upset. That woman was circling like a vulture all night, especially when she thought there might be drama between Shawn and me.

For a beautiful, successful woman, she needs to get a life.

When we got back to the building around midnight, Shawn asked me to come up to his place. He said he had news to tell me, and from the serious look on his face, I knew it wasn't going to be good.

"I've been offered an opportunity," he said, pouring us both a glass of water. "The bank wants to send me to

New York for a training program in their brokerage division."

My stomach dropped. "New York?"

"If I do well, I can stay and work in their Manhattan office. It's exactly the kind of career advancement I've been working toward."

"I didn't know you were working toward anything like that," I said, and immediately regretted how that sounded.

"Well, I did tell you about it when we first met, but you've been a little preoccupied," he said gently. "But this opportunity came at a good time."

He means that it makes it easier to have space between us and to dump me, out of sight, out of mind.

"When would you leave?"

"Next week."

Next week. I felt like he'd punched me in the stomach.

"Tara," he said, stepping closer and taking my hands. "I care about you. More than I should. But your life is complicated right now, and maybe this is the universe telling us both to take a step back."

He kissed me then, soft and sweet and final. "I should probably let you get some sleep."

I took that as my cue to leave. When I got back to my apartment, both kids were out with friends. Instead of lying awake worrying about everything that's falling apart in my life, I went straight to bed and slept like the dead, with a little help from Benadryl. Sometimes I pretend to be itchy so I can justify taking drugs to fall asleep.

"Mom! Get dressed, Kelso will be here soon for brunch!"

Willow's voice from the kitchen jolts me out of my brooding. I check my phone and realize it's already almost eleven. I was supposed to meet Patrick for lunch, but I completely forgot.

"Coming!" I call back, downing the rest of my coffee.

I head upstairs to get ready, pulling on jeans and a sweater while texting Patrick: "So sorry, family thing came up. Can we meet later at the cidery? Around 6?"

His response comes back immediately, but it's not in English. A string of foreign words fills my screen, and that is a very different alphabet.

I text back a question mark.

"Sorry, wrong person. See you at 6! ☺ "

I send back a smiley face, but I'm left staring at my phone, wondering what he said and who he was texting in Vietnamese at eleven in the morning on a Sunday. Not that I am a linguist, but I am putting together the clues, and that seems logical. The mystery of Patrick's trip just became even more intriguing, but I don't know why I even care.

I finish getting ready and head downstairs to meet Willow's boyfriend. At least one of us should have our love life figured out, even if she is dating someone older than her mother's practice boyfriend.

Ex-practice boyfriend, I guess.

I join Willow in the kitchen and find her at the stove flipping pancakes while Birch sets the table.

"Morning, Mom," Birch says, but he looks distracted. "I need to run over to Shawn's and grab my charger. I left it there the other night."

"Wait. Shawn might be busy... and you could just text him to leave it by the door on his way out."

Birch stops walking to the front door and looks at

me more closely. "What happened? Didn't you guys go to that party together?"

Willow turns from the stove, spatula in hand. "Yeah, what's going on? You look like someone stole your puppy."

Speaking of puppies, I still haven't taken possession of Mitzi. Cassie is having a hard time letting go. I can totally relate.

I feel a stab of guilt. I should never have let my kids get attached to Shawn. This is exactly why I didn't want them meeting the men I was dating—now they're going to be hurt too when he leaves.

"It's nothing dramatic," I say, trying to sound casual. "Shawn got a job opportunity in New York. He's leaving next week."

"What?" Birch's face falls. "But we were going to work on my college applications together. He said he'd help me with my essays."

My heart breaks a little more. "I'm sorry, honey. I should have been more careful about letting you two get close. This is my fault."

"Mom, it's not your fault," Willow says gently. "These things happen."

Birch grabs his jacket. "I'm still going to get my charger. And maybe say goodbye like a normal person."

After he leaves, Willow pours more pancake batter into the pan. "So, are you okay? You really seemed to like him."

"I'm fine," I lie. "Actually, I have a fun weekend planned with Patrick from the cidery. We're going to Berkeley Springs."

"Mom—"

A knock at the door interrupts whatever Willow was

about to say. "That's Kelso!" she says, her whole face lighting up.

I open the door to find a tall, lanky guy with messy brown hair and kind eyes behind wire-rimmed glasses. He's wearing a vintage NASA t-shirt and jeans that look like they've been worn for twenty years straight. He's cute in an endearingly nerdy way, like a young Bill Gates crossed with a friendly science teacher.

"Mrs. Silverthorne! So nice to finally meet you," he says, extending his hand with a genuine smile. "I'm Kelso Mitchell. Thank you for letting me crash your Sunday brunch."

"Please, call me Tara. And you're not crashing—Willow's been excited for us to meet."

After Birch comes back (he doesn't say another word about Shawn), we settle around the table with our plates, and Kelso launches into conversation with the enthusiasm of someone who genuinely loves what he does.

"I have to say, your daughter is brilliant," he tells me. "She's got this incredible idea for a business that could actually change things for women."

"Oh?" I look at Willow, who's blushing.

"Mom, remember how you're always complaining about how uncomfortable the shoes are at your job? How they're beautiful torture devices?"

"Every single day," I confirm.

"Well, I've been designing comfortable shoes that can actually compete with fancy brands like Monet. Shoes that look just as elegant but don't destroy your feet." Willow's eyes are shining with excitement. "Kelso helped me work out the engineering aspects—the arch support, the materials, the weight distribution. And I consulted with Aunt Beth about the foot health side."

My mouth falls open. "You talked to Beth about this?"

"She's the one who encouraged me to pursue it," Willow continues. "I want to take a year off from college to really develop this business plan, then apply to design school. Or maybe do a double major in engineering and design. Or maybe even a triple major adding something in the health sciences, like physical or occupational therapy."

Kelso nods enthusiastically. "The market research shows there's a huge gap between comfort and style in women's footwear. We could really make a difference."

I stare at my daughter, feeling like an idiot. Here I've been worrying about her throwing her life away for some guy, and she's actually planning to revolutionize the shoe industry.

"Willow, this is... this is incredible. I'm so sorry I didn't know about any of this."

"You've had a lot going on, Mom, but I'm pretty excited about it."

Birch says, "Yep, Willow's going to take over the world."

"Did you know about this?"

"Of course," he says, grabbing another pancake. "She's been working on this for weeks. Meanwhile, I can't even decide what I want for lunch most days."

"You'll figure it out," Kelso says kindly. "I changed my major three times."

As I listen to them talk, I'm struck by how mature Willow seems, how well she and Kelso complement each other. Yes, he's older, but he treats her like an equal, not a child.

I know someone who might be very interested in investing in this kind of venture. Someone who's been in the shoe business his whole life and might appreciate some fresh thinking…. and working with someone who is not his jealous ex-wife.

Chapter 36

"I am very sad to see you go, but I understand this completely," Didier says, sitting across from me in his office. "You will have the money to take the time to know what your heart wants, non?"

I nod, feeling lighter already. "It's time. I should have done this weeks ago."

"And I am so sorry to hear that Shawn with the hard body is leaving town," he continues, shaking his head sadly. "At the party Saturday, he seemed so happy, so in love. I think he will be back, you know."

My chest tightens. "I don't think so. He got a great opportunity."

"Bah!" Didier waves his hand dismissively. "New York is not a faraway planet. Love will bring him back."

I'm not sure about that, but I appreciate his optimism. "Speaking of love, how are things with Roxanne?"

His whole face lights up. "Magnifique! I must thank you again for introducing us. And the old people she lives with — they are so cool, as you say. I spent the night, and when they found this disheveled Frenchman on their couch in the morning, they did not even seem to care! Vinny spent the day teaching me to make the chicken marsala."

After Didier leaves, I go back to my office and pack

up my personal items from my desk. There's not much — a small succulent, a photo of the kids, and the shoe-shaped pen holder I bought to make the space feel more like mine. The beauty of a mostly made-up job is that there's no need for two weeks' notice or training a replacement.

I leave the office building feeling lighter and head to Cassie's to pick up Mitzi.

"Okay, I am ready to let her go," Cassie says, handing me Mitzi's leash and a small bag of toys. "Everly will want to see her… and so will I, but this is so helpful, Tara. I may get a full night's sleep, but are you sure you want yours interrupted?"

I clip the leash on Mitzi, and she immediately starts wagging her tail. "I'll be fine. Maybe I can get her on a different schedule. Ready for a walk, girl?"

The early November day is perfect — crisp and sunny with leaves crunching under our feet. Mitzi is a little slow, but walks like a pro for an old girl. She has a steady little trot, and it's so cute to watch her ears flopping around.

As we pass the cidery, I can see Patrick through the window, pacing back and forth while talking on his phone. Even from outside, I can tell he's agitated, and I spot Bobbi, his ex, sitting at the bar looking equally upset.

I keep walking. I don't need that drama right now. Whatever they're arguing about, I just want to focus on the Berkeley Springs weekend. Hot springs, spa treatments, good food — it sounds exactly like what I need to clear my head.

Patrick was acting a little weird last night when we met at the cidery, checking his phone constantly and seeming distracted. But we had some laughs, and I sampled their new seasonal ciders. He's probably perfectly normal—people argue with their exes and get upset about business problems all the time.

Look at Didier with the modern-day Marie Antoinette.

And there are plenty of reasons someone might go to Vietnam. I've heard it's a cool place to visit with amazing food and beautiful beaches. Maybe we can go there on our next trip after Berkeley Springs. Todd was never into more exotic locales.

I put Mitzi in her carrier so we can take a longer walk because she seems to enjoy being out and about, watching the world go by. She loves to stop and sniff something I can't see or smell every few minutes, but her little legs can only handle so much walking.

As we walk, I find myself feeling better than I did yesterday when Shawn broke his news. New York isn't another planet, as Didier pointed out. Shawn needs to follow his dreams—he's young and has his whole life ahead of him. Maybe this is exactly what we both need.

I'm so lost in thought that I don't realize where I've walked until I look up and see the familiar glass building where I used to work. Somehow, I've come full circle back to where I started the day.

That's when I spot Roz outside on a bench, smoking a cigarette and crying.

I wave at her, and she hesitates before waving back. I walk over with Mitzi, who immediately perks up at the sight of a new person.

"Hey, are you okay?" I ask, settling beside her on the bench.

Roz wipes her eyes with the back of her hand. "Oh,

you know. James checked into rehab yesterday, so now I have Maple full-time. And I need to work, but I can't afford daycare for her. James and I had the schedule figured out, so we didn't need it. But now…"

"Can any of your other sons help?"

Roz lets out a bitter laugh. "Right. As I said, my sons are useless. The only one who is halfway decent is Tommy, and he and his wife already have four kids. They don't need another one, especially one who asks a million questions and wants to play dress-up all the time. Her life may be topsy-turvy, but Maple has gotten a lot of attention and the best care."

"I can see that. Does she go to preschool?"

"Three hours a day, but that's not nearly enough. And Tommy and his wife are already complaining about having to drive her because they live on the other side of town."

I hug Mitzi closer, feeling her warm little body against my chest. She's sleeping peacefully, completely trusting and content. Before I can second-guess myself, I hear my mother's voice in my head: "Really, your cure for a broken heart is a geriatric dachshund and a little girl with no mother and a father in rehab?"

My mother can be a real bitch sometimes, and I don't care what she thinks, but to be fair, she didn't say a word, and I am just projecting. I am too old to run every decision through my mother's virtual moral filter. It's been a little cloudy lately anyway.

"What if I helped?" I say before I can change my mind.

"What do you mean?"

"What if I were Maple's babysitter? I could pick her up from preschool, keep her until you get off work."

Roz stares at me. "Tara, I can't pay you. And how would you even do that? You work too."

"Actually, I just quit. And I don't need the money—I'm about to get a settlement from my divorce. What I need are positive things in my life." I scratch Mitzi's ears. "And what's more positive than hanging out with a cute little girl and a quirky little dog?"

"Are you serious? You'd really do that?"

"I'm serious. Maple is a sweetheart, and honestly, I know it's not the most modern thing to say, but I don't really want to be a career woman, at least not right now. I like taking care of small beings who need me."

This whole "helping other people" thing feels pretty great. I realize now what a self-centered person I was becoming… trying to be someone I'm not to get back at Todd.

So dumb.

"So, when can I start?" I ask.

Chapter 37

"Mrs. Tara, look! Mitzi is wearing a princess crown!"

Maple holds up the little wiener dog, who's sporting a plastic tiara from the dress-up box and looking remarkably patient about the whole situation. Her tail is wagging, so I think she's enjoying the attention.

"She looks very regal," I say, snapping a photo with my phone. "Should we have a royal tea party?"

It's Thursday afternoon, and I'm discovering just how much I've missed this—the pure joy of playing with a little person who finds magic in everything. Maple and I have spent the last hour building a fort out of couch cushions, reading picture books, and now apparently crowning my new dog as royalty.

I'm leaving for Berkeley Springs with Patrick tomorrow night, and I'm looking forward to the getaway, even though I have to leave Mitzi with Willow. Some time away from the city, away from all the reminders of Shawn, sounds perfect.

"Can Mitzi have some tea?" Maple asks, carefully setting out plastic cups and saucers on the coffee table.

"Of course. What kind of tea does a princess dog drink?"

"Cheese flavored!" Maple giggles.

I laugh and think about my kids when they were little. Now Willow is constantly out working on her business plan with Kelso— they've practically moved into the library, surrounded by sketches, spreadsheets, and engineering calculations. And Birch has been busy with school, friends, and visiting Todd at his fancy, furnished apartment downtown.

Both kids have visited their father a couple of times, and they say he seems better—calmer, more like the dad they remember from before Nicole entered the picture. Still no word on Nicole's fate, but that's up to the courts and her lawyer now.

It's good that the kids will have more time with Todd now, though it means less time at home with me. Maybe having Maple around will help fill that void until I figure out my next move.

Mitzi settles into my lap, still wearing her crown, and I scratch behind her ears. She's been the perfect companion—content to nap while Maple plays, but always ready for a walk or a game of fetch with her squeaky hamburger toy. Her running is more of a waddle, and she only does like three fetch sessions, but it's good for her to get a little exercise.

A knock at the door interrupts our tea party, and Maple jumps up excitedly. "Is that my Granny Roz?"

"I don't think so, sweetie. She's still at work." I check the time—it's only three-thirty.

When I open the door, my heart does a little flip. It's Shawn, holding a small duffel bag. I see a much bigger suitcase sitting in the hallway.

"Hey," he says, his smile a little uncertain. "I wanted to stop by before I left. My train's at six."

"Hi, I'm Maple," Maple comes running over, still holding her plastic teacup. "Look, we're having a tea party with Princess Mitzi!"

Shawn's face lights up when he sees her. "Wow, a real princess dog! That's amazing." He crouches down to Maple's level. "And who are you? Are you a princess too?"

"No, I'm not a real princess! I'm staying with Mrs. Tara while my daddy is away. He's sick."

I watch Shawn's expression change as the pieces click into place. His smile falters slightly, and he looks up at me with a question in his eyes.

"This is James's daughter," I say quietly.

Shawn's jaw tightens almost imperceptibly, but he keeps his voice gentle when he turns back to Maple. "Well, I'm sure your daddy will feel better soon. And it looks like you're having lots of fun with Mrs. Tara."

"We are! Do you want some cheese tea?"

"I would love some, but I can't stay very long." He accepts the tiny plastic cup she offers him and pretends to take a sip. "Mmm, delicious!"

Maple beams and skips back to the coffee table to pour more pretend tea. Shawn straightens up, and I can see the conflict in his expression.

"It's not what you think," I say quickly.

He sighs, looking suddenly defeated. "I know. Well, I don't know anything, but it's like you to help someone who needs it. It's..." He rubs the muscles in his neck, which seem to be tensing as we talk about his least favorite person.

I glance over at Maple, who is lost in her pretend world with Mitzi, and say, "Shawn—you were right about James. He's in rehab now."

He nods and says, "Nice. That's on brand for him." He watches Maple carefully arranging cookies on a plate for Mitzi. "She's adorable. And she's lucky to have you looking out for her."

I don't even know what to say, and I know it won't keep him here anyway.

"Maybe I'll stop by when I come home for Thanksgiving weekend," he says, but his tone suggests he's not sure about anything anymore. "But who knows, maybe Daddy will be better by then."

The way he says "Daddy", with just a hint of bitterness that he's trying to hide, makes my chest ache. I want to explain everything, to make him understand that this isn't about James at all. It's about a little girl who needs stability and love while her father gets the help he needs.

But he knows all of that, and I can still see in his eyes that he's already pulling away, already building walls to protect himself from more disappointment. And maybe he's right to do that. Maybe this is too complicated, too messy, too much drama for someone who's trying to start fresh in a new city.

"Have a safe trip," I say instead. "And good luck with everything."

He nods and heads toward the door, then turns back one more time. "Take care of yourself, Tara."

After he leaves, I sink back onto the couch next to Maple, who's now trying to teach Mitzi how to curtsy.

"Was that your boyfriend?" she asks innocently.

"No, sweetie. He was just a friend saying goodbye."

"Oh. He seemed sad. He liked the cheese tea, but maybe he needs his own wiener dog."

I laugh despite the heaviness in my chest. "You know what? I think you're absolutely right. Who doesn't need a wiener dog?"

Tomorrow I'll be in Berkeley Springs with Patrick,

soaking in warm water and trying to enjoy some escapism.

I just wish cheese tea were enough to make me feel better.

Chapter 38

Saturday morning in Berkeley Springs is exactly what I needed.

I'm walking next to Patrick through the charming downtown area, window shopping at the cute boutiques and galleries, and for the first time in weeks, my mind feels quiet. Maybe it's the country air, or maybe it's just being somewhere that has no memories of Shawn attached to it.

Last night was... nice. Really nice, actually. The inn Patrick chose is lovely—a historic building with exposed brick walls and antique furniture that manages to be elegant without being stuffy.

Our rooms are on different floors, not even close to each other, which made it clear that Patrick isn't expecting anything from this trip. It was refreshing not to have that pressure, even though there is no reason why something can't happen if I want it to, right?

We had dinner at the inn's restaurant—perfectly cooked steaks and a local singer who was a little cheesy but charming in that small-town way. After dinner, we took a long walk through the quiet streets, talking about everything and nothing. When we got back to the inn, Patrick walked me to my door and kissed me goodnight, sweet and gentle, not demanding anything more.

The shoes he gave me are sitting in my room right

now—delicate little ballet flats in soft, blush pink leather. "I saw these in a market in Ho Chi Minh City and thought of you," he said. "Much more comfortable than those torture devices you have to wear at work."

I didn't bother telling him that I gave up the high heels pretty soon after starting the job, and now I am unemployed.

I slept better than I have in weeks. No tossing and turning, no checking my phone for texts that weren't coming, no replaying conversations in my head. Just deep, dreamless sleep.

Okay, yes, I took a Benadryl again. I'm not that relaxed.

"Oh, look at this place," Patrick says, stopping in front of a glass-blowing studio. Through the large windows, we can watch an artist shaping molten glass on the end of a long rod, the orange glow dancing across his face as he works.

"That's amazing," I say, "but that looks so hot it's scary."

It's not my thing, but Patrick is completely absorbed, studying the technique with the same intensity he probably brings to perfecting his cider recipes. "The temperature control must be incredibly precise," he murmurs.

"I'm going to wander around a bit more," I tell him. "Meet you back here in a few minutes?"

He nods, still transfixed by the glassblower's work.

I slip away and head toward the building I've been curious about since we arrived—the Berkeley Springs State Park bathhouse. It's a large, utilitarian concrete structure that looks somewhat out of place among the charming Victorian buildings, but I know this is where the famous warm springs are housed.

Inside, a friendly woman with graying hair tied back in a practical ponytail greets me. "First time visiting our springs?"

"Yes, and I'm not sure what to expect."

She leads me down a hallway lined with doors. "Let me show you one of the rooms so you can see what you're in for."

She opens a door to reveal what looks like a large concrete bathtub built into the floor, maybe eight feet long and four feet wide, deep enough to stand comfortably. "We fill each tub with the natural spring water, which comes out of the ground at 74 degrees. It heats up to about 102 once you're soaking in the enclosed space."

"It's more intimate than I expected," I say, looking around the small, partially underground space with the tiny window facing the footpath outside.

"Most people find it very relaxing. You can wear a bathing suit if you prefer, but many of our guests go in nude—it's completely private, just you and whoever you're sharing the experience with."

I feel my cheeks flush slightly. "How long are the sessions?"

"Thirty minutes is standard. Would you like to make a reservation?"

"Yes, for two people this evening? Maybe around seven?"

"Perfect. I'll put you down for the seven o'clock slot."

When I get back to the glass studio, Patrick is holding a wrapped package.

"I couldn't resist," he says, carefully unwrapping a stunning glass bowl. It's about the size of a salad bowl, but the glass is swirled with deep blues and greens that seem to move and flow like ocean water. Threads of silver run through the colored glass, and the rim has been shaped into gentle waves. When the light hits it, the whole piece seems to glow from within.

"Patrick, it's beautiful!" I take it carefully, amazed by how substantial it feels despite looking so delicate. "The colors are incredible."

"I thought it would look perfect in your apartment—something to remind you of peaceful places when city life gets overwhelming."

I'm touched by the thoughtfulness of the gift.

"I wanted you to have something special from our trip." He looks pleased with himself.

"Thank you. I went and booked us a session at the warm springs bathhouse for seven tonight, after an early dinner. I hope that's okay?"

His face lights up. "That sounds perfect. I was hoping we'd get to try the springs—that's what this place is famous for, after all. Good thing I brought my swim trunks."

As we continue our stroll through town, the glass bowl cradled carefully in my arms, I find myself relaxing even more. This is what dating should feel like—easy, comfortable, without all the emotional drama and complications that have defined my recent relationships.

Except I am kind of bored.

Am I so addicted to drama now that a pleasant time with a nice man feels boring?

Chapter 39

Dinner at the inn's restaurant is pleasant enough. Patrick seems to prefer eating here rather than exploring the other restaurants in town, and I'm not complaining — the food is good and it's convenient. We managed to get an early table, which gives us plenty of time to walk across the courtyard for our bath experience afterward.

It feels a little geriatric to be eating this early, but this whole town is a little back in time, so it's fine.

We both order the fish special, and Patrick is telling me about the spa services at the inn.

"They have couples' massages and mineral bath experiences that are supposed to be different from the state park springs," he says, cutting into his fish. "We should try it tomorrow. Or you could do something separately if you're more comfortable with that."

His phone rings before I can respond, and he glances at the screen with a frown.

"Seems like you have a lot to keep you busy," I say, trying to keep my tone light.

"Sorry, I really need to take this." He stands up and walks toward the entrance, answering as he goes.

I can hear him speaking what I assume is Vietnamese, and his tone sounds angry. He's pacing in the parking lot now, throwing his free hand in the air as he talks.

He seems angry when he talks to anyone but me. Hmm…

I'm dying to ask him why he went to Vietnam, but when I tried on the drive here Friday night, he just said it was for business, didn't elaborate, and changed the subject. I let it drop because, honestly, I shouldn't complain. I'm on a nice weekend getaway with a pleasant, handsome man, and it couldn't have come at a better time. Besides, it's definitely Todd's turn to deal with the kids and any drama that comes up this weekend.

And Patrick's travel destinations have no bearing on my life, but it's hard not to be curious.

I butter another roll and try not to stare at Patrick through the window. What's that saying, "not my circus, not my monkeys?"

Instead, I focus on the family at the center table. They have four kids of varying ages, and the mom is up dancing to the singer's music with her two youngest children. The dad is feeding the baby from a jar, and an older girl is looking at her phone but making funny faces at the baby to get him to laugh.

I shouldn't be jealous, but it's such a nice domestic scene. Of course, full-on chaos will probably ensue when they try to get all those kids to go to sleep later. I think about Mitzi, and how I have my own responsibilities waiting for me at home. I hope she's okay with Willow. And Maple—I know all I've done is put a Band-Aid on that problem.

Patrick comes back looking slightly frazzled. "Sorry for the interruption. Work stuff."

We finish our meal, and he glances over at the family table where one of the younger kids has started crying loudly.

"Jeez, that looks like a nightmare," he says, wincing as the child's wails get louder. "That's why I never wanted kids. Too much work, and now they're all shrieking."

I don't say anything. I have no intention of having babies with Patrick or anyone else at my age, but his comment still feels unnecessarily harsh. Those parents are doing their best, and honestly, the crying stopped after about thirty seconds. I don't normally care if kids are being loud in public, unless when they yell "Mom", they are talking to me. Otherwise, it's just background noise.

We pay the check and head back to our rooms to change into our swimsuits. I slip into my black one-piece and grab a towel, feeling oddly nervous about this whole experience.

The bathhouse attendant, a different woman from this morning, gets us set up in our reserved room. The concrete space feels even smaller with two people in it, and it's already getting hot.

"This is romantic," Patrick says as the door closes behind us, but the sterile concrete room feels more like a prison cell than a romantic hideaway to me. Maybe the inn's spa will be cozier tomorrow, but this is fine for tonight.

The tub is filled with the warm spring water, and we ease ourselves in. The heat is intense but not unbearable, like being in a very hot bathtub.

Patrick moves closer and starts kissing me. While I'm not opposed to it, I feel a little weird about getting intimate in this space with so much skin showing and concrete walls echoing every sound. I know I could sleep with Patrick if I wanted to, but I don't have any burning desire to do so.

And definitely not in the warm springs at the state park.

I don't feel ready now that the charade of this whole non-monogamous dating thing is over. I need to think about my heart instead of my… well… you know…

I think about Shawn for a minute, wondering what he's doing right now, probably enjoying cocktails at some trendy Manhattan bar with a hot banking woman from his training program—and push the thought away just as quickly.

Patrick stops kissing me and sways slightly.

"Are you okay?" I ask. "It is getting very hot in here."

He jokes about me making him hot, but his face looks pale. I move toward the small window that opens onto the walking path to get some cool air flowing in when I hear a splash behind me.

I turn around, thinking he's joking around, maybe pretending he wants to have a water fight, and then I realize he's not moving.

"HELP!" I scream, lunging toward him and trying to drag him up. "SOMEBODY HELP!"

The door bursts open, and the two bathhouse attendants rush in.

"We got a fainter!" one of them yells. "It's always the men—they can't handle the heat!"

Between the three of us, we manage to get Patrick out of the tub, but he hits his head on the concrete edge as we're pulling him out. There's a small cut on his forehead that's bleeding, and he's still unconscious.

"I'm calling 911," the other attendant says, already on her phone.

The paramedics arrive within minutes and insist that Patrick needs to go to the emergency room to be checked for a concussion. He's conscious by then but groggy and confused.

"I'll ride with him," I say, even though I feel like a terrible person for wishing I didn't have to. As I climb into the ambulance in my damp clothes, I can't help thinking that emergency rooms really kill the whole relaxation buzz.

I was hoping to escape more drama this weekend, and I am probably going to hell for not wanting to support a man with a potentially cracked head because he's kind of boring… and not the someone else I'm trying not to think about.

But if I do decide I want to see more of Patrick, I would like to know why he's so angry all the time.

And secretive.

Chapter 40

I'm curled up on my couch with Mitzi and a soft throw blanket, trying to read a book, but I can't concentrate. My mind keeps wandering back to the ridiculous scene at the bathhouse yesterday.

I wouldn't wish for anyone to drown or sustain brain damage, but I have to admit I'm kind of glad Patrick's fainting spell killed the mood. After spending three hours in the emergency room waiting for his tests to come back normal, any romantic tension that might have existed between us evaporated completely, and that was fine by me.

I don't want to be thinking about Shawn and sleeping with someone else.

I stayed in his room overnight because I didn't know who else to call, certainly not his ex, and then drove us both home this morning. Patrick was embarrassed and worn out from the whole experience, and if there was any chance I might have weakened and slept with him, the concussion definitely killed that possibility.

Not that there would have been anything wrong with it, but I don't feel the same about Patrick as I do about… someone else.

When I dropped Patrick off at his apartment near the cidery, Dinah happened to be taking her Sunday walk and spotted us. Once she heard what happened, she immediately offered to sit with Patrick and make sure he was okay.

"And of course Vinny will send over some meatballs," she added. "Nothing cures a head injury like some good meat."

After I got Patrick situated, I pulled Dinah aside and told her about the additional Vietnam discussion and those odd phone calls. And how I keep catching him yelling and getting angry.

"That doesn't sound like the Patrick I know, and I told you I don't know anything about his business dealings," she said with a frown, "but you know what? I'll show that text he sent you by accident to my nail technician. She's Vietnamese. It can't hurt, and it's probably just some boring work stuff."

"Okay, but I guess it doesn't matter. Patrick's a nice guy, but there's no spark."

Dinah patted my arm. "Right, then why do you care about why he went to Vietnam? If he didn't light my fire, I wouldn't care if he went to Timbuktu. Honey, you've had enough excitement for one weekend. Go home and relax with that sweet little dog of yours."

"I don't know why I am so curious. Something just seems off, and I can't put my finger on it. I hope he's not in any danger."

Dinah told me not to worry, and I gave up for now and took her advice.

So here I am at home, finally relaxing, when my phone rings.

It's Roz.

"Hey, I hope you don't mind me calling on a Sunday," she says, and I can hear the smile in her voice. "I had a great date last night and it turned into an overnighter, so my son and his wife kept Maple at their house."

"That's wonderful! You deserve some fun." I wish she wouldn't leave Maple with her uncle, but I need to be careful about being too interfering.

"I hope you won't judge me, but it's honestly the best date I've had since my husband passed away."

"I thought you said they wouldn't babysit Maple?"

"Not as a regular thing, but they have so many kids that one more on the weekend doesn't really matter. And Maple likes playing with her cousins."

"How's James doing?" I ask.

"He's angry, but I think he's going to try to make this work. It's early days yet." She pauses. "Would you mind picking Maple up at my son's house? I'm having such a good time that I don't want to cut it short, but I'll be home before her bedtime."

I hesitate because I am enjoying my solitude, but I don't like Maple being with her uncle's family. "Of course I don't mind. I'll get her and bring her back to my place until you get home."

"You're a lifesaver, Tara. Really."

She gives me the address, and I load Mitzi into her carrier. Twenty minutes later, I'm pulling up to what can only be described as a redneck nightmare.

The yard is littered with broken toys, empty beer cans, and maybe old car parts. The house itself is a small ranch with peeling paint and several windows that appear to be covered with plastic instead of glass. I can hear screaming and yelling coming from inside, and I spot two little kids playing in the backyard wearing what looks like dirty pajamas and no shoes, in November.

I knock on the front door several times before a man answers. He's holding a beer and looks annoyed to be bothered.

"Yeah, what do you want?"

"I'm here to pick up Maple. Roz's granddaughter?"

His expression clears slightly. "Oh yeah, the extra kid. Hold on."

He turns and yells into the house, "BRENDA! That lady's here for Maple!"

A woman appears behind him, cigarette dangling from her lips. She looks Mitzi up and down with disdain.

"How old is that dog? She looks almost dead," she says with a laugh.

I clutch Mitzi's carrier tighter. "She's fifteen, but she's perfectly healthy."

The woman brings Maple to the door, and I'm relieved to see she looks unharmed, just tired.

"One more kid doesn't matter around here," Brenda says with a shrug. "We barely noticed her."

I take Maple's hand, appalled by their casual indifference. As we walk back to the car, I look back at the house in horror, wondering how these people could be related to sweet Roz.

"Mrs. Tara," Maple says quietly as I buckle her into the car seat I bought to drive Maple around. "I'm hungry. They didn't have any breakfast except cereal with no milk."

My heart breaks a little. "Don't worry, sweetie. We'll get you something good to eat as soon as we get home. Maybe some pancakes? And some nice fruit?"

As we drive away from that awful house, I make a mental note to have a conversation with Roz about alternative childcare arrangements. Maple deserves so much better than to be treated like she doesn't matter, and that may be the least of the problems in that house. It didn't look safe for adults, let alone the kids.

"Mrs. Tara?" Maple says from the backseat. "Can Mitzi have pancakes too?"

"Of course, sweetheart. Mitzi loves pancakes."

This child is an angel, but I am getting in pretty deep now, and I can't let her continue to be cared for by those horrible people, even if it is only once in a while.

But now that it seems Roz has a new boyfriend, she will need more help with Maple. And I don't blame Roz—she's had a rough life with her messed-up sons and losing her husband.

So why do I feel ridiculous for taking on this responsibility?

At least I don't have to worry about explaining it to Shawn anymore.

Chapter 41

"Come on, you need to treat yourself to a nice pedicure," Dinah says, practically dragging me toward the nail salon. "Mitzi is fine sleeping at home, Maple is at preschool, and we need to find out what that mysterious text means."

The salon is owned by a group of Vietnamese women whom Dinah has known for years. It's a cozy place with rows of pedicure chairs and the constant chatter of multiple conversations in Vietnamese mixed with English.

"Mrs. Dinah! So good to see you!" A petite woman with perfectly manicured nails rushes over to greet us. "And you bring new friend!"

"This is Tara," Dinah says. "We're here for the works, but we also need your help with something."

The woman (her name tag says 'Lily') brings us glasses of ice water and a plate of fresh fruit as we settle into the pedicure chairs. The warm water feels amazing on my feet. Like the hot springs, but without the concrete and head injury.

"So, what kind of help you need?" Lily asks, clearly excited. "I love to help with problem."

Dinah explains my situation—the mysterious boyfriend (I didn't bother correcting her label) who went to Vietnam, the strange phone calls, and the accidental text message. Lily's eyes light up with each detail.

"Ooh, this is like TV show! Show me the text!"

I pull out my phone and find Patrick's message—those Vietnamese letters that made no sense to me, no matter what order they're in. I hand it to Lily, and immediately her face changes. The excitement drains away, replaced by alarm.

She calls over two other technicians working on other customers. "Mai! Hoa! Come look at this!"

The other women hurry over, leaving their customers soaking. When they see my phone screen, they all make the same distressed faces.

"Oh no," Dinah says, looking back and forth between their expressions. "I can't even imagine what it says that would shock you ladies. You hear just about everything in here."

Lily looks around nervously. "We need to talk in back room. Come, come!"

She gestures for us to follow, but we both have wet feet, so we shove them into the flimsy salon flip-flops. Dinah almost falls over getting out of her chair, and I have to steady her as we shuffle toward a small break room in the back of the salon.

Once the door is closed, Lily whispers urgently, "The text say: 'I'm almost ready to make the drop. Don't shoot.'"

Mai nods gravely. "This very bad. Your boyfriend, he maybe working with Vietnamese mafia organization."

"The—" Hoa starts to say something, but Mai quickly puts her hand over her mouth.

"No! Don't say name! Very dangerous!"

I stare at them in disbelief. "That seems unlikely.

Patrick is a nice guy—he owns a cidery. He took me to a beautiful inn and brought me shoes from his trip. Why would he be in the mob?"

All three women freak out again at the mention of shoes.

"The shoes!" Lily shrieks. "Are these the shoes you wearing when you come in here?"

"Yes, the ones he brought me from Vietnam. They're sitting by the pedicure chair."

Hoa runs back to the pedicure area and grabs my shoes like they are going to detonate any minute, and we all peek out into the salon to watch her promptly throw them out the front door onto the sidewalk.

"Hey!" I protest, but Mai is shaking her head vigorously.

"No, no, very bad! They might have insect inside!"

Dinah and I look at each other, confused. "Insect?"

Hoa comes back from disposing of my shoes. "She means bug. Like listening device."

"Why would he be spying on me?" I ask, my mind reeling.

"Maybe he mistakes you for law person. Like FBI. This happened one time with the mafia. Very bad things happen." Lily says.

Dinah waves her hands. "Tara's not in the FBI! She was a housewife for twenty years, and she just quit a little retail job selling shoes—"

I wince and say, "My ex-husband is a lawyer."

Dinah is eyeing me like maybe I am a secret agent all this time, and the other women are flipping out again.

"Ohhh!" Mai gasps. "Maybe your ex is lawyer for rival drug lord. Or maybe drug deal is to go down at the shoe store. You have any suspicious customer?"

"I said she just quit!" Dinah insists.

But as the words leave her mouth, I realize something that makes me wonder a little. Or it's more likely I am being swept up by the general paranoia. But what if I'm the naïve housewife of twenty years and I've been tricked?

"Actually," I say slowly, "I didn't tell Patrick that I quit my job."

The room goes dead silent except for the hum of the nail dryers from the main salon. All four women are staring at me with expressions that range from concern to outright terror.

What the hell have these women seen in their lives beyond the gels and acrylic nails?

"Oh, honey," Dinah says, sinking into a plastic chair. "I think you might be in some trouble. It's all my fault for introducing you."

"This is insane! Dinah, you can't be buying this. Maybe he just likes giving gifts, although it is odd, and the text is a little hard to explain, especially the shooting part."

We finish our pedicures in relative silence, though I catch the nail technicians whispering to each other in Vietnamese and glancing at me nervously. When we're done, I reluctantly retrieve my shoes from the sidewalk where they were unceremoniously thrown.

I examine them carefully, turning them over in my hands. They look like normal ballet flats to me—soft leather, simple design, nothing obviously suspicious about them.

"We need to take these to someone who knows about shoes," Dinah declares. "Let's go see Didier. He's an expert."

I'm sure Kelso would be a better insect or bomb detector, but I don't want him to think his girlfriend's mother is several pancakes short of a stack.

Twenty minutes later, we're standing in Didier's office while he examines my potentially bug-infested footwear.

"Ah, mes amies!" he says, clearly delighted to see us. "I was just thinking about Roxanne. Did you know she brought me authentic French macarons yesterday? She learned to make them from watching the YouTube videos! And tonight, I am teaching her to make coq au vin at your house, Dinah! Vinny is so excited to learn a French recipe. Maybe they add to their catering business, non?"

"That's wonderful, but we have a situation," Dinah interrupts, explaining about Patrick and the mysterious text.

Didier holds up the shoes, turning them this way and that. "These look fine to me. A little cheap in the workmanship — the stitching is not very precise. But I do not know of any drug lords or FBI people." He pauses thoughtfully. "We should ask Kenneth. If there was any danger, he would notice this. He thought the UPS man was Macy's spy. Do you need security? I will pay for it."

"No!" I say, exasperated. "This needs to stop. I just won't wear the shoes or see Patrick again."

"You should bring the shoes and the text to the police station," Dinah insists.

"Just because gossipy nail ladies watch too many true crime shows? They'll just lock me up in the loony bin!" I throw my hands up. "And who knows how good Patrick's Vietnamese is? Maybe the text said something innocent, and it autocorrected. Did you see how many squiggles and dots go with those letters? Maybe a squiggle means 'don't shoot' and a missing squiggle means 'have a good night'. And anyway, he's just a casual acquaintance — yes, one that I dragged out of a hot tub and whose head I smacked on concrete, but that's the extent of our relationship."

I grab the shoes from Didier's desk. "Now let's go home. Thanks for looking at these. And indulging these delusions." I roll my eyes at Dinah and add, "And we can stop by the library," I tell Dinah as we head for the door, "and get you some crime mystery novels to keep your overactive imagination occupied."

Didier calls after us, "If you change your mind about security, just let me know! I will send big men with guns."

As we walk to the car, I can't help but wonder if there is a Vietnamese mafia. The nail ladies seemed to think so. I could Google it, but then the FBI will see that I was interested… what the hell am I saying?

But, oh my God, maybe the nail ladies know some mafia members who live in Richmond. Like a cell in hiding? No one would suspect that. Does Todd have drug lord clients? He does make an awful lot of money.

Maybe we should also stop at the liquor store on the way home, too, and erase this whole experience from our memories.

But who was Patrick telling not to shoot?

Chapter 42

It's a beautiful November afternoon, and I'm sitting on a bench at the playground, watching Maple go down the slide for the twentieth time while Mitzi naps in my lap. A couple of weeks have passed since the great Vietnamese mafia conspiracy, and I'm starting to feel like myself again.

I love this—taking care of Maple and Mitzi, being needed, having a purpose that doesn't involve spreadsheets or uncomfortable footwear. Maybe I should do something with pets or children when I figure out my next career move. Though honestly, I'm not worried about it. We already have an offer on the house. Our neighborhood is very sought after, and homes don't go on the market often. The realtors have buyers practically salivating to drop millions on a mansion.

So, I have money now, and a lot more is coming.

It's funny to think that a few months ago, I had three men in my life, and now I have none. Shawn moved to New York, James is in rehab, and Patrick is an alleged mobster. Also, very boring. I can't help but laugh at the absurdity of it all.

I glance around the playground, wondering if this is where single people meet these days. There are a few dads here, but they all seem to be chasing toddlers or pushing strollers with infants. I definitely don't need any more kids right now, or heaven forbid, married men!

I check my phone and realize I'm almost late for my lunchtime Zoom call with Robert and Beth to discuss Thanksgiving plans and our increasingly nutty mother. My siblings don't know about Mom's crush on her real estate partner yet, and I'm not sure I'm ready to drop that bombshell.

Plus, who knows if it's more than a crush now?

I pack up Maple and a sleepy Mitzi and head home, getting connected to the call just as I walk in the door. Robert's face appears on my phone. He looks frazzled, which is his default state these days.

"Sorry, I'm late," I say. "I was at the playground with Maple."

"Who's Maple?" Beth asks, appearing in her own square. She's clearly on a lunch break from her podiatry practice. I can see medical equipment in the background and a Tupperware container on her desk.

"Long story. She's the daughter of a friend who's going through some things. I'm helping with childcare."

"That's nice," Robert says, then immediately gets distracted by something off-camera. "Sophia! Please don't put Play-Doh in Oliver's hair!"

My brother works from home writing children's books while his wife, Moneca, is the CFO at Monet Shoes. They have four young children—Sophia, who's five, Oliver, who's three, and one-year-old twins named Aria and Tyrion.

Apparently, they binge-watched Game of Thrones during the twin pregnancy.

"Where's Moneca?" I ask.

"Board meeting," Robert says, looking exhausted. "I don't know how she does it all. I can't even figure out how to braid the girls' hair properly."

"YouTube tutorials. I use them all the time." Beth suggests helpfully.

"For what?" I ask, hoping it has nothing to do with her medical practice.

"Embroidery. What do you think I am looking at, a refresher course on how to remove bunions with kitchen utensils? I went to medical school, Tara. Cadavers are so easy to learn on, they don't complain that you're hurting them or doing it wrong."

Robert grimaces. "Can we please not talk about dead feet while I'm eating lunch?"

"Everything's connected to feet," Beth says. "Your whole body depends on proper foot health. Did you know that foot problems can cause back pain, hip issues, and even headaches?"

"Anyway," I interrupt before Beth can launch into a full podiatry lecture, "we need to figure out Thanksgiving. I vote for Beth's house since Robert and I both have overflowing households."

"Yeah, I'm fine with that. I don't have to cook, right?" Beth asks. "Because you know if you make me responsible for the meal, I'll just order everything from a catering place."

"Sounds great to me," Robert says. "And it's your turn to have Mom and Dad stay with you. They drove Moneca crazy last year when the twins were infants, and we just can't handle houseguests. We walk a fine line between normalcy and a full-on dumpster fire. One little thing could tip us into the flames."

He makes the explosion noise and the poof gesture with his hands. So dramatic.

"Speaking of Mom and Dad," I say carefully, "has

anyone talked to them lately?"

"Dad called yesterday," Beth reports. "He spent twenty minutes explaining the statistical probability of turkey-related food poisoning if we don't cook the bird to exactly 165 degrees."

"What about Mom?"

"She's been weirdly quiet," Robert admits. "Usually, she's called me five times by now to discuss the menu and lecture me about getting the kids' hair cut before family photos."

This would be the perfect time to mention Mom's super-late midlife crisis, but some conversations are better in person.

"So, are you bringing any of your men?" Beth asks with a grin. "Mom's been asking about that young guy she met."

I let out a bitter laugh. "The men have all dropped off like dead flies in a patio bug zapper. Shawn's in New York, James turned out to be a racist former cop who's now in rehab, and Patrick might be involved with the Vietnamese mob."

Both my siblings stare at me through their screens.

"The Vietnamese mob?" Robert repeats slowly.

"It's a long story involving mistranslated text messages and potentially bugged shoes."

"I'm sorry, what?" Beth says. "Did you just say bugged shoes? As a foot doctor, I have to know more about this. How can you bug a shoe?"

"Never mind. The point is, I'll be coming alone. Well, not alone. I am bringing two teenagers, one cute, nerdy engineer, and a very old wiener dog.

"Well, we know Beth isn't bringing anyone," Robert says with a smirk. "She's very secretive about her love life."

"Actually," Beth says, and there's something different about her tone that makes both Robert and me lean closer to our screens, "as a matter of fact, there will be someone new at Thanksgiving. And you all better behave yourselves."

The silence stretches for a full ten seconds before Robert and I both start talking at once.

"Wait, what?"

"Who is it?"

"How long has this been going on?"

"We're finally going to meet the mysterious someone?"

Beth just smiles and shakes her head. "You'll find out soon enough. And that's all I'm saying."

After we hang up, I sit staring at my phone screen, trying to process this development. Beth, my secretive sister who's never brought anyone to a family gathering, is finally introducing someone to the family.

This Thanksgiving is going to be very interesting.

Chapter 43

The house is complete chaos, and I'm starting to wonder if volunteering to do all this Thanksgiving prep was a mistake. I am not much of a cook, but I don't want bland catering food, and Robert and Moneca are surely not whipping up any pies.

Birch is home from school and playing video games at maximum volume in the living room. The sounds of explosions and gunfire are punctuating every conversation, making it impossible to think straight.

And sadly, it makes me think of Shawn and how he could be here in this domestic scene, playing games with Birch and helping in the kitchen.

But I do have helpers. Willow is prepping vegetables while Kelso sits at the island, talking animatedly about their business plans.

"I'm so excited that Didier is going to sell his share of Monet Shoes and invest in our company. What a bold move for him!" he says, practically bouncing in his seat. "It's going to change everything for us. He's a mega successful businessman and such a nice dude."

"Well, he needs to get away from Dominique anyway," I say, chopping celery more aggressively than necessary. "And he's so rich he can afford to take a break and start something new."

Willow looks up from the carrots she's dicing. "No,

Mom, I think he's just so happy because he's in love with Roxanne."

She's probably right. When Didier called me last week, he could barely contain his excitement about the shoe company investment. Apparently, Kelso has been socializing the idea around town, trying to find investors. Todd offered to help financially, but Willow and Kelso decided they wanted to go outside the family, and Todd doesn't have that kind of capital.

Mitzi is stationed hopefully by the counter, waiting for food to fall, while Maple sits at the kitchen table drawing pictures of turkeys and pilgrims for our Thanksgiving placemats.

Yes, Maple will be with us for the holiday. Roz is going with her new man to his daughter's house in North Carolina, and I don't mind having her. Though I have to say, this new boyfriend of Roz's seems to like to travel, which could become a problem. Roz deserves happiness, but Maple deserves stability.

It's nice to worry about other people's problems for a change.

Speaking of other people's problems, I finally talked to Patrick last week. He'd been calling, and I was avoiding him at first, but then I met him at the cidery and told him what happened with the accidental text message.

He laughed so hard he nearly spit out his cider. "I botched the Vietnamese so badly," he said. "I was trying to communicate with my business partners, but I think I accidentally said something about shooting? I copied the same text to the right person, and they were cracking up at my poor language skills. I can speak and understand much better than I can write."

Turns out Patrick is starting a chain of nail salons. He has a friend from Vietnam whose four sisters want to start a business in the US. He was over there working with them on business plans, sourcing supplies, and helping with immigration paperwork.

I realized this must be the potential competition the nail salon ladies were complaining about. Yes, I get a pedicure every week now. It's become my new form of therapy, and they are up in arms that a new salon is coming to town, just up the street from theirs.

When I told Patrick what the nail technicians thought his text said, he shook his head. "I don't know if it's good or bad that my competition thinks I'm a Vietnamese mobster."

We laughed about it but parted as friends. Patrick seemed to get the hint that there was no chemistry between us, and he's still self-conscious about fainting in the hot tub.

After leaving the cidery that day, I made the mistake of looking at Shawn's social media while waiting for a traffic light to change. I've been trying not to stalk him online, but he seems to be having a great time in New York. There's one very pretty woman who appears in all his recent photos; someone who probably understands his generation's cultural references and has healthy, baby-making eggs.

I texted him once, just to see how he was doing. He wrote back the next day, saying everything was going well, asked me to say hi to all the kids and neighbors, and mentioned that he'd be home to see his family at Thanksgiving. "Maybe I'll stop by to say hi," he added.

I didn't tell him we're having the holiday at Beth's house.

"Mom, we need more cranberries," Willow says, interrupting my internal monologue. "And more pie crusts. And probably more chocolate."

"We're serving chocolate on Thanksgiving?"

"No, I just got my period, and I'm craving a big Hershey's bar."

"Right. I need to run to the store. Does anybody else have any cravings?"

Maple looks up from her latest turkey masterpiece and says, "I like chocolate too. What's a period? Maybe I want that too."

Willow gives her a cookie from the jar on the counter and says, "Trust me, you don't."

I am not prepared for a sex education lesson, so I take off my apron, fluff my hair in the hallway mirror, and grab my keys. As I'm waiting for the elevator, I hear a door open behind me and turn to see a woman about my age going into Shawn's apartment. She has the same warm eyes and confident posture.

That must be his mother.

I try to get on the elevator quickly when it arrives, but she turns and looks directly at me.

"You must be Tara," she says with a knowing smile. "How about we grab a coffee?"

My heart starts pounding. Why is she being so direct? Is she mad at me for robbing her son out of the cradle? Or, oh my God, her mother told her about the shower incident.

"I'm Angela," she says, extending her hand. "Shawn's told me so much about you."

We end up at the coffee shop, even though I'm supposed to be at the grocery store, and I find myself surprisingly at ease with this woman who raised the man I can't stop thinking about.

"So, you're the famous Tara," Angela says with a warm smile. "I guess things got complicated for you two when he accepted the training program in New York. But I have to say, I'm proud of how well Shawn is doing. This was exactly what he needed to get out of his rut with a dead-end job and a... complicated relationship."

The women in Shawn's family do not beat around the bush.

"He looks happy on Instagram," I say, then immediately feel my face flush. "I mean, not that I'm stalking him or anything. I just... occasionally check..."

Angela laughs. "Honey, we all do that. But you know what? Just because I know what's best for him as his mother, he seems sad when I talk to him on the phone. You know how hard it is to see your kids go through stuff and face hard decisions."

"Yes, my daughter dropped out of Harvard after half a semester." I smile but realize that the mention of Harvard sounds so braggy. "Do you really think Shawn is sad?"

"I do, unfortunately. And speaking of embarrassing family moments, I owe you an apology for my mother's behavior at Shawn's apartment that morning. Walking in on you two in the shower like that was completely inappropriate."

I nearly choke on my coffee. "Oh, that. Yeah, that was... memorable."

"My mother is a hypocrite," Angela says with a laugh. "She pretends she's going to Bible study twice a week, but I know for a fact she's visiting some man named Earl who lives in her senior community." She raises her eyebrows meaningfully. "Apparently, Earl has been teaching her how to play poker. And I am guessing it's the racier version, if you get my meaning."

"Your mother has a boyfriend?"

"She's getting more action than I am. But that's beside the point." Angela leans forward. "The point is, she had no business judging you for your age when she's out there living her best life with Earl the poker teacher."

I can't help but smile. "I guess all families are complicated."

"They are. But here's the thing about Shawn—I had him when I was seventeen, and he's an only child, so he was raised around a lot of adults. He's always been an old soul, more mature than his years would suggest."

"That's what I noticed about him, too. He's nothing like other guys his age. I would never normally be interested in someone so young. It just kind of happened. I know that's a clichéd excuse but…"

"No, I get it. And I think that's why this whole thing with you has been so hard on him. He doesn't connect with people easily, but when he does, it means something."

I stare into my coffee cup, not sure what to say.

"Look, Tara, I don't need blood grandchildren. I just need my boy to be happy. And when he talks about you, even when he's trying not to, I can hear something in his voice that I've never heard before."

"But there are so many complications. My kids, my age, his career…"

"Complications can be worked through if two people care enough about each other." Angela reaches across the table and squeezes my hand. "The question is, do you care enough?"

"I do," I whisper. "But I'm scared I'm holding him

back from the life he should have."

"I understand, and I want him to be successful and take advantage of opportunities, but at what price? And in my experience, everything is figureoutable."

Before I can answer, my phone buzzes with a text from Willow. "Mom, where are you? We ran out of ingredients, and Kelso is trying to make stuffing with cornflakes."

I laugh despite the emotional weight of our conversation. "I should probably get back. My daughter's boyfriend is apparently improvising the Thanksgiving dinner prep."

"Of course. But Tara?" Angela stands and gives me a hug that feels surprisingly maternal. "Shawn's coming home for Thanksgiving. He'll probably stop by the apartment. Maybe don't overthink it so much."

I once again don't offer up any details about my Thanksgiving plans.

As I drive to the grocery store to get a cart full of holiday meal ingredients and chocolate, I can't help but wonder if Angela is right. Maybe I have been overthinking everything.

Maybe some things are worth the complications, and Shawn just needs time and space.

Those are two things I really hate. Quick closeness is much more appealing.

I really thought Angela was going to tell me to keep my old lady hands off her son, but it was just the opposite.

But I can't move to New York, can I?"

Chapter 44

Beth's house is a stunning old townhouse on Monument Avenue, all gleaming hardwood floors and soaring ceilings. It's also exactly the kind of place where you worry about children spilling things on priceless antiques.

Beth looks slightly panicked as she watches Robert and Moneca's kids, Sophia and Oliver, race around the living room at full speed.

"Maybe we could get everyone to color?" she suggests desperately, pulling out a stack of coloring books. "Willow, Kelso, could you help corral the little ones?"

Willow and Kelso are already setting up at the coffee table with Maple, who's carefully coloring a turkey, her new favorite artistic subject, while Mitzi snoozes contentedly on the velvet couch.

At least the furry older kid seems manageable, unless she pees on the expensive furniture.

In the kitchen, my parents are holding court while the turkey finishes cooking. Dad is in his element, quoting probability statistics about everything from food poisoning to traffic accidents.

"Did you know that 46% of all kitchen fires occur on Thanksgiving?" he announces cheerfully.

Mom is looking at her phone, and she absentmindedly says, "Is that so?"

"Liz, honey, you really need a break from work. You've been putting in so many hours lately. Please put the phone away and enjoy the day."

I give Mom a pointed look, but she just pops her phone in her purse and busies herself with arranging appetizers on a platter, completely ignoring my glare.

The one bright spot has been meeting Beth's girlfriend, Carmen. She's a lovely woman in her early forties with short silver hair and kind brown eyes, and she works as a therapist at VCU. Everyone was surprised but happy when Beth finally introduced someone to the family.

My phone starts ringing, and I see it's Roz calling. "I should take this; it might be about Maple."

I step into the hallway and answer. "Hi Roz, Happy Thanksgiving!"

"Hi, honey, can I talk to Maple for a minute?"

I bring the phone over to Maple, who's excited to hear from her Granny Roz. After a few minutes of chatting about turkeys and her new coloring friends, Maple hands the phone back to me.

"How's your holiday going?" I ask, walking back toward the kitchen.

"It's nice, but..." Roz's voice sounds strained. "Sam wants me to go on a three-month cruise around the world with him. He's retired and has the money for it, but I just can't leave right now. Not with Maple needing stability and James still in rehab."

My heart sinks. "I'm sorry, that must be a difficult position. Did you give him an answer?"

"No, I don't have the guts to say yes or no. Unless the cruise ship allows little kids, I'm screwed. And I don't think a family vacation was the kind of trip he had in mind."

"I'm sorry, Roz. Let's talk more when you get home. Speaking of family, do you think James will call for Maple today?"

"I hope so. He's struggling, but that little girl is a bright spot for all of us."

After I hang up, Beth appears beside me. "Everything okay? You look worried."

We both glance over at Maple, who's now receiving a tutorial from Sophia on how to color inside the lines, while Oliver is ripping his coloring book into little pieces, and Mitzi is trying to grab them with her mouth.

"It's complicated," I say quietly. "Roz is torn between a relationship and taking care of Maple. And I can't keep this child indefinitely; I'm not even a family member."

"But you love her now."

"Of course I do. That's what makes this so hard."

As if on cue, my phone rings again. This time it's James.

"Maple," I call softly. "Your daddy's on the phone."

I sit with her on Beth's elegant sofa while she talks to her father, her face lighting up at the sound of his voice. After a few minutes, she looks up at me.

"Daddy wants to talk to you."

I'm about to take the phone when I hear Mom's voice from the foyer.

"Look who was outside!"

I turn to see her walking in with Shawn behind her, and my heart nearly stops. He looks amazing, a little thinner maybe, but those green eyes are the same, and he's wearing a sweater I've never seen that makes him look older and more sophisticated.

"Why were you outside?" Dad asks, looking at Mom

with innocent confusion.

"Oh, I had a work call," Mom says breezily.

"On Thanksgiving?" Robert questions, raising an eyebrow.

I choose to ignore the implication there and focus on the phone in my hand, where James is saying, "Hello? Tara? Are you there?"

But I'm also looking at Shawn, whose face has completely dropped as he takes in the scene of me sitting with Maple, while James is calling my name on the phone.

Shawn stands there awkwardly, looking like he doesn't know whether to stay or go, when Maple suddenly yells out cheerfully, "Daddy says I'm going to stay here for a long time with Mrs. Tara until he can be with us!"

The room goes completely silent except for the sound of the twins babbling in their highchairs, and Mitzi growling at shredded paper. Everyone is staring at me now—my parents, my siblings, Carmen, even Willow and Kelso have stopped coloring. Birch looks unsure how to greet his long-lost gaming buddy.

And Shawn's face has gone from dropped to disgusted.

This is definitely not how I imagined this moment going, although I didn't tell him where I was going to be today.

Shawn turns and walks toward the front door, and I follow him out onto Beth's front porch, completely forgetting that James is still on the phone waiting for me to respond.

"Your mother texted me and told me where you'd be and that you were hoping I would show up today. I guess she was wrong."

"Tara?" James's voice comes through the speaker. "Are you there? What's going on?"

Shawn reaches over, takes my phone, and says curtly, "She'll have to call you back," before hanging up.

"That was childish!" I snap.

"Childish?" Shawn's eyes flash. "I came here to spend some time with you and your family. I've missed you. But I can see you have other entanglements that have grown significantly since I left."

"What about the girl in all your photos? You seem to be having plenty of fun without me."

"I am having a good time in New York," he says, his voice getting colder. "And yes, that woman is interested in me. You know what? Maybe I should go for it, because if anything, things are a bigger mess here than they were before I left."

I was going to explain that Maple is a little child who was just trying to repeat what she was told, and I haven't even talked to James about any long-term arrangements yet. But maybe it's none of Shawn's business.

My voice is rising now. "That child needs someone stable in her life, and I am not going to push her aside because you're jealous of her daddy, who is obviously not coming to live with me!"

"Nothing is obvious anymore, Tara." Shawn starts walking down the front steps.

As he reaches the sidewalk, I can't help myself. "May I remind you that this whole non-monogamous dating thing was YOUR idea! Just go screw everyone in town, I don't mind!"

My voice carries across the quiet street, and I suddenly realize that the stuffy elderly couple next door has stopped greeting their arriving grandchildren to stare at us. The woman actually gasps and puts her hand to her chest as if she's witnessing a domestic violence incident.

Perfect. Now Beth's refined neighbors think I'm some kind of deviant having a public breakdown on Thanksgiving.

Shawn doesn't even turn around. He just keeps walking down Monument Avenue, his hands shoved deep in his pockets, leaving me standing on my sister's front porch in my festive Thanksgiving dress, feeling like the biggest fool in Richmond.

The neighbor whispers something to her husband, who immediately ushers their grandchildren inside. Great. I've managed to traumatize an entire Monument Avenue family gathering, but… no… actually, they can kiss my ass. Sometimes things happen, and you have to deal with them.

"You people don't even know what non-monogamous dating is!"

I stand there for another moment, watching Shawn disappear around the corner, before slowly walking back inside to face my own family's concerned stares and call a man back who had better not want anything from me. I am doing all I can for his daughter, but Mrs. Tara's polyamorous shop is closed.

Even the "one man at a time" shop is locked up tight.

Chapter 45

I'm driving through Richmond's Monday morning traffic, heading to the rehabilitation facility where James is staying, and my mind keeps drifting back to Thursday night.

After that disastrous scene on Beth's front porch, I somehow managed to get through the rest of Thanksgiving dinner. I explained to Maple that Daddy and I got disconnected and would talk again soon, deflected my family's concerned questions, and helped clean up while trying to ignore the worried glances everyone kept shooting my way.

But around ten o'clock that night, after everyone had gone home and I'd gotten Maple settled in bed, I found myself standing outside Shawn's apartment door.

I texted Willow in her bedroom and let her know I was stepping out and to listen for Maple. She just wrote back and said, "Okay." I'm sure she knew where I was headed.

Shawn answered at the first knock, like he'd been expecting me.

"I'm sorry, but I couldn't leave it like that," I said.

He stepped aside to let me in, and we talked for hours about everything—his career, my fears, the impossible timing of it all, the baggage I've accumulated, the life he deserves to have.

And of course, all that closeness and real talk caused us to end up back in his bed, where I didn't think I would ever be again.

"You know what I see when I look at you?" he said as we lay tangled together afterward. "I see someone who takes care of everyone around her. You're a good mother, Tara. To your own kids, and now to Maple too. But we have way too much baggage for a couple who have only known each other for a couple of months."

When I didn't answer right away, he said, "You know I'm right."

That's when I started crying, and I'm crying again now as I pull into the parking lot of the rehabilitation center.

We both knew Thursday night was goodbye. He needs to stay in New York and build his career. I need to figure out my life and take care of the people who depend on me. We were just prolonging the inevitable.

I wipe my eyes and check my makeup in the rearview mirror before walking into the sterile, institutional building.

James looks better than I expected. Healthier, more clear-eyed, though he seems nervous as I sit down across from him in the visiting room.

"How are things going?" I ask.

"Good days and bad days," he admits. "But more good ones lately. I can't thank you enough for taking care of Maple. She sounds happy."

"She is happy. That's actually what I wanted to talk to you about." I take a deep breath. "Your mother has an opportunity to travel with her boyfriend on a long cruise. And I'd like to keep Maple while she's gone, if that's okay with you. But I need some kind of legal status to make decisions for her, if you agree."

James runs his hands through his hair. "Tara, I really liked you. I mean, I still do. But you don't need a guy as messed up as me in your life."

"This isn't about you, James. This is about Maple."

"I know, but..." He looks down at his hands. "I have no excuse for what happened with Shawn's cousin Marcus. I was drunk, I was angry, and I made a terrible decision that hurt an innocent kid. I've been working through it here, but I can't take it back. Obviously, none of that is Maple's fault, but I have a feeling that your continued involvement with me and my family has fucked up things with Shawn."

"He's gone now. Back to New York."

James looks up sharply. "Right, because of me and Maple. My mother shouldn't have involved you at all."

"Look, I wanted to help because I am lucky to be in a position to offer help. And it gives me a purpose at a time when I'm feeling a little lost. As for Shawn, it's complicated."

"Shit." He shakes his head. "Are you sure you want to take on my kid after all of this?"

I think about Maple's laugh, the way she curls up with Mitzi for naps, and how she carefully arranges her crayons by color before she starts drawing.

"You made a mistake, and you're doing something to make your life better. Maple still needs you, but she needs you to be well. She's just a little girl who needs consistent, loving care. And I can provide that, along with a whole extended family of people who will love her, too."

"Then yes," he says quietly. "Yes, I'll sign whatever papers you need. Temporary guardianship, whatever it takes. She's lucky to have you." He rubs his face, and now that I look more closely, I can see the effects of being in detox and working through his problems. "I'm lucky to have you… for Maple. When her mother died, I knew we were screwed. I am very grateful you came along. But what I really want to know is who is going to take you to cool rock shows now?"

I stand up to hug him and say, "I have a lot of higher priorities, but I promise I'll let you know how things are going with the swaying guy and the drunk cowboy."

We smile at the absurdity of it all, and on a more serious note, I add, "I do believe people come into our lives for a reason. Just get well, you've been through a lot. They say it takes a village, and I have quite the village for Maple."

Chapter 46

Christmas at Robert and Moneca's house is usually happy chaos, but this year feels different. Maybe it's because I'm officially Maple's temporary guardian now, or maybe it's because everyone keeps tiptoeing around me like I might spontaneously combust.

The past month has been a whirlwind. Roz left on her cruise two weeks ago, crying as she hugged Maple goodbye, but clearly excited about her adventure. Maple told her to have fun, and she would draw her a picture every day she is gone.

Willow and Kelso's shoe company got their first meeting with a potential manufacturer, thanks to Didier's connections.

Birch has been splitting his time between Todd's downtown condo and my apartment, which works well since Todd seems much happier in his bachelor pad.

And Roxanne and Didier are engaged. I know it's rather insane, but his divorce isn't final yet, and I think he just wanted to give her a beautiful ring and let her know he is serious. I hope it works out for them. I have never seen Didier so happy. He also sold his share of Monet Shoes to Dominique. I was shocked—it's his family's business, but hopefully their daughter will take over one day when she's grown. He seems very relieved to be moving on to something else and to be rid of his prickly business partner.

Everything is going well for all my people, and I couldn't be happier, but right now I'm hiding in Robert and Moneca's master bathroom, staring at a pregnancy test and trying not to hyperventilate.

This is impossible. I'm forty-two years old. I haven't had a period in two months, but I attributed that to stress and possibly early menopause. The nausea I've been having? Grief? The exhaustion? Taking care of a four-year-old and a geriatric dachshund?

But Moneca noticed me turning green at the smell of her Christmas morning bacon and quietly slipped me the test with a knowing look.

Well, and also after quizzing me about Shawn and what happened on Thanksgiving.

I guess she keeps pregnancy tests on hand. That woman is so organized.

The doorbell rings downstairs, and I hear the voices of more guests arriving late for our family gathering. Great. More witnesses to my life implosion.

"Tara!" Robert's voice calls from outside the bathroom door. "Everything okay in there?"

"Fine!" I call back, my voice cracking. "Just... using the bathroom!"

"For twenty minutes?" That's Moneca now. "Honey, come out. Whatever it is, we can deal with it."

I think Moneca knows what it is, but she's trying not to "out" me in case I decide to tell everyone I had an explosive case of diarrhea, which would be easier than announcing a pregnancy.

"Is she sick?" That's my mother's voice. Perfect. "Tara, open this door right now!"

"Maybe she's having a panic attack," Beth suggests.

"I could climb through the window. Carmen, help me get the ladder."

"Please don't climb through any windows," I say weakly.

"Aunt Tara, are you pooping?" That's definitely Sophia's five-year-old voice, followed by Oliver shouting, "POOPING!"

"Kids, go downstairs," Moneca says firmly.

There's a knock, different from the others. Gentler.

"Tara?" It's a voice I haven't heard in person for a month. "Can you please come out? I drove all the way from New York to see you."

My heart stops. "Shawn?"

"I called him," Robert admits through the door. "You've been miserable, and frankly, so has he based on our phone calls."

"You've been talking to Shawn? Why is everybody in my family always talking to Shawn but me?" I ask, incredulous.

"Weekly," Robert says. "Someone had to keep tabs on both of you stubborn idiots, and I was elected as the one least likely to screw everything up."

That's for sure, but do they really like Shawn that much? And does he see himself as a potential part of this wacky clan after all?

I look down at the pregnancy test in my hands. Two pink lines. Unmistakably positive.

I'm pregnant. At forty-two. With Shawn's baby.

"Tara," Shawn's voice is closer to the door now. "Whatever's going on, we can figure it out. I miss you. Maple cornered me downstairs and told me that you're sad sometimes. No one wants you to be sad. And you need to be happy for that little girl, too. For all of us."

I can't let Maple see me sad, he's right. I am supposed to be providing stability for that child, but that doesn't mean I want Shawn to martyr himself so everyone else can be happy. He has a new life, and I am already poised to blow it up with my news.

Maybe if he knew, he would run back to his car and be on the Jersey Turnpike before we serve Christmas dinner.

I sigh and say, "Where's Maple?"

"Downstairs, teaching Mitzi how to wrap Christmas presents," Kelso reports.

I take a deep breath, unlock the door, and step out into a hallway full of expectant faces. Everyone I love is here—my parents, my siblings, my children, Shawn looking nervous but determined in a Christmas sweater I've never seen.

I hold up the pregnancy test before I chicken out. If he's going to reject me, he can do it publicly. I am not interested in another heart-to-heart at his place that ends with sex and even more heartbreak.

"So," I say, looking directly at Shawn, "remember when you said my life was complicated?"

The hallway erupts in chaos. My mother starts crying and fanning herself with her hands. Dad immediately begins calculating the statistical probability of pregnancy complications at my age. Beth is already googling her favorite obstetrician colleague on her phone and telling him to stop it. Robert is grinning like an idiot, and Moneca is hugging everyone within reach.

Even my kids don't look upset, although this is clearly a shocker for them. Birch's eyes are definitely popping.

Why does everyone think my being pregnant with

the baby of a twenty-five-year-old guy who isn't even my boyfriend is good news? I am already the mother of two teens, a foster mother, and a dog mother.

I really have the mother thing well covered.

And Shawn? Shawn is just staring at me with the biggest smile I've ever seen.

"Does this mean you're staying?" I ask him.

"Try and make me leave," he says, stepping closer. "We're going to need a bigger apartment."

I am crying again because of the stupid hormones, and also, he looks so sincere and sweet, and oh my God, but he has to stay in New York. I bet no one in my family is thinking of that little complication while they are picking out baby names and offering to babysit.

"But what about your program? Your job?"

Everyone quiets down since this is the most pivotal moment, and he says, "The program is over at the end of January, and I have already accepted a job offer from a company that has brokerage operations in Richmond. My company wasn't happy about giving me free training, but the new company is going to reimburse them for it, so everybody is happy."

Carmen says, "Wow, you must be as good at your job as you obviously are at… other things."

Yes, Carmen impregnating a woman in her forties is an accomplishment. Shawn's guys can swim.

Chapter 47

One Year Later

It's Christmas, and here I am standing in the entryway of what used to be Cassie's grandmother's house, watching Birch and Shawn hang more garland in the entryway while Maple "helps" by handing them pieces of tape that immediately stick to everything except what they're supposed to.

"Mrs. Tara, can I put snowflakes on Mitzi?" Maple asks, holding up a packet of sparkly white stickers.

"Sure, but just a few. She's getting old and doesn't like too much fuss."

Mitzi, now sixteen and moving even slower than before, is napping in a sunny patch by the window, occasionally opening one eye to supervise the party preparations.

The house is perfect for us. It's a 1920s colonial with enough bedrooms for our growing family, a big backyard for Maple and Mitzi to play in, and a guest cottage where Cassie lives with Everly. It solved everyone's housing problems in one fell swoop.

"Tara, where do you want the food?" Cassie calls from the back door, carrying a tray from the catering van that had just pulled up.

"Just put everything on the dining room table. Roxanne and Didier insisted on handling all the food themselves."

The guest list for tonight's housewarming/Christmas party reads like a cast of characters from the strangest romantic comedy ever written.

My entire family will be here, including my parents, who seem genuinely happy after weathering Mom's crisis. Turns out her flirtation with Peter at the real estate office never went anywhere, and she and Dad are both finally retiring next month. They're talking about buying a small place in Florida, which I'm sure will provide endless statistical fodder for Dad about hurricane probabilities and alligator attacks.

Beth and Carmen are doing wonderfully. Carmen fits into our family like she's always been there, and Beth seems more relaxed than I've ever seen her. They're talking about moving in together officially.

Roz is on another cruise. Apparently, she and her boyfriend have decided to travel the world for months at a time at least once a year. She video calls Maple every few days, and the arrangement is working well for everyone. Maple is adjusting beautifully to our chaotic household, especially now that she's a big sister.

That's not to say that she doesn't have her moments of meltdowns and whining like all children, but she seems secure now that she has her own room and a stable home and family.

"Mom, where did you put the good wine glasses?" Willow calls from the kitchen. She looks so grown up these days, living in her own apartment downtown near VCU, where she'll start design school in the fall. The shoe company is really taking shape—they've got three investors now and a provisional patent on their comfort technology. Kelso is renting my old apartment for the remainder of the lease, but Willow was adamant about having her own space. I'm proud of her independence.

"They're in the china cabinet," I call back, then turn to Shawn. "Are your mom and grandmother settled in?"

"Yeah, they're upstairs, freshening up. Grandma's already complained about the music being too loud, and we haven't even started the party yet."

Shawn is happy with his new job. It's less money than he would have made staying in Manhattan, but less cost of living and stress, too. And he gets to be with us.

All of us.

Birch is living here now full-time, and he has changed high schools. It was a bold move, but he was ready for a change, too, and he likes being able to walk to school. He has become more interested in science, thanks to Kelso's influence, and he's applying to both local and out-of-state colleges.

James is out of rehab, and he and I have joint legal custody of Maple. He couldn't bear to take her away from the secure foundation I've built for her.

He's doing well, and as long as that's the case, our arrangement will work well. He's looking for a new line of work that doesn't involve law enforcement or alcohol. He's staying at his mom's place so that he can keep Maple there during his time with her, and it's familiar for her and full of only happy memories.

And yes, Shawn has accepted this. James is still not his favorite person, but he knows what it's like to grow up without a dad, and he can't imagine life without a loving, stable mom.

Plus, have I mentioned that Maple is just the cutest, sweetest little thing?

Shawn even said James could come here for

Christmas, but we decided he would take Maple tomorrow. He wants to celebrate the holidays with his other sober friends, and those are important relationships to maintain.

The doorbell rings, and I hear familiar voices on the other side of the door. Dinah and Vinny arrive first, followed by Lotto Lenny, who's carrying what appears to be a case of champagne and a bag of scratch-off lottery tickets.

"Only the finest gifts for youse people," he announces. "Nice place, maybe I should look in this neighborhood. Feels like New York a little bit with the old houses."

Maybe he's tired of being the only lottery winner in the family, and the only one still living way below his means. He does still have the Buick, though. It's kind of like an extension of him at this point.

Didier and Roxanne are bustling around the kitchen, both of them glowing with happiness. They're getting married next month, and Roxanne's catering business is booming. She's completely transformed Vinny's little take-out operation into something that could genuinely compete with the big Richmond caterers, and it will preserve the Bertellis' legacy, long after they're gone.

"Mes amis!" Didier exclaims to our new guests, wearing an apron and kissing everyone on both cheeks. "This house is magnifique, non? Much better than that little apartment." He looks at Shawn and says, "Not that I was ever there when Tara lived there. I was not part of the men harem. I have business meetings there now with Kelso and Willow."

Shawn smacks Didier on the back and allows him to do the cheek kisses, even though I know it weirds him out a little.

Soon, the house is full of voices and laughter. Robert and Moneca arrive with all four kids, who immediately scatter to find Maple and cause chaos. My parents come bearing a casserole dish, and I'm sure Dad is talking about the traffic on I-95 and the holiday accident statistics to anyone who will listen. Beth and Carmen bring flowers, wine, and big smiles.

Now Shawn's mother, Angela, and his grandmother have joined us downstairs. Grandma has an audience in the living room, telling everyone about how she always knew Shawn would "come to his senses about that nice girl."

I guess she's gotten over the shower incident, or her daughter shamed her into apologizing, which she does every time I see her.

I still can't believe everyone is okay with our age difference, but I am learning that there are no rules and happy couples come in many forms.

As I watch everyone mingle—Roxanne showing Carmen her engagement ring (apparently both Carmen and Shawn have been ring shopping, but Beth and I aren't supposed to know that), Lenny explaining lottery strategy to my father, Kelso and Willow excitedly discussing their business plan with Didier, I realize something.

I don't want any job right now except for wife and mother. For the first time in my adult life, I'm exactly where I want to be, doing exactly what I want to do.

If that makes me a bad feminist, oh well.

But I don't think it does. I think it makes me powerful. I haven't given in to midlife divorce cliches or other people's expectations.

But I have been thinking about writing. I always loved it as a kid, and let's face it—I've certainly accumulated enough material for a memoir. Adventures of City Girl: How I Went from Suburban Housewife to Urban Mama in One Chaotic Year.

"What are you thinking about?" Shawn asks, slipping his arms around me from behind, holding our little bundle of baby, who has just woken up from his nap and is looking for me, his food source.

"Just... all of this. How crazy the past year has been."

"Good crazy or bad crazy?"

I lean back against him and watch Maple chase Oliver around the coffee table while Mitzi barks encouragement from her dog bed.

"You know it's the best kind of crazy."

Aspen giggles, as if agreeing, and I take him from Shawn as he puts away all the coats and starts taking drink orders.

Yes, we kept with the tree name thing—it was irresistible.

I whisper in my baby boy's ear, "So what do you think? What adventures await us next?"

Aspen grabs my hair and laughs again, and I know someday he will love hearing the stories of how he came to be a part of this big, eclectic bunch.

But whatever comes around the bend for us, we'll face it together—me, Shawn, our children, our family and friends, and who knows who else we might collect along the way.

Change is the new normal for me, and honestly? I wouldn't have it any other way.

THE END

Novels by Carol Maloney Scott

Rom-Com on the Edge Series

Dazed & Divorced (Book 1)

There Are No Men (Book 2)

Afraid of Her Shadow (Book 3)

The Juggling Act (Book 4)

Accidental Makeovers (Book 5)

Let's Hear it From the Boys (A Short Story Collection)

Love Pixies Series

Love Pixies (Book 1)

Spooky Matchmakers Series

Nobody Tells Lia Anything (Book 1)

Something Molly Can't See (Book 2)

Meet the Family Series

The Funeral Date (Book 1)

The Parent Feud (Book 2)

The Wedding Bells (Book 3)

Join Me On The Edge

Join her on "The Edge" for giveaways, cover reveals, excerpts, contests and members-only content at carolmaloneyscott.com/

As a member of my Edgy Readers Group, you will receive:

- Advance Reader Copies!
- News on upcoming releases!
- Exclusive contests and giveaways!
- Updates on projects and new series in the works!
- Polls asking for your opinion!
- Shenanigans!
- Wiener dog pictures!
- Excerpts!

I can't wait for YOU to join the party!

Acknowledgements

When Kindle Vella first became a thing, I was excited and thought it looked like a great opportunity to share serial stories and experiment with that form of fiction writing.

So, I jumped in and spent more than a year focusing on my content on the platform.

I published a three-book series, Meet the Family (comprising The Funeral Date, The Parent Feud, and The Wedding Bells), based on my original Kindle Vella story, The Funeral Date. This has been my best-selling and most loved series to date, which was very exciting and continues to bring me new readers.

But then there was Adventures of City Girl, another Vella that had a bunch of published episodes.

I published this one as Season 1 of the story, in keeping with the serial theme that mimics the structure of a television series. Instead of finishing the story with Books 2 and 3, like I did with The Funeral Date, Adventures of City Girl left readers hanging, waiting for Season 2.

When Kindle Vella went away and all the Vella authors were left with partially finished stories, I couldn't decide how I wanted to handle it. Should I do Seasons 2 and 3, or did that not make sense anymore since I was abandoning the whole serial concept?

After much internal debate, I removed ACG Season 1 from sale, finished the story, and packaged it as the standalone novel you just read.

I hope you enjoyed it!

As a woman who spent a number of years as a clueless, divorced person trying to figure out her next moves, Tara's story is one of the many paths I have seen others take who were in my shoes.

And as with all my novels, there is always a little bit of me in there.

I want to thank all the women I met on my journey who were also starting over. I would like to think that we learned a lot as we supported each other on our scary, but sometimes exciting, journeys to new and improved lives.

I thank my husband, Jim, for being my HEA and inspiring me to be bolder and put myself out there in the world. I don't know if I would have ever started writing in my forties if we hadn't met.

My son, Nick, who is now 30 (I don't understand how this happened), is working on a rebrand of my author business, and I am very excited to see what his talented creative mind comes up with.

And Jaime, my stepdaughter, who attends a lot of book

events and festivals, has inspired me to start selling my physical books in real life. I have a plan to begin attending author events and meeting readers IRL in 2026. If you have a favorite event, let me know and I will try to be there.

I wish I could bring my adorable furry assistants, Benny and Moose the wiener dogs, but they are quite high-maintenance and would be very distracting. I hope you enjoyed the character of Mitzi – when I was writing her scenes, I was thinking of my beloved Daisy, and what she would have been like had she lived longer into her old lady years. I still miss her every day.

And thanks to all of my readers – there is no feeling like knowing that you have entertained strangers and that you are connecting with people who do not know you.

What a gift.

About The Author

Carol Maloney Scott, author of women's humorous fiction, is a happy wife, proud mom and stepmom, and a wiener dog fanatic.

She is a lover of donuts and a hater of mornings. After unearthing a childhood passion for telling stories, she can once again be seen carrying around a notebook and staring into space.

Her stories are witty, fresh, and real—just like life.

Join her on "The Edge" for giveaways, cover reveals, excerpts, contests, and members-only content at The Edge.

Please check out her social media sites and say hello!
    Website
    Amazon
    Goodreads
    Facebook